The Secrets of Pain

PHIL RICKMAN was born in Lancashire and lives on the Welsh border. He is the author of the Merrily Watkins series, and *The Bones of Avalon*. He has won awards for his TV and radio journalism and writes and presents the book programme *Phil the Shelf* for BBC Radio Wales.

PHIL RICKMAN

'Phil Rickman is one of my all-time favourites.
I love everything he's done, from horror to mystery to super-
natural thriller – often all in the same book'
DIANA GABALDON

'No-one writes better than Rickman about the shadow-frontier
between the supernatural and the real world'
BERNARD CORNWELL

'Rickman writes mysteries in the classic sense, cleverly
combining the supernatural and criminal elements to
illuminate the darkest corners of our imaginations'
JOHN CONNOLLY

'I like Merrily. She's got vices, she likes a smoke, she swears,
she's not easily fooled and she's nobody's pushover'
BARBARA NADEL

'A completely new approach to crime'
BARRY NORMAN

'A haunting quality beyond crime fiction'
RUSSELL JAMES

'FIRST CLASS'
GUARDIAN

'FIRST RATE'
DAILY MAIL

'WONDERFUL'
DAILY EXPRESS

'TERRIFIC'
THE TIMES

'First rate. We don't praise our home-grown thriller writers enough.
It's high time we praised Phil Rickman' *DAILY MAIL*

'Compassionate, original and sharply contemporary, one of the best
crime series around' *SPECTATOR*

'The clever combination of modern idiom and the timeless echo of
history leaps from every page. You are there with poor Merrily every
step of the way' *DAILY EXPRESS*

'Feuds, intrigues and murder. A most original sleuth. Terrific'
THE TIMES

'A first class thriller with a difference' *GUARDIAN*

'Conveys evil like no other writer... A major talent' *SFX*

'Tough-minded, atmospheric mystery'
BARRY FORSHAW

'A dark no-man's-land where murder mingles with
superstition. Complex, absorbing, fascinating'
ANDREW TAYLOR

PHIL RICKMAN

The Secrets of Pain

CORVUS

First published in Great Britain in 2011 by Corvus,
an imprint of Atlantic Books Ltd.

1 3 5 7 9 10 8 6 4 2

A CIP catalogue record for this book is available from the British Library.

Hardback ISBN: 978-1-84887-273-8
Trade paperback ISBN: 978-1-84887-274-5
eBook ISBN: 978-0-85789-474-8

Printed in Great Britain by the MPG Books Group.

Corvus
An imprint of Atlantic Books Ltd
Ormond House
26-27 Boswell Street
London WC1N 3JZ

www.corvus-books.co.uk

The Secrets of Pain

FEBRUARY

They came for me in darkness
They were black-eyed, grey and thin

Lol Robinson, '*Mephisto's Blues*'

1

White Hell

THE HOUSE WAS right next to the road, wherever the road was.

And out in front there was a woman.

Not exactly dressed for the weather, thin cardigan all lumpy with snow. Stumbling about in Bronwen's lights and the blinding white hell, waving her arms. And they were going to run her down, cut her in half.

'Gomer!' Danny roared. '*No!*'

The snow was coming down like rubble now, had been this past four hours, and if Danny couldn't see through it there was no chance that Gomer could. When Bronwen lurched and the snow sprayed up, Danny was thinking, *Oh Christ, it'll be all blotched red.*

Then they'd stopped. Apart from Bronwen's grumpy chuntering, there was silence. The front door of the house was wide open, yellow light splattered over the snow like warm custard on ice cream. Some of it reaching Gomer, sitting at the wheel in his old donkey jacket, with his cap and his sawn-off mittens and his muffler and the snowlight in his glasses.

'What we done?' Danny heard his own voice, all hollow. 'What we done, Gomer?'

Oh God. Leaning on his side door, breaking through the crispy layer of snow. New tractor, out for the first time with the snowplough. This superhero routine of Gomer's, coming out in the dark to clear – *for free* – the roads that Hereford Council wouldn't go near… well, you learned to live with that, but how long before he was a danger to other folks and hisself?

You ask Danny, it was starting to look like the time had come.

A slapping on the door panel, Gomer's side.

'*Who's that in there?*'

Danny went, 'Woooh.'

Sagging in blind relief. It was her. Gomer, meanwhile, totally relaxed, was letting his window down, the ciggy glowing in his face.

'We help at all?'

'... dies of frostbite, what do he care? Long as *he's* bloody warm!' The woman, entirely alive, glaring up at the cab, hair all white and wild. 'Not *you*. Him in there, look.'

Glancing behind her just as the front door of the farmhouse got punched shut from inside and the warm light vanished.

'En't that typical? He won't do nothin', 'cept toss another bloody block on the fire. *Serve the buggers right. Let 'em get theirselves out.* Then back to his beer.' She was standing back, snow over the tops of her wellies, squinting, then she went, '*Gomer?*'

'Ah,' Gomer said. 'Sarah, is it?'

'Gomer Parry Plant Hire! Thought you was *long* retired, boy!'

Danny was too cold to smile. Gomer had an angry puff on his roll-up. Long as the ole boy had his ciggies, the cold never seemed to bother him. Least, not as much as the idea of folks thinking he was too advanced in years to be driving heavy plant through a blizzard. His voice was distinctly gruffer as he drew out the last half-inch of ciggy.

'Problem, is it, girl?'

'Some fool in a car, it is,' this Sarah said. 'Come whizzin' clean off the road on the bend back there. Slides across, crashes through the gate and straight down the bloody hill!'

'You sure?'

'Sure? I was at the bedroom window, Gomer, couldn't hardly miss him. Straight through! Headlights all over the snow, then they've gone, look. Well, there en't no way out of there. Ends in forestry.'

'So, let's get this right, girl,' Gomer said. 'There's a car or some'ing gone down over this yere hill, and he's vanished?'

'Likely buried already, and *we* en't got no gear to haul him out. Can you get through in that thing, Gomer?'

It was like the whole cab was bulging with Gomer's outrage.

'*This thing?*'

Danny sighed.

'Gomer, mabbe we should call the—'

'En't *nowhere*…' Gomer tossing the last millimetre of ciggy into the snow '… on God's earth this girl can't get through.'

Danny, defeated, looked up at the falling sky. Snow and ice had come hard and bitter after Christmas, right after the floods. Over a month of running out of oil, on account of the tankers couldn't get through, and starving rats raiding your vehicle from underneath, dining on your electrics. A brief respite early in February and then, just when you thought you'd seen the end of winter, the bastard was back with both fists bunched, and Gomer Parry had got hisself a big new JCB tractor called Bronwen and something to prove.

Danny climbed down and found the car hadn't gone crunching through the gate after all.

'Some fool left him open.'

He climbed back in, slammed the door. No warmer in here. Bronwen had a cracking heater, only Gomer wouldn't use it in case he nodded off at the wheel and some bastard magistrate had his HGV licence off him.

'Shouldn't be no gate there at all,' Gomer said. 'No fence, neither. Common land, it is. Bridleway. Only Dickie, see, he reckons if he d'keep fencin' it off, one day folks is gonner forget it don't belong to him.'

He lowered the plough: tracks in the headlights, but Danny saw they were filling up fast. Gomer set about clearing the field entrance in case they came back with something on tow.

Danny said. 'Dickie who?'

'On the pop half the time. Dickie *Protheroe*. Her's gotter hold it all together, ennit?'

'Ah, so that's Dickie Protheroe's new wife, is it? Never seed her before.'

'Course you en't. On account of Dickie's in the pub and her's back yere *holdin' it all together.*'

'Aye,' Danny said. 'Fair play to her.'

Pulling snow out of his beard, thinking whoever was down there could be badly hurt, or worse. Could've hit a tree or a power pole.

'Land Rover, them tracks,' Gomer said. 'Long wheelbase. Only one set o' tracks so he en't out.' He sniffed. 'Right, then. We go for it?'

Ten minutes from midnight when they went in, and the windscreen was near-opaque. Like being inside a washing machine when somebody'd overdone it with the powder. Hoping to God this wouldn't end in no pink snow, Danny dug his hands into his pockets. Warming himself inside with thoughts of the Pyramid Stage at Glastonbury on a hot night at the end of June, coloured lights in rippling sequence, the strobes going, the ole Strat hard against his thigh as he went sailing off into the solo from 'Mephisto's Blues'.

Well, it *could* be, if only Lol would realize how much he had to offer... if the boy could just overcome that persistent low self-esteem.

What the hell, life was good.

Had been good.

'You all right, Gomer?'

'Course I'm all right.'

Bronwen went grinding on between leafless trees turned into great white mushrooms. Humpy, glistening ground and a teeming sky, the countryside like a strange new-made bed, all the familiar creases filled in.

A slow, downward slope, now, the snow-level rising either side of them. Not going to be that easy getting back up.

'Oh, hell!'

Patches of grey stone in the lights.

'All right, boy, I seen him.'

'What the hell is it, Gomer?'

'Looks like an ole sheep-shelter.'

Gomer brought Bronwen grunting to a stop and Danny made out the roof of a vehicle behind the broken wall, a wedge of thick snow on top. How the hell did he get behind the bloody wall? Danny lowered his window.

'You all right there?'

No reply. He glanced behind. The incline they'd just come down would look dangerously steep on the way back. He turned back to find shadows moving silently on either side, just beyond the lights. Danny stiffened. How many of the buggers were in this yere Land Rover, and why wasn't they calling out? Like, *Thank God you come*, kind o' thing.

'En't bein' funny, Gomer, but I don't altogether like the looks of this, to be honest.'

The shadows were spreading out, circling and crouching like a pack of wolves. Five of them at least, murky grey now in the swirling night.

A sudden massive bang on Danny's side of the tractor.

One of them was there. All black, no face.

BANG! BANG! BANG! BANG! on the panel.

The man was in camouflage kit. Gloves, balaclava. No glint of eyes behind the slit.

Danny got his window up to just a bit of a crack. Looked at Gomer across the grey light in the cab. In the past year, two JCBs had been nicked from this area. All right, not hijacked, just stolen out of their sheds, but there was big money in a brand new tractor and a first time for everything.

'Don't wanner make a thing 'bout this, Gomer, but how about we don't get out till we finds out a bit— *No!* Gomer!'

'Balls!' Gomer was leaning across Danny, mouth up to the crack at the top of the window. '*Gomer Parry Plant Hire.* You all right, there?'

Oh Jesus... Like these were the magic words, the key to not getting dragged out into the snow and having the shit beaten out of you while the lovely new tractor you'd called Bronwen and had blessed by the vicar got shipped out to Lagos.

Danny was going, 'Look, pal, we—'

When the voice came out of the snow.

'Yow know who we are.'

Aye, *that* kind of voice. Full of clouds and night and a bit of Birmingham, and now Danny could see two solid shadows, either side of the camouflage man. Gomer coughed, a bit hoarse.

'This a hexercise, pal?'

Silence. Then a short, little laugh.

'Give the ole man a coconut.'

'What I figured,' Gomer said. 'Only, Sarah back there, see—'

'... so yow just turn this bus around, yeah, and bugger off.'

All the breath went out of Danny in a steam of relief.

'I should just do it, Gomer. These guys, they don't make a habit of flashin' their ID.'

'Put your lights out, *now*,' the camouflage man said. 'Then fuck off and forget you seen anything.'

Danny shifted uncomfortably in his seat. You wanted cooperation, you didn't talk *quite* like this to Gomer Parry. Five foot four and well past seventy, but you just didn't. Everybody knew that.

'And you might find it easier if you put that filthy cigarette out.'

'Now listen, boy—'

'Just do what he says, eh, Gomer,' Danny hissed. 'You can complain to the Government later.'

Gomer said nothing, just let the windows glide up, putting the tractor into reverse and reaching out for the lights.

Only, the mad ole bugger didn't switch them off, he threw them on full beam, making a starburst in the snow, and – *Jesus!* – Danny was jerking back as Bronwen swung round hard, on a slide. In the lights he'd seen what he'd seen – what he *thought* he'd seen – before the tractor lurched and bucked and went snarling back along the track they'd made earlier.

8

Danny and Gomer didn't speak at all till they'd managed to make it up the hill and out the gate and onto the road again. Then Danny sat up and looked hard into Gomer's thick, misty specs.

'We really see that?'

'Hexercise,' Gomer said gruffly. 'That's all it is. Kind o' jobs they get, they gotter be hard, ennit?'

'Well, yeah, but, Gomer…'

'*Hexercise,*' Gomer said. 'That's what we tells Sarah Protheroe. Her'll know.'

'You reckon?'

'And we don't say nothin' else. All right?'

Danny was shivering. He'd go along with that. Anything. But what they'd seen in the white hell… in other circumstances it could have been almost funny, but in a late-February blizzard, in the minutes after midnight, it was enough to scare the shit out of you.

Especially the way the fifth man had been just standing there laughing, bollock naked in the snow.

Part One

MARCH

Empty your septic tank
Take it to the bank

Lol Robinson, 'Wasted on Plant Hire'

2

Longships

THE BAD STUFF started with Jane insisting on getting the drinks. A Lotto thing – she and Merrily had both had ten-quid paybacks on the same number. Jane wanted to buy Lol and Danny Thomas a beer. Which was nice of her. She seemed determined these days, Lol thought, to do more things that were nice, as if she had something to repay.

He watched her at the bar. The tight jeans, the sawn-off white hoodie and the area of soft skin exposed between the two. Merrily had said, *If you could just, you know, keep an eye on Jane…?*

She'd been thinking about the weather. They all had, since the Christmas flood, a continuing source of unease in Ledwardine. Mid-evening on a Friday, the Black Swan was less than a third full but sounding crowded to Lol because of all the voices raised against the punch of the wind and the fizz of rain on the leaded windows.

Big weather. *More* big weather.

He'd seen it coming well before dark, the sky over Cole Hill chaotic with ripped-up cloud and flarings of wild violet beyond the church steeple. The last taunt of winter. Or maybe the first sneer of spring. The floods, then the snow, then more snow and now, just as you thought it was over, the gales.

And yet it was an ill-wind because, out of the black night and the white noise of the rain and his anxiety, suddenly *the lines* happened, like they'd been blown into his head.

The chorus had been hanging around for weeks, begging for an opening trail of memorably bleak images to illustrate the raw emptiness before love walked in. The rhyme was a bit bumpy, but maybe that was OK, maybe even good.

The wind is screaming through the granary
It turns the springtime into January.

This was the granary, where he'd lived for a time, at Prof Levin's studio over at Knight's Frome. The perpetual January of a lonely bed. Lol pulled over a beer mat, found a pen in his jacket, saw Danny's eyes lighting up over the shoe-brush beard.

'Cookin', boy?'

Lol reversed the beer mat, steered it across to Danny then drew back as the gale pushed like a big hand – *whump* – on the leaded pane directly across the room. No let-up. The lines had probably arisen from his failure to prevent Merrily driving out into the storm… or at least letting him drive her. What if there was no Merrily? What if there'd *been* no Merrily? The void at the core of the song: *I can't define my sense of need.*

Danny was gazing at the beermat like it was Mozart's scorepad. Before Gomer Parry had rescued him, he'd been a struggling Radnorshire farmer with fading dreams. Also, three vintage guitars, a couple of ancient amps, a decibel-dazed wife and a sheepdog called Jimi.

He looked up.

'I'm hearin' it, boy, sure t'be.'

The grin reappearing in the beard, though still a little wary, like a poacher's flashlight in the undergrowth. Not long after Danny had joined Gomer Parry Plant Hire, Lol had been looking for a lead guitarist, someone good but not too expensive. After two sessions in Danny's barn over at Kinnerton, he'd said, *You want a proper contract or will a handshake do?* Danny grinning like a little kid, his muddied hand already out.

'Should be in your barn, recording this,' Lol said. 'Under the storm noise, everything shivering.'

'Storm noise in a barn en't never as good as you imagines. Ole wind got his own backbeat, see, never plays to yours.' Danny nodded towards Jane at the bar. 'Growin' up?'

'I suppose.'

Getting the drinks herself was important to Jane. Doing it legally was still a novelty. Barry, the manager, was behind the bar, and everybody in the Swan knew Jane. Some of them even liked her.

The wind came back, a fighter in the ring, leaving you no time for recovery, and Danny picked up on Lol's anxiety.

'You're worried about your lady.'

You had to love the seventies rock-band jargon.

'It's not blowing over, Danny.'

'Hard to blow an ole Volvo off the road.'

It had been mid-afternoon, after the first Severe Weather Warning, when Merrily had come across to Lol's house, looking unsettled and facing an hour's drive to the mountains the other side of Brecon. This was Huw Owen, inevitably. For reasons Huw hadn't disclosed and Merrily couldn't fathom, he'd wanted her to talk to his students at the grim, disued Nonconformist chapel up in the Beacons where he taught ordained priests how to mess with the unmentionable.

'I'll give Huw a call, anyway.' Lol had his mobile out. 'Make sure she…'

'Makes you feel better, boy,' Danny said, 'do it.'

In Huw Owen's rectory, thirty-plus miles away, the phone rang out. Maybe they'd already left for the chapel, which probably didn't even have a phone. Huw liked to awaken in his students a sense of isolation and vulnerability. Lol killed the signal.

'Nothing.'

But Danny Thomas was listening to something else, his long grey hair pushed back behind one ear. He caught Lol's eye, lifting a cautionary forefinger. Lol heard a drawly voice from Off.

'… *what I said, George, I said the old totty-meter's flickering into the fucking red.*'

15

Then liquid laughter. Lol turned towards the bar. Kids, you'd think, but they weren't. About five of them, late twenties to early forties, talking in low voices, but their London accents lifted them out of the background mush.

'*Clean off the fucking dial, George. I mean, will you just look at that...*'

'*... he on about?*'

'*His fanny-meter's gone off.*'

'*Ask the barman for a Kleenex.*'

'*Not kidding, George. I'm in love.*'

'*You're rat-arsed.*'

'*I think... I think I feel a wager coming on...*'

None of them spoke for a few seconds. Apple logs shifted on the hearth. Danny looked at Lol. Red mud was still flaked in his heavy-metal hair. He'd been here in the village all day, working with Gomer on extra flood defences down by the river.

A wager. Lol could imagine florid men, squires and their sons, in three-cornered hats, with lavish waistcoats and long bendy pipes, under these same beams on Jacobean nights when the Black Swan was young.

'*How much?*'

'*Hundred? Two?*'

'*You're not scaring me, George. I'll go three.*'

'*Bloody confident tonight, Cornel.*'

'*He's bladdered. He won't—*'

'*All right. Listen. I'll persuade her into the paddock for nothing, and then... why don't we say three-fifty if I get her upstairs? However—*'

'*Yeah, but that doesn't prove—*'

'*However... any tricks, any remarks from you bastards that might put her off, and you pay up anyway. Deal?*'

'*That's—*'

'*Deal?*'

'*Don't fall for it George.*' Mild Scots accent. '*He'll probably offer to split it with her if she plays along.*'

'*He won't, Alec, because we'll be listening to every word.*'

16

At some stage, probably when money came into it, the banter had shed its forced humour. At the other end of the bar, Jane was handing Barry a ten-pound note, leaning forward, exposing a widening band of pink skin just below the small of her back.

As the daylight faded, their cars would arrive on the square like Viking longships floating into a natural harbour, the top-of-the-range Beemer, the Porsche Boxter, the Mercedes 4-by-4.

Barry the manager, like half the village, was in two minds about them. They had – nobody could argue about this – seen the Swan through a bleak winter of recession, and yet…

Like they own the place. That old cliché. You heard it a lot around Ledwardine but it was only half right, Lol thought. You didn't need to own a playground.

Only one man in Ledwardine actually seemed interested in owning the village. Lol had never actually met Ward Savitch, but you couldn't fail to be aware of his presence, usually on Sunday mornings. Used to be church bells, now it was shotgun echoes.

The new hunter-gatherers. Paying guests of Savitch, who'd bought the old Kibble place, known as The Court, a farmhouse with fifty acres. Savitch was everywhere now, grabbing marginal land – woods and rough country, like he was reclaiming his heritage. In fact, he was building himself one. Came out of London just ahead of the big recession, with all his millions in a handcart. Now the fifty acres had more than doubled, holiday chalets had gone up. Shooting and paintballing weekends, for those who could afford them. Some were corporate jollies, designed to freshen up tired executives – Savitch clearly exploiting his old contacts.

Not many posh cars outside tonight, though. A couple of these guys were staying here at the Swan – overspill – and the others had come down from The Court on foot, intent on serious drinking. Some of them still in their designer camou-flage trousers bought from one of the few retail chains in the county that were no longer on nodding terms with the Official Receiver.

'Day's shooting supervised by Kenny Mostyn and the kids from Hardkit and they think they're fighting fit,' Barry had said one night when it was quiet. 'Well… fit enough to take on a five-course champagne dinner and a few gallons of Stella.'

Barry knew about fighting and fitness. Retired from the SAS at forty, still went running in the Black Mountains most week-ends. He was on the portly side these days, but only portly like a bouncer.

'But – what can I say? – it keeps the lights on. Most of these guys, it's just about getting pissed and bringing me pheasants they've shot. Who loses?'

'Apart from the pheasants?' Lol had said.

Glad that Jane hadn't been there.

But not as much as he wished she wasn't here now.

Keeping an eye on Jane… this was getting increasingly delicate.

She'd been Lol's friend before he even knew her mother, back when she was just an insecure kid, in a new place, and he was a part-time recluse in a cottage down Blackberry Lane. But Jane was eighteen now, approaching her last term at school, finding herself some space. Wasn't as though Lol was her dad or even a dad figure. Not exactly a dad-figure kind of person.

Jane had said she was just popping to the loo, would get the drinks on her way back. But Lol had noticed she hadn't actually gone to the loo. Directly to the bar. Purposeful.

He pushed his chair back so he could see her talking to the lanky young guy with the deep chin and the big lips. Because of all the voices raised against the rattle and hiss of the weather, you couldn't hear what was being said as the guy bent down to her, like he was offering her a lollipop.

'Stay calm, boy,' Danny said. 'This is the Swan on a Friday night. She can just walk away.'

But she hadn't. She seemed to be listening, solemnly, then smiling right up into the big-jawed face. Wearing that close-fitting white top, half-unzipped, over very tight jeans. The small band of pale flesh and the navel.

'... *hand it to Cornel,*' one of the older bankers-or-whatever murmured to another. '*Eyes in her knickers already.*'

Lol looked helplessly at Danny. You could see the three lagers Jane had bought sitting on the bar top behind her left elbow, giving her a good excuse to prove she was not here on her own.

Jane could walk away from this any time she wanted.

But no, she went on talking to this Cornel.

Very much a woman, and smiling up at him.

'Oh God,' Lol said. 'What do I do about this?'

3

Wet Cassock

THE GREY MONK was still there, in the ladies' lavatory, his face fogged and his arms spread wide.

A déjà vu moment and it made Merrily feel unsteady. The wind was whining in the rafters, buzzing in the ill-fitting glass of the leaded window, whipping into the thorn trees around the chapel. All the different rhythms of the wind.

Had this *ever* been a friendly place? Its stone looked like prison stone. It stood mournful as an old war memorial in a shallow hollow on the yellowed slopes where the SAS used to train. Nearer to God? All it felt nearer to was death.

She glared at the grey monk by the side of the door, where he lived in the plaster. Where you'd see him in the mirror as you tidied your hair. According to Huw, he'd been a Nonconformist preacher who'd roamed the hills sick with lust for someone's wife down in Sennybridge. He'd been found dead where the women's toilet now stood, head cracked open on the flags.

The point being that he was said to have left his *imprint* there, later known, because of its general shape, as the Grey Monk – Huw explaining how most so-called ghostly monks were not monks at all, just a vagueness in the electromagnetic soup suggestive of robe and cowl.

Merrily saw herself in the mirror standing next to the monk. She was thirty-nine years old. Were the crow's feet becoming webbed or did she just need more early nights? She nodded to the monk and walked out to where Huw was waiting for her at the top of the passage, standing on his own under a small, naked bulb, spidery filaments glowing feebly through the dead flies and the dust.

The course students had all gone into the chapel. Merrily shut the doors on them. The only chance she'd get.

'OK. I was absolutely determined not to ask, *but…*'

'It'll be obvious, lass,' Huw said. 'Also, good for you. A chance to step back and see how far you've come. Rationalize it.'

'It can't be rationalized. It isn't rational. You taught me that.'

Huw put on his regretful half-smile. His dog collar was the colour of old bone. Huw's collars always looked like they'd been bought at a car-boot sale, maybe a hearse-boot sale. Merrily remembered the first time she'd heard his voice, expecting – Huw Owen? – some distant Welsh academic with a bardic lilt, but getting David Hockney, Jarvis Cocker. He'd been born in humble circumstances just down the valley here, then taken away as a baby to grow up in Yorkshire.

'All right,' he said, 'It's *partly* on account of you being the first woman ever to get sent here for deliverance training.'

Which he'd hardly been happy about at the time. Walking her over the unwelcoming hills, telling her what a turn-on women priests were for the pervs and the creeps. As for a woman *exorcist…*

'Two on this course,' Huw said.

You could tell by his tone that he hadn't been impressed. The hanging bulb glowed the colour of wet straw. The wind was leaning on the new front door at the top of the passage, and Merrily had an urge to walk through it, out onto the hill. Try and keep a cigarette alight up there. Or just keep on walking into the rattling night, back to the car, foot down, out of here, with the wind behind her.

'So what do you want me to tell them?'

'Just answer their questions, best you can. Feel free to down-play everything. We don't want to put the shits up them.'

Then, suddenly, impulsively, Huw sprang up on tiptoe and

headed the bulb, setting it swinging like a censer. In its fibrous light, his smile looked slightly insane.

'Although we do,' he said. 'Obviously.'

The women on the course were a brisk, posh girl and a squat, quiet matron in her fifties who Huw said had been governor of a women's prison. If it wasn't for the hungry female clergy, a third of the churches in England and Wales would probably be nightclubs and carpet warehouses. They had the confidence of being needed, these women.

'So why are you all here?' Huw said. 'Eh?'

Over twenty clergy in the body of the chapel, mostly young middle-aged. The higher number on the course reflecting not so much an increased interest in exorcism, Merrily was thinking, so much as the trend for deliverance *panels* within each diocese. Health and Safety. Back-up. Decisions made by committee.

There was a kind of formality about them. No jeans, no sweatshirts, more dog collars than Crufts. But somehow it felt artificial, like fancy dress. The only obvious maverick here was Huw himself, so blatantly old hippie you expected flecks of spliff down his jacket.

'I'm serious. Why were *you* picked for this – the one job the Church still gets all coy about? And Dawkins on the prowl, knife out.'

Somebody risked a laugh. Huw gazed out. Now they were out of fashion again, he wore a ponytail, grey and white, bound up with a red rubber band. He was sitting next to Merrily, behind a carafe of water, at a mahogany table below where the lectern used to be.

'You...' Levelling a forefinger. 'Why've you come? Stand up a minute, lad.'

The guy into the second row was about forty, had narrow glasses and a voice that was just as soft and reasonable as you'd expect.

'Peter Barber. Luton. Urban parish, obviously, high percentage of foreign nationals. The demand was there. I was invited by my bishop to consider the extent to which we should address it.'

'And how much of it do you accept as valid, Peter? When a Somali woman says she thinks the Devil might be arsing about with her daughter, what's your instinct?'

'Huw, we discussed this. I have a respect for everyone's belief system.'

'Course you do, lad.'

Huw glanced at Merrily, his lips moving slightly. They might have formed the words *Fucking hell.* The wind went on bulging the glass and swelling the joints of the chapel.

'How many of you are here because you've had what could be called a psychic or paranormal experience?'

Silence.

'Nobody?'

Someone coughed, smothered it. Merrily felt Huw wanting to smash all the lights. Then the woman who'd been a prison governor stood up. She wore a black suit over her clerical shirt. Her lapel badge said *Shona.* Her accent was lowland Scottish.

'I've been close to situations which were difficult to accommodate. We had a disturbed girl with a pentagram tattooed on the side of her neck, who we found was organizing Ouija-board sessions. Something not exactly unknown in women's prisons and not invariably stamped upon.'

'Because at least it keeps them quiet,' Huw said.

'Not in this case. We had disturbances bordering on hysteria, which spread with alarming speed. Girls claiming there were entities in their cells. The equilibrium of the whole establishment seemed to have been tipped. The prison psychologist was confident of being able to deal with it but eventually our chaplain asked me if he could bring in a colleague. From the deliverance ministry.'

'When was this?'

'Five or six years ago. I'd been reluctant at first, expecting him to… I don't know, subject the girls to some crude casting-out thing. But he just talked to them, and it gradually became

24

quieter. No magic solution, and it took a number of visits by this man, but it *was* resolved.'

'Never an exact science, lass.'

'I was impressed. Wanting to know how it had been achieved. When I took early retirement a couple of years later and sought ordination, that incident kept coming back to me. So here I am. A volunteer.'

Huw nodded and didn't look at Merrily. If the first guy had seemed unlikely to go the distance, it would be hard to fault this woman on either background or motivation. Merrily watched Huw bend and lift the carafe with both hands and tip a little water into his glass.

'So in other words,' he said, 'you're a set of dull buggers.'

Outside somewhere, a branch snapped. Huw took an unhurried drink.

'Men and women of common sense and *discretion*. Selected for their *stability*. Safe pairs of hands. Individuals who won't embarrass the essentially secular element inside the modern Church. No mystics, no evangelicals, no charismatics.'

Merrily stared at Huw. That was a *bad* thing? He shrugged lightly.

'Well, aye, we don't want crackpots. We don't want exorcisms prescribed like antibiotics, to cure shoplifting and alcohol abuse. Ideally, we don't want them, in the fullest sense, at all. But let's not dress this up...'

Merrily watched his fingers flexing on the mahogany tabletop then taking his weight as he leaned forward.

'This is no job for a digital priest. At some stage, if you decide to go ahead with this particular ministry, you'll be pulled into areas you never wanted to go. You'll be affected short-term and long-term, mentally and emotionally and spiritually. Every one of you's guaranteed to encounter summat that'll ruin your sleep. I don't want any bugger leaving here thinking that's not going to happen.'

She was aware of him glancing into the bottom left-hand corner of the chapel, where the shadows were deepest and you couldn't make out the faces.

'Which is why I asked this friend of mine to come over. Through the rain and the gales.' Turning to look at Merrily, who couldn't kill the blush and frowned. 'This is Mrs Watkins, deliverance consultant for the Diocese of Hereford. Successor to one of the most experienced exorcists in the country. Quite a responsibility. So… we have to ask, how did a young lass get a job like that? Safe pair of hands? I don't think so, though she is now. No, she were hand-picked by the Bishop of Hereford at the time, because…'

Huw. Glaring up at him, not moving her lips. *For God's sake…*

'Because he fancied her,' Huw said. 'It were a glamour thing.'

Merrily had come in jeans and a cowl-neck black sweater with her smallest pectoral cross. *Nowt formal,* Huw had said on the phone. She sighed.

'Runner-up in the *Church Times* Wet-Cassock competition. Never going to live that down.'

'*Runner-up.*' Huw sniffed. 'That were a travesty.'

Only half of them laughed. You could almost see the disdain like a faint cloud in the air around the posh girl who was probably planning a paper on how the Virgin Birth and the Resurrection were part of the same complex metaphor.

'With Merrily, you can't see the damage, but it's there.'

Huw wasn't smiling now. She noticed that his face was thinner, the lines like cracks in tree bark.

'Tell them about Mr Joy, Merrily. Tell the boys and girls what Mr Joy did to you.'

And then he turned away so he wouldn't see her eyes saying no.

1

Talk About Paris

CORNEL – WAS THAT his first name or what? *Cornel.* You had to *try* and laugh. He didn't even need to open that wide, loose, red mouth to be screaming, *Look at me, I'm from Off.* That too-perfect combination of plaid workshirt and Timberland-type boots... and the Rolex. Or whatever it was. Some flash old-fashioned status watch, anyway, and he'd be thinking all the country girlies would be like, *Take me, Cornel... take me away in the Boxter and show me the penthouse.*

Well, not *quite* all of them.

'I've never been up there myself,' Jane said. 'The Court... it's like real mysterious to us.'

The localish accent rolling out nicely, not too pronounced. If this wasn't so serious it could almost be fun.

'Mysterious,' Cornel said.

Did he actually say *myshterioush*? Was he really that pissed?

Probably. Jane looked up at him, hands on her hips.

'So go on...'

'What?'

'Like what *happens*?'

'What do you think happens?' Cornel said.

'I don't *like* to think.'

Cornel grinned down at her. There was that sour, too-much-wine smell on his breath. More unpleasant, somehow, than beer or whisky. Kind of decadent and louche.

'You're really tall,' Jane said stupidly. 'You know that?'

'I was breast-fed. For months and months.' He looked up from her chest. 'So my mother tells me.'

'You got a gun, Cornel? Of your own?'

'Two, actually. One's a Purdey. You need another drink.'

'So, like, what do you shoot?'

'Things.'

'*Things?* What, like bottles off walls and stuff?' Jane could see Cornel trying to not to snigger. 'Well, *what*?'

The wind came in again. Lights flickered.

'Darling,' Cornel said. 'We get to shoot pretty much anything that comes within range… pheasants, rabbits, those little deer… pussycats…'

Below bar-level, Jane felt the fingers of her right hand bunching into a tight little fist. There'd been talk in the village of cats going missing.

'Wow,' she said.

'What happens at The Court is anything you want… basically. 'Cause you're paying for it. Or, rather, the bank is.'

'Oh.' Jane did the vacant look. 'Which bank you with? Is it…' Putting a finger up to her lower lip. 'Is it the NatWest? Or like that one with all the little puppet people and the tinkly music?'

'Uh-huh.' Cornel smiled, shaking his head. 'Landesman's. New kids on the block, very progressive.'

'You do credit cards and stuff?'

Cornel sighed.

'And what do *you* do, girlie?'

'Hairdresser,' Jane said. 'Well, trainee. But one day I'll be doing it big time in Hereford. Or London, mabbe.'

'Hmm.' Cornel was swaying a bit and wrinkling his nose like he was figuring something out. 'Don't know anybody in Hereford, but I did once handle some finance for a chain of salons in London… and Paris? Paris any good to you?'

'Paris?'

Jane blinking, like she didn't dare believe he was serious.

'And Milan, now, I think,' Cornel said. 'You look like you need a drink. A big one.'

'Had too much already,' Jane said.

'Maybe you'd rather have one somewhere else?'

'Dunno really.'

'Where we can talk about Paris.'

Jane's left hand was on the damp mat on the bar top, and Cornel's much bigger hand was over it and squeezing gently. She pulled, not hard, but the hand was trapped.

She looked up at Cornel and giggled. His eyes were well glazed. It was unlikely that she'd get any more out of him. Probably time to end this.

The odd times when it was needed in an establishment as relatively sedate as the Black Swan, Barry was known for acting with speed and economy and a glimmer of steel. But Barry was on the phone. Lol tensed. The inglenook coughed out smoke and soot.

'You seen him before?' Danny said. 'Do we know if he's got a room yere?'

Lol shook his head.

Telling himself it would be OK. That this was Jane. Jane who'd once expressed the hope that some myopic Japanese stockbroker would accidentally blow off Ward Savitch's head.

'Hell's bells!' The main door had sprung open, the wind pushing in James Bull-Davies. Last squire of Ledwardine, partner of Alison Kinnersley, Lol's ex from what now seemed like another, distant lifetime. 'Bloody *night.*'

James thrust the door shut against the gale, shaking drips from his sparse hair, as Lol heard Jane's unmistakably dangerous laughter, like pills in a jar. Cornel was grinning and Jane's expression was kind of, *Oh you…* Almost affectionate, like they'd known one another a long time or she was as pissed as he was.

Lol looked at Danny. Danny sighed.

'All right, then, boy, we'll both go.'

He was halfway out of his chair when the weather took over. A wall of wind hit the Swan, the candle-bulbs shivering against the oak panelling. Lol saw Jane's free hand reaching out to grasp the end of Cornel's leather belt.

'Bastard's bloody pulled,' one of his mates said.

'George, she's pulling *him*. Doesn't that give us a get-out?'

Both of these guys smiling now, as Cornel let Jane tow him along the bar towards the door to the stairs, looking into her eyes with what Lol interpreted as a kind of grateful disbelief as he and Danny moved in. Then the whole bar was doused in sepia.

Power drop-out. Somewhere in the room, a woman did a theatrical scream, and Lol froze. All he could make out was a shadow-Jane trying to stand a beer glass on the bar. Then a roar.

'*Shit!*'

As the lights came flickering back, he saw Cornel jerking up and away, movements fractured like an early movie.

Jane's smile was wide and wild, but her voice was shaky.

'… from the pussycats.'

Her face pale and strained, and she was breathing hard but clearly determined not to run, as Cornel came at her, his head like a red pepper, big lips twisted.

'… *you little fucking…*'

'No!'

Lol flinging himself between them, hands out.

Saw it coming, twisted sideways but still caught the fist on the top of the shoulder, which really hurt, then saw Cornel's colleagues closing around him, with a sickly wafting of wine-breath.

'Now, hold up…'

James Bull-Davies wading in. Stooping a bit these days, though it might have been the weight of whatever he kept in the fraying pockets of his tweed jacket.

'Might one suggest you chaps cool off outside?'

'… fuck's this?'

'Ladies present,' James said briskly.

'*That* bitch?' Cornel's face thrust into James's. 'You saw what she did?' Close to screeching, losing it. '*Saw* that, did you? *Did* you?'

Lol saw an extensive dark stain on the front of Cornel's jeans.

'Shouldn't render you impotent for long,' James said mildly. 'Big man, little girl, be disinclined to make a fuss, myself.'

Somebody laughed. The inglenook was oozing smoke like some ancient railway tunnel.

'All right. Enough now, lads.' Barry was here, in his quiet suit, his slim bow tie. 'Accidents happen in the dark. If you'd like to leave your trousers at reception, sir, we can get them cleaned for you.'

Cornel was looking at Jane, his eyes sunk below the bony ridge of his sweating brow.

'I'll be seeing you,' he said, 'girlie.'

Lol felt Jane shaking and put an arm around her and steered her back to the table by the fire. She smiled slackly.

'Cocked *that* up.' Lifting up her hands, all wet. 'More on me than him.'

'What did you say to him, Jane?'

'I was just, you know, so pissed off at the idea of them coming in all *droit de seigneur* kind of thing – and he was obviously legless. So I thought I'll get him talking, see what I can get out of him?'

'That's why you wanted to go and buy the drinks?'

'Oh, Lol, it was an impulse thing!' Her face shone. 'Like, it's important to know, don't you think, what Savitch is letting them get away with? Like, if we're going to get the bastard closed down before he turns the village into the blood-sport capital of the New Cotswolds—'

'Jane, he's *investment*. A lot of people love him.'

'*Nobody* loves him! And we don't want that kind of invest-ment. We've got archaeological remains, we've got the strong possibility of a Bronze Age henge with actual stones. We could have *loads* of tourism – worthwhile tourism, not these... scum.'

'All right, they love his money,' Lol said sadly.

'They just think they might *need* his money, so they don't like to tell the bastard where to stick it.' Jane glowered for a moment, then looked up, wary. 'You're not going to tell Mum about this, are you?'

Lol sighed.

'So what *did* he tell you, Jane?'

'Actually, it's not funny. *I* was, like, what do you do at The Court, and he's going, Shoot things, of course, and I'm like, *Things? Go on.* And he thought… I mean, I could see he thought I was…'

'What?'

'Like turned on by it? The way some women are. The hunt-ball floozies? He said they'd shoot anything that got in the way. Deer… pussycats, he said.'

'Probably exaggerating to try and sound hard.'

'I could tell he was waiting for me to go, Oh, I'd love to come and watch you wielding your weapon. Lol, they're— Oh shit, look at him now…'

Lol half-turned, pain spinning into his shoulder where he'd caught Cornel's fist. Cornel was standing next to the door to the stairs. His eyes seemed to be physically retracting under the shelf of his brow as he looked around the room in the half-light, plucking at the damp patch on his trousers.

'Wherever you are, you little bitch,' he said mildly, 'I just want you to know this isn't over.'

Lol looked around. Maybe only he and Jane had heard Cornel, because there'd been a sudden scraping of chairs, exclamations and then a hollow near-silence in the bar as a small circle formed around Barry in the centre of the room.

'*Where* was this?' James Bull-Davies snapped. 'Say again.'

'Oldcastle?' Barry said. 'Have I got that right? Beyond Credenhill, but before you get to the Wye. Don't know any details. Mate of mine with an apple farm was just passing it on in case we saw any police action. Cops are all over there, apparently.'

'Yes, but who—?'

'Oh, Mansel…?' Barry stepped back. 'Gawd, James. That mean he's a relation?'

'Cousin. Of sorts.' James straightened up, bit his lower lip. 'Hell's bells.'

A flaking log rolled out of the fire up against the mesh of the fireguard. Danny Thomas came back and sat down, pushing fingers through his beard.

'Barry just had a call from a mate. Feller been found dead. Farmer.'

Lol said. 'What... storm-related?'

'Sounds like way too many coppers for that,' Danny said.

5

Gangland

Up against the brick wall under a bleary bulkhead lamp, Bliss was struggling into his Durex suit. Big, wide puddles in the yard, four of them rippling like something tidal in the lights and the remains of the gale. The fifth puddle much smaller, not rippling at all, the colour and consistency of bramble jelly.

Farmers. Never felt comfortable around farmers, not even dead farmers.

'Boss...'

Terry Stagg came lumbering out of a litter of uniforms and techies shielding the body from the wind, Bliss looking up from the flapping plastic.

'DCI know about this, Terry?'

Realizing this was the very last question he'd normally ask. This was getting ridiculous. He peered at Terry Stagg's eyes in the lamplight. Terry was working on a beard to cover up his second chin. His eyes looked tired. And faintly puzzled?

Shit.

'Boss, it was actually the DCI who said to get you out. Be more convenient for DI Bliss were her actual—'

'Bitch.'

Stagg said nothing. Bliss turned away, nerves burning like a skin rash. Probably digging himself an even bigger pit.

'My impression was that the DCI won't be coming out tonight at all,' Stagg said. 'Which is unusual, given the social status of the deceased.'

'Don't question it.' Bliss zipped the Durex suit from groin to throat. 'Give thanks.'

He plucked the elasticated sleeve away from his watch: just gone nine. Taken him the best part of half an hour to get here from home. Blown-off branches all over the roads, one lacerating the flank of his car as he squirmed past on the grass verge.

'So this is…?'

'Mr Mansel Bull, boss. Fifty-seven. Farmer, as you know. Old family.'

'Double-page spread in the *Hereford Times* kind of old?'

'Maybe special supplement,' Terry Stagg said.

'Not short of a few quid, Tez. Lorra leckie going to waste, or is that you?'

The yard was ablaze with lights on sensors, like a factory, and alive with bellowing creaks, the smashing of blown-open doors, the restive moaning of the cattle in the sheds – Bliss thinking all this was like the sounds of his own nerves amplified.

'Billy Grace?'

'On his way,' Terry said. 'Allegedly. But we do have time-of-death to within half an hour or so. Mr Bull'd gone to a parish-council meeting arranged for seven, but called off due to the conditions. Sounds like he came directly back. Walking into… something.'

A council meeting explained the suit and tie, what you could see of it under a glistening beard of blood. Hard to say if his head was still even attached. Was that bone? Was that an actual split skull? Bliss stepped back. You never quite got used to this.

'Who found him?'

'Brother. Heard the cattle moaning in the shed, so he had a walk up. With his shotgun.'

'Oh aye?'

'Not loaded, he *claims*. Lives in the big bungalow down towards the river. Mr Bull lived here, on his own.'

'On his *own* – in *that?*'

Security lights on the barn opposite flushed out mellow old brick and about fifteen dark windows on three storeys. Oldcastle

Farm. The house and buildings wedged into a jagged promontory above the Wye, embedded like a fort. Georgian or Queen Anne or whatever, had to be big enough for a family of twelve, plus servants.

'Divorced. For the second time, apparently.'

Terry looking sideways at Bliss. Mr Bull was face-up to the lights, eyes wide open in his big, bald, dented head, like he couldn't believe the way death had come racing at him out of the wind and the night.

'Where's the brother?'

'In the house. Waiting for you.'

'He see anything?'

Terry Stagg shook his head.

'All right.' Bliss hunched his shoulders against the wind. 'So where we up to, Tezza?'

'Covering the lanes, pubs, for what that's worth now. They'll be well away.'

'They?'

'Mr Sollers Bull thinks a gang. He'll explain.'

'Where's Karen?'

'House-to-house. Well... farm-to-farm. In the four-by-four. With a couple of uniforms, just in case.'

'Good, good.'

Karen was connected: farming family. Where Bliss came from, a farmer was a bloke with a shared allotment and a chicken.

'Obviously you've searched the buildings.'

'With Mr Sollers Bull. And the house. Did I...?' Terry Stagg coughed. 'Did I say Mr Sollers Bull was not very happy?'

'*No.* You amaze me, Terence.'

Terry said, 'In the sense that... he reckons he and his brother both reported intruders.'

'When?'

'Two occasions in the past month. He says we laughed.'

'*We* laughed?'

'The police.'

'The police laughed. Fuck me. Excellent.'

'I mean, that's what he says.'

'Might this explain the DCI's generosity in letting the under-ling take charge, d'you think?'

Thinking, *nice one, well-timed, Francis*, as a vehicle came coughing and grumbling up the tarmac drive. Dr Grace's Land Rover Defender.

'Also,' Terry Stagg said, 'when I told him you'd be in to talk to him later on, Mr Sollers Bull said... He seems to know who you are.'

The vehicle's engine had been switched off but was clinging to life. In the instant of its last shudder, the wind died and it was like they were standing in the vacuum of quiet at the eye of the storm.

'Fame at last. I'm made up.' Bliss's own voice came bouncing back at him from across the yard. He lowered it. 'What are you saying?'

'He knows your father-in-law.'

'Oh.'

Billy Grace was hauling his kit up the drive. Bliss went to meet him.

Shit. The downside of having a complicated private life in a small county.

Every other Saturday, work permitting, he'd collect his kids from the in-laws' farm. Trying to time it so he'd be bringing them back just before Kirsty got in from shopping or wherever. In the hope that he could leave them with his mother-in-law, a woman he could handle, more or less.

Unfortunately, he'd pulled this one too many times. Last Saturday, the door had been ajar at the farm holiday cottage where Kirsty was living, and the kids had gone running inside. He'd considered just buggering off, but in the end he'd gone in to find the stove lit, all very cosy, smell of quality coffee – sour reminders of his own kitchen with all its comforts now plundered.

And here was the plunderer in person: Mrs Bliss. Only, this was the Mrs Bliss of ten years ago – the *future* Mrs Bliss reborn. All made up, short black skirt well up the thigh. *See what you threw away.*

'You had another hour, at least,' Kirsty said, when the kids were out of the room. 'But then you always did get bored with them quite rapidly... what with an eight-year-old's lack of interest in the vagaries of the Crown Prosecution Service.'

Vagaries? She'd been rehearsing, evidently.

'Kairs—'

'Or do you have a *date* tonight?'

Date. Not a word they'd ever used between themselves. That little tweak of petty triumph on Kirsty's lovely pulpy lips.

She knew something. She bloody *knew something.*

'Gorra be off, Kairsty,' Bliss said. 'Be the Easter holidays next time I come, so we can make it a different day if you want. I could maybe take them over to Aberystwyth or somewhere.'

'You never did put yourself out much, did you, Frank?'

Finding his arms folded – classic defence stance – Bliss let them drop.

'It's not *that* frigging convenient. Couple of hours each way, and with Easter traffic—'

'I think,' Kirsty said, 'that you know what I'm talking about.'

'I've gorra go.'

'The thing is...' she stood up slowly '... isn't it against the rules? I mean, when it all comes out, won't one of you have to move to another division? Isn't that how it works?'

Bliss had felt the blood draining out of his face so fast that his cheeks actually felt cold.

'Now, look... I don't where you think you're going with this, but—'

'Oh, you do, Frank.'

Bliss's mind was going like a washing machine: oh shit. *Shit, shit, shit.* Where had she got this from? Which one of his beloved colleagues had sniffed it out? How was this even *possible*?

'You're mental, Kairsty, you know that?'

Safest to go on the offensive. An advantage of being separated
was the way you could bring a row directly to the boil, knowing
you could slip away, with nothing lost, before the first plate hit
the wall.

'I don't think so.' Her eyes cold as quartz. 'I mean, I could
almost feel insulted if that cow's as far as your ambition goes,
but being I know what a sad little sod you've become, it doesn't
surprise me a great deal, Frank, to be honest.'

'I'm going.'

Bliss's palms starting to sweat.

'Calling the shots now, is she, on your private life?'

'Think whatever you want.'

'As I understand it, with a male officer and a woman, it's
always the man has to move, isn't it? Or have I got that
wrong?'

'What exactly do you want off me?'

And she'd smiled. Generously.

'Just want you to own *up* to it, Frank, that's all.' Oh, the satis-
faction in her eyes. 'Dad's solicitor says that makes it a lot easier.
Play your cards right, it *might* not come out in public.'

Oh sure.

'Just makes it easier, that's all,' Kirsty said.

'And costlier. For me, anyway.'

Kirsty had shrugged, Bliss feeling like his insides had been
flushed out with cold water. Kirsty blamed the police for everything that had gone wrong between them. She was wrong about
that, and she probably knew she was wrong, but this was convenient, and she'd use it.

'Close friend, Billy?'

Dr Grace, who was *very* well-connected, glanced over his
shoulder at Bliss. 'Not particularly a friend at all, Francis, but
everybody's at least acquainted in this county. Except, possibly,
for uncouth incoming Scousers like yourself.'

'You mean a Masonic thing?' Bliss said.

Dr Grace declined to reply, turning back to his work, lifting a distended flap of skin like he was opening a Jiffy bag full of blood, and Bliss turned away.

'Big family, mind, Billy. Branches everywhere. The Bulls, Bull-Morrises, Bull-Davieses…'

'Small county.'

'And a big house for one man.'

'Two marriages, Francis. Both childless. *Not* what a farmer wants. Well, now, I'd say that was pointing at him as culprit, but not the kind of man to have his sperm tested. Almost certainly would've been a third wife. Never a man to look back, Mansel.'

'He didn't see this coming,' Bliss said.

'Ah now…' Billy Grace turned, beaming, a loose, shambling man with big white teeth, a wild, neon smile. 'Actually, he *did*. He must've been facing directly into it.'

'What you offering?'

'Not a penknife, Francis. Machete, more like.'

'That's urban, Billy.' Bliss took a step back. 'That's frigging gangland.' *Mr Sollers Bull thinks a gang.* 'Go on then, doc. Give me the guesswork.'

Billy Grace lurched to his feet. Thimbles of blood on the fingers of his surgical gloves.

'The neck – one blow, looks like. A single slash. I'm guessing that came first, while he was still on his feet. The blows to the top of the head would've put him straight down.'

Billy took a couple of long strides into the middle of the farmyard, all the uniforms and techies moving away as his right arm went back for role-play.

'If you imagine he's standing here when the blade makes contact, *slamming* into the windpipe. Not exactly what you'd call a butcher's strike, but the sheer impact of it would leave the poor bastard reeling, spouting blood and tissue everywhere. A great dollop… as you see.'

Billy gestured at the separate puddle. Bliss felt queasy.

'Poor old Mansel tottering away, couple of metres and then…' He began to back off unsteadily. '*Bang*, on the skull, and Mansel comes down like a block of flats.'

Bliss said, 'And the killer…?'

'Just watches.'

'Watches?'

'Well, obviously, I don't know that, but… I'll be able to give you a full list of injuries and possibly confirm the sequence tomorrow, but if you want to take a closer look…'

'For now, I'll take your word. So the killer knew he'd killed. There was serious intent…'

'Hardly trying to fend the poor chap off.'

'And then slinks away. With his big knife.' Bliss turned to Terry Stagg, the wind in his face like barbed wire. 'First light, we go over the whole frigging farm, inch by inch. I also think we're gonna have to drag Howe away from her dinner party, or wherever. Gorra mad bastard here.'

'Or someone pumped up with drugs.' Billy's teeth shining with carnivorous glee. 'Whoever he is, Francis, *I* wouldn't like to face him in an alley.'

Terry Stagg said, 'Mr Sollers Bull… you need to know…'

'Where is he?'

'I suggested he went home. You go down to the fork in the drive, turn right—'

'Where've I heard that name before, Terence? Sollers Bull…'

'TV?' Stagg said. 'Pictures in the papers? I've been trying to tell you.'

Bliss turned. Billy Grace was grinning.

'Oh shit,' Bliss said. 'He's got *form.*'

'That might be how you see it, Francis,' Billy said. 'But to quite a few people hereabouts, he's a bloody hero.'

6

Exhaust

Even now, even in a room full of priests, it was hard to relive. Years later, it would still start burning in her memory like acid. If it caught her in the night, she'd have to get out of bed and pray. Recite St Patrick's Breastplate, the way she had the night Denzil Joy died.

'Let me set the scene for you,' Huw Owen said to the students. 'When Merrily were appointed as deliverance consultant, the man she replaced was the last Diocesan Exorcist. His name were Canon Dobbs and he couldn't be doing wi' namby-pamby terminology like *deliverance*.'

He paused, looking down to the darkest part of the chapel again.

'An austere owd bugger, Dobbs. Former academic. *Not* a supporter of the ordination of women. Merrily's a university dropout who received her calling in the last days of a wonky marriage – he got killed in a car crash. Was there an element of guilt after that? I wouldn't like to spec—'

'Huw—'

'Always an element of summat, in't there? We're all on the threshold of imbalance. As this job keeps reminding us.'

She saw his left hand quiver. And again he looked out towards the shadows in the left-hand corner, where Merrily could see a man now, leaning back, an arm thrown across the back of the empty chair next to his.

'Anyroad, Canon Dobbs felt it were his duty to expose the

upstart bint to the kind of evil the very existence of which would be denied by the progressive bishop who'd appointed her. And – happen – by some of you. Lass?'

Huw extended an arm. Merrily stood up.

'Erm… I don't know whether anybody here's ever been a nurse. Or knows one. But I've found it's always useful to listen to nurses.'

A rush of wind hit the chapel and there was a distant splintering, all heads turning except for Huw's.

'Not least because they've seen most things relating to death. This, erm, this is about a death. It was my first deliverance job and probably should've been Canon Dobbs's last before he retired, but he was… unavailable.'

Merrily was already uncomfortable. All she had to do was lift the cellar hatch of memory, just a crack, and out it sprang again, and she could almost feel it on the underside of her wrist.

Scritch-scratch.

The smell coming back at once: *cat-shit and gangrene,* one of the nurses had said.

'Mr Joy was a hospital patient in Hereford, and he didn't have long. I was called out in the night because the nurses said he was asking for a priest and the hospital chaplain wasn't available. The truth was that it was the nurses who needed the priest.'

The nurses who didn't like to touch Mr Joy. The nurses who had seen the way he used his wife when she came to visit.

The nurses who never could forget the sensation of his fingers when they bent over him to take his temperature or change one of the tubes.

Scritch-scratch. On the soft skin on the underside of the wrist.

'But I was new at this,' Merrily said. 'I told them it wasn't my job to judge him, only to try and bring him peace. Something was still insisting, back then, that there was no such thing as an evil presence.'

A hand went up. Shona, the woman who'd been a prison governor, hair like a light brown balaclava.

'You mean your own life-experience or your training?'

'Look,' Merrily said. 'Here you are at the bedside of a dying man. *He's* dying, you're a priest, there to bring comfort. How can you do that if you accept that he's infested with evil? So you go with the rational view. No such thing as an abstract, incorporeal evil. You need to relax.'

He can enter you without moving, that man, one of the nurses had said.

Merrily's hand instinctively moving to the pectoral cross. Don't shudder. Do *not* shudder now.

'Cut to the car chase, lass,' Huw said. 'And don't omit the exhaust.'

She told them the rest. Well, most of it.

Trying to convey that sense of all the light in the room being sucked sourly into a man on the very rim of extinction, whose touch was like an enema.

'Looking back, it leaves me asking a number of questions. Fierce sexual energy coming from an old, dying man – can that be explained medically? Possibly it can, I'm not qualified to say, but the nurses didn't think so, and nurses, no matter how compassionate, can be very cynical people.'

It was quieter now, the wind in remission.

'The psychological explanation,' Merrily said, 'might be that here was a man who'd enjoyed exploiting women sexually, degrading them. A man in search of increasingly perverse pleasures – to what extent you want to demonize this is up to you.'

Huw was looking at her, head on one side. *OK, I'm coming to it.*

'You can usually find a rational explanation, but there has to be a cut-off point. You need to recognize when you're trying too hard to explain something away, because that can be when you're most vulnerable. And if it reaches *you*, there's not much hope for whoever you're trying to protect.'

Shona said, 'When you say "if *it* reaches you"…?'

'What do *I* mean by *it*? Not sure. But I think if you're unable

45

to accept the premise of an external evil, you may not be able to deal with some problems. I think… looking back, I don't think I handled it forcefully enough. I let the psychology make too many decisions. And afterwards I failed to draw a line under it, as a result of which… something… seemed to be hanging around, for some time.'

Looking at Shona, hoping she'd ask another question, move the thread.

Nobody spoke.

'I felt unclean. Bad dreams. Night… sensations. Subjective, you might say, psychological. I've since encountered criminals, accepted as being disturbed, and this was just an ordinary old man. Yet Mr Joy was a notorious case in that hospital. Canon Dobbs had had dealings with him before and could have done so this time, but he set me up.'

She didn't want to go into the burning of garments, and no way was she going to tell them about the essential advice which had come not from Huw but from an old woman who'd lived in a care home and who'd been surrounded by some very dubious books. Wouldn't help anybody. Although it had helped her.

Maybe seeing she was floundering, Huw stood up.

'The point being,' he said, 'that it might've been years before Merrily encountered owt as extreme as that – if ever. Make or break, and Dobbs is expecting break. I'd still say that were irresponsible of him.'

Heads turned at a slow creaking sound from outside, some distance away but ominous.

'Another tree coming down,' Huw said. 'Nowt we can do.'

'It's like a series of doors,' Merrily said. 'You start off opening the psychological door, and sometimes that's as far as you need to go, and it ends with prayers and a blessing. But quite often, several doors down the line, you'll come to one that a psychologist wouldn't go through.'

She drank some water.

'I don't know, to this day, whether Mr Joy was afflicted with some violent sexual anomaly which had more or less eaten away his humanity. Or whether that had opened him up to *something else*. But you don't have to. That's why we have the rituals and the liturgy. To an extent… just do it. Without it, you'd be off the rails.'

The posh girl – did the card say *Bethany*? – had her hand up.

'What happened finally? Were you there when he—?'

The wind had started up again but now it was less ferocious, as if slightly dismayed at what it had done. The big gust which had brought down the tree had also driven clouds away from the moon. It flared suddenly in the lowest window and lit the face of the man at the back. Briefly, before he slid into the adjacent chair.

The man at the back of the chapel had flat, grey hair and his eyes still looked like they'd been sewn on. No bags, no wrinkles. A soft-toy's eyes.

Bloody hell.

'He died that night,' Merrily said. 'I was there, yes. Nurses will often tell you stories about the dying being… helped over. Claiming they can see the faces of people they've known. Parents, old friends, grannies. Brain chemicals, if you like, comfort visions. Lots of rational explanations, but it keeps happening. Someone to beckon you over.'

'And was there someone waiting for Mr Joy?'

'At the end, he was conspicuously disturbed. As if he could see something which… didn't seem like his granny.'

'Did you see anything?'

'No. And I came away, as I've implied, with a quite acute sense of failure. Sat and smoked a cigarette with the ward sister. Both of us fairly shattered after watching an old man who'd scared us all… go out in a state of abject terror.'

Shona said, 'And when, subsequently, you felt that something of this man hadnae gone away… do you think this sense of failure might've been a contributory factor?'

'Haunted by my own inadequacy?'

Nobody followed up on this. Merrily glanced at Huw, sitting with his eyes half-closed. She had that sense of being set up, manoeuvred into place, as surely as she had with the late Canon Dobbs.

'Were you afraid,' the girl, Bethany, said, 'when you thought something was coming for him?'

'Hard not to be. *He* was.'

'Afraid for your immortal soul? Or afraid that you weren't going to be able to handle the job?'

'Mmm.'

'And what did you do about that?'

'I don't know,' Merrily said. 'It's never gone away.'

Huw was nodding.

'You're *always* afraid?' Bethany said. 'Whenever you're asked to deal with…' Her face, at last, showing dismay.

'Pretty much,' Merrily said.

Glancing towards the guy at the back, half expecting to see a spiral of smoke. Remembering a summer afternoon in a big church in the Malvern Hills, the vicar there finishing off his cigarette, leaving little cylinders of ash at the foot of the lectern. Remembering what he'd said that day.

Not a lot frightens me. I can deal with most physical pain, emotional pain, stress.

He'd probably done his training up here in the Beacons, and the exercises prior to selection. It was said they had to run up to fifty miles with an eighty-pound pack and when they took their boots off their socks were thick with blood. *I can achieve separation from the weakness of the body,* he'd said that day in his church.

It was fairly clear now that he hadn't been expecting to see her here. Maybe hoping to slide away quietly when the session had ended, so they wouldn't have to meet? The moon had screwed that.

He looked up at last, and their eyes met, and his were small and almost flat to his head like a teddy bear's, and his smile was tentative, wary.

7

Old Evil

FALLEN TREES HAD restructured the landscape. Two of them were down on the hillside below the chapel, the biggest near the bottom of the track, just before it joined the main road. A crackling, skeletal mesh in the blurred moonlight.

Huw Owen was standing on a crag with a lambing lamp. Like one of Holman Hunt's rejected sketches for *The Light of the World,* Merrily thought. Below him, a bunch of the deliverance students stood staring dumbly at the tangle of branches, like this was an act of God. Huw smiling thinly, as if he knew that it was.

Not that it would affect the students. They'd all walked up from the pub and the guest houses and B & Bs in the village, Huw from his rectory. Only someone who'd arrived late enough to have to park her old Volvo right outside the sodding chapel…

Bugger.

'What this probably means,' Merrily said, 'is that I won't get home tonight.'

The wind had died back to a murmur, like distant traffic. Huw came down from his crag.

'Couple of lads'll be up wi' chainsaws, I expect.'

'When?'

'Soon as it's light. I'll make you a bed up. Won't be silk sheets or owt, mind.'

She followed him across the rough and sodden grass, popping

49

the studs on her waxed coat, not liking to think what kind of damage there might be back home in Ledwardine. Huw stopped and looked back at her.

'Country life. Like town life, wi' extra shite.'

'Don't like Jane being on her own in the vicarage. I know she's eighteen, but in my mind she's ten.'

'She's got Robinson just across the street.' Huw came to a wooden stile, waited, patting Merrily on the shoulder as she drew level. 'You did bloody well tonight. Wouldn't've worked the same coming from me.'

He balanced his lambing light on one of the stile's posts and climbed over. She called after him.

'You're a bastard, Huw.'

Huw picked up the lamp, and the lamp picked up a razored track leading down towards the stone rectory, a grey boulder with a scree of crumbling outbuildings. Merrily scrambled up on the stile, the wind whipping at her hair. This was nothing – an hour ago she'd've been on hands and knees.

'You didn't tell me Syd Spicer was on the course.'

After the session was over, she hadn't gone looking for the man with teddy-bear eyes, she'd waited for him to approach her. But he never had. She hadn't seen him leave. Old skills.

'He rang me up. Asking if he could sit in for one day.'

Merrily looked down at him from the top of the stile.

'When was this?'

'At the weekend.'

'He say why?'

'Not in any detail.'

'Would I be right in thinking...' Merrily climbed over and sat down on the step of the stile '... that Syd no more expected to see me here than I expected to see him?'

Huw stood gazing out, beyond the rectory, to where the moon had pewtered the hills.

'I didn't tell him I'd asked you to come, no. I figured... since you worked with him last year, I figured he'd trust what you had to say.'

'In relation to what?'

'Whatever problem he's got.'

'Which is…?'

The step was soaked through; Merrily pulled her coat under her bum. This was obviously going to take a while. Across in the rectory, a light blinked on.

'That'll be Spicer now,' Huw said.

'He's in your bloody rectory?'

'He were stopping t'night here anyroad.'

Two lights were on now in the rectory. Merrily folded her arms.

'You see, what strikes me as odd is that when I was invited down to Syd's parish in the Malverns, it was because he, basically, did not do this stuff. Had no time for any of it.'

There are leaps I can't make, he'd said to her.

And Merrily had said, *You're worried by the non-physical.*

And he'd said, *Samuel Dennis Spicer, Church of England.*

Name, rank and number. You could pull out all his teeth and that was the most you'd get from the Rev. Syd Spicer, former sergeant with 22 SAS, the Special Air Service, Hereford's finest.

The UK's finest, come to that. Some said the world's.

Huw sat down at the other end of the step.

'Remind me about the time you worked with him. Briefly.'

'Series of road accidents in the Malverns, near his rectory. All in more or less the same place. Survivors saying they'd swerved to avoid a man on a bike.'

'Who wasn't there. And Spicer didn't believe that.'

'Kept saying he had a problem with paranormal phenomena,' Merrily said. 'He wanted me to look into it, do the roadside blessing bit and reassure local people that it was sorted. Which led to—'

'I know what it led to. Did he believe at the end? When it was over?'

'Probably not. So if you're asking whether I'm surprised to see him on a deliverance course, yes, I am.'

Huw said, 'I were also wondering why he hadn't gone to you in the first place.'

'Over *what*? What did he tell you?'

'He said – and I quote – an *old evil* had come back into his life. And he needed to deal with it.'

'Exhaust. That's why you set me up to talk about Denzil Joy?'

'Don't get me wrong, lass, I think it were a useful exercise for all of 'em. It's the most explicit case of possible demonic possession I've heard of in a while, and I thought you'd tell it well, and you did. None of them buggers is going to forget about Denzil. But whatever it is it's likely in your manor, and I thought you should know about it. And I thought he should be reminded about you.'

'Syd isn't expecting to see me again tonight, is he?'

'Aye, well... he'll think you've gone. He won't know your car's trapped behind a tree.'

'Huw, you're a—'

'Bastard, aye.'

Even the weather played into Huw's hands.

'I take it, Merrily, that when that business were on in the Malverns, Spicer wasn't frightened.'

'No, he wasn't.'

'He is now.'

'You reckon?'

'A man who's served in likely the hardest regiment in the entire history of the British Army.' Huw stretched out his legs into the dark, greasy grass. 'Now then, lass, what could possibly scare the shit out of *him*?'

8

Neglect

BLISS HAD COME alone, parking outside a metal gate at the top of the drive, eventually having to climb over because he couldn't work the bolt in the dark. A spotlight speared him as he hung astride the shivering tubular bar. At the top of the drive, a door had opened. A man stood there. Green gilet, high boots.

'Police,' Bliss said.

Feeling like a twat as he came down from the gate, stumbling to his knees. The countryside could always bugger you up when it felt like it. He stumbled towards the bungalow, built of old brick like the big house – an outbuilding, possibly a converted coach house.

'Mr Bull?'

A nod, maybe.

'Francis Bliss, Mr Bull. West Mercia CID.'

Bliss pulled off his beanie, held up his ID. The guy in the doorway didn't look at it.

'You're the man who married Chris Symonds's daughter.'

'I am, yes.'

Bliss sighed. Maybe they'd met at one of the agonizing county functions Kirsty had dragged him to, some creaking conveyor belt of dinner jackets.

'Chris is a friend,' Mr Bull said. 'I see him often.'

Well, that could hardly be more explicit. A blast of wind caught Bliss as he stowed away his ID. Loose bits of his life getting blown in his face.

'Mr Bull, can I say that I'm very sorry—'

'For my loss?'

Bliss said nothing.

'You can take your routine commiserations, Inspector Bliss, and insert them into your rectum,' Mr Bull said.

Bliss nodded wearily and followed him into the house.

Grief took many forms, aggression one of the commonest.

Low-energy bulbs laid a mauve wash on the kitchen. It had costly customized fittings and strong new beams of green oak. When a phone started ringing, Sollers Bull unplugged the lead from the wall.

'Everybody who needs to know knows.'

'Next few days will be difficult,' Bliss said.

'*Days?*'

Sollers Bull stood gazing into wide windows that looked to be triple-glazed. Nothing much to see but the reflection of himself and Bliss and a double-oven Aga in tomato red. Sollers had told Stagg he'd spent the early evening at a staff meeting at his farm shop. It checked out.

'Chris says you consistently neglected your wife, Inspector,' Sollers Bull told Bliss's reflection. 'Neglect seems to be your force's forte.'

'Where's *your* wife, Mr Bull?'

'Not your concern.'

'Well, you know, actually it is,' Bliss said quietly. 'With an extremely violent killer on the loose.'

'Then why aren't you out there looking for him?

Mr Bull turned at last to Bliss. A wedge of stiff dark hair was razored clear of his ears, a tiny diamond stud winking out of one of them – the one that TV cameras always caught when, with his handsome head held high, Sollers was striding in and out of court.

Bliss said, 'Your brother reported intruders on his land.'

'We both did. On separate occasions. Did you know that?'

'I… no.'

'Doesn't particularly surprise me, Inspector Bliss, because *preventing* crime—'

'Look…' Bliss held up both hands. 'I understand your distress and your anger, but alleged trespass isn't necessarily police business at all, let alone CID business. For a start, it has to be trespass with *intent*—'

'And preventing crime is low-priority stuff nowadays, isn't it? Counts for nothing in the target culture. Nil points.'

You got this every day now, every little twat nicked for a minor offence accusing you of using him to make the figures tally.

'Mr Bull, we don't like the target culture any more than you, and I try not to let it get in the way of being a good copper. I'm not saying if I'd heard about your intruders we'd've come rushing over with a chopper and an armed response unit, because our resources are limited at the best of times but…' Bliss drew out a chair from under the kitchen table but didn't sit down '…I think I need to know about it now, sir. Don't you?'

Sollers Bull crossed the room, switched off the main bulbs, as if to dim his anger. The moon was in and out, now that the storm was over. Through the window you could see poplars waving blackly, like they were fanning away shreds of cloud.

Mr Bull, sharp face scarred with shadows, told Bliss he'd seen two of them, around the end of last week, Thursday, perhaps. Two men and a vehicle. 'Wasn't quite dark. I could quite easily have shot one.'

'Probably as well you didn't, though,' Bliss said patiently. 'You don't *know* this was down to the people you saw. Whom I'm presuming you didn't recognize… or did you?'

'I don't know who they are, but I know *what* they are.'

'Who did you speak to, Mr Bull, when you rang the police?'

'Rang what I thought was Hereford police and it turned out to be some anonymous call centre… might as well have been in fucking Delhi, like the rest of them. Sometime later, I actually received a call back to ask if the intruders were still in the vicinity because the police were *rather busy…*'

'Yeh, well,' Bliss said. 'We both know that's not satisfactory, and if I was Chief Constable I might well talk to the Home Office about things being done a bit differently. But I'm just a lowly foot soldier. What exactly did your brother see?'

'Is he still there? Still lying out there in his yard?'

'When I left, but probably not now. There'll be a post-mortem in the morning.'

There was a bottle of single malt on the table. Sollers Bull pushed it at Bliss. Bliss shook his head. Not falling into that trap.

'Tell me about the vehicle.'

'Pickup truck. White or light blue. Mansel saw it on the track two nights together. Raced away when they saw him. I've told all this to your sergeant—'

'Which is why the whole area's taped off. In case there are tyre tracks and footprints.'

'We've both been over it several times since then. And delivery vehicles.'

'We can eliminate them. It's still worth it.'

Sollers Bull eyed him over his glass.

'Wasn't worth it when we had a quad bike stolen last year, was it? Or when Gerry Morgan's chain-harrow took a walk the week after Christmas. I bet you don't even know what a chain-harrow *is*, do you, Inspector?'

Bliss moved on. Might know what it was, but he was buggered if he knew what it looked like.

'Mr Bull, you said you didn't know who they were but you knew *what* they were…'

'Did I?' Sollers poured himself a drink. 'Probably because I'd been reading in the local rag how the Hereford murder rate's doubled the past year or so.'

'Still means a lot less in Hereford than it does in New York. Or Birmingham, even. And if you're pointing out that the last two killers were East European… well, so were the victims. And both were urban. Aren't even any migrants round here, yet. Are there?'

It had been too dark on the way here to see the fruit fields, the frames for the polytunnels where the seasonal workers were employed, the caravans and dorm blocks where they lived. But they wouldn't even have started planting yet.

'A percentage of migrants are career criminals, we all know that,' Sollers Bull said. 'Easy pickings over here. Organized credit-card theft, fiddling cash machines. Driving through a farm and lifting anything not nailed down.'

'Did *you* see any signs of a break-in?'

'Inspector Bliss…' Sollers Bull regarding him with scorn. 'We en't yet been able to count the livestock.'

Bliss was silent. Sollers sipped his whisky.

'Don't the police have two men of East European origin awaiting trial for rustling?'

'Yeh, but I think that's in Evesham, Mr Bull.'

'Not all that far away.'

'It's a fair way from small-time rustling to taking a man's life.'

Bliss was recalling another case, unsolved, where sheep had been slaughtered in a field and then butchered on the spot. Somebody's idea of a takeaway. Bliss thought of butcher's knives. *Check it out.*

He said, 'You think your brother came back earlier than expected after his council meeting was abandoned… and walked in on a robbery in progress?'

'Nothing else makes sense to me.'

'Seems odd he should be all alone in that big house.'

'His marriage ended.'

'No kids?'

'No children from either of his marriages.'

'Housekeeper… cleaner?'

'A local woman comes in most days. I've given your sergeant her details.'

Bliss said, 'We do need to know if he had enemies.'

'He was well liked and well respected by everyone who knew him. A traditional farmer. An old-fashioned farmer. A man of the land – *this* land. Bred to it.' Sollers looked down at the tabletop as if the contours of the land were marked out on its surface. 'We both were.'

'Bridge Sollers,' Bliss said.

At least he knew his place names.

'And Mansel Lacey,' Sollers said.

Both villages – hamlets – within a few miles of here.

'Something to live up to, Mr Bull.'

'That sarcasm?'

'No,' Bliss said, surprised. 'No, it wasn't.'

Sollers Bull lowered his head to his hands, massaging the edge of his eyes with the knuckles of his thumbs.

'Let's talk again tomorrow, shall we?' Bliss said.

He drove up to the fork, parked with his engine running, headlights on dipped, and got out his mobile. Signal was a bit wonky.

'Mansel Bull,' he said. 'Farmer. Machete job, Billy Grace reckons.'

'I know,' the DCI said. 'I've just talked at length to Stagg.'

Addressing his superior, Bliss felt acutely strange. Up to a few months ago, he was routinely editing his thoughts before opening his mouth.

'Sollers Bull,' Annie Howe said. 'That would be…?'

'Gobby hunt supporter nicked by the Met for pouring red paint on John Prescott's second-best Jag.'

'Fighting for his heritage. A hero.'

'Malicious damage is malicious damage, Annie. And still a cocky twat. Who, as you can imagine, doesn't like the police much. Especially me.'

'Stagg said.'

They'd been in the remains of Bliss's sitting room when the first call came through. Kirsty's old man had been in with Kirsty's key while Bliss was at work and had nicked the flame-effect fire. Bliss had been filling a paraffin stove when Terry Stagg had come through on Annie's mobile.

Be more convenient for DI Bliss.

True enough, in that Bliss was nearer the door. Whenever Annie came round she'd arrive just after dusk, leaving her car in a cul-de-sac two streets away. Strategic. Kirsty was right. If it came out, one of them could end up behind a desk in Carlisle.

No guesses which.

'We need to watch Stagg,' Bliss said. 'Ma'am.'

Hadn't yet said a word to her about Kirsty's suspicions. Best to keep quiet until he knew for sure that the bitch wasn't flying a kite.

'What else did Sollers Bull say, Francis?'

'Reckons it was a robbery gone wrong. All but accusing migrant workers from the fruit farm across the road.'

Figuring this might rattle Annie's PC cage a little.

'That would be Magnis Berries?'

'That what it's called?'

'Named after what was a Roman town,' Annie said, 'which used to stand somewhere round there. How close is it to Oldcastle?'

'Half a mile? I doubt there are many people employed there now. Probably not even got the polytunnels up yet. You think we should go in, see what vehicles they've got?'

'Check it out discreetly tomorrow. Maybe find out if anyone's in charge. During the season, it could be the biggest centre of population between there and Leominster.'

'Yeh, OK.' Bliss sat watching the bare brown hedge, like a complex circuit board in his headlights. 'What time will you get back tomorrow?'

She was in court at Worcester: three brothers accused over the near-fatal stabbing of a father-in-law.

'Verdict early next week. I might look in on you tomorrow, but no point in me getting involved if I'm back in court on Monday. You pleased?'

'Made-up, Annie. Where are you now?'

'Home. Thought it was best.'

'What about tomorrow night?' he said.

'I'm not sure.'

See, that was what he was scared of, too. The idea that something which neither of them had expected to last... really wouldn't last.

'Didn't catch that, Annie,' Bliss said. 'I keep losing the signal.'

9

Towards the Flames

SYD SPICER HAD the fire going nicely in the parlour.

'This looks like sycamore,' he said to Huw. 'Good burner, easy ignition. And a bit of oak to keep it going all night. Well-dry, too.'

'Stored for three years, the oak,' Huw said with disinterest.

Merrily was observing Syd. Hyper. Striding around Huw's Victorian parlour then diving at the fireplace and rearranging a log to funnel the flames. The pensive figure in the darkest part of the chapel – *that* had been the Syd Spicer she knew: this was not. Same voice, though, flat as old lino.

She looked at Huw in his leaking armchair, his face mapped by shadows. The parlour was still in winter mode, with two baskets of logs and a heavy curtain drawn across the main door. Whitewashed walls ochred with smoke.

'Tell you what…' Syd was back on his feet. 'I'm just thinking, if you've got a chainsaw, Huw, we could get Merrily out.'

She sat down on the sofa. If he wanted her out, she no longer wanted to go. Sunk into the ruins of his armchair, Huw shook his head.

'Take you bloody hours on your own, lad, in the dark. Dangerous, even on your terms.' He started easing off his walking boots. 'Make your calls, Merrily. Ring Jane. You'll only be on edge. Go in t'kitchen. Rayburn's on.'

'I've no big secrets.' Merrily looked at Syd, then back at Huw. 'But if you two want to talk… Can I make you some tea?'

'Aye, that'd be nice. Two sugars for me.'

She'd never been in Huw's kitchen before, and it was a small surprise: clean, and not as basic as you'd imagine. New pine cupboards and a larder fridge. Odd domestic touches – spice rack, even. Feminine touches. Maybe his cleaner? There was no woman in Huw's home, as far as she knew. Not since the death of Julia, the love of his later life.

The Rayburn was doing warm, throaty noises. She filled the kettle, found the pack of Yorkshire tea bags then called the vicarage on her mobile. Answering machine. Called Jane's mobile: answering service. Called Lol at his cottage in Church Street: no answer, no machine.

Bugger. Since the great Christmas flood, Ledwardine had seemed vulnerable in a way it never had before. Changing times, a climate in destructive flux. Jane… variable. Something not quite right, lately. She rang Jane's mobile back, left a message: *'Just call me.'*

Syd had a daughter, too, around Jane's age and problematical. For once, he seemed to want to talk about her.

'Em's been clean for most of a year. Though we remain watchful.'

Stretching in his chair. Couldn't seem to keep still. He'd shown no actual surprise when she'd turned up with Huw, but then he wouldn't. But watchful, oh yes. He always would be, until his teddy bear's eyes were closed by someone else.

'Where's she now, Syd?'

'Back home. With Fiona.'

'Which is still down south?'

'For the present.'

Syd was from some part of London, his wife from Reading. He'd virtually promised her they'd go south when he came out of the army, but his ordination had changed everything, the way it often did. And, like so many SAS men, he'd grown fond of the place that he'd kept coming back to with his mission scars.

Only problem being that, by the time Syd had become a curate there, Hereford had developed its own little drug culture, and Emily was a born addict. No safer, as it turned out, in Malvern. In the end, Fiona Spicer had taken her back to Reading in manacles, while Syd, bound by his faith, had stayed on.

'But it's going to be all right.' Syd sat with his hands clasped between his knees, staring into the fire, rocking slightly. 'It's working out.'

'You're finally leaving Wychehill?'

'I've left.'

'I didn't know that.'

'Not been gone long.'

'So, erm…'

'Oh God.' Syd stretched his socks towards the flames. 'I know what you want, Merrily, and I really can't help you. Hands are tied. You know how it is.'

'Not really.'

Huw sniffed, sank lower into his chair. In the poor light, its leaking stuffing was the colour and texture of his hair.

'Bloody old Huw,' Syd said, like Huw wasn't there. 'He's a cunning bastard. Can't say I wasn't warned. Hasn't explained, has he?'

'What?' Merrily didn't look at Huw. 'I'm not getting any of this, Syd. Either you're taking over my job and they haven't told me yet…'

'I wouldn't go near your job in a radiation suit, Merrily. It's simply that where I am now makes direct consultation with anybody outside of certain circles… inadvisable, at best.'

'You *are* still in the Church?'

'To a point.'

'Jesus,' Huw said tiredly. 'Weren't for me to tell her. He's gone back where he came from, lass.'

'What, the…?'

'Bit irregular,' Syd said. 'The Regiment doesn't like old warriors crawling back. Nobody wants a loser who can't cut it on the outside, with a yen to start jumping out of helicopters again, but the current guy did his back in on an exercise, and they needed a stand-in for a while.'

'They've made you…?'

'Temporary chaplain.' Syd plucked his mug from the chair arm. 'Saves sending a civilian on the Vicars and Tarts for the sake of a few months.' He smiled. 'That's the course they have at Sandhurst for clergy new to the army.'

He leaned back, his eyes half-closed.

'Interesting times. Not often commented on, but the growth of the secular society's not good news as regards the Regiment. Especially when you're dealing with an enemy that welcomes martyrdom.'

'Taliban.'

'Among others.'

Syd sat up, drank some tea, leaned back again, pushing out his feet to the fire. He'd once told Merrily that there was a harsh kind of mysticism at the heart of the SAS. Something to do with the miracle of survival against immeasurable odds. Ninety per cent training and preparation, nine per cent luck and one per cent something you'd call on at breaking point. The lantern in the storm.

'I know what I'm doing,' Syd said. 'First rule – don't throw the Big Feller in their faces.'

Merrily nodded. It made sense.

'Always a surface cynicism about all things religious,' Syd said. 'Which is healthy. But, in the end, these are not ordinary sol-diers. They live by a very strong faith. Faith in themselves, faith in their mates. There's also what you might call a monastic quality, and if a particular kind of inner spark is allowed to go out, they're open to a certain creeping disillu— *Shit!*'

Syd jerked his feet back from the hearth. His socks were smouldering. He stamped his feet lightly on the edge of the hearth, then rubbed them together and carried on talking.

'If you come over too evangelical, you're well stuffed. But you do have to come over like a priest, not a mate. They'll always respect an expert.'

'This mean you sometimes have to go abroad with them, Syd?'

'You make your own decisions on where you might be needed.'

'I mean, how dangerous is it for a priest? Stupid question?'

'Frustrating more than dangerous. If threatened, for instance, you must never resist or exercise violence. You go willingly into captivity. And no shooters. What's kind of amusing, if you go on exercise with the boys, they don't like to think you're getting off with light kit, so they give you a cross to carry, size of an old Heckler and Koch nine-mil.'

'And if it's touch and go, lad,' Huw said, 'wi' a crazed Taliban warlord?'

Syd let his chin sink into his chest, peered up, coy.

'Every SAS chaplain worth his kit knows thirty-seven ways to kill with a wooden cross.'

There was a silence. The elephant in the room had a big D tattooed on its hide. Merrily sipped her tea, looking for an approach.

'Why did you want to do it?'

'It was the right time. Iraq, Afghanistan. War, but not the kind of war people care about. You hear a lot about the dead, but not much about the damaged.' Syd put a thumb to his head. 'Up here, you know? The NHS got no answer to that – not much of one, anyway.'

'You think you can help?'

'In a small way. Makes me feel more useful than... you know...'

'A parish.'

'It's still a parish. Except this is one where I can see the point of it.'

'You're based at Credenhill?'

'Army villa, fully equipped.'

'On your own?'

'For the present. However, Emmy's no longer at college. On account of being four months pregnant.'

'Oh.'

'Nah...' Syd sat up. 'It's good. This is the *good* thing. She gets married beginning of May – to a boy who'll soon be a baby barrister, how perfect is that? Then Fiona moves back in and we get to think about a future.'

'Well.' Merrily smiled. 'Things do turn around, don't they?'

'Told you it was OK to smoke in church.'

He wasn't smiling, he was wearing a smiley mask. He didn't seem frightened, though. He seemed in control.

Right, then...

'So, Syd... you're here because you have a deliverance issue related to your SAS ministry?'

'Blimey.' Syd stretched his arms over his head. 'Is that the time?'

There wasn't a clock in here and probably insufficient light to see his watch. Syd was on his feet.

'Samuel Dennis Spicer.' He yawned. 'Church of England. As was. Goodnight, all.'

10

Male Thing

THE LOGS HAD reddened and collapsed into glowing splinters, the air outside fallen to near-stillness. Merrily stood up and went to the window. Across the valley, clouds had cleared and the hills were moon-bleached, but you couldn't see the tip of Pen-y-fan the way you could from the chapel.

'Of course,' Huw said from the sunken chamber of his chair. 'You're a woman.'

'We all have our cross to bear.'

'They don't have women in the SAS.'

'You're saying that's why he won't talk to me?'

'He's back in the army, his ministry's governed by the buttoned-up bastards in the MoD. Not that he said much to me, either.'

'An evil. What do you think that might be? As I recall, that's not one of his words. He doesn't do melodrama. But, yeah, I can see why you might think he's scared. He's a bit manic, isn't he?'

'You're hardly going to see him trembling or keep running to the bog.' Huw sat up, reached down to the hearth for the pot and poured more tea. 'But, aye, that fact that he'll say nowt to you more or less confirms it. It *is* Regiment-related. So very much on your patch.'

'Although it *has* moved since Syd was a soldier.'

In Syd's time, the Regiment had still been based on the southern edge of the city where it had been established during World War Two by an army colonel, David Stirling. The camp known ever since as Stirling Lines. Still producing highly trained commando units, parachuting in to operate behind enemy lines. That famous motto: *Who Dares Wins.*

Strangely, in the city, it had been more anonymous. The townsfolk part of a conspiracy of silence. But now it had moved a few miles out, to the former RAF base at Credenhill. Now everybody knew where to find the SAS: out in the sticks, with a high fence and armed guards.

Merrily came away from the window.

'Topographically they're in the county and in the diocese. But not part of either. The SAS are a little island of their own.'

'So if Spicer has a problem involving a spiritual evil he has to deal with it himself. Doesn't that bother you?'

'In what way?'

'He does one day on a deliverance course and thinks he knows enough to wing it on his own?'

'Mmm. See what you—'

Merrily's mobile was chiming in her bag. The kid had always chosen her moments.

'Where are you?'

'In the pub.'

'I'm assuming not on your—'

'With Lol. And Danny Thomas.'

'Good. Listen, flower, I've got a bit of a problem.'

Telling Jane why she'd be spending the night at Huw's rectory.

'Jesus,' Jane said. 'Gormenghast?'

'So when you get in, maybe you could ring and assure me that all the doors are locked, things like that. Or you could even stay in Lol's spare room…'

'And become the subject of evil gossip? I'll be… fine.'

Hesitation?

'You sure?'

'Wind's dying down. A few slates gone in the village, that's all. You want me to take a walk round the vic—?'

'No! If there's nothing obvious from inside, just—'

'You want me to hang on in the morning, till you get back?'

'No, get the bus. I'll call you anyway, about eight.'

'OK.'

'And get Lol to see you home and check—'

'That there's nobody around. Yes. I will. I'll do that.'

Now that *was* wrong. Normally it would be, *Don't be ridiculous, this is Ledwardine.*

'Owt up, lass?'

'Don't know.' Merrily dropped the phone into her bag; maybe she was overtired. 'You think when they're officially adult, it's going to be easier. That they'll be more restrained. But the only real difference is that now they can *do* things. Shake foundations.'

She told Huw about the Ledwardine henge issue – indications of a Bronze Age earthwork around the village, concealed for centuries by apple orchards. It was clear that elements inside Hereford Council would prefer that nothing was found on land they hoped to develop, thus turning Ledwardine into something approaching a town. Jane – obsessed with ancient sites, planning a career in archaeology – was furious. And Jane was eighteen. Jane could vote and express opinions.

'She's also enraged about a very rich man called Ward Savitch inviting other rich people to kill our wildlife. And she feels… I don't know. She was a bit screwed-up when we arrived – fifteen, dad dead, mother adopting a deeply uncool career. And yet she's been happier in Ledwardine than anywhere, and now she can see it coming apart. The village is a divided place now. Not a happy place.'

'And you've to keep walking the fence.' Huw fell silent, gazing into the embers from the depths of his chair. Then he got to his feet. 'I'll go and make some more tea.'

When he returned with the teapot it was after midnight and Jane had rung back to say all was well: doors barred, cat fed, no signs of storm-damage at the vicarage.

Still detectable traces of *let's not worry Mum unnecessarily*. But short of listing every conceivable mishap and pedantically putting them to her, one by one, there wasn't a thing you could do about it.

The tea was strong, as if Huw was determined neither of them would get much sleep tonight.

'You read the new guidelines?'

'Mmm.'

A circular last week, underlining the need for full insurance. Be sure your clerical policy covered deliverance and all the possible repercussions.

'It's a farce, Merrily. Rules and procedures and targets. Like the NHS. Health and Safety. It can't work like that. I've been thinking… might be time for me to pack this in. The courses.'

'You've said that before.'

She moved to the chair vacated by Syd, up against the dregs of the fire. Lighting a cigarette and leaning back into a padded wing so that most of her face was out of Huw's line of sight. You tended to think it was only the intensity of his work that had kept him going after Julia's death.

'What would you do?'

'Happen retire. Write me memoirs.'

'That would explode a few comfort zones.'

Huw leaned back with his hands behind his head.

'I'm starting to think we could be close to fucked this time, Merrily. I go into Brecon – even Brecon, and I can feel it. Apathy, scorn… even fear. Of what we might be underneath. Used to be the worst we were was irrelevant, now we're taking the shit for militant Islam and a handful of kiddie-fiddling Catholic priests. We're either naive and laughable or we're part of a sinister old conspiracy to control people's minds and have sex with their children. And all the time there's Dawkins standing on his citadel of science, pissing on us over the railings.'

Merrily let the smile show.

'Did I just hear a snatch of your fantasy final sermon?'

Huw's eyes lit up for just a moment, like in the old days, and he laughed.

'Bugger off to bed, you cheeky cow, or you'll be fit for nowt in the morning.'

She nodded and stood up.

'Keep an eye on him,' Huw said.

'Syd? He's a grown man.'

'Credenhill's no more than… what? Eight miles from you?'

'You think this could actually be something at the SAS camp? Not going to get in there, am I?'

'I never saw you as a defeatist,' Huw said.

The room Merrily'd been given… she figured it wasn't supposed to be a guest room. Syd would have the guest room. This was… a woman's room? Nothing you could quite put your finger on. No frilly pink shade on the bedside lamp, no extra mirrors, no fleecy rugs.

The lamp had a parchment shade, making a pale sepia circle around two books: a hardback New Testament and an Oxford paperback edition of Aquinas's *Selected Philosophical Writings*. The bed was a double bed. Merrily guessed this was the room where Huw had slept with Julia – a room that he didn't use any more.

Wearing a sweater over bra and pants, Merrily switched off the lamp and walked over to the sash window. The view was down the valley towards the few remaining lights of the village of Sennybridge. The landscape looked disarranged, like rumpled bedclothes after a restless night.

The way the weather got inside the landscape. The way it got inside people. Even Huw.

New deliverance guidelines. Another generation of dull buggers appointed by careful bishops. She couldn't lose that grainy mental video of Huw in the passage at the chapel heading the old stained light bulb, and she had a disturbing sense of disintegration: Jane leaving home for some university next autumn, Lol's career reviving after the years of oblivion. Even though he only lived across the street, Merrily wasn't seeing as much of him this year, now that Danny Thomas's barn, over the border, had become his rehearsal room.

Well, that was wonderful, obviously. Life was good for Lol, good for Jane... if she could let go of Ledwardine.

Merrily stood at the window, arms wrapped around herself, watching the lights in the valley going out.

Part Two

*...then my sight began to fail
and the room became dark
about me, as if it were night...*

Julian of Norwich
Revelations of Divine Love

11

Stable Doors

MID-MORNING, DAY THREE of the Mansel Bull investigation, and the police press officer was on the phone to Bliss. Elly Clatter, this was, ex-local journalist from the Black Country and a nice enough woman if you didn't mind being treated like a maladjusted kid at play school.

'Normal way of it, Francis, my duck, I'd be suggesting you maintain a dignified silence. Only it looks to me like this is starting to become a bit of an issue.'

An issue. This year, everything was a frigging *issue*.

'And he's saying what, exactly?'

Sollers Bull. The first formal interviews since his brother's murder. *Hunt hero Sollers Bull*, in the Tory tabs. Twat in Bliss's book.

'He hasn't said anything yet. He's doing TV and radio in about an hour. But if he says what we think he *might* say, we're going to need to be ready with some answers.'

'Not me again, Elly, I've done enough.'

Couple of pressers over the past two days. *This was a particularly savage and pointless crime. We know the killer left the scene with a considerable amount of blood on his clothing and on his person. Somebody out there knows who this is. This is an individual nobody should be hiding.*

Trite crap. Hated the telly, particularly.

'You can relax,' Elly said. 'It'll just be a quote from a police spokesperson at this stage. All we need from you, Frannie, or your colleagues, is some background, so we can formally say, no, we're *not* turning a blind eye to petty crime in the country-side, and yes, we *do* investigate all reports of suspicious behaviour.'

'Shit, Elly, I've gorra—'

Bliss broke off. Eyes were raised all over the CID room. Must've been shouting. Normally he'd be in his own office, but that wasn't the best place to find out if people were dissecting your private life.

'If you cobble something together,' Elly said, 'I'll mess around with it, read it back to you, then take it upstairs for clearance. How's that sound?'

'Or you could just tell the media that DI Bliss has told Mr Bull to go and— '

'Now, Francis…'

'Sorry.' Bliss lowered his head into Billy Grace's report: *divided trachea, several blood vessels…* 'I'm not gerrin a lorra sleep, Elly. I'll talk to the DCI, get back to you, all right?'

'He seems to be an impulsive sort of man, this Mr Bull,' Elly said.

'Yeh.'

Bliss had a few of the back-stories on his laptop. THE BLOODING OF PREZZA – *Daily Express* on the red-paint incident. A *Telegraph* feature on the saintly Sollers's battle to defend a thousand-year tradition. Pictures of Sollers in his fox-hunting kit and his ear stud. Bliss looked up and saw that Elly Clatter hadn't gone away.

'What?'

'I'd be a bit a careful, Frannie. You just see him as a man with form, but in hunting circles it's a medal. Him and that Otis Ferry?'

'Both members of the Jumped-up Twats Club.'

A moment's silence. From opposite corners of the CID room, Terry Stagg and Karen Dowell were staring at him.

'You ever think you might be working in the wrong part of the country, Francis?' Elly Clatter said.

About half an hour later, Bliss rang Annie Howe at headquarters in Worcester. From his office this time. Door shut, voice lowered. Annie was still only half-available, required to be on hand in case she was recalled to the Crown Court. She'd been quite helpful meanwhile, which was still a whole new experience for Bliss.

'Sorry,' she said. 'We tried. Either they know nothing or they're not playing.'

'Or the translator's crap,' Bliss said.

'She's actually a very good translator, I'm told.'

It had been Annie's idea – and not a bad one – to approach the two men facing rustling charges in Evesham, offer them a deal in return for information on who might be lifting stock in Herefordshire. A network couldn't be ruled out.

'Both came over as seasonal workers,' Annie said, 'but don't seem to have been at any of the Hereford fruit farms.'

Bliss and Stagg had been over to the Magnis Berries farm first thing. Still a pre-season skeleton staff: local manager, six workers. Everybody living off-site, the whole place locked up all night.

'Stuffed, then,' Bliss said. 'They could've come from anywhere... Birmingham... Newport... Gloucester...'

'Widen the net, then. Talk to West Midlands, Gwent. What about general crime? No pointers there?'

'Farm thefts are up. Stolen quad bikes, chainsaws. Diesel drained from tanks. Widespread metal-theft. Some organized poaching, but no recent rustling of farm animals, no violence. We'll keep trying.'

The press conferences had shaken out sightings of two unfamiliar pickup trucks on private land – one up towards Bredwardine, one seen turning round at Lulham like he was a stranger who hadn't known it was a dead end. This was the best so far, but still not worth much.

'Meanwhile,' Bliss said, 'Mr Bull is doing interviews.'

'Talking stable doors? Accusing us of giving rural crime low priority? Don't react. I mean it, Francis.'

Bliss found himself wondering what Annie was wearing.

'Where are you tonight?'

'Jury's still out, and we're warned to expect an overnight.' She was always careful on police phones. 'Might make it over there before close of play. Failing that, I'll be home this evening. If you need me for anything.'

'Home.'

'Malvern.'

'Right,' Bliss said.

The lunchtime TV news had pictures of grey fields, barbed wire and police tape. It said the hunt for the killer of a farmer in the Wye Valley had been *stepped up*.

What they always said when there was no new line. Bliss switched off. He'd brought Karen Dowell and Terry Stagg into the office, with a pot of tea and a few sandwiches.

'We're going to get a hard time over this, aren't we?' Terry said.

Sounding almost pleased. Bliss extracted an egg sarnie.

'But it's not totally our fault, is it, Tezza? As we're severely undermanned, underfunded and overburdened with bureaucratic shite. I think we need to quietly point this out to the media.'

'Quietly, how?'

'I was thinking you, actually. When you go back out there, I thought you could find out which pub they're occupying, join them for a butty, exchange a few confidences. You've got the look of a boozer, Tez, it's the veins in your nose. They like that. Maybe you could find out what Sollers is telling them on the side, and what *they* think of him.'

'You don't like Sollers Bull, do you, boss?' Karen said.

A wholesome country girl, but smart.

'Karen, what were his relations with Mansel, do you think?'

'Big old family.'

'It's not the frigging *Royal* family, Karen.'

'It's near enough, in this county. You should know, you married into the fringes of… all that.'

Bliss scowled.

'Sorry,' Karen said.

'I was sensing a distance, between Sollers and his brother,' Bliss said. 'The way he kept telling me what a well-respected man he was. No conspicuous affection.'

'With respect, boss, he wouldn't show that in front of you.'

'But they weren't *mates*. Big age gap. Not exactly grief-stricken, is what I'm saying. *And* he's very likely going to inherit a big slab of prime riverside acreage, plus a small mansion. Mansel had no wife left, no kids.'

'I heard that's why they're history,' Terry said, 'the wives.'

'That's what Billy Grace thought. Mansel wanted an heir to Oldcastle but refused to believe it might be his fault he didn't get one. Bottom line, looks like Sollers could be in line for most of it. They *were* partners.'

'You want to be a bit careful, boss, that's all,' Karen said. 'Under the circumstances.'

'I'm doing me *job*.' Bliss threw up his hands. 'He's got form.'

'He was nicked for exercising his countryman's right to protest about what he considered to be an unjust law.'

'*You* think he's a hero, do you, Karen?'

'I think he's clever. University, then business college? Big on diversification – farm shop, restaurant…'

'We frequent his restaurant, do we?'

'No, but my mum works there.' Karen split a Kit Kat. 'What's the DCI's line? Something this big, I keep expecting her to come stalking in, rapping knuckles. But she stays in Worcester. Odd, that.'

'She's been in court.'

'Not over the weekend. I mean, she *was* here, but not for long.'

Terry Stagg said, 'Maybe keeping out of the line of fire. Let the DI cop the flack.'

'Not the only odd thing, when you think about it,' Karen said, thoughtful. 'She does that spell as acting-super here and then gets offered Thames Valley, which – unless I've got this wrong – would've been about six months under a superintendent coming up to retirement. *On a promise.* Why didn't she go for that? Not the Howe we know, is it?'

Terry Stagg smiled greasily through his unsightly stubble.

'Maybe she has other things she wouldn't want to leave behind.' Grinned at Bliss. 'Father's daughter?'

'OK,' Bliss said, 'let's just…'

'That's crap.' Karen shaking her head. 'Even I don't think she's bent.'

'That case…' Terry brushing crumbs off his tie '… maybe she's finally getting herself seen to.'

Shit. Bliss was looking down at his desk, turning over the forensics, feigning lack of interest, when he heard Karen go, 'It's not you, is it?'

His gut went tight as a drum.

His head came up very slowly – a struggle to frame some flip reply, until he saw she was looking at Terry Stagg.

A joke. How many of these frigging jokes could his heart take? He watched Stagg shudder.

'Why is Karen trying to give me nightmares, boss?'

'She's actually not bad-looking,' Karen said. 'In her austere way.'

'Karen…' Terry Stagg blinked. 'That woman's a metal coat hanger with tits. It'd be like, you know, with a plastic doll or something? Staring over your shoulder with glazed eyes. Anyway, nobody's yet proved to *me* she's not a lezzer.'

'*How* many times we been through that?' Karen said.

'Does a brilliant impression of a woman who hates men.'

'Gay women cops, Staggie – man-friendly. Always. Am I right, boss?'

'Sorry, Karen?' Bliss tried not to look too concerned either way. 'I was just wondering how Terry knows so much about having sex with a plastic doll. That was a very telling detail about the way their eyes stare over your shoulder.'

Karen giggled.

'Sod off,' Terry Stagg said, going not quite red. 'Boss.'

Bliss relaxed. As best he could these days.

***

He stood fingering the loose change and the car keys in his pockets, unhappy about the way Annie Howe's uncharacteristic professional restraint had been spotted. Had they also noticed how readily she'd trusted him to handle a major inquiry of national interest?

'Karen?'

On their own now in his office, Terry Stagg heading back to the crime scene.

'Mmm?'

'Karen, look, I'm gonna come over all pathetic now. Is there any kind of rumour going round? About me.'

'What? About being gay?' Karen grinned, then saw his face. 'Sorry, boss, I'm not sure what you're asking me. If you mean Kirsty... a wonky marriage's hardly got novelty value in this place.'

'Nothing else? I apologize for sounding girlie.'

'Thank *you*.'

'Well?'

'Unless I've failed to pick up on something, I'd say the pressure of a high-profile murder investigation, combined with your domestic issues, is making you just a bit paranoid.'

'So nothing?'

'Nothing. Frannie, I'd know. And if I knew, I'd tell you.'

Should've kept his gob shut. She'd be curious now. And Kirsty... Kirsty still knew something. But from whom? Who'd found out about him and Annie and passed it on?

'Things'll get better, boss,' Karen said.

'Yeh,' Bliss said, as Gwyn Adamson, office manager on the Mansel inquiry, came over with an envelope.

'Couple of things, Francis. One's an eyewitness report from a petrol station at Leominster. Bloke apparently was dropped from a car and then escorted by two men into a four-by-four. As he was getting in, someone pulled a bag over his head.'

'When was this?'

'Last Wednesday night. Two nights before Mansel was killed. No indication of duress. Witness thought it was a joke. However this…' Gwyn handed Bliss the envelope '… is more interesting. Came in the lunchtime post, just addressed to Police, Hereford. *Could* be a crank job, but…'

Bliss accepted a folded sheet of A4. Computer printout.

The word BLOOD all over it.

12

Act of Sacrifice

THESE WERE TWO *pains that shewed in the blessed head: the first wrought to the drying while his body was moist, and that other slow, with blowing of wind from without, that dryed him more...*

The sky, through the scullery window, was scored with raw pink cloud. Easter was coming, and Easter Week at the end of March would sometimes mean snow. Nobody here would be surprised after what last winter had hurled at them.

...and pained with cold, more than my heart could hold... and The shewing of Christ's pains filled me full of pains.

Merrily folded down the corner of the page, shut the paperback. It was still scary. It had the feel of reportage. Informed, forensic, almost dispassionate reportage. Nothing quite like it before or since.

There'd been a few blank faces when she'd brought it out in church yesterday, Palm Sunday.

This had been after the evening meditation, attended by the more thoughtful, committed parishioners, all ten of them.

'Julian of Norwich.' Holding up the paperback. 'A woman. Mother Julian. A nun. An anchoress, or recluse, and a mystic. In 1373, when she was just thirty, she became very ill and nearly died, and that was when she experienced the series of visions she discusses here.'

Or fever dreams, hallucinations, whatever.

'Leaving us with this profoundly, harrowing, gritty account of what crucifixion must really have been like. Which, erm... I was thinking we could use as a basis for the Good Friday meditation.'

A suitably sombre prelude to the proposed vigil in the church through Saturday night to Easter Day. Amanda Rubens, the bookseller – looking a little nunlike herself in a long black dress – had probably spoken for most of them.

'And you really want us to dwell on wounds and killing... exactly a week after what happened at Oldcastle Farm?'

It had been all over Ledwardine by the time she'd arrived home from Brecon. Ten miles was nothing in the country. Ten miles was somewhere you could see, across the fields, between the trees.

Although she'd never met or heard of Mansel Bull, she knew a relative, James Bull-Davies, last remnant of the Ledwardine squirearchy. And Gomer Parry had once dug a pond for Mansel. And Jim Prosser in the Eight Till Late, his brother-in-law had had a sheepdog pup off Mansel less than a year ago. Merrily's own grandad had farmed at Mansel Lacy after which the dead man, apparently, had been named. Connections everywhere: an act of sudden, blinding violence ricocheting like a pinball around the countryside, setting off vibrating lights, jarring the whole table.

The Sunday papers had pictures of a red-brick farmhouse on the edge of an orchard above the Wye and a smiling thickset man leaning on a gate.

This morning, a new *For Sale* sign had appeared in Church Street to join the existing four. All of them reactions to the winter and the fatal flooding which had turned the church into a no-go area on Christmas Day. The mopping and the mourning into New Year, when the snow came.

And then the bitter winds, driving the sleet, heralding the murder of Mansel Bull at Oldcastle, whose high chimneys you could see from Cole Hill in the lifting of the morning mist.

Some weeks, during the frozen months, there had been no actual meditation in church. Too cold in here, even with all the heat on. They'd just sat around, in their coats, and talked.

Ledwardine shivering in chill fatalism, and the village still looked raw and flaking. Not much energy here, except around The Court, where Ward Savitch hosted upmarket action weekends and shooting parties to reawaken hunter-gatherer instincts in men from Off.

'Obviously we should do it,' Gus Staines had said.

Gus was a plump little woman with a semi-permanent goblin smile. She'd come up from London in January to join Amanda, her long-time partner, who had been making an adequate and decorous living here in the New Cotswolds... until the weekend visitors began to be repelled by the snow and the electricity kept failing, and the shops didn't get supplied so often.

'We've all gone soft,' Gus said stoutly. 'We *should* throw ourselves into the full horror of the Crucifixion. The violence and the misery. Because that's the reality of what people do to each other still. This is not the time to turn away.'

Merrily had glanced over to where Jane was sitting on the edge of the circle. Jane had been to the meditation most weeks since Christmas. Not saying much, which was probably just as well. She didn't say anything now, but she looked mildly interested. And then...

'It's a magical ritual,' she'd said last night. 'You're playing with the Big Forces here. Community shaman.'

'Dear God.'

'Resurrection of Christ, resurrection of Ledwardine. Correct?'

The kid was sitting, as she often did, on a cushion at the edge of the hearth with the reddening log fire behind her, Ethel the black cat on her knees, the eyes of both glittering like LEDs.

'The role of the shaman being to lead the tribe out of the dark. Like, out of the tunnel of winter onto the sunlit hillside of spring. Pain and death, a vigil through midnight and then, boom... catharsis... *Easter!*'

'Sod off, Jane.'

'You're going into denial already?'

'Not exactly *denial...*'

'Easter was the most profound of all seasonal festivals way before Christianity. Even the Last Supper has pagan origins. And, like... I think you said Julian of Norwich actually *wished* for her illness... invoking mortality in the hope of rebirth? Experiencing those visions in like the delirium of near-death?'

Merrily sighed.

'It's all totally valid,' Jane said. 'The village has lost its mojo. You need to kick-start the ancient engines. And some asses.'

Jane looking down, slowly massaging Ethel under the chin. Ancient engines. They'd been here before. The creaking and stirring of old Ledwardine, spiritual sap seeping eerily into centuries-dead oak timbers. Jane's favourite picture of herself was the one taken by Eirion, her boyfriend, in Coleman's Meadow, bare arms raised to the sun. Handmaiden of the Goddess.

'Needs to be seriously harrowing, Mum. Like, when a place gets into disaster mode, expecting the worst all the time, the worst just seems to go on happening. Unless you step in with an act of sacrifice.'

'Jane, how can I put this? We don't actually want to scare people?'

Although we do, obviously, Huw Owen said now in Merrily's head, watching a bulb swing like some sinister censer.

Merrily had spent an hour underlining passages in *Revelations of Divine Love*. Normally on a Monday afternoon, she'd have driven into Hereford to go through the deliverance diary with Sophie, but the Monday before Easter was for planning and organizing the weekend ahead.

There was also a parish council meeting on Wednesday. Uncle Ted, senior churchwarden, had a proposal to create a permanent café in the church. Turn it into the heart of the village again, he said. Also make some money. So what would happen to the silence? Where would you go when you needed to be alone with something that didn't judge, didn't question, didn't ask you if you wanted to buy a raffle ticket?

Merrily looked up, out of the scullery window at the lesions in the sky. The sky was momentarily blurred. Maybe she needed glasses. A middle-age thing. It would come, sooner rather than later. Now she had an adult daughter. *God...*

The phone rang. She shut her eyes for a second before picking up.

'All right, lass?'

'Fine, thanks.'

Hadn't spoken to him since Saturday morning. A sparse breakfast, just the two of them, Syd Spicer having left silently before first light, as they'd both known he would.

'Just had a call.'

'What did he want?'

Merrily watched the daffodils still huddled in their buds. You didn't have to be psychic.

'He's laughing. "Huwie," he says, "just a slight problem here, mate, a mere technicality..."'

'A *mere technicality*. He said that?'

'And laughed.'

She could hear the laughter. It would be artificial. She felt for a cigarette, still staring out of the window. Under the winter-bleached church wall, banks of snowdrops were only now beginning to droop next to the emerging daffs.

'And what *was* the technicality?'

'If a man feels... let's say *oppressed* by the perceived proximity of someone who's passed on, someone who, in life, was known to him but who was, shall we say, a flawed person, how is it best to get this presence off the premises?'

'Requiem eucharist? You might expect him to know that.'

'He said there could be complications. Here comes the technicality. He suspects there could be what he describes as strongly negative energy behind the manifestations.'

'Plural?'

'Plural, aye. Suggests a chronic case.'

'Is this one of his, erm, flock?'

'Declines to be specific. But why else the secrecy? I reminded him I wasn't his spiritual director. I said Hereford Diocese wasn't my patch, I said he needed to talk to somebody else.'

'And *he* said…?'

'He said he thought that when you were describing the case of Mr Joy you hadn't finished the story. He wanted to know what nobody else had the nous to ask about. What you did afterwards to keep Mr Joy out of your life.'

'I see. *That* negative.'

'Cry for help, Merrily.'

'If that's a cry for help, it's pitched too high for my hearing. Look…' She pulled the last cigarette out of the packet. 'I was *new* to it then. I was very scared. I'd listened to an old wives' tale from an old woman who'd dabbled in areas I was supposed to abhor, and…'

'And it worked.'

'Something worked. Well… so far.'

'It worked because you did it in the right spirit.'

'You could argue…' Merrily stared at the church wall, with all its lichens and life forms '… that the right spirit would be not to have done it at all. The purer soul does it with considered prayer. This was… something else.'

The cold finger was on Merrily's spine. Up sprang the spidery figure of a creepy old woman in a care home whose name was Anthea but who only answered to Athena.

'And you told him, did you?'

'What I knew of it. Threw in a couple of defensive penta-grams, point up. See what reaction I got to that. He said nowt, seemed to be writing it down.'

Merrily remembered discussing Athena's advice with Huw afterwards. How it bordered on what Jane would call magical ritual, and Huw had asked her if she realized how many so-called magical rituals had come out of the medieval Catholic Church.

She wondered if Syd had noted what she'd told Huw's students about not necessarily analysing everything in depth.

That's why we have the rituals and the liturgy... just do it.

Still not sure how true that was.

'How does this feel to you?' Merrily asked.

'Feels wobbly. Temporary. I don't like it, but if the bugger won't come clean...'

'It's personal, isn't it? It's him.'

'Or connected to him.'

'Is he going to come back to you afterwards? Tell you – man to man – if it worked? Because he isn't going to come to me, is he?'

'Happen you should smother your pride and give him a call.'

'I haven't got his new number.'

'I have it here,' Huw said. 'Give him a day or so, then call him. I think it were bloody hard for him to give away much as he did. I reckon he's in a bad way.'

'Thanks,' Merrily said.

13

Killing Fields

THE CORE SQUAD, in the CID room in front of the box. All the blinds up on a heavyweight early-evening sky. A gathering dismay in the room. Bliss howling.

'What are these bastards trying to *do*? It's like it's been orchestrated.'

He'd come in halfway through the replay of the national news. He sat down, shaken.

'How far it was planned is of no great importance at the present time,' Annie Howe said. 'It's happening, and we need to respond to it.'

Annie had returned in a rare sparkling mood, the Worcester jury having come back unexpectedly with a nice result: two out of three guilty on the stabbing. The DCI's fizz had survived the national TV news, but the extended version on *Midlands Today* was something else.

'*... poisoned our towns.*'

On the screen, some fat bastard bulging out of his tweeds.

'*... and now it's overflowing into rural areas. All the time, we see strangers in old vans, clearly up to no good, but we know we're wasting our time reporting it, because it'll be ignored... simply ignored.*'

Cut to camel-coat-and-headscarf woman by a five-barred gate.

'*Obvious why they don't care. Coming out here's jolly time-consuming, and everybody knows they can meet their arrest and conviction targets far quicker and more cheaply in the towns.*'

'Trouble is, she's not far wrong there, is she?' Bliss said.

'Though we won't be expressing those sentiments outside of this room, will we, Francis?' Annie Howe said quietly, not looking at him. 'Karen, run the item again from the beginning, would you, please? We need to know who they all are.'

Karen Dowell played about with the remote, brought up the current *Midlands Today* Barbie-and-Ken presentation team.

Man: '*With the hunt for the brutal killer of a Herefordshire farmer in its third day, a rural pressure group has been accusing police of failing the countryside.*'

Woman: '*And, as Mandy Patel reports, the attack's been spearheaded by the brother of the murdered man, who says West Mercia Police repeatedly ignored reports of intruders on their land.*'

Familiar shots of the middle Wye Valley looking bare and wind-scoured. Patel's voice describing how the mood in Herefordshire had swung from horror to rage, as the vision cut to an obvious protest meeting. Bunch of people at a raised table, draped in banners. Apart from Sollers Bull, Bliss recognized nobody.

Annie said to Karen, 'Who's the man in the red waistcoat?'

'Can't remember his name, ma'am, but I'm pretty sure he's the county chairman-elect of the NFU. And the guy next to him...'

'Is Lord Walford?'

Karen nodded.

Bliss said, 'Who the fuck's Lord Walford?'

'Old Tory peer, boss. And Sollers Bull's father-in-law.'

'Also a former member of the police authority,' Annie said, 'Where's this happening, exactly?'

Walls of light wood, spotlights from exposed rafters. Pine tables.

'The restaurant at Sollers Bull's farm shop,' Karen said. 'Out on the Leominster Road. My mum works there, part-time. Got to say I've been around here all my life, ma'am, but there's quite a few people I don't think I've ever seen before.'

'Yes, well, me neither,' Annie Howe said. 'Which possibly lends credence to their claim that it's a national movement.'

'Freeze it,' Bliss said. '*There* – isn't that one of those ageing boy racers from *The Octane Show*?'

'Smiffy Gill,' Terry Stagg said. 'Lives just over in Wales.'

'Just the kind of flash twat who'd throw his driving gloves into the ring for this shite,' Bliss said.

Above the panel of nobs at the raised table, a sign, green on white, covered half the wall.

COUNTRYSIDE DEFIANCE

The camera pulling back from the sign, the reporter saying, in voice-over, '*The organizers insist this is not a spin-off from the Countryside Alliance but a new response to what they say is an urgent situation.*'

'Hold it there,' Annie Howe said. 'Man at the back, black hair, receding jawline. Tim… Tim somebody. Member of the police committee.'

'Who's *he* supporting?' Bliss said.

'Who indeed? Sorry, let it run, Karen.'

New voice, a woman, not local.

'*This is not political, but it's certainly a matter of…*'

Now you saw her. Fortyish, short red hair, tailored suit.

'*… pride and tradition. This county, like every county in Britain, has its roots in agriculture, but in Herefordshire the roots are still close to the surface, not yet buried under tons of concrete.*'

The caption said:

Rachel Wiseman-France.
Coordinator, Countryside Defiance.

Bliss made a note of it as the woman said: '*With the hunting ban and four-by-fours road-taxed to the hilt, people who live and work in the countryside already felt they were being systematically penalized. Now they not only fear for their livelihoods, but their very lives.*'

The reporter's voice came back: '*The brother of murdered farmer Mansel Bull is also talking of a climate of fear in the Welsh*

Border hills and is accusing West Mercia Police of turning a blind eye to rural crime.'

Sollers Bull was standing outside his restaurant between two flags, a Welsh dragon and a cross of St George.

'My brother's death left us shattered. Not only the family, but the whole county. I've had dozens of phone calls, letters, emails from farmers and country dwellers, and most of them are saying the same thing.'

Sollers wore a dark suit, black tie. Spoke quietly, even hesitantly, letting a local accent leak through and stumbling over the odd word. No hint of the aggression he'd displayed to Bliss. No ear stud today.

'Only days before he was killed, my brother reported seeing strangers on our land, behaving in a suspicious manner. So he phoned the police. Who did not *come out to investigate.'*

Sollers paused. No mention of migrants this time, Bliss noticed. He knew that any hint of racism and the BBC would never speak to him again.

'... and even after the murder, I was appalled to be told by a senior officer that we could not have expected any more attention than we got.'

Annie Howe and Terry Stagg both glancing at Bliss. DCs Vaynor and Toft exchanging smiles, maybe even smirks. Bliss scowled.

'What was I *supposed* to say? Yeh, I'm really sorry, we should've sent an ARU?'

Rachel Wiseman-France was back.

'The point is that some police divisions have special squads for dealing with gun and knife crime and offences in urban ethnic communities. But rural crimes, time after time, go undetected, because too many police have absolutely no knowledge of life outside the cities.'

Karen Dowell looked at Bliss, raising a despondent eyebrow, as shots appeared of uniformed police and SOCOs in Durex suits standing by a van at the entrance to Mansel Bull's farm. The camera lingering for just an instant too bloody long on a full-length shot of Bliss pointing at something and smiling. God, he hadn't noticed that first time round. Smiling at a murder scene. Bliss kept his eyes on the TV, knowing that every bastard in the CID room would be covertly observing his reactions.

What he saw next, as the picture cut back to the people in the restaurant, made him want to kick the screen in.

He turned away, nails digging into his palms, as Rachel Wiseman-France said, *'The last thing we want is to be accused of taking the law into our own hands. But are we really going to stand by and see our precious countryside turned into killing fields?'*

At a signal from Annie Howe, Karen cut the sound on the male presenter reading out a précis of the press statement put out by Elly Clatter about how West Mercia were fully committed to the policing of rural areas and nobody would rest until the killer of Mansel Bull was caught. Annie moved in front of the screen.

'OK, you all know what we've said to the media. After what we've just seen, we all know it's not going to be good enough, long-term. I have a meeting with the Chief Constable tomorrow, and I'd like to be able to tell him we're moving towards a quick result on this. But… clearly we're not.'

'Killing fields?' Bliss snarled. 'Frigging *killing* fields? Who *is* that woman? Anybody know anything about this Countryside Defiance?'

Bliss looked at Karen Dowell, who shrugged.

'Ask around, shall I, boss?'

'There's a new pressure-group formed every other week,' Annie Howe said. 'Probably latching onto this for their own political reasons, with the telegenic Mr Bull as a useful figure-head. However… they do seem to have the support of certain influential people in the county, which is obviously not going to make things any easier for us.'

Bliss looked at Annie, in her black Crown Court suit and her white silk shirt. His lover, now, unbelievably.

But his friend?

Later, in his office, Bliss showed Annie the letter posted to *The Police, Hereford*. 'Gwyn Adamson's inclined to think it's a crank thing. I'm not sure.'

To the Detective investigating the Murder of Farmer Bull.

I cannot tell you who I am for personal reasons. While my girlfriend and I were parking at the entrance to a field last Friday night, we both saw a man covered with blood. He was coming towards us as I pulled in and when he saw us he turned and ran. I had the headlights on full and we saw that there was blood all over him. I am sorry that I cannot reveal my identity but I swear this is the truth.

I did not think to look at the exact time but it was about 8.00pm. This is all I can tell you. I hope it helps you catch him. I am unable to give you a better description of him because of all the blood.

'This has been processed, presumably?' Annie said.

'It's a copy.'

'Where was it posted?'

'In town.'

'Could be on CCTV, then. If we can tie it down to a time margin, could be a simple process of elimination.'

'Already being done,' Bliss said. 'What strikes me is the way he calls Mansel *Farmer Bull*. Heard that a few times the last couple of days. Some local people called him Farmer Bull in a humorous kind of way because he looked so much like an old-fashioned gentleman farmer – tweeds, waistcoat, cloth cap.'

'That been in the papers?'

'Not that I'm aware.'

'So this person's probably a local. Fairly intelligent, no spelling mistakes or dodgy grammar. We could be looking at a neighbour. In a car. With a girlfriend. So if he's married… What've you done about it so far?'

'Extended the search area. Nasty night, so there'll be tracks.

Also, if this bloke they saw was well splattered with Mansel's blood, he's likely to've sprinkled some of it around.'

'We need to find whoever sent this,' Annie said. 'This guy thinks he's told us all he knows, but half an hour's questioning we could get twice as much. Let's put out an appeal. Person who sent a letter posted in Hereford. No details.'

'OK, will do. Interesting they saw only one man. Could be significant?'

'Unless they split up, took off in different directions.'

'There's also a report come in of a man at Leominster being taken away in a four-by-four with a bag over his head. But that was two nights earlier. Maybe a joke.'

'Yeah, well, from now on, we ignore nothing that happens in the sticks,' Annie Howe said.

'Yeh. Um…' Might as well tell her. 'Don't think you've ever seen Kirsty, have you?'

'Apart from in the wedding picture that used to be on your sideboard.'

'She looked different then. Longer hair. And it's dyed now. Dark red.'

Annie looked at him, a forefinger extended along one pale cheek.

'Dark red hair? Black coat?'

'You noticed her, then.'

'On the box? Oh God, Francis.'

'Yeh.'

'Who was the man, with her?'

'Her old man, Chris Symonds. Interesting the way they were sitting at the table right underneath the Countryside Defiance banner.'

'So they knew they'd be on TV, and you'd see it.' Annie folded the photocopy of the letter and stood up, allowing her hand to brush briefly against Bliss's. 'Come over later, if you can.'

14

Not Going

BORDERLIFE: THAT WAS when the knife really went in.

A quarterly glossy, full of ads for luxury stuff that few local people would buy even if they could afford it. But then, *Borderlife* wasn't aimed at local people. Getting off the school bus, Jane had seen the spring issue on the rack at the Eight Till Late. Hadn't *wanted* to buy it, obviously, but the know-your-enemy instinct had kicked in with the picture of Ward Savitch on the front, sitting on a vintage Fergy tractor with The Court in the background, all misty, and the blurb *Just Call Me A Reformed Townie.*

OK, Jane had never actually met Savitch. Didn't really want to, either, in case he turned out to have, you know, some level of basic charm or a prosthetic leg. But she was building up a file of news cuttings, background for the exposé in a proper publication.

Borderlife had four pages, including about six pictures of the countryside looking lush, the enemy looking smug.

THE SAVITCH EFFECT
Lorna Mantle meets the man
at the heart of the New Cotswolds

Jane had the magazine open on the floor by her bed and was lying across the width of the duvet, tensing up already.

How many lives must have been changed for ever by a quick flip through the property pages in a dentist's waiting room. 'Yes, I owe all this to a broken tooth,' Ward Savitch laughs, showing me around an estate that now extends to over 300 acres... and growing.

The advertisement for The Court at Ledwardine wasn't the biggest on the page, but there was something about it that told the jaded City broker: *This is the one.*

'I think it was the fact that I'd simply never heard of the place,' he says. 'I'd inspected properties all over Gloucestershire, Oxfordshire and Berkshire with an increasing sense of seen-it-all-before. But Herefordshire was a revelation.'

They all said that. Jane wrinkling her nose in distaste. What they meant was that Herefordshire was still up for grabs, whereas the Cotswolds had been firmly grabbed, no bargains left.

The term 'New Cotswolds' as applied to the pre-recession rush to buy property in Herefordshire is not always used approvingly, but Ward Savitch sees it as a challenge. 'This county has a wealth of customs and traditions in danger of being lost for ever. I want to see growth of a kind which supports the old traditions and helps develop a society that will preserve them in a sympathetic and *lasting* way.'

Made you want to vomit.

After an extensive restoration of the former farmhouse and its grounds and outbuildings, Mr Savitch began breeding pheasants and organizing shooting weekends. Then, as he acquired more land, new luxury chalets were concealed in the dark woods, giving upmarket holidaymakers a taste of the wilds.

The action-holiday market was also catered for, with paintballing events, canoeing on the river, quad bikes and rough shooting. Many of the guests enjoyed themselves so much that they didn't want to leave and went on to buy their own homes in the area, finding that it was possible to live on the Welsh Border without giving up their highpowered business ventures.

'I realized there was a new energy here,' says Mr Savitch, 'and became more excited than I'd ever been in my life. I saw that, with the decline of agriculture, the countryside was literally being left to rot – by the damned townies. Well, you can call me a *reformed townie* – I've seen the light. In the Internet era we can do anything here that can be done in a city – and better.'

To prove this to City power-brokers, Mr Savitch has been organising hugely popular 'freshen-up' weekends aimed at London-based professionals damaged by the recession and and desperate to make a new start.

Cornel and his mates? They were damaged all right, but not in ways they'd accept.

Ward Savitch certainly exudes an infectious vitality as he drives me in a bumpy old Land Rover across fields and along forestry tracks, where every chalet – and *chalet* is a poor term for these luxurious holiday homes – comes with over half an acre of wooded land, and full Wi-Fi broadband. They all have solar panels and Ward has plans for a small wind farm on the edge of his estate.

'Oh, I'm as green as the next man,' he says. 'But I'm not into gimmicks and all that old hippie "good life" nonsense. The countryside isn't a place for running away to. It's a place to *progress* to. Surveys show that the largest proportion of incomers to Herefordshire in the past year have been from London.

'Many are people with money, eager to invest it somewhere they can see it having an effect,' says Mr Savitch. 'I've lost nearly two stone since moving here and sleep better than I've ever done. Coming to the Border – I expect that to add at least fifteen years to my useful life.'

Useful life?

Solar panels and windmills for phoney green cred? Who *was* this Lorna Mantle? Had Savitch opened a bottle of vintage champagne afterwards and shagged her in the barn? Jane wasn't laughing, because it got worse.

***

The Savitch effect is already visible in the economic health of the county, in the demand for country-sports equipment and outward-bound accessories.

'Mr Savitch has done great things for my business,' says Kenny Mostyn, proprietor of camping and country sports suppliers Hardkit, who provides instructors at The Court. 'I won't deny we were in trouble before he came – the bank was pulling the plug – but we now have four flourishing retail outlets either side of the Welsh Border.'

'Ward has been good news for us,' says Lyndon Pierce, who represents Ledwardine on the Herefordshire Council. 'He's pre-served the village economy in difficult times, and even attracted new business ventures. And this is just the start. A broad eco-nomic base means we should be able to go ahead with a major expansion programme that might otherwise have been in danger.'

At the bottom of the piece it said:

SEE FOR YOURSELF what Ward Savitch has achieved when The Court at Ledwardine is open to visitors over the Easter holiday period, culminating in a Family Fun Day on Bank Holiday Monday.

He had it all worked out. Winning the battle for hearts and minds. It was *sick.*

Jane slid the magazine under the bed, rolled onto her back, and a rogue sob came up like a hiccup. She lay looking up at where, when they'd first moved here and she'd claimed the attic as her apartment, she'd painted the white plastered spaces between the timbers in primary colours. The Mondrian Walls. The big statement. *This is me, this is my space.*

Just a kid, then. Not yet getting it that Ledwardine was all about bones of oak and creamy white skin and didn't need chemical colours.

Or anybody like Ward Savitch. Ever.

Now there were sheets of white card taped between the

timbers. She'd spent every evening for most of a week putting this together, using blow-ups of a large-scale OS map. Here was the village with the orchard marked out, as it had been centuries ago: a great circle around a much smaller community. The orchard still enclosing much of a Bronze Age henge. Roots of old apple trees wrapped around buried stones. It *had* to be.

She sat up, took the mobile from the bedside table and rang Neil Cooper, of the county archaeology department, at home. He answered on about the twelfth ring.

'OK, look,' Jane said, 'I'm really sorry to be ringing you at night again, and I know your wife thinks we've got a thing going, but I need—'

'No, she doesn't, Jane,' Neil Cooper said. 'She's seen you. She knows I'm far too much of a slippers-and-cocoa kind of guy for someone like you. In fact, Russell Brand would probably be too—'

'Yeah, yeah, very amusing.'

Jane squirmed to the edge of the bed where she'd lost her virginity to Eirion Lewis. He was at university now, in Cardiff, came over most weekends, bless him, didn't want to lose her. *Russell Brand?*

'We're moving as fast we can, Jane,' Coops said, 'but like I keep telling you, it's not the only dig in the queue.'

Nearly all archaeology these days was rescue archaeology. They only ever got to look at places about to be buried for ever under a housing estate. What worried her was that if the council sanctioned plans for a superstore and upmarket housing – and Savitch had to be in on that somewhere – the henge would stay buried, like for good?

'So what you're saying *is*…'

'It's now looking doubtful this summer.'

'So, like, if I wind up at uni in September, I miss everything.'

'Jane—'

'Sorry, I expect you've got things to do. I'll go.'

'I *will* keep you informed. I realize how much this means to you.'

Jane lay down with her head hanging over the side of the bed. Couldn't seem to sleep these nights.

It was OK till you turned eighteen. OK to sound off about things you hated, knowing there was nothing you could really do about any of it. All those years of thinking how great it'd be when you were officially adult and nobody could restrict you any more. When, in fact, *not* being able to do anything was actually a kind of freedom. If you stood up now and accused your local councillor of being bent – which he *was* – he'd have you in court. The village and the henge… she'd tried to discuss it with some of the guys at school, and they didn't get it. Didn't *remotely* get it. None of them could wait to get the hell out of the places they'd grown up in, dreaming of London and Paris and New York and LA.

Maybe it was a pagan thing, that sense of place. That sense of attachment. Although even Mum was picking up on it now.

Jane had Googled Julian of Norwich last night and discovered a woman who, in an age when God was generally feared, had found the old guy polite, compassionate and…

… had even talked of *Mother God.* Which the theologians said was no more than a recognition of God's nurturing of mankind. But, hey, come *on,* how far was this really from *Mother Goddess?*

All the blood was running to Jane's head, almost on the floor by now, in a nest of hair. This whole university thing was like some insidious conspiracy by the lousy Government, just a way of keeping you off benefits for another three years, while hitting you with mega tuition fees. By the time she was out of it, there'd probably be thousands of qualified archaeologists who were all going to be Indiana Jones and…

Jane's head hit the floor.

… she didn't have to go.

Shocked and excited, she wriggled back onto the bed then rolled off it, stood up, went to the window. The village lights were coming on, twin lanterns either side of the main door of the Black Swan, fake gas lamps on the square. The lights you could see, the lights you couldn't.

Jane's eyes widened.

Wasn't going?

That simple? A decision already made? On some level, it had been decided?

Holy shit.

She was breathing very fast now. OK, maybe not a question of deliberately fluffing the A levels. Probably make a point of doing well, getting the grades, just to show she could do it. And then just *not going*.

No shame in that. It was actually kind of radical. She could just go out and get a job. Any kind of job that would allow her to stay in Ledwardine and fight for what mattered.

Jane felt suddenly still inside and terrifyingly clear-headed. She needed to be absolutely direct about this. No shit. She'd give it a few minutes, then go down and tell Mum before she could change her mind. Hadn't Mum, after all, dropped out of uni after getting pregnant? Hadn't she even been known to say – long after Dad's death in the car crash alongside the woman he'd been shagging – that maybe it was all *meant*?

Jane stood gazing down at her village. Which needed her. In this sick, withering world, it needed all the energy it could get.

She saw a small shadow emerge from the vicarage gate. Mum, in jeans and sweater, tripping across the market square. Of course – off to meet Lol in the Swan, like it was still the early days of their relationship, courtesies to observe. What was the *matter* with them, hovering around one another still? Everybody hovering, nobody *doing* anything.

OK, give them an hour or so and then go across to the Swan. Telling Mum in front of Lol, that would diffuse the effect.

Still in her cloud of *knowing*, Jane went downstairs to the kitchen, talked it over with Ethel, the cat.

Ethel was like, *Yeah, but what about your career?*

'It's just a word, Ethel.'

Jane stood for an uncertain moment in the cold kitchen, then went over to the fruit bowl on the dresser and took out an apple. Cut it in half – crossways – to reveal the pale green pentagram at its heart. Carried it out into the garden and held it in the cup of her hands, open to the rising moon, only a misty grey-blue smudge, but it would do.

She stood in the silence, expanding the apple pentagram in her mind until she was standing in the middle of it, watching it widen and become a white-golden aura, eventually enclosing the whole of Ledwardine.

And then Jane prayed to the Goddess, to become a channel for the cosmic energy which would make things happen.

15

Dead Game

Lol said, 'Would Barry have to kill me with his bare hands if I put that on the fire?'

Merrily followed his gaze to the basket in the inglenook, black and ashy.

'The big log?'

'The only log.'

He was right. She couldn't remember ever before seeing only one log in the inglenook at the Black Swan, famous for its apple-wood fires, smoke-sweetened air over the cobbled square. She shivered. In the beamed and panelled lounge bar, only half the wall lights were on. Enough for the eight or so customers whose sparse voices made soft echoes.

'You might not like what Savitch is doing,' Lol said, 'but you really notice when one of his wealthy hunting parties leaves the village.'

'Barry's *that* dependent on them?'

Lol shrugged. He was wearing his fraying grey Gomer Parry Plant Hire sweatshirt. He had a spiral-bound notebook – his lyrics pad – and, beside it on the table, a pint she guessed was shandy, not yet half-drunk.

'Smoking ban,' Barry said from behind the bar. 'Cheap supermarket booze. And now Fortress Hereford. Yeah, we *are* getting dependent on them. Seven fewer five-course dinners, bar takings down by a third. Put the bleedin' log on, Laurence, I can always saw up an oak settle.'

Lol left the log alone. Merrily stared at bulky amiable Barry in the black suit and the bow tie.

'Fortress Hereford?'

'All farm doors locked at nightfall, shotguns loaded. Tell me I'm wrong. Tell me there's another reason we're nearly empty.'

'What, because of—?'

'Having your quad bike nicked is one thing, but getting killed like Mansel Bull is not a case for *Farm Watch*, as we know it.'

'It's not Texas, either,' Merrily said. 'Not yet.'

'Civilization, vicar, has a thin skin. This is still a frontier. Face west, nothing but lonely Welsh hills. Don't take much to send us to ground. See this?'

Barry slapped down a glossy flyer showing the winding Wye seen from above. A man in a hunting coat stood with his back to the camera, a riding crop in one hand. Under the photo it said:

WORTH FIGHTING FOR?

Under that:

COUNTRYSIDE DEFIANCE

Lol's eyes flickered.

'Who *are* they?'

'The woman we saw on the box – Wiseman-France – she's dined here a time or two, with clients. Professional PR, management consultant, not sure which, but you get the idea. You know the type. Move in and tell the hicks their interests are being ignored at national level because they're not making their voices heard with sufficient eloquence.'

'Mmm.' Merrily nodded. 'Then they offer their services free to give themselves a certain status in the community. Make them feel they belong. She's created it, has she?'

'She ain't created the mood, but she's given it a name,' Barry said. 'Don't have to be thousands of people behind it, just a few dozen of the right people. The thousands will follow. And the money.'

'Savitch?'

'Put it this way… it was one of his minions brought the flyers in. I'm told it also comes in different languages. When the shooting parties come in from Europe, America, Japan they learn that the spiritual home of hunting since the eleventh century is under threat. You ask me, Defiance is pulling donations from US hunting and gun lobbies.'

'*This* is Savitch?'

'Probably excites him. Life on the edge can be quite sexy when you're living behind big walls with big guys around and a game-keeper in the lodge with a rack of shotguns.'

'Spoken by a man who knows all about life on the edge,' Merrily said.

'This and that.'

'You know Syd Spicer?'

It just came out. Barry's expression didn't change. Lol glanced at Merrily, curious. You could hear the *tunk* of a pool game over in the other bar. Barry came round the bar, raked over the fire in the dog-grate, picked up the apple log and dumped it on top.

'The last good log,' he said. ''Scuse me a minute.'

Lol's spiral-bound lyrics pad was half-filled. Merrily remembered him buying it in Hereford, maybe two weeks ago, after a rare lunch at All Saints.

'You're, erm, cookin'? As Danny would say.'

'We need to get the album out before summer.' Lol had a cautious sip of shandy. 'It's not just about me any more.'

Probably meaning not Danny so much as Prof Levin. Hard times for a producer with a studio and overheads, now that a band could make a perfectly professional album with digital kit in someone's spare bedroom. She knew Lol was worried about Prof going back on the booze, if only out of boredom.

'And, um…' Upturning his pencil, letting it slide through his fingers to the pad. 'I've had another approach.'

'Sorry?'

'An agency. Nu-folk stuff – reputable. They could break me into tours, have me headlining middling events next autumn, and…' Lol leaned back. 'There we are. Serious money.'

'Oh.'

With downloads and burn-offs, the profits were in gigs again.

'I said maybe I'd get back to them,' Lol said.

'Of course.'

'I won't, obviously.'

'Lol, don't let—'

'It's not just that. I mean, it's not *just* you.'

Merrily felt like the stone flags were falling away beneath her chair. That what he was saying was *not* what he was thinking.

Lol said, 'I don't actually *want* to be rich. You know that.'

'I do?'

'Well… be nice, in a way, to be so loaded you could buy out Ward Savitch. But realistically…' Lol put his hands on his knees, stared down at them. 'I've been handed a second chance, right? So I want things to be different from what they might've been if I'd made it first time. Partly because there's going to be less time. And also… Like, when Prof says, we need more *body* on this album and why doesn't he see if Tom Storey's available, I'm going, no, there's actually this guy called Danny Thomas who's an ex-subsistence farmer and isn't *quite* as good as Tom Storey, but is good *enough*…'

'You didn't tell me that, either. You didn't tell me Prof wanted to get you Tom Storey.'

Unlikely to be an idle promise, because Prof had been around a long time and knew these ageing rock gods from way back, and some of them owed him favours. Merrily felt starved. What else hadn't he told her?

Lol said, 'Just we've not had that much time to talk lately, have we?'

'Because you've been at Danny's barn night after bloody—
You just didn't *want* to tell me, did you?'

'You have enough to—'

'So we have separate problems now? We keep our problems
to ourselves? We keep them *apart*? Now you don't need me to
bounce this stuff off because you've got Danny?'

'I don't want a row...'

'Jesus, Lol... you *never* want a bloody row.'

Merrily jerked her chair back. What was the matter with her?
She *liked* Danny Thomas. She was glad that Lol was working
with a local guy. But was he turning down tours only because he
thought it would be incompatible with the life of a woman tied
to a parish?

'I like it here,' Lol said. 'I like being a guy living in a village
where one day you're playing music, the next you're doing...
something else.'

He pulled over the lyrics pad, pencilled a circle around something, then pushed it in front of Merrily. She read:

When life's become a bitch
Dig out another ditch
Find some recovery
Back in the JCB

Referencing the times he'd spent helping Gomer Parry. She
wasn't really taking this in. She was thinking, *This is a test. It
had to happen one day. The Christian thing would be to persuade
him to do the tour.*

She saw a man walk into the bar, carrying a black bin
liner.

'Look,' Lol said, 'I've agreed with Barry to do a few more gigs
here – at the Swan.'

'And would that be a *living*?' Merrily clutched her head. 'All
right, I'm sorry...'

'And maybe something outside in the summer, with more
music. Other people.'

'A music festival? In Ledwardine?'

'Too big a word. We're thinking no more than one day… and a night. Just an idea. Well, Danny's idea. He has Glastonbury dreams. I was going to see what you thought before we took it any further, because… festivals of any kind haven't always gone well here, have they? Anyway, it would be useful to have the album finished and mastered and out there, before it happens. *If* it happens.'

'Does the album have a title yet?'

'*A Message from the Morning.*'

'Oh God, I knew that. What's the matter with me? Lol, look…' Merrily reached across the table for his hand. 'Maybe we should grab half a day. Drive over to Wales. Talk about all this. And other things.'

Lol said, 'What's up with Barry?'

Merrily turned her chair around. Barry was back and the man was holding up the bin liner. Barry was wiping his hands on a towel.

'He's not happy, Lol.'

Lol said, 'Why were you asking him about Syd Spicer?'

'It's a long story.'

The guy put the bin sack on the bar.

'For you, Barry.'

He was gangly, long-faced, jutting jaw. And not sober. Barry looked up, doing his professional beam.

'Is this roadkill, sir, or did one of you finally learn how to shoot?'

'Dinner.' The guy slapped the bag on the bar. 'My dinner for tomorrow, Barry.'

He wore a camouflage jacket, newish. He had a loose, rubbery mouth.

'I wanna eat it,' he said.

Merrily saw Lol look up, frown.

'I thought he'd gone back to… wherever he came from. I thought they'd all gone.'

'Guest of The Court?'

'They love to find bits of lead shot in their dinner,' Lol said. 'Real men.'

'Do us a favour, sir,' Barry said, 'Take it round the back. Not everybody likes dead game in the bar. Especially when it's over a month out of season.'

'It never fucking *is*, landlord!'

'Then it's probably unfit for human consumption,' Barry said calmly. 'Round the back, eh?'

'I need to eat it.'

'We'll talk about it round the back.'

'I can only thank God Jane's not here,' Merrily said.

She saw Lol wince.

16

The Rule

HALFWAY ACROSS THE square, under the amber wash of the fake gas lamps, Jane lost the certainty. Not cold feet exactly, just the need for a second opinion. Why ruin Mum's night? She hadn't seen Lol for days.

She slipped into the shadowy sanctuary of the little oak-pillared market hall, pulled out her mobile and called Eirion's phone.

Eirion's answering service kicked in.

'It's me,' Jane said.

She'd give him two minutes to call back and then walk across to the Swan, see what kind of mood Mum was in. Let the fates decide.

She was alone under the stone-tiled roof of the market hall which sometimes looked even more ancient than it was, like a prehistoric burial chamber. In her plan of the Ledwardine henge, the market hall was just off-centre, maybe marking a confluence of energies. A fair bit of energy had been expended here, all those shadowy couples exploring each other's bodies up against the pillars.

Which made her think about Eirion at university, with all its temptations, although he'd sworn to her…

Sod it. Jane tucked away her phone and walked across to the Swan, reaching the bottom of the three stone steps just as the door opened. She backed away as someone stumbled out, the porch lamp lighting his face and his slobbery mouth.

Oh God, no.

Still *here*? Weren't they all supposed to have gone home to their penthouses? How long did these bloody courses go on?

Still here, still pissed.

I'll be seeing you… girlie.

Bad, bad news. Jane slid into the alley which led to the Swan's backyard. He might not even remember her, probably tried it on with a few more women since then, but it wasn't worth the risk. She stood leaning against the wall, waiting for him to go.

Obviously *not* the time to talk to Mum. Too many negative signs.

The phone shuddered in her pocket. She eased it out of her jeans, moving further into the alley, holding it very tight to her ear.

'I was finishing a curry,' Eirion said. 'Some things must never be interrupted. And, before you ask, yes, it was a vegetable curry. Not easy to obtain in this part of Cardiff.'

'Well, that—' Footsteps, someone grunting. 'Irene, I'll have to call you back.'

'Jane—?'

'Sorry.'

She killed the signal, edged a little further against the wall. There was a sigh and a liquid splatter. Steam and stench. *Gross.* Jane turned away and waited until it was over, expecting him to go once he'd finished, but…

Damn, damn, damn. He was coming into the alley. Jane moved all the way into the inn yard. There was an old brick toilet block at the end, long out of use. Jane slid around the side of it, stumbling into a pile of rubble.

Only just making it in time. The kitchen door was opening. A splash of light. Jane saw Dean Wall standing in the doorway, wearing an apron. A local thug, basically, unless he'd changed since she'd been at school with him. Somehow, he'd persuaded Barry to take him on as an assistant chef, which probably meant he was responsible for sweeping the yard. Essentially, only a few years, a degree from the LSE and probably a Swiss bank account separated Dean from Cornel, who was standing on the step, one arm inside a plastic sack.

'Tomorrow's dinner, mate.'

Something was pushed at Dean, who went kind of *duh*, but it was crisply overlaid by Barry's voice.

'I'm sorry, mate.'

'Don't apologize, Barry. Just take it.'

'You misunderstand. I told you once, I'm not accepting this. This is the country. There are rules.'

'Wha—?'

'Rules. Take it away.'

'No, *mate*,' Cornel said. 'In the country, there aren't *any* fucking rules that can't be broken.'

'Son, you don't know anything about the country.'

'You reckon?'

'Season ends on February the first, and it's now very nearly the end of March. That make sense to you?'

'What?'

'Pheasants. The rule.'

'Did I mention pheasants? *Did I?*'

Jane saw white moonlight rippling in the black plastic of a bin liner, bulging. Cornel was holding it up with both hands, something hanging out of it.

'It deserves to be fucking eaten,' Cornel said. 'By me. That make sense to *you*?'

Barry didn't move. Cornel pulled the bin liner open at the top and held it out to him. Barry stayed in the doorway, very relaxed-looking, not touching the bag.

'How'd you kill that? You all get together and beat it to death?'

Jane couldn't see what it was and didn't want to. She felt herself going tight with hate.

Cornel said, 'You're really not gonna—?'

'Goodnight, son.'

Barry at his most no-shit.

'Wha'm I s'posed to do with it?'

Almost screaming now.

'I should put it back in your car boot, mate, and dispose of it very discreetly.'

'You're no fun, Barry. You're *no fucking fun.*'

'Actually,' Barry said, 'this is me at my most fun. You want to see me at my most *no* fun, you'll leave that thing behind on these premises. You get where I'm coming from?'

There was a scary kind of deadness in Barry's voice. Jane had heard stories about what Barry had been known to do, the odd times it had got rough in the public bar. The yard went momentarily black as the door was shut, and – *oh, shit* – the mobile started vibrating in Jane's hip pocket. She was gripping the phone through the denim as Cornel totally lost it, started snarling at the closed door.

'This is not over. It's *not fucking over!*'

Just like the other night. *I just want you to know it doesn't end here.* Only losers walked away. Limited repertoire. Tosser. Jane stayed tight between the perimeter wall and the toilet block, trying to breathe slowly in the stale-beery air, not wanting to think how Cornel might react if he found her here, witness to his humiliation. Again.

The moon showed her Cornel's foot coming back, maybe to kick the closed door, and then it got confusing.

'Didn't handle that very well, did we, Cornel?'

Another voice. Someone had come into the yard from the alley.

'Pick it up, eh?'

An ashy kind of voice. Not Barry. A bit Brummy.

'I thought you'd gone,' Cornel said.

'Thought? Yow *don't* think, Cornel, that's the problem. Now pick it up. Take it somewhere and bury it, then go and cry yourself to sleep.'

Cornel's voice came back, petulant.

'Why are you *doing* this to me?'

'Go home any time y'want, mate. No skin off my nose.'

'You're just a—'

A movement. Not much of one. A chuckle. Then a short cry, more shock than pain.

'*Uhhh!*'

'Ah, dear, dear, you're really not ready. Didn't see that that coming either. Not as hard as we thought, eh? Long way to go, Cornel, still a long way to go, mate.'

Jane breathed in hard, through her mouth, and the breath dragged in something gritty.

'I've told you,' Cornel said. 'I'll pay the extra.'

'It's not about money. It's about *manhood*.'

An indrawn breath, full of rage, a scuffling, like Cornel was finding his feet. Jane tasted something disgusting, realized she was inhaling a cobweb full of dead flies.

Cornel was going, 'You sanctimonious fucking… *Awwww…*'

From the yard, a bright squeak of intense agony. Piercing violence lighting up the night like an electric storm, and Jane, choking, clawing at her mouth, was really scared now, sweat creaming her forehead. Trying to meld with the toilet wall, breathing through her nose, holding her jaw rigid, not even daring to spit.

'Come and see me again, look, when your balls drop,' the guy said.

This kind of tittering laugh. A sound you'd swear was the guy clapping Cornel on the back in a *don't take it to heart* kind of way.

Departing footsteps, light and casual in the alley, but in the yard there was only retching and then Cornel going, '*Shit, shit, shit, shit…*' like he was walking round in circles, while Jane clung to the jagged stones in the toilet wall, her head ballooning with a suffocating nausea.

'*…shit, shit, shit…*' from the alleyway now, receding.

Cornel had gone.

Jane sprang away from the wall, coughing out the cobweb and the flies, coughing and coughing, wiping her mouth on her sleeve as she went staggering out into the warm smell of new vomit in the yard.

She was at the top of the alley, where it came out onto the square, when she saw Cornel again.

He was on his own, dragging the black bin sack across the cobbles like some vagrant. He was moving jerkily, his body arched. Jane saw him stop. She saw him pick up the plastic sack with both hands, his gangly body bending in pain like an insect which had been trodden on.

Cornel dumped the sack into one of the concrete litter bins on the square, ramming it in hard before walking crookedly away.

Jane didn't move until he was long gone and the village centre was unusually deserted in the amber of the fake gas lamps.

Beyond the glow, gables jutted, like Cornel's chin, into a cold, windless night sky, and the church steeple was moon-frosted as Jane moved unsteadily across to the concrete bin.

17

Get the Drummer Killed

'YOU DON'T HAVE to take that crap,' Barry said. 'There comes a point where you just… you realize you just don't.'

He'd come back from the kitchens looking dark-faced, angry, and that was rare. A few more customers had come in since, and Marion, the head barmaid, had taken over. Barry had poured himself a Guinness and come to sit with Merrily and Lol.

'Behaving like a servant is one thing. Being treated like one is something else.'

'He'd killed a pheasant?' Lol said.

'Don't matter. None of it matters too much now, anyway. When the worst happens, I'm not going to be around.'

He got up suddenly, unhooked a big black poker, turned over the last big apple log, and the flames were instantly all over it. Barry came and sat down, rubbing soot from his hands.

'The worst?' Merrily said.

'I apologize.' Barry drank some Guinness, wiped his lips almost delicately on a white pocket handkerchief. 'There's no reason at all for me not to tell you. Savitch is buying the Swan.'

Pool balls plinked off one another in the Public. Lol put down his pencil.

'When you think about it, it was only a matter of time,' Barry said.

'I didn't…' Lol's voice was parched. 'The Swan's for sale?'

'Way things are now, Laurence, any pub's for sale. Every day, somewhere in Britain, another one shuts down.'

Merrily stared into the fire. After Christmas, it had become known that the Black Swan's elderly owner had handed it over to her son, who ran a building firm. The building trade would revive, but the future for pubs…

'Savitch put in an initial offer last week.' Barry's voice was flat. 'Ridiculously low, and it got turned down, of course. But that was just round one. He'll be back.'

'Why's he doing this?' Lol said. 'Why not just, you know, *live* here?'

'He's a businessman. The place you live, you want it to look like an enterprise, not a loser's refuge.'

'This can't happen,' Lol said.

'It could happen tomorrow, mate, if he doubles his bid. Which I'm sure he can afford to. But I think he'll wait.'

'What can we do?' Merrily said.

'Pray?'

'What are his plans, exactly?'

'Village is set to grow. Maybe he's on a promise. All too friendly with Councillor Pierce these days.' Barry leaned his chair back against an oak pillar where a wall had once divided the bar into two rooms. 'End of the day, we're just the little people. These things don't happen on our level, do they? I mean, the word is he'll ask me to stay on, but that's… not for me.'

'I'm so sorry, Barry.'

'Nah, I'll be all right. Not sure about Ledwardine, though.' Barry settled into his chair, evidently more relaxed now it was out. 'So what's the problem with Syd Spicer, then, Merrily?'

'Didn't think you wanted to talk about him.'

'I didn't. Now, suddenly, it seems like light relief. One of your lot now, last I heard.'

'Actually, one of your lot again. Been made chaplain at Credenhill.'

'Has he now?'

'You didn't know?'

'They don't put out a newsletter. Chaplain, eh? *Padre*. Well, well.'

'Barry, could I ask you something in general? About the Regiment?'

Barry shrugged, his jacket tightening, a sleeve rising to expose a purplish scar snaking up his wrist from the palm of his left hand.

'I'm sorry if it—'

'Nah, nah, just it's usually teenage boys. How many men you killed? How many times you been tortured? It can get wearing.'

'Just that Syd once told me… he said there was a kind of mysticism in the Regiment. His word.'

'Oh, I see. This is about the things you do on the side.'

Much of the time, Barry's broad face was smooth and bland, but his eyes were the eyes of a far thinner, warier man. Maybe a colder man. He sucked some froth from his Guinness.

'Not quite sure what you mean by mysticism. There's a lot of *myths*.'

Merrily waited. The old apple log was well alight and it felt warmer in here now, almost like old times. But this was the last good log.

'What can I tell you?' Barry said. 'There've been geezers I knew, up against a wall, who've prayed their hearts out and the wall never moved, know what I mean? And there's a bloke I know survived against all the odds, and he's seen it as a miracle and gone hallelujah, praise the Lord, born-again.'

'What about superstition?'

'Rabbits' feet? Not treading on the cracks in the minefield?' Barry shook his head minimally. 'Small obsessions can get you hurt.'

'Fear of the unknown?'

'You don't give in to it. If you're in a tight situation, personal fears take a back seat because you're concentrating on how to deal with it.'

'What if it's something a man knows he can't get at? I'm wondering at what stage he would think he was going mad.'

'Blimey,' Barry said. 'What's this about? Only, generally speaking, we don't do mad. All right. What I'd say is you might start by eliminating the possibility of there being, say, something in the water – practical stuff.'

'And when you've eliminated the rational, the hallucinatory…?'

'We talking about Syd here? Only he's a bleedin' vicar.'

'Not all vicars feel able to take the funny stuff on board. Don't all take *God* on board any more. At what stage do you think he might seek help?'

'On a mission, you rely on your mates, your gang. The circumstances would have to be very special for you to venture outside. You read Frank's book? Frank Collins?'

'Should have, shouldn't I?'

Frank Collins: former curate at St Peter's, Hereford. Ex-SAS. Occasionally spoken of among Hereford clergy, warily.

'Wish I'd known him,' Merrily said. 'But he was dead before I came here.'

By his own hand. Gassed himself in his car. She'd heard it said that he'd become depressed after writing the book about his time in the SAS and his conversion to Christianity. It hadn't been well received – by the Regiment, not the clergy.

'Some weird stuff in that book,' Barry said. 'How God spoke to him through the radio. There's one tale in there of a guy who knows his best mate's bought the farm in the Falklands on account of he's appeared to him in his house, thousands of miles away, all dripping wet. Made me shiver a bit, that. I served with them both. Frank, too. Blondie, we called him.'

'I'll read it. Did start it once, but life intervened. Did, erm… did Frank Collins find the same level of support in the Church as he had in the SAS?'

'Evidently not,' Barry said.

'I see.'

'In the Regiment, you rely on your mates not only because they're your mates but because each of you's got special skills. Abilities the others respect.' He looked at Lol. 'Like in a band. Only a band where, if you forget your chords, you might get the drummer killed.'

'Good analogy,' Lol said. 'I'm guessing.'

'We don't like to rely on guesswork,' Barry said.

Some nights, Lol would just go back to the vicarage with Merrily for coffee or hot chocolate.

This wasn't going to be one of them. They both knew that, as they walked out onto cobbles already slick with black ice. Almost touching, not quite. They never publicly held hands in Ledwardine, not even after dark.

A few icy stars were out over Cole Hill, a wreath of them above the church steeple. Merrily shivered with cold and unease, watching Lol beside her, head down, the lyrics pad under an arm, a hole in an elbow of his Gomer Parry sweatshirt. The Ledwardine village musician, one day playing music, the next following a JCB down to the riverbank with a hand shovel. She could almost hear his thoughts echoing across the cobbles: *what kind of fantasy is this?*

Lol had never really been much of a pub guy. Didn't drink much, didn't play darts or pool, didn't have *mates*. It was only after his Christmas concert at the Swan that he'd achieved a degree of openness in Ledwardine. After he'd been lured out to play his music in front of his neighbours. And now...

I've agreed with Barry to do a few more gigs. Here at the Swan. And maybe something outside in the summer.

'If Savitch can't get it cheap enough, he might not bother,' Merrily said at the entrance to Church Street. 'I mean, what's he going to do with it anyway, to make it show a decent profit... on his scale?'

Wishing, as soon as it was out – like with a lot of things she'd said tonight – that she'd kept quiet.

'You know exactly what he'll do,' Lol said. 'He'll make it into some kind of après-shoot retreat for his corporate clients... and for all the wives and girlfriends who don't want to stay in a chalet, however luxurious, on a muddy farm. He'll build up the restaurant and double the prices. It'll just... regularize things.'

They stood and contemplated the clutch of lights down Church Street, where the holiday homes – sixteen at the last count – would be in darkness until Easter weekend. One of the *For Sale* notices had acquired a cross-strip saying SOLD. Had Savitch bought that, too?

Merrily saw Lol bent over his guitar in a corner, his music drowned out by the laughter of loud-voiced, *faux*-rural thugs.

'They look out from their penthouses across all the lights,' Lol said. 'And they can't see it but they know it's there… all those thousands of square miles of it, all dark and empty. It just… it starts to irritate them. They're thinking, what's it *doing*? We're the masters of the universe, why isn't it giving *us* anything?'

Merrily was nodding gloomily. Had it ever been otherwise, since Norman kings designated thousands of acres as hunting ground? Great slabs of it going to the barons, who settled and grew, in their brutal way, to love it and eventually became the old squirearchy.

The Bulls and the Bull-Davieses.

Until they, in turn, started to lose it under the weight of inheritance taxes, leaving it prey to the new money. Savitch.

Cycles of exploitation.

The last fake gas lamp on the square was behind them now. A merciful mesh of shadows claiming them for its own. Lol brought out the keys to the terraced cottage where Lucy Devenish used to live. The folklorist. The guardian of the soul of the village. Jane's first mentor.

'I suppose what gets me,' Lol said, 'is that most people don't seem to mind. The first time somebody off the TV comes to stay at the Swan, bit of glamour, they're all in favour of it. It's brought the village alive… but not in the right way.'

'A bit of glamour,' Merrily said. 'Maybe we all need that.'

Her eyes felt damp.

Lol held open the front door for her. Inside, the wood stove was burning a surprising terracotta red.

Merrily's black woollen top was off before they reached the sofa.

18

An Island in the Night

'ACTUALLY, I DO think he did it,' Bliss said. 'What's wrong with that? It's me job to suspect people.'

Staring up at the plaster moulding around the bedroom ceiling. The curtains were undrawn; you could see blurry lights in the big houses on the hillside across the road.

Cosy. An upstairs flat in a classy Victorian villa set back from the main road out of Great Malvern. Bliss liked it here – at the moment, more than anywhere, especially his crappy semi on the flat side of Hereford. OK, if he was called out in the night it'd take him maybe forty minutes to get back, and he'd need to leave at seven a.m., anyway. But it was worth it. Wasn't it?

'Francis, you...'

Annie Howe peering at him, her eyes all soft and woolly and useless without her contacts. It was worth it just for that.

'... you can't simply accuse a man of murder because he doesn't like you. Sometimes *I* don't like you. You can be an intensely annoying person.'

'Part of me appeal, Annie.'

Bliss watched a light go out across the road, and then the hillside was as blank as those years of mutual blind distrust. Fast-track Annie, man-hating bitch, daughter of Councillor Charlie Howe, ex-copper, bent. All the poison darts Bliss had aimed at her back. Why *should* she like him?

He felt, unexpectedly, flimsy. What was she supposed to see in a twat who couldn't hold anything together, not his job, not

127

his family? Like Kirsty said, *You never did put yourself out much, did you, Frank?*

True, in a way. He and Annie had fallen into bed within days of Kirsty leaving, both coasting on the euphoria of a crucial result, a key arrest. A cop thing. How much staying power was there in that?

'What's the matter?' Annie said.

Chris says you consistently neglected your wife, Inspector.

'Francis…?'

She moved away from him. She'd put her nightdress back on, all creased. She was his superior. Better-educated, better-connected, better-looking. *Coat hanger with tits?* Was Stagg blind?

'We said when this began that there'd be no analysis,' Annie said softly. 'One day at a time. We also said that.'

But there *were* no days, only nights. Cover of darkness. Cover of Christmas. It should have been his emptiest Christmas ever. Instead, he'd spent the days in work, the nights with Annie. In January they were spending two nights a week together, one at her place, one at his – Annie parking around the corner, walking, all muffled up, to the back door. *We're all right*, she'd said, *as long as nobody finds out. As long as we're never seen together. As long as we don't go out together. As long as we don't ever do that thing where you drive a hundred miles into Wales or somewhere and have lunch and walk by the river, because there's always some bloody copper, who used to be in this division, on holiday.*

Bliss cleared his throat. Badly wanting to tell Annie about Kirsty, get her input, see if she had any idea at all who might've rumbled them. But Annie's job was as important to her as his was to him. If he told her, she'd restrict their meetings, and he couldn't stand that, because this was the only thing preventing him exploding into gases and shrapnel.

'Right, then, Francis…'

In the glacial light from the street lamps he saw that she'd arranged two pillows against the bedhead, sitting back into them, a nipple's areola vanishing back into the white cotton. Reaching to the bedside table and finding her glasses and putting them on to watch him across the post-midnight greyness. Return of the Ice Maiden.

'Tell me about Sollers Bull,' she said.

Gut feelings were no longer encouraged. No place for them in teamwork. Even Bliss was suspicious of gut feelings. Other people's, anyway.

'See, even when I was talking to him, I could feel it. I could see him in a pair of them green nylon overalls that farmers wear for mucky jobs.'

'Pulling them off, I suppose, as he ran through the fields into the headlights of our correspondent and his girlfriend.'

'I wanted to go back with a warrant to search his house. I wanted to talk to his hidden wife. Maybe she knows, maybe she doesn't or maybe she just suspects.'

'Stay away from her, Francis. Until you have something stronger, anyway. The bottom line is… he has an alibi. Several.'

'The staff at his caff? It's still borderline. Time of death's not that certain, and it's not that far away. You didn't see the rage in him. Something about it that was wrong for the situation… skewed.'

Anger was always useful for concealing a hole where grief ought to be, but it was also a good outlet for the hyper excitement that lived in you for hours after you'd done something enormous.

'I was thinking at first that if there was no real pain there it was because half of him'd be well chuffed at getting the farm.'

'Perhaps that's all it was,' Annie said. 'We don't even know he didn't get on with his brother. OK, different kinds of men – the traditionalist and the young progressive. University education, big ideas.'

'Enough to cause a rift, when he starts shaking off the steadying hand.'

'Even if they did hate one another, who's going to tell you? Not the family, and not the wider community.'

'Somebody will,' Bliss said. 'Always somebody with a grudge, a chip.'

'We get his DNA, for purposes of elimination?'

'Yeh.'

'You feel threatened, Francis?'

'Me?'

'He's put you very much in the firing line. A symbol of what's gone wrong with the police in this area. Urban cop.'

'Strange as it may seem, Annie, it wasn't that urban where I grew up. Not then, anyway. There *are* fields up there.' Bliss lay back. 'Countryside frigging Defiance. Where did *that* come from?'

'I Googled them. Much of it's hunting-based. Aimed mainly, I'd guess, at attracting younger people to the cause. The traditional fox-hunting image of a retired colonel and Camilla Parker-Bowles as was... is not terribly evident on their Web site.'

'Who's behind it?'

'Don't know. They're also using Facebook and Twitter. Sollers Bull in hunting pink is a gift. Good-looking and a little bit dark and edgy. He was always like that.'

'Oh?'

'I didn't know him well, but I did know him. From his days in the YFC.'

'*You* were in the Young Farmers?'

'I was a young farmer's girlfriend for a while. He was a friend of Sollers. This was when I was about sixteen. We were at the same parties, occasionally. He was popular with girls who... had more going for them in the looks department than I ever did.'

'Don't sell yourself short.'

'I'm a realist. Anyway, I didn't know him well enough to get behind the image.'

'He's a liar,' Bliss said. 'He was acting. On TV. Just like all those husbands who break down in front of the cameras: *Please find the monster who killed my lovely wife.* And all the time you're looking at him.'

The lights were all out in the houses on the hillside, traffic was sparse. Bliss had that feeling he used to get as a kid, of being on an island in the night. It was not unpleasant.

'He did it, Annie.'

'I'd be very careful, at this stage, who you share your suspicions with. It's a small county and Bull has friends all over it.'

'Including my soon-to-be-ex-father-in-law.'

'Did you know that your in-laws knew Sollers Bull?'

'Be surprising if they didn't. The farm's only ten minutes away and Chris Symonds has social ambitions. Always asking me if I was up for promotion.'

Annie slid down in the bed, a long thigh against his.

'You're obviously up for something,' Annie said.

Overslept.

It was six-thirty and fully light when the mobile trilled by his side of the bed. Bliss awoke spooned into Annie's back, experiencing the usual half-shock at whose back this was. His hand had barely found his phone before Annie's phone made its Nokia noise on the other side.

'Karen, yeh?' Bliss said.

Watching Annie fumbling for her glasses, peering at her screen. In Bliss's phone, Karen Dowell didn't dress it up.

'Shit,' Bliss was clawing the sleep out of his eyes. 'Where?'

'City centre, more or less. East Street?'

'A woman. You did say a woman?'

'No, boss, I said two.'

Part Three

*When I was still young, I thought it
a great pity to die. Not that there
was anything on earth I wanted
to live for…*

Julian of Norwich
Revelations of Divine Love

19

Icon

Just gone eight, and the city was stirring irritably under a blotchy brown sky, East Street sealed off, end to end.

A barrier was moved to one side, the tape dropped, letting Bliss through to where Terry Stagg was waiting with a blurry excitement on his brick-dust face.

'Briefly, Tez.'

'Two females. Mid-twenties? We're thinking East European.'

Bliss stood in the middle of the street, looking down to a private parking area for office workers, lawyers, hairdressers. You could see the screens projecting from behind a blank yellow end wall. East Street ran narrowly between the city centre and the Cathedral Close. A few discreet shops, refurbished terraced housing, offices, the rear of the Shirehall and a lone bijou black and white property used by chiropractors.

'And why are we thinking that?'

'Apart from general appearance,' Stagg said, 'one's wearing this kind of a locket thing, silver, with a little religious-looking picture inside and some foreign words.'

'Foreign words.'

'I was off sick when they ran the course on migrant crime.'

Bliss wrinkled his nose. Thousands of East Europeans around the county now: mainly honest, decent migrant workers, a percentage of migrant layabouts and a handful of migrant heavy-duty wrongdoers. There'd been a short course for cops on the kind of societies they came from, their favourite crimes – the more violent ones usually practised against other migrants who were usually reluctant to give evidence.

'How long's *he* been here?'

A silver Beemer was parked up by the little black and white place. The Havana cigar box on the dash identifying Billy Grace's urban transport.

'Quite a while,' Terry Stagg said. 'He likes the ones where he gets noticed.'

The private parking area was almost a little square. Uneven levels, low brick walls and the arse-ends of buildings in need of repair. A weeping birch tree grew incongruously at its centre and its horizons were tarted up by the tower and steeple of St Peter's and the Shirehall's little cupola with its flagpole and Union Jack.

'This where it happened – or were they dumped?'

'Unlikely,' Terry Stagg said. 'Blood and gunge over a fairly wide area.'

'Who found them?'

'Elderly bloke from over there.' Terry nodding at a modern-ized brick terrace. 'Woke up to screams and yells not long after midnight.'

'You mean… we actually came out here last night?'

'No, he didn't report it. Thought it was kids, pissed. Seems he's complained twice in recent weeks and, um, no action was taken. And you don't go out to remonstrate any more, do you?'

'I presume the DCI's en route?' Bliss said.

A practised insouciance – getting good at this. Annie'd given him ten minutes' start so they wouldn't be seen arriving together.

'And presumably we're knocking on doors. Those windows overlooking the car park? Pubs, clubs, night workers, minicab firms.'

'And CCTV,' Stagg said. 'The whole city centre.'

'Good,' Bliss said. 'Right, then. Let's go and put me off me breakfast.'

Turned towards the tape and the canvas, and Terry handed him the Durex suit, and they walked down past the offices of the Hereford Herd Book Society, whatever that meant.

Sollers frigging Bull would know.

Most of the video had been shot, but they were still taking stills from different angles. Images to wither your soul. Breathing in all the degrading smells of violent death, Bliss heard a man distantly protesting, 'No, I *work* here, of course. Come in early because I have *clients*. How long am I supposed to hang around? Can't you at least…?'

'Twat,' Bliss said.

It came out a bit choked up, surprising him. It wasn't the horror as much as the sad banality: the two red shoes shed in different places, the blue vinyl handbag sprung open, letting out lipsticks and tissues and photos, left where they'd fallen. He saw a picture of a middle-aged couple, hand in hand on the edge of a field, with a white dog.

'Only one handbag, Slim?'

'Nothing else here.' Slim Fiddler, head SOCO, came up like a hippo from a swamp. 'And I can't imagine they shared.'

The first body… it was as if she'd been thrown like discarded clothing over a low wall, maybe the foundation of a demolished outbuilding. She was wearing jeans and a black fleece, half off. A thin arm was draped over the bricks, the hand already bagged. You could only see one of her eyes; it was like sun-dried tomato.

'Looks like the head was banged repeatedly into the sharp edges of the bricks,' Billy Grace said. 'The other one… is less of a big-production number.'

Beaming the way only Billy Grace ever beamed.

The other one lay a few paces away in a patch of scrubby grass. The pink fleece and the way she was half-curled made her look like a prawn, Bliss thought, a giant prawn, for God's sake. One hand down between her legs.

'Sexual assault?'

'Probably.' Billy bent down. 'Dress ripped here. Didn't do *that* herself. But the rest of it, as you can see, is far less... frenzied... than the other one.'

Her face was unmarked. It was a doll's face – not a baby's doll, more like one of those Russian dolls where one was inside another and so on. The hair was brown with gold highlights.

'Probably died quite quickly,' Billy Grace said. 'I'd guess she fell back on the corner of that brick – see the blood there? Then perhaps somebody pulled her away, let her fall again.'

'But the other one... fought harder.'

'To the end, I'd imagine.'

Billy straightened up. Under his unzipped Durex suit, he wore a blazer with a badge, old-fashioned rugby-club type.

'Not a lone assailant, is it?' Bliss said.

'Unlikely.'

Bliss returned to the first and bloodiest body, took a breath and bent to the poor kid, examining her neck. A few scratches there, that was all.

'Where's the locket?'

'Came off, Frannie.' Slim Fiddler led him to a patch of weeds. 'Try not to touch.'

Bliss squatted to where the leaves had been parted, making eye contact with the Virgin Mary in light blue and gold. The locket was silver, tarnished.

'Very possibly Romanian,' he said.

An unusual silence. Bliss half turned. Billy Grace was peering at him over his half-glasses, eyebrows raised. Bliss scowled.

'Piss off, Billy, I'm norra complete friggin' moron. It's from an icon, Russian Orthodox kind of thing. The Romanians are big on icons of Our... of the Virgin.'

Could have told him how once, aged seventeen, just, he'd had to take his ma and his most devoutly Catholic auntie to this exhibition of icons in Liverpool – was it the Walker Gallery? Not long after he'd passed his driving test, anyway, so he'd been quite happy to relieve the old man of the chore just to get his mitts on the car keys for an afternoon.

Bliss stood up and backed off to view both victims in the context of the location. The violence was… careless. Almost impersonal, like storm damage.

'They've been left like rubbish, Billy. Like fly-tipping. No attempt at concealment. Not what rapists do. Rapists, if they've killed, they make *some* effort to cover up.'

'That include gang-rapists? Drunk.'

'I dunno. Something's not quite right.'

'Be able to give you a more formal verdict on the sexual aspect later today.'

'Won't be me, Billy. I'll be off back to Oldcastle. Where I might even get left alone for a bit. DCI'll be here soon. This is the big one.'

'You think so? Mansel Bull's a pillar of the rural community, whereas these pitiful young things…'

'Careful, Billy.'

'I'm too old to care, Francis. This your mistress now?'

What?

Bliss tensed, but didn't look at him. Up in the street, Annie Howe, in her light grey trenchcoat, was getting out of her Audi, bringing her mobile to her ear.

Just a figure of speech, that was all. Not a chance in a million that Billy Grace knew or even suspected. Just a frigging stupid, flip remark.

Bliss turned his back on the crime scene to walk slowly, as if reluctantly, towards Annie.

'No!' he said. 'No, listen, that's not what's gonna happen…'

'Don't be stupid.'

Back in the Audi. Bliss in the passenger seat, all the windows up. Annie behind the wheel, no make-up. Bliss hunched himself up against the passenger door, explicit body language for anybody watching: he didn't want to be here with this woman.

'Apart from anything, you know exactly what it's gonna look like.'

'Actually, I don't think it will,' Annie said. 'That's the point. This is a double murder. By any criteria, the biggest case. It's also going to be immensely high-profile, controversial and politically sensitive.'

'And urban.'

'Nobody's going to make that distinction, Francis. And, anyway, it's what God wants, so we have to live with it.'

She'd been talking to the Chief on the Bluetooth, driving here. Fait accompli. Fit-up. The church clock at St Peter's began to chime the hour. Annie passed a folded paper across to Bliss, under dash-level.

He stared at her.

'I don't *like* the friggin' *Guardian*. It's all opera and foreign stuff.'

'It's the *Daily Mail*. I had to pick it up on the way here. Just read it, will you?'

Sourly, Bliss opened the paper out to a double-page spread. A panorama of Oldcastle Farm on its bank above the Wye, photographed across the fields between bands of police tape.

RURAL IDYLL OR KILLING FIELDS?
Police 'don't want to know'

In another picture, the Countryside Defiance banner. In the middle of the page, a shot of a man sitting with his head in his hands. The caption,

Sollers Bull: shattered.

'If it's painful, you can skip to the end,' Annie said.

'Not sure I can move me reading finger that fast.'

Annie turned away, tapping the steering wheel slowly with her nails. Bliss sighed. Near the bottom of the story, it said:

West Mercia police confirmed last night that the detective leading the inquiry, DI Francis Bliss, is an incomer from Merseyside.

'DI Bliss has been with us for several years now,' a spokeswoman said, 'and we're fully confident both of his ability and the extent of his local knowledge.

'We consider the claims made by Countryside Defiance to be ill-founded and obstructive.'

'So just get on with it,' Annie said. 'And be nice to the television people. Look, it's the best solution. Except, possibly, for me, but I'll cope.'

'Two incident rooms?'

'You get Gaol Street. I'll be taking a caravan over to Oldcastle.'

'Will there be a generator and a primus stove?'

'You'll also get some extra bodies from Worcester and two translators, that's been agreed.'

Translators. Wonderful. Bliss could foresee long hours of watching people's eyes for traces of guilt while listening to the soundtrack of a foreign film without the subtitles.

'And you can have Karen Dowell.' Annie Howe went on looking out of the windscreen down the length of East Street. 'Look, I'm adapting to instructions, Francis. It's what I do. Adapt. Known for it. Off you go. Get the bastards before they can leave the country. Oh— There are two Lithuanian nationals in the cells, apparently, brought in pre-dawn, drunk and incapable. That'll be a start for you.'

'Thanks, I'll eat them later.' Bliss shouldered open the passenger door. 'Just remember what I said, Annie.'

'About what?'

'You *know* what.'

Bliss stepped out, looked up into the sheeny sky, scraped with brown clouds like the chickenshit on a new-laid egg.

'Annie… check him out, yeh? Just… check him out.'

20

Who We Are

Despite the metropolitan fantasies of a few power-crazed councillors, Hereford was still a big village. When a very bad thing happened, Merrily was thinking, ordinary life didn't yet accelerate around it. Something lurched, shifted down a gear.

With East Street sealed off, traffic concertinaed, it had taken her ten minutes to get from the top of Broad Street to the Cathedral Gatehouse. You could walk it in two. She'd left the old Volvo in the Bishop's Palace yard, meeting one of the canons, Jim Waite, who explained what had happened.

Slaughter was the word he'd used.

He hadn't said, *Where the hell is God in this?*

Up in the gatehouse office, Sophie was at the window, gazing down into Broad Street, then across the Cathedral Green towards Church Street. Both of them linked into the – hitherto more obscure East Street.

The killings must have happened close to the centre of Hereford's medieval triangle of big churches: All Saints, St Peter's, the Cathedral. An alleyway linked East Street directly to the Cathedral Close, winding past the house once occupied by Alfred Watkins, the antiquarian.

And where the hell *was* God? A question that the previous owner had pencilled into the margin of her second-hand copy of Frank Collins's *Baptism of Fire*, the book she'd been reading till after one a.m.

'It'll become commonplace here sooner than we know, Merrily.' Sophie turned sharply away from the window, her glasses swinging on their chain. 'Like Birmingham and Manchester. Society's losing all cohesion.'

She went to sit down at her desk. She'd had her hair cut shorter for spring – too soon, as it had turned out. She was still wearing the winter cardie long after its time. She looked – unusual for Sophie – lost.

'One only has to look into the hopeless faces of the drunks in Bishop's Meadow. Lost souls in a purgatory of disillusion and charity shops.' Both Sophie's hands were placed flat on the desk, as if for stability. 'I have no doubt that the vast majority are decent people, trying to earn an honest living. But they're not the ones who create the need for a policeman almost full-time on the door at Tesco.' She looked down at herself. 'Dear God, stop me, Merrily.'

'Questioning the impact of social change isn't *quite* the same as joining the British National Party,' Merrily said.

Sophie winced.

'And we don't know what's happened, yet, do we?' Merrily said. 'We don't know if it's a sexual thing or a robbery or a… private matter.'

'A *private matter*. That's just it, isn't it?' Sophie said. 'We don't know what they've brought with them. We don't understand what kind of demons drive them. And we do need to, because we're not London, we're a country town. *We know who we are.* Or we always used to. Now, one can feel a… a weight of silent resentment. And an apprehension.'

'But that…'

Merrily had been about to say that it wasn't exactly new. In the Middle Ages there'd been resentment in the city about the increasing Jewish community, even the revered bishop Thomas Cantilupe railing against them.

No, forget it. She wandered over to the window, looked down at the Cathedral Green. Seasons slowly shifting out there, winter retiring into the mist, spring blinking warily in the tepid sunshine. Then the clouds took it away, and she saw a lone daf-fodil, still in bud, flattened by someone's shoe.

'The Bishop's been quiet lately.'

'He's increasingly tired. I think he'll probably hang on until the autumn, then we'll hear something.' Sophie stood up. 'I'll make some tea. I've itemized your calls, in terms of apparent priority. Three inquiries in the past week, none of which I felt you needed to be alerted about. One's that rather querulous person who seems to think you can get her grandson off heroin by… exorcizing his inner junkie. I've taken the precaution of quietly alerting her parish priest and suggesting she talks it over with him.'

'Thank you.' Merrily sat down. 'Nothing from the Holmer?'

A fortnight ago she'd been called out to a single space in a factory parking area where a manager, newly divorced, had – like poor Frank Collins – asphyxiated himself in his car. Several workers had claimed that they'd felt him sitting next to them in their own cars if they parked there. The local vicar had dis-missed it as hysteria.

'Nothing.' Sophie shook her head, filling the kettle. 'In fact, you really didn't need to come in.'

'Well, I came in because… I need to make a possibly tricky phone call.'

For some reason, it was easier from here. Like you had the weight of the Cathedral around you. And Sophie to consult. Pretty much the same thing.

'It's Syd Spicer. Now at Credenhill?'

'Ah, yes,' Sophie said.

'How long have you known?'

'Since the Bishop approved it. It's been announced now, has it?'

You were inclined to forget that her principal role was as the Bishop's lay secretary, guardian of episcopal secrets.

'I've been a bit naive about all this, Sophie. Until a few days ago, it didn't strike me that to become a chaplain you had to actually join the army. Or rejoin.'

'Yes, that's a requirement.'

'Problem?'

'Well… I suppose I can tell you. We were in two minds about his suitability. Since leaving the city for Credenhill, the Regiment does seem to have become more remote from us. Not even in the same parliamentary constituency. So Hereford, technically, is no longer a garrison town.'

'Appointing one of their own as chaplain makes them more remote?'

Sophie said nothing. Merrily looked at the phone. Much of the incentive had gone. She looked up at Sophie.

'OK, can I tell you about this?'

Lol had had to force himself to go back to work this morning. Couldn't bear to finish the one about the village musician who found recovery in the back of a JCB. When the knock came on the front door, he was messing with the lyrics for 'The Simple Trackway Man', one he was trying to persuade Danny to sing. A homage to Alfred Watkins, the Hereford man who discovered ley lines.

> *I am a simple trackway man*
> *Who walks the lanes by ancient plan*
> *Leading the people from beacon to steeple*
> *And steeple to stone*
> *And all the way home.*

Back in the 1920s, Mr Watkins, controversially, had traced possible cross-country tracks connecting prehistoric ritual sites – stones and circles and burial mounds – and the medieval churches built on ancient sacred enclosures. Most of his research had been done in his home county and Danny's native Radnorshire. Unlocking the British countryside for future generations who wanted to connect again with the land. Jane's hero.

Lol's song had been written carefully in the vernacular, borrowing material from Watkins's classic work, *The Old Straight Track*. He was quite proud of it. A song that should've been written decades ago, to be sung in folk clubs and on village greens at Whitsuntide. Or by chains of walkers stepping out to refresh themselves and the countryside at Easter. Mr Watkins as some unassuming, low-key pied piper of the border hills.

Sitting on his sofa, with the Boswell across his knees, Lol sang 'Trackway Man' to the wood stove glowing ashy pink against the morning sunlight.

Across the fields where gates align
Ole scarecrow gives us all a sign
Where stand of pine marks sacred shrine
And secret dell hides holy well.

He saw the man in the cap walk past the front window, didn't take much notice, and it was about half a minute before the knock came, as if the man had walked past the door towards the village square and then either had remembered something or had second thoughts and turned back.

Answering the front door, Lol didn't recognize him at first. He wore a rust-coloured gilet and a leather cap. Incomer wear, nothing unusual. He had his chin up and his hands behind his back. He had a quick, efficient smile.

'Lol Robinson?'

'Yes.'

'My partner introduced me t'your music.'

'Oh… right…'

The hand came out, a leather glove removed.

'Ward Savitch. Is this convenient?'

'Too much reticence can be counterproductive,' Sophie said. 'You deserve at least an explanation.'

They were looking at the SAS base on Google Earth. Half surprised to find it there, this unexpectedly large network of utility buildings, parked vehicles. A community probably bigger, if more compact, than the village of Credenhill. You pulled back, and the wide view was all open countryside, apart from the wooded slopes of the hill itself, close enough to overlook the base.

'You feel like you're breaking the Official Secrets Act just doing this, Sophie. Like they're going to know, and the door will fly open and men will be there with automatic rifles.'

Sophie looked severe.

'When they were at the old Stirling Lines, they were part of the city. Part of the community. Mrs Thatcher liked to call them *her boys*. But, essentially, they were *our* boys. Part of Hereford since the Regiment was formed in 1941. That's a long time.'

'But the glamour years only began in the 1980s.'

After the SAS had travelled from Hereford to rescue hostages in the Iranian Embassy in London, abseiling down the walls from the roof live on TV.

'And we were always *discreet*, Merrily. When a new recruit came off the train and asked for directions to the army base, he *wasn't told*.'

'I've heard that.'

'We all knew where it was, but we didn't tell just anyone. The Regiment was inside the city itself, but it was anonymous. And yet a presence.'

'Like the Cathedral?'

'Call Spicer,' Sophie said abruptly. 'He used you. I'm tired of seeing people *used*.'

Merrily looked at her, curious. Was she thinking that nobody had been murdered on the streets of Hereford when the SAS was still in town?

She picked up the phone, put in the number Huw had given her. And was almost grateful when there was no answer, no machine, no voice-mail.

Last night, she'd told Lol about Syd at the chapel. Lol had met him once, at the end of a very dark night in the Malverns, when Syd had been very much in denial. Merrily had said, *You really don't see anything bordering on the paranormal?* and Syd had said, *You mean you do?*

She let his phone ring for half a minute before hanging up.

Tried twice more before lunch and also called home to see if there were any messages on the machine. Sometimes, if she'd had to leave early, Jane would leave one for her. Jane, whose mood last night, when Merrily had got in from the Swan, had been changing like traffic lights, flickering erratically, *red-amber-red-amber*. Like she'd wanted to talk about something, but couldn't. Said nothing this morning, either, and you wondered if it would be better or worse when she went to university.

Not that Merrily had wanted to talk last night. Better not to mention Savitch's bid to buy the Swan until it actually happened. With the vague hope that it wouldn't.

'Sophie... in Canon Dobbs's day – was there ever any involvement with the SAS, back then?'

'In what way?'

'I don't know. I'm just wondering if there's any precedent.'

'I can check the records.'

'Perhaps it wouldn't be there. If there was anybody less forthcoming than the SAS, it was Dobbs, so the combination of the two...'

Sophie's smile was transient, and it probably wasn't nostalgia.

At twelve, they switched on the radio for the national news headlines and, for the first time since New Year, Merrily heard the nasal tones of Frannie Bliss.

'*... horrific crime, and we wanna talk to anybody who was in or near the centre of the city last night between the hours of eleven and one a.m. Doesn't matter whether or not they think they've seen anything significant, they may still have information that could be useful to us.*'

Frannie – how was he doing? Merrily had invited him round for a meal a couple of times since his marriage had finally collapsed. Both times he'd said he was busy.

The phone rang and Sophie turned the radio off.

'Gatehouse.' A pause. 'The *Cathedral* Gatehouse. In Hereford. Who is this?' Sophie listened. An eyebrow rose fractionally.

'Ah... one moment.'

She put the call on hold.

Merrily said, 'Me?'

'Picked you up on 1471. From Credenhill.'

'Syd?'

'His wife,' Sophie said. 'Mrs Spicer, I'm putting you through to Mrs Watkins.'

What did she know about Fiona Spicer? Very little. Except that SAS wives who survived the course were rarely insubstantial women.

'I think we almost met once in the Malverns. My name's—'

'Yes, I realize who you are now.'

Voice low and steady and not exactly friendly. Neutral southern-English accent. Merrily pulled the Silk Cut packet from her bag, stood it on the desk in front of her. Sophie frowned.

'I ran into Syd a few days ago. I'm sorry. I didn't realize you were... back with him.'

Christ, what did this sound like? Merrily stared at the packet, extracting a spiritual cigarette.

'I'm not back with him, Mrs Watkins. This is a visit.'

'Is, erm... is Syd there?'

'No.'

Merrily waited. After a couple of seconds, the silence suggested that Mrs Spicer had gone.

No – a mobile. She'd picked up the number from the house phone, but she was calling back on a mobile. Merrily looked at Sophie, back behind her desk, making no pretence of doing anything but listening.

'Mrs Spicer, it's the first time I've used the Credenhill number. I got it from Huw Owen, my spiritual director. Syd consulted him and – indirectly – me, about something, and I just wanted to follow up on it.'

'Did you?'

Something wrong here. Merrily lit the spiritual cigarette. Sometimes it worked.

'Do you, erm, know where he is, Mrs Spicer?'

'He can't be far away. His car's here.'

'You *are* at the house?'

'I'm at the house, yes. The army house. He'll be across the road. Attending to his *flock*. Fortunately, he's not very SAS when it comes to hiding spare keys, so I was able to go in and take a look around.'

'First time you've been?'

'To this house, yes. I'm in the garage now.'

'Syd said you'd be moving in soon.'

No response.

'Mrs Spicer—'

'My husband worked with you once before,' Mrs Spicer said. 'Your name and number are written inside a book entitled *Deliverance*. A book much thumbed. Pages folded over.'

'That would make sense.'

'But you haven't spoken to him today.'

'No.'

A silence, then…

'Mrs Watkins, something's disturbing me. Would it be possible for us to meet?'

'Of course. Should I come over?'

'Perhaps I should come to you. I'm staying in Hereford, at a B and B. You're at the Cathedral, are you?'

'In the gatehouse. Above the entrance to the Bishop's Palace.'

'I'd rather come to the Cathedral itself. Where's quiet?'

'Do you know the Lady Chapel?'

'I can be there in about half an hour.'

The dead line was for real this time. Sophie was sitting on the edge of the desk, pale and watchful as a barn owl on a branch. Merrily handed her the phone to hang up.

21

Liberal of the Old School

WHEN DC DAVID Vaynor came in, all seven feet of him if you included the big hair, Bliss was waiting for the pictures of the dead to come up on his laptop. Cleaned-up pictures of the cleaned-up dead, done before the PM, before the craniums came off. Pictures you could show to people with no loss of breakfast.

'We might've got them, boss,' DC Vaynor said.

'Shut the door, son.'

Bliss closed his lappie, Vaynor ducking into the office. Despite being a Cambridge honours graduate, or some such, and wearing a tweedy sports jacket, he wasn't a bad lad. Locally born, working class, good contacts – where they counted. Maybe these sloppy old sports jackets were all he could get to fit him.

'Right, then. Go on.'

'Goldie Andrews, boss? On the Plascarreg?'

'Couldn't be that easy, Darth. Could it?'

'Goldie's been scuttling around the estate asking if anyone's seen her lodgers.'

'Female lodgers.'

'Sisters.'

'Where'd this come from?'

'The new launderette at the front of the Plas? My cousin's wife, it is, runs that.'

'Good *boy*. Names?'

'Marinescu. Maria and Ileana.'

'Jesus, that sounds right, the *escu* bit.' Bliss began tapping lightly on the lid of his lappie. 'How long they been missing?'

'Just the one night. Not normally a cause for upset, except they don't do things like that. Also… it's rent day and apparently they owe Goldie for two weeks. I just rang her up to confirm, took it straight to Sergeant Wilton, and he said to come in and tell you right away.'

'Goldie's lodgers… *yes*…' Bliss came to his feet. 'The bottom line here being that it's not exactly unusual for Goldie's lodgers to be on the game, is it?'

'Unusual for them *not* to be on the game.'

'She know they might be dead?'

'She will by now, it's all over the radio, TV, Internet…'

'Right, then.' Bliss pulled his jacket from the chair. 'Let's go and have a chat. They can send the piccies to me phone.' He beamed. 'Nice one, Darth. Write yourself out a commendation.'

'Cheers, boss. Do you, um… want me to…?'

'Yeh, yeh, come along. But I might just go in on me own at first, to chat to Goldie.' Walking out, almost bumping into Karen Dowell. 'Thing is, that woman owes me… quite a bit. Karen.'

'Boss, we have a reliable sighting in the Grapes in Church Street, from half-nine, and then the Monk's Head, ten-nish.'

'Lovely. Get Elly to put out an appeal for anybody who saw them in either. Karen, me and Darth's off to Goldie's on the Plas. If you could tell Brian Wilton, it looks like we'll need forensics. And when the pictures come in from the morgue, could you get them sent to me phone?'

Known, inevitably, as the Plascarreg Hilton.

It had once been a row of 1930s brick-built terraced houses, here before there was an estate. Goldie had got the first for peanuts, renting out the bedrooms to working girls, buying out the neighbours one by one as the new estate got developed at the bottom of their backyards and the value of the houses sank.

The sign outside said *Abbey View*, possibly referring to Belmont Abbey, which you were unlikely to see from anywhere on the Plascarreg without a platform crane, although on a clear day you could spot the Tesco tower.

Bliss let Goldie weep for a while. Two weeks' rent she'd never see, that wasn't funny. Eventually she looked up, over her lace hanky with the border of red flowers like little blood spots.

'Shoulda knowed. Soon's I seen it was you at the door.'

'Nothing's set in stone yet, Goldie.'

'You's the angel of death, you are, boy.'

Couple of years now since two teenage boys in a stolen Transit had booked in for the night, paying in advance with hot cash from an armed robbery at a petrol station in the Forest of Dean. Two boys, one seventeen, one fifteen, and a bottle of Gordon's. Oh, and an old .38 revolver with which they'd played Russian roulette and, at just after three in the morning, one had lost.

'I never said you wasn't understanding, mind,' Goldie said.

'How long the girls been with you, Goldie?'

'Four, five months.' Goldie set light to a roll-up. 'We connected straight off, see... The Roma?'

'What? Oh, yeh...'

Romany, Romania? Who knew? Goldie's origins were obscure. She'd come down from a caravan in the Black Mountains. Before that, it was a caravan somewhere in the South Wales valleys. Some element of gypsy back there – you could see it all over the living room, the brass ornaments and the illustrated plates and the gilt pendulum clocks.

'We had a...' Goldie mouthed the ciggy, touched forefingers in the air. 'Like that, we was.' The cig waggling. 'Movin' in yere, it was like comin' home. Her kept sayin' that, her did.'

'Who?'

'Maria, was it?' Goldie pulled out the ciggy, ruby and emerald rings winking. Breathed out some suspiciously herbal smoke. 'She've got the best English. She do's the talking.'

'So they were here for the winter, yeh?'

In summer Goldie did B & B. Difficult to imagine anybody

wanting to spend a holiday on the Plascarreg. But then, there were holidays and holidays. In winter, it was long-stay guests, cheap deals, all meals out.

Bliss watched the skin around Goldie's eyes crinkling like bits of old bath sponge.

'Lord above, Mr Francis, this can't be right. They's good girls.'

'Of course.'

A liberal of the old school. All Goldie's girls were good girls.

Bliss's iPhone was buzzing.

'Gissa sec, Goldie.'

No message, just the pictures which somehow, when viewed on his phone, made him feel like a sick voyeur. Snuff-porn.

'Goldie, I'm gonna have to ask you to take a look at a couple of photos.'

'I en't their *ma*.'

'You're all right, we've had them, you know, prettied up a bit.'

'Oh, dear Lord.'

Goldie breathed in, slow and phlegmy, then pulled her glasses from their electric-blue plastic case. Bliss flicked from one pic to the other a couple of times and chose the least horrible. Goldie pushed her unlikely blonde ringlets behind her ears, and he handed her the iPhone.

'Take your time.'

Sitting next to her on the old studio couch, slabs of polished wood, somehow coffin-coloured, set into the armrests. Waiting for her nod and then flicking to the other picture, which was not so nice because of the eye. Given time, they'd've found a glass eye.

Bliss counted five clocks ticking before Goldie leaned back and crossed herself.

'Which is which, Goldie?'

'The one with the eye... that's Maria. The one with the English. Lord above, what's happenin' to this town?'

'When d'you last see them?'

'I'm not sure. Yesterday morning? They left... I dunno, about ten?'

'To go where? Where'd they go when they left here?'

'Town. Where's anybody go?'

'They say where in town?'

'Just town. Was they interfered with?'

'Where would they go at night?'

'Pubs? Clubs? I don't know. They only goes out one night a week. Safer yere. We all knows each other on the Plas.'

'They got any family… anywhere in this country?'

Goldie shook her head.

'None?'

'Come over to work on the strawberries, ennit?'

Figured. Thousands of them came across from Eastern Europe to work in the polytunnels.

'Last year?'

Goldie nodded.

'And didn't go back?'

'A lot don't.'

'What did they do after that? Did they get more work?'

'This and that.'

'They work for you, Goldie?'

'Bit of housework.'

'I mean outside work.'

Goldie's eyes were narrowing.

'I've always tried to help you, Mr Francis.'

'And I think it's been mutual. If not *more* than mutual. And, in case you forget, this is a *mairder* investigation.' Bliss leaning on his accent. 'We're nor'all that interested in lifting anybody for minor stuff.'

'They never done no outside work for me.'

'Never? Not even when they ran out of cash and couldn't pay the rent? You never suggested how they might pick up a few quick twenties apiece?'

'I'm tellin' you they done cleaning work, an' that was it.'

'Where?'

'Used to be at one of the stores, on the Barnchurch. The factory-outlet place, you know? Wasn't full-time, and then they got let go.'

'When was that?'

'When it closed down.'

'Yeh, that would figure. *When?*'

''Bout a month ago?'

'All right, I'll ask yer again. Any reason to think they might've been doing night work, freelance?'

'They wouldn't. I'm tellin' you. They was religious girls.'

'What about friends? They have friends among other East Europeans?'

'Not many, far's I know.'

'Boyfriends?'

'No.'

'Attractive girls, Goldie.'

'No boyfriend I *knows* of. They went around together. They looked out for each other.'

'All right.' Bliss stood up. 'Let's see their rooms.'

'Room. They had one room between them.'

He followed her into the hallway. Two neighbouring hallways once, the dividing wall turned into an archway. A reception desk in one corner had a steel grille to the ceiling – well, this *was* the Plascarreg. One staircase had been taken out, so the other was isolated in the middle, Hollywood baronial.

'Anybody else in residence just now, Goldie?'

'It's quiet, it is. We got a few comin' in for Easter.'

'Anybody staying here in the past week?'

'Occasional one-nighter.'

'And the odd one-hourer?'

Goldie was like she hadn't heard. The bedroom doors had big plastic numbers. They went from Room Three to Room Five, Bliss noticed. Room Four was where they'd had to scrape teenage brain cells off the ceiling. Superstitious old girl, Goldie.

She led him along a corridor with three different carpets, stopped at Room Seven, unlocked the door with her master. Bliss put out an arm.

'We're gonna stay in the doorway, Goldie. Nobody goes in till crime-scene gets here.'

'This en't no crime scene, Mr Francis! I objects to that!'

'It's just that we'll need to examine all their things very care-fully. Yeh, it's likely whoever attacked them it was a random thing, but it may not be. We also need the passports, papers, all that sort of stuff. We need to find the relatives.'

The room had dingy yellow walls, two beds, two single ward-robes. But it was tidy. There were two holdalls with shoulder straps under the window, Bliss keen to get inside them, but he didn't move. A wardrobe door was open. The clothes he could see looked clean, new even.

'What sort of girls *were* they, Goldie? All right, good girls, but...'

'Polite. Tidy.'

'You can do better that that. You have long chats with your guests. Old-fashioned nights with the tarot.'

'I'm a people person. It's why I opens my house.'

'If they had worries, they'd confide in you.'

'I likes to think.'

'So...?'

'Course they had worries. They worried about their family back home. They was expected to send money back, but there was never enough. Not what they expected. I done readin's, set their minds at rest.'

On the window sill was a small framed picture of a couple on a sofa, smiling. The window overlooked a playground, a swing with the chains cut off near the top so it looked like a gallows.

'You know what I'm after, Goldie.'

'They didn't have no enemies, if that's what you're gettin' at. How could girls like that have— *Was* they messed with? You can tell me that.'

Good question.

'I can't, actually,' Bliss said. 'Not yet. But we do think there might be more to it. You said they worked on a strawberry farm. Which one?'

'Couple, I think. One out near Ledbury, but they left because of the... you know, gettin' pushed around and messed about.'

'Messed about how?'

'You know what conditions is like in these places. Next thing to slave labour. They was passing out, and if they asked for water they got it in an ole petrol can. Disgustin'.'

'They're supposed to've cleaned up their act,' Bliss said, cautious. 'The worst ones.'

'You believe that, you'll believe anythin'. Maria, she told me one of the other farms there was a woman raped by two of the foremen. Took in a shed and raped.'

'But nobody reported it.'

'*Course* nobody reported it. They knows their place. They got no status. Young fellers, they din't do what they was told they got the shit beat out of them, and the women was raped. 'Less they gived it up willin'. Them as gived it up willin' got the easier work. You must've heard what goes on.'

Everybody had heard the stories. Karen Dowell had come close once to getting a Polish girl to give evidence against this Albanian minibus driver who was demanding a weekly blow job for getting her to work on time. Then she'd disappeared. They could disappear very easily.

Bliss said, 'So the girls got out.'

'They moved to that place out on the Brecon Road. Magnum?'

'Magnis.'

A complex chime went off downstairs. Bliss thought it was one of the clocks.

'Doorbell,' Goldie said.

'Could be my lads. So they moved to Magnis.'

'To be near Hereford.'

Coincidence was a lovely thing, but maybe this wasn't much of one: it was a small county and Magnis was close to the city.

'When was this, Goldie?'

'Last summer.'

'They stay the course this time?'

The bell went again.

'I better let your men in,' Goldie said.

'They'll wait.'

'They left there, too,' Goldie said. 'The sisters.'

'Something happen to them?'

'I don't know.'

'Were they staying here when they worked at Magnis, or did they live at the camp?'

'At the camp. They come yere when they left.' She didn't look at him. 'I felt sorry for them, I did. They wanted to go home. They was thinking how to raise enough cash to go home. I'll go down, let your mates in.'

Bliss waited at the top of the stairs, looking at the holdalls, one pink, one tartan. Never had liked strawberries.

22

Ground To Air

THE LADY CHAPEL was a serene shrine to motherhood, recently renovated in quiet golds, muted tints, the gilded panels of its altar screen illustrating the domestic life of the Blessed Virgin Mary.

Merrily was alone. Someone had left a newspaper on a chair: today's *Telegraph* folded at 'The Killing Fields of Middle England'. She picked it up, sat down next to a Madonna and Child panel where the infant Jesus had the face and the haircut of a middle-aged estate agent. Did one killing make them killing fields? And when did the Welsh Border become Middle England?

The paper had been left here as if it was part of the Countryside Defiance campaign. Fortress Hereford, all farm doors locked at nightfall, and don't expect any help from the police.

Something not right about this. Why were people erecting fences, spreading panic?

Answer: they weren't local people. Local people were cautious, but they didn't panic.

There was a colour picture of Mansel Bull's brother, Sollers, in hunting pink and then, downpage, a small shot of Frannie Bliss caught side-on getting out of his car, the now-trademark dark blue beanie covering his close-mown thinning hair. At the foot of the story it said, *DI Bliss, who came to Hereford from Merseyside, could not be contacted last night, but a spokeswoman...*

West Mercia's brief quote in support of its officer was

lukewarm, a formality. *Bastards.* Merrily tossed the paper back onto the chair.

Maybe the woman in green Gore-Tex had seen the annoyance on her face; she'd stopped a few paces away. Merrily stood up.

'Oh, I'm sorry, I didn't hear you coming.'

Shoulder-length straight dark hair under a black woolly hat. Cursory make-up. She lowered a leather shoulder bag to the flags, turned candid brown eyes on Merrily.

'You're angry.'

'Mmm.'

'Yeah, well, me too,' Fiona Spicer said.

It was about surviving marriage to a man who would vanish overnight, usually for weeks at a time, and sometimes she didn't know where in the world he was, or why, or when she'd see him again, or if.

'Exciting boyfriends, for a while.' Fiona Spicer's voice was thoughtful and seldom lifted. 'But, as husbands... problematical.'

Most people, this might've been small talk, ice-breaking stuff: the partner's little quirks, how Fiona had known Syd before he joined the army. How they'd met on holiday, a teenage seaside romance, exchanging letters for a couple of years before they even saw each other again. And it got no better.

'For more than half my marriage, my husband's keeping secrets from me – me and the rest of the country. Where he's going, what he's doing there.' They'd moved to the corner near the votive stand where three candles were alight. 'I thought all that was over, when he left the Army. But part of them doesn't leave, ever. He'd keep going to the window, as if he was looking for a reason to walk out. Sometimes I'd wake up in the night, and he'd be at the window in the dark.'

'They come out of the Regiment at forty, is that right?'

'At Sam's level. You get a hazy kind of honeymoon period before they start wondering what they're for. If their life has meaning any more.'

Fiona took off her wool hat, laid it on her knees.

'I suppose I was luckier than most. Just a few months of agonizing before he hit God like a ground-to-air missile.'

'*Syd*?'

'God's warrior. All gunfire and smoke. As if saving a soul was the same as rescuing a civilian from terrorists. He did settle down, eventually. Probably as a result of Emily going off the rails.'

'You must be relieved all that's over.'

'One problem ends, another opens up. Suddenly… it's like the old days again: secrecy, lies, obfuscation.'

'Because he's back in Credenhill?'

'He was never *at* Credenhill. But, yes. Back to the Regiment. Assuring me it was going to be entirely different this time. First and foremost, he'd be a priest. And that would be different. I almost believed the bastard. Then the curtain came down again. The vagueness, the false optimism. Everything's *fine*. Everything's going to be *all right*. And you know he means *afterwards*.'

'After what?'

'You tell me, Mrs Watkins. Sam kept your number in his car.'

'*Sam?* Oh…'

Samuel Dennis Spicer. SD. Thus, Syd.

Fiona was gazing up at the sanctuary, the Virgin at home. Two elderly couples filed through an oak door in the richly panelled screen to the right. The Audley chantry – the Thomas Traherne chapel now, recreated to honour, in new stained glass, the seventeenth-century poet and celebrant of the mystical Welsh Border countryside. Who had also, as it happened, been vicar of Credenhill.

'Did he know you were coming here?' Merrily said. 'To Credenhill?'

'I rang last weekend, suggesting I might come over, get things organized… and there was immediate resistance. Oh, there were things he needed to do to it, it was still in a mess. Well, I *like* a mess, gives me a sense of purpose. Hell, I'm supposed to be living there in a few weeks. No… he didn't know I was coming. Compliance is an essential virtue for a Regiment wife, but I'm fifty-one, for Christ's sake. I've been through that phase.'

'So you went to see Syd, without giving any indication that you were coming.'

'It was easier in the old days, when they were in Hereford. All that high fencing, like a prison, but it was still in the city. Credenhill, you feel more exposed. Still, I found the house easily enough, end of the row, near a little wood.'

Fiona had parked the car, gone up and knocked on the door. Ready for Syd saying this really wasn't convenient and maybe she could come back in a couple of hours. But there was no answer.

Fiona had her hands in the pockets of her jacket. Like Sophie, she was overdressed for the weather – even a scarf, as if she'd learned from experience that you couldn't trust signs of warmth.

'So you let yourself in,' Merrily said.

'I know where he hides things like spare keys. *Not* under the step. And I didn't do anything furtive, which always gets noticed.'

The two couples came out of the Audley chantry and Canon Jim Waite appeared, said 'Hi, Merrily,' and then guided the visitors into the Lady Chapel. Merrily nodded at the chantry door.

'Why don't we go in there? I'll tell you what I know.'

She talked about Syd at the Brecon chapel, sitting in the shadows, asking no questions. And afterwards at Huw's rectory, that unconvincing airy optimism. *It's going to be all right. It's working out.* How they'd decided, she and Huw, that there was probably a security aspect to whatever was troubling Syd.

'Always a good get-out,' Fiona said. 'And that's it, is it?'

'There's a bit more. He phoned Huw yesterday to inquire about certain deliverance procedures.'

They were on separate wooden benches, Merrily by the windows, Fiona by the door, staring bleakly into a stained-glass starburst Godface of blinding white.

'Let me get this right. Deliverance is exorcism?'

'Yes.'

'To get rid of spiritual evil.'

'Sometimes. Syd suggested to Huw that an old evil had come back to haunt him. Would you have any idea what that might be?'

'There was a book dealing with it. *Deliverance*. It was with two other books on the back seat of his car, in the garage. The car wasn't locked, which is how I got your number.'

Fiona hadn't answered the question; Merrily didn't push it. Fiona said Syd had told her the Credenhill house was a mess, but it had actually been very tidy. Everything in its place. Not the places Fiona would have put things, but all very neat.

He'd lied, to keep her away. Why?

'Not another woman. He'd've told me.'

Her face was flushed, but only by the sun through the firework blaze of extreme stained glass. The new Thomas Traherne windows, four of them, were small and ferocious, with individual dominant colours: the almighty white, the crucifixion red, the pagan green. *You never enjoy the world aright,* Traherne had written *...till you are clothed in the heavens and crowned with the stars.*

You had the impression that it had been a long time since Fiona had found anything in the world to enjoy.

'I made myself some tea,' she said. 'Sat down in the living room for a while, thinking he'd be back. When he didn't come back, I started to look around. Some of it... You could come back to the house and take a look if you wanted to. If you have the time.'

'If he's back, he won't be overjoyed to see me there.'

'If he's back, he can bloody well live with it.'

No raising of the voice, just a hoarse, fur-tongued undertow, thick with history. Fiona was looking into the second window, which had an ephemeral Christ figure in a shaft of light, arms wide, head bowed, crucified without a cross.

'Do you know anything about the house?' Merrily asked. 'Who lived there before? I mean, they're not old houses, are they?'

'It's army housing, end of a row, detached. You think there's something wrong with the house?'

'It might be one explanation. If it was a house where... perhaps people couldn't settle, where successive occupants felt unhappy, had marital problems, sickness... then new people living there might well get a sense of that.'

'You're so matter-of-fact about all this, aren't you?'

Fiona shook her head slowly, as if her senses were adjusting to the atmosphere of another planet.

'I'm familiar with it, that's all,' Merrily said. 'But Syd didn't have much patience with any of it. Out of his comfort zone.'

'They don't do comfort,' Fiona said. 'Neither do I. But – I'm sorry – this is beyond reason. This is mad.'

'What did you find?'

Fiona unwound her scarf as if it was choking her. The green glow of the end window lit the side of her face, making her look faintly sick.

'I went upstairs. If it was going to be my home, I had every right. Have to work out where to put the furniture, much of which is still in store.'

'Sure.'

'The house has three bedrooms. Two were full of boxes of stuff, waiting to be unpacked. The master bedroom... well, it was empty. As if it had been burgled or something. No clothes in the wardrobe. And the dressing table... all the drawers had been pulled out, as far as they'd go. All empty.'

'I see.'

In the green window, a figure – possibly the poet, Traherne himself – was running along a path towards a conical wooded hill. Fiona was slowly winding the ends of her scarf around her hands, pulling it tight.

'That means something to you?'

'It might. Go on.'

'The mirror had a dust cloth draped over it, although there was no visible dust. The whole room was extremely clean and bare. The bed had been pulled away from the wall, almost into the middle of the floor, the bedclothes pulled back but not removed. Oh— and there was no carpet. It had been rolled up and put into one of the other bedrooms. And… there was a trail of white, making a circle around the bed.'

'Salt.'

'A lot of salt. How did you know?'

'Salt's part of the mix for holy water, sprinkled during a clearance. An exorcism, if you like. But it can also be used on its own.'

'Christ.'

'Anything else?'

'And on the wall, opposite the window, there was a large wooden cross I'd never seen before.'

Probably to catch the first rays of the morning sun.

'Sam's never done much of that – crosses and pictures. Nothing ostentatious. He says you should hold whatever you have in your… your heart. The only thing he used to keep in the bedroom was his Bible. Not a Gideon-type Bible in the bedside cabinet, this was a massive old family Bible, half the size of a paving slab.'

'An heirloom?'

'No. He bought it. Just before he was ordained. Symbolic, I suppose. Something big and heavy that you couldn't just slip into your pocket. A necessary burden. I..' Fiona spread her hands. 'I don't know. With Sam, there were always things you didn't ask. It had brass bindings and a lock, and he used to keep it on top of the wardrobe and get it down to dust it every Sunday. The odd thing is that it wasn't there. There was nothing on top of the wardrobe. Not even dust.'

'What did you do?'

'I got out of there. I felt… quite cold.'

Fiona took both her hands out of her scarf and laid them on top of it. Her wedding ring was iridescent in the blazing stained-glass light. Merrily stood up, turned to watch the figure that might be Thomas Traherne moving away along the path up the wooded hill which might be Credenhill. Traherne had been the vicar at the church below the hill. She had a strong feeling there was history here that Fiona wasn't yet prepared to disclose.

'Those things you didn't ask...'

'I don't have the knowledge. Do I?'

'How about if I ask them?'

'That might be helpful. If you don't mind.'

'OK.' Merrily picked up her bag. 'Your car or mine?'

23

Swab City

BILLY GRACE HAD found bruising around the pubic area in both cases but no traces of semen, and no internal damage. Neither Maria nor Ileana Marinescu had been raped. Or, it seemed, had recent sex of any kind.

'So... was there an attack with *intent* to rape?' Bliss said to the class. 'Or was it something random? Group of lads coming back from the pub, spot these two on their own, maybe wander over, see what's on offer.'

'Maybe simply thinking they were prostitutes?' Darth Vaynor said.

They had decent CCTV now, of the girls entering and leaving the Grapes in Church Street at 9.45 p.m. On their own, both times. Nobody following them.

'Very drunk, presumably, the attackers,' Rich Ford said, the veteran uniform inspector. 'And then it gets progressively out of hand.'

About fifteen of them in the incident room, including seven uniforms and Slim Fiddler and Joanna Priddy from crime-scene.

Rich Ford, months off retirement, glanced over his shoulder, cleared his throat.

'Perhaps I should mention that while the two Lithuanian gentlemen helped into the hospitality lounge in the early hours were completely pissed – one vomiting profusely all over the reception desk – neither had any blood on him. We did manage to talk to them this morning before they were checked out, and it was fairly clear that neither of them had seen – or at least remembered seeing – anything untoward.'

Statistics showed overwhelmingly that most crimes against economic migrants in Hereford were committed by other migrants. Maybe retribution for non-payment of business protection or the required percentage for procurement of employment. Neither of which seemed to apply to the Marinescu sisters.

'However, if this is to do with some existing conflict we know nothing about,' Rich said, 'there's likely to be retaliation, isn't there? Could be trouble on the streets tonight – and that could give us an in.'

'If the girls *had* been on the game,' Bliss said, 'we'd have to consider the possibility that they'd intruded on someone else's street corner or pub of choice… or failed to cough up the agreed percentage of their earnings to the pimp.'

'Which in this case would be Goldie,' Darth Vaynor said. 'And we don't have any reason to think Goldie's lying about them not being involved in prostitution.'

Slim Fiddler grunted.

'Less they was doing a foreigner?'

'Can't be ruled out,' Bliss said. 'Or, as Darth said, that some-body *thought* they were on the game. We'll come back to that. Let's just deal with the second possible motive – robbery.'

Turning to Brian Wilton, the office manager, who brought up on the monitor a picture of the pale blue handbag found in Bishop's Meadow down by the river. A twin to the one Bliss had seen in East Street.

'Contents emptied out,' Brian said. 'Wallet-type purse found in the Cathedral Close, empty. Bits of make-up kit also picked up between the Cathedral and the river.'

'Likely to be DNA,' Slim Fiddler said. 'We're still waiting.'

'Also, that lays a bit of a trail.' Bliss went over to the blown-up street map, tapped it with his pen. 'Quickest way from East Street to the Cathedral Close is through this little alleyway, almost directly across the street from the car park. Curves round past the old Alfred Watkins house into the Cathedral grounds. We might assume that, after killing the Marinescu sisters, the attackers ran across East Street, into the alley, going through the bag as they went.'

'Why take only one bag?' Karen Dowell said. 'If the other was left in East Street and there was a few quid left in the purse...'

'I don't think we ever really considered this was about robbery, Karen, I'm just gerrin it out the way. What else? Any ideas?'

'Personal?' Rich Ford said. 'They've committed some offence against their family?'

'According to Goldie Andrews, they have no known family over here, and they didn't mix much with other migrants.'

'What about non-compliance?' Darth Vaynor said. 'They were invited to work for somebody but, being religious, they declined, and...'

'Maybe.' Bliss wrinkled his nose. 'Have to be more complicated, though. Like that they were threatening to come to us. And how often does *that* happen?'

He waited for more, got blank faces. They were talking to the Romanian authorities, but the suggestion so far was, as Goldie had thought, that the Marinescu girls were from a fairly rural area and maybe not exactly sophisticated.

Bliss was still pretty sure, mind, that there was a lot of stuff Goldie hadn't told him, maybe in connection with the fruit farm. Time to float this one.

'It'll surprise none of you to learn that these girls came over to work in the tunnels. In the last instance, Magnis Berries, off the Brecon Road. So... what do we know about Magnis Berries? All shut when me and Terry called in the other day, and no particular reason to take it further at that stage.'

Silence.

'Aw, come *on*, children, what've we *heard*?'

'No suicides,' Brian Wilton said. 'Unlike some similar establishments.'

'Rumours of intimidation? Threats, bribery? Think back to the van driver who demanded his weekly blow job for getting a woman to work on time. Pretty scary for a couple of young lasses from a village in rural Romania.'

'It's a newish establishment,' Karen Dowell said. 'They seem to have started up with full knowledge of the kind of reputations that some fruit farms had got themselves for bullying and poor working conditions. Brought in local people as supervisors. I don't suppose they pay any more than the others, but we're not getting rumours.'

'Then why did the girls leave? We need to find out.'

Karen said, 'If we're descending on Magnis Berries, that'd be rubbing shoulders with the Mansel Bull inquiry. I believe the farm's being extended onto what used to be Mr Bull's land.'

'It is?'

'I learned last night that he sold it a month or so ago. Causing a bit of controversy locally, as you'd expect.'

'Absolutely.' Bliss was blinking hard. 'Right. Well, not too much is clear at the minute, but I still don't expect this to take long. We've gorra lorra DNA to play with. So – need I say – any excuse to snatch a sample from any bugger, we grab it. Welcome to Swab City.'

⁕ 'OK, Karen.' Assembly over, Bliss shut the door of his office, waved her to the spare chair, sat down behind his desk. 'Give.'

'The bit of controversy?'

'Indeedy.'

'You're going to get overexcited now. This is only from my mum, right, so it might need some more looking into.'

'I see Mrs Dowell as an impeccable source, Karen.'

Karen sighed.

'Magnis Berries, the parent company, is in the Vale of Evesham. Well established, fairly responsible. So what you hear – or what you *don't* hear – is pretty reliable. It's still a shit job, but nobody at Magnis gets a bucket of muddy water thrown over them when they pass out from the heat.'

'But just because it's not too bad for the *wairkers*...'

'Once it gets out that a few hundred migrant workers are going to be housed in huts and caravans, creating a new community twice the size of any of the local villages, and all the fields spread with plastic... you've got trouble. And as it's now about to almost double in size again...'

'Double? Sollers Bull agreed to this deal?'

'Nobody locally knew that ground was even for sale until the deal was done. Which is not exactly normal procedure, if you want to get the best price...'

'Yeh, yeh.'

'Point is, Sollers didn't get a chance to disagree. The deal was done by Mansel Bull. On the quiet.'

Bliss leaned his chair back on two legs, his elbows against the wall.

'Mansel Bull... very quietly, behind his brother's back, sells a chunk of his farm to Magnis Berries?'

'I think it was no more than about twelve acres, but he also brokered a deal for three other neighbouring farmers to sell pieces of *their* land... probably for well above the going rate. Which, in a time of deep recession, would overcome any resistance they might have. The few enemies he'd make would just be incomers from Off, the roses-round-the-door types.'

'And Sollers.'

'Sollers... came round,' Karen said.

'It was me, I'd be nursing a grudge the size of Wales.'

'Boss, bear with me. He, like, *physically* came round? To Magnis Berries? I mean, quite often. Oh hell, look, this is from my mum, right? And if it ever got out she was the source she'd lose her job so fast—'

'Yeh, yeh.'

'I mean, it's not a major secret that Sollers puts it about, and although he—'

'Hang on...' Bliss was sitting up. 'Sollers puts it...'

'Bit of a celeb?' Karen said. 'Plus, the number of women turned on by hunting pink and riding boots is still considerable. He's discreet, naturally, with a useful marriage to protect.'

'Lord Walford's daughter.'

'In hunting circles, that means a lot.'

Bliss was breathing hard.

'Karen, could you possibly… spell this out? Whereabouts has Sollers been putting it?'

'This is only—'

'Hearsay, yeh. I love hearsay. Just spit it out.'

'Some of the migrant girls… always hoping it'll end in a fairy-tale marriage and a lovely home in England?'

Bliss shot forward, the front legs of his chair clacking to the floor.

'You're telling me Sollers Bull was shagging the *wairkers?*'

'It only once got dicey, when a certain Polish girl… I understand he went back a few times too many, and she got the wrong idea. Shows up at his restaurant one day, demanding to see him. Which was how my mum first got a glimpse of the situation. I think she must've collected a good pay-off, this girl, 'cause she apparently went home to Warsaw or wherever soon after that. Anyway, it was dealt with.'

Bliss was tapping his desk, rhythmically, quite fast.

'He was practically accusing migrants of killing his brother.'

'That would be male migrants, boss.' Karen's eyes were opaque. 'I expect you'll have to pass this on to Ma'am, though, it being not your case any more.'

'Sure. Although, naturally, I'll need to visit Magnis Berries first, ask some questions about their two murdered employees.'

'That restaurant…' Karen looked unhappy '… there's a lot of irresponsible gossip. I don't know if he goes to the farm any more. It probably gave him a scare, the Polish girl. I think maybe you should pass this *directly* on to Ma'am, don't you? It's the way things are done?'

'The Marinescu sisters,' Bliss said. 'Very attractive girls. But also religious. Maybe a little naive.'

Karen stood up and opened the door and then shut it again.

'Just be careful, Frannie. You know? Let the DCI run with it?'

'Your ma's job is safe in my hands, Karen.'

Bliss's fingers still going tappy-tap-tap on the side of the desk, like a little dynamo.

Alone in his office, Bliss Googled Magnis Berries, found a discreet Web site with the head of some Roman-looking god wearing a wreath of strawberries, blueberries and blackcurrants. There was only one number, in Evesham. Bliss tapped it in, got a chirpy lad's voice.

'Magnis Berries. My name's Robin, how can I help you today?'

'My name's Detective Inspector Bliss from West Mercia Police, Robin, and you can help me by putting me through to Batman.'

'It's Bat*woman*, sir,' Robin said.

Bliss waited on hold, listening to the inquiries unrolling on the other side of the door, Darth Vaynor talking intelligently to someone in London connected with the Romanian embassy. In his left ear, some half-familiar classical music from Magnis Berries, then a crisp, educated female voice.

'Alex Goddard.'

'DI Francis Bliss, Ms Goddard, West Mercia CID, Hereford. You're the MD?'

'Inspector Bliss...' A bit snappy, not intimidated by cops. 'I've already told one of your officers that we have very few people working in the Wye Valley at this time of the year, and my manager has assured me he knows nothing that would help with your investigation.'

'Cross purposes, Ms Goddard. This is not the Mansel Bull inquiry, this is two of your former employees. The Marinescu sisters?'

'If they're *former* employees, I don't see how... What have they done?'

'Got themselves beaten to death in Hereford.'

'Oh, good God.'

'As you were their last formal employer, I'm interested in the circumstances under which they left.'

'Inspector, these people come and go in great numbers, and while they're the first at one of *our* farms to become victims of violence...'

'As far as you know.'

'My instructions to all the managers is that anyone found fighting or attempting to intimidate other workers should be summarily dismissed.'

'Is Wye Valley your biggest farm? I was thinking, with the whole firm being called Magnis Berries...'

'We adopted the name last year. Magnis was the name of the Roman town discovered not too far away, and it gave us an identifiable corporate image. In fact, several of our other farms are two or three times as big.'

She gave Bliss the manager's name, *Roger Hitchin*, and the unlisted number. Not that he planned to ring first; he and Karen could be there in ten minutes.

But then Brian Wilton came in to tell him that a couple of young women had arrived in response to their appeal for anyone who'd seen the Marinescus in the pubs around East Street. Then Elly Clatter rang through about the inevitable press conference, a necessary chore, timed for two p.m. Magnis would have to wait.

Of course, it might all come to nothing.

Bliss was tingling to his fingertips.

24

Demons

Lol found Barry in the Swan dining room, putting out menus. Just had to talk to somebody about this.

'It's like you've gone to hell and here's Satan in a cardigan, offering you tea and scones.'

'It's the way he is,' Barry said. 'Taps into what he sees as the prevailing mood. Now, what you accusing me of?'

Five tables were laid out with traditional stiff white cloths and napkins furled like water lilies. Lol counted another six tables, bare wood, redundant now, pushed against the oak panelling.

'All I'm saying is only four of us knew about it. Danny Thomas, Merrily… and I didn't even tell her until last night.'

'Making me the most likely one to've blabbed to Savitch.' Barry pulled a dining chair away from a table, waved Lol to another. 'What *exactly* did he say?'

'Tells me his partner likes my… fine music.'

'Brigid? That woman keeps a flat in the Smoke because she can't go a week without a night at the opera. With all due respect, Laurence, I doubt she regards what you do as music at all.'

'Good at this, though, isn't he? Knows his folk festivals, too… Super idea, actually, Mr Robinson. Obviously, never be a Glastonbury here, but perhaps a smaller-scale Cropredy, or a Green Man? Real ale… good Herefordshire cider. Marvellous.'

'Google is a wonderful thing,' Barry said. 'What's he offering you?'

'A site. He's thinking one of his larger meadows, up near the bridge. Lots of parking.'

'How much?'

'I may have misunderstood, but I think it was free.'

'Tribute to your status here, Laurence, though he'll want a percentage.'

'Barry, I don't *have* any status here.'

'Nah, the gig during the flood won you a bunch of new friends. Always been great public affection for the dance band on the *Titanic*.'

'They all drowned,' Lol said. 'The dance band.'

'Well, that's true, yeah.' Barry opened out a napkin. 'You got a problem here, no getting round that.'

Lol recalled Savitch's face exploding into a wide, disarming smile. He'd expected arrogant, distant, and had got ordinary, reasonable. Very scary.

'He said people had him all wrong. As if he was trying to distance himself from the blood-sport side. How keen he was to revive the whole tradition. More about Merrie England than hunting and shooting.'

'Merrie England? Like when the countryside was a recreation area for the aristocracy?'

Barry's smile was like the coal-chip smile on a snowman. Lol understood he'd been brought up in South London foster homes. His dad had died in Wandsworth Prison.

'So what was your response, Laurence?'

'I'm sorry, Mr Savitch, your ethos is not in the spirit of the music we're trying to promote. In fact we hate everything you stand for.'

'And you *actually* said…?'

'I said it was a very generous offer, but it was early days yet. And he invited me to visit his establishment on Thursday. Media launch for the family open day he's having on Easter Monday. He gave me two tickets.'

'You and Merrily?'

'Me and my partner.'

'He wants the vicar, trust me. Two birds with one. Sooner or later he'll make a donation to Merrily's church. He'll wait for an opportunity. Urgent repairs needed in the belfry, something like that. Something that gets him noticed, yet doesn't look like profligate largesse.'

'I've never heard you use so many big words before, Barry.'

'Funny how despair can inflate your command of English. Of course, if you do turn down his offer, that would look a bit...'

'Perverse.'

'But, equally, if you say yes...'

'I'd be in his pocket. So I'm not going to, am I?'

'Idea's planted now. He could go on to hold a bigger event, with big names. Yours not among them.'

Barry's hands were efficiently twisting the napkin into another lily. Lol watched, fascinated.

'They teach you that in the SAS?'

'Yeah, but with necks,' Barry said.

In the end, they went in separate cars, Fiona's blue Honda Jazz leading Merrily north-west along those pale, seemingly point-less new roads which hinted at clandestine development plans. Then familiar wooded hills with an early-spring greening like fresh mould, an occasional long view across the hidden Wye to the notched belt of the Black Mountains.

The side-window down, but the breeze couldn't blow away the voices

Huwie, he says, just a slight problem. A mere technicality.

A circle of salt. Had Syd also forced himself to visualize the golden rings around and above his body, mentally enclosing himself in an orb of light?

Received wisdom. Received madness from a spidery old woman named Anthea White who called herself Athena and lived in an old folks' home with her occult library. Supplemented with suggestions from the handbook of the Christian Delivery Study Group. *Much thumbed, pages folded over.*

Open all the cupboard doors, take out all the drawers, cover the mirrors.

... a chance to step back and rationalize it.

Huw again, with chapel echo.

'It *can't* be rationalized,' Merrily hissed, as if he were sitting in the car with her. 'It isn't rational.'

Carly Horne, the skinny one with black hair slanting down over one eye, thought Bliss talked like that comedian.

'Yeh, I know,' Bliss said. 'Lily Savage.'

Carly said, 'Who?'

Karen Dowell smiled. Bliss didn't ask. They were in the least grotty interview room. He sat down next to Karen.

'So you heard it on the radio news.'

'Stations I listen to don't do news, to be honest,' Carly said. 'Taylor Magson told me – this bloke at college? He knows which pubs we do and when I said I remembered these Russian girls, he was like, hey, you better go tell the cops?'

'Romanian,' Karen said. 'The girls were Romanian.'

'Got us an afternoon off college, anyway.'

'What courses are you on?'

'I'm doing secretarial, she's beauty therapy, jammy cow.'

The other one was heavy and sullen-looking. Her hair was cut short and the acid colour of lemon cheese. Her name was Josceline Singleton. She had on a high-necked top and pink leggings.

'You know those pictures you showed us,' Carly said. 'Was that them dead?'

Bliss gave her a rueful smile.

'That's really sick,' Carly said.

Karen said, 'How long you been going in the pubs, Carly?'

'Years, but I don't drink much, to be honest, when I got college next day.'

'So this is the Monk's Head,' Bliss said. 'Lounge bar. Ten o'clockish?'

'Bit later, when these women come in. There's only one bar now, since they started doing live music, weekends.'

'You ever see these girls before?'

Carly shook her head.

'Were they on their own?'

'Yeah. They looked kind of, you know, isolated? I used to feel pissed off about them coming over here taking our jobs and stuff, but I feel sorry for them now, I do. When you read about them having to live like seven of them in one room? That's why I went over and talked to them, really. Well, I was on my way to the lav, to be honest, and I like bumped their table?'

'Oh.' Bliss sat up. 'So you actually talked to them.'

'Talk to anybody, me. I mean, we didn't discuss the government and stuff, it was just like, so where you from, kind of thing? And then she comes out with this place I en't never heard of, so that was a bit useless. I don't think they wanted to talk, to be honest. Same with a lot of these ethnics, they don't really wanner mix with us, do they?'

'It's the language,' Josceline Singleton said. 'They don't know a word of English.'

'Except *benefits*,' Carly said. 'That's my dad. He's a bigot, he is.'

Bliss said, 'You told the sergeant some men followed them out.'

'Yeah. A few blokes in the pub was looking them over?'

'How d'you mean?'

'Like, you know, grinning at each other, making fists and stuff? Kind of, give *her* one. You know?'

'And then followed them out? What time was this?'

'Not sure. Maybe about quarter past eleven?'

'How many of them?'

'How many, Joss? I wasn't counting, to be honest. Wasn't like they was good-looking or anything. And quite old. Three? I think there was three. They was ethnics, too.'

'How do you know that?'

'You can just tell, can't you?'

'Would you recognize them again?'

'You don't really take them in, do you, 'less they're a bit fit.'

'All right,' Bliss said. 'I'm gonna leave you with DS Dowell. I'd like you to try very hard to describe these men – how old, how tall, what they were wearing…'

'Yeah,' Carly said. 'All right. I mean, when you think about it… could've been any of us, couldn't it? Like, murdered?'

It was Jane, with her growing feel for the landscape, who'd pointed out that Credenhill existed on three different levels.

The village itself was strung out aimlessly – modern housing, a line of convenience stores set back from the main road. It was looking already like the suburbia of a much-extended Hereford which it might one day become.

An ignominious future, in the shadow, literally, of its impressive ancient history.

Merrily and Jane had once walked up the huge afforested hill to the east, which carried the remaining earthen ramparts of the biggest Iron Age hill fort in the county. Not much to see now, but some historians said Credenhill had once been the Celtic capital of what became Herefordshire, an elevated fortified community with a population of more than three thousand.

It had once looked down on the later Roman military town of Magnis, long gone. Now, as you followed the winding track, you could see down below, when the trees were bare, a spread of low buildings, vaster than it looked from the road. A quiet, self-contained community, with intersecting roads and parked trucks.

The third and most modern Credenhill, to which the elite warriors of the British Army returned, some of them seared and scorched and riven by demons. Applauded from afar, but not allowed to talk about it.

Except to people like Syd Spicer.

Merrily slowed when the gates of the camp appeared on her left. Two police cars were parked alongside one of the buildings, armed guards at the entrance. None of this, to Merrily's knowledge, outside of routine. The army housing was across the road. She followed Fiona's Jazz into the estate, which was like any other housing estate except somehow quieter. Parking behind the Jazz outside an end house next to a wooded field, she guessed their arrival would already have been clocked by somebody, somewhere.

All the hundreds of times she'd driven past. Never actually stopped here before. You didn't. You just didn't.

Memories of the Frank Collins book were with her now. Frank, a Christian in the SAS, bothered by the old question of God and warfare. In the end, he'd justified it simply to himself: soldiers killed to prevent innocent people dying. The Regiment as knights, trained to deal with evil. Frank had been raised among tough kids in working-class Newcastle, breaking the law like the others. She guessed he'd been a good priest.

Merrily came out of the old Volvo with a ridiculous caution, as if she might be in someone's cross hairs. For no obvious reason, she pulled the collar of her woollen coat across her dog collar and buttoned it.

It was all very quiet. She looked around and saw nothing moving on the estate, no curtains twitching. No wind. A sky like tarnished brass.

Further along the main road was the turning to Credenhill Church, raised up on the right. Strange connection, coming here direct from the chantry where Thomas Traherne's vision burned in stained glass. This was a tiny parish in his day, averaging about two baptisms a year, but it would be wrong to think he wouldn't recognize the place now. He'd know the fortified hill at once and the vista across the Wye Valley to the Black Mountains. On the Welsh border, the big things didn't change.

He might wonder, though, about the metal frames for polytunnels which she could see in the distance to the south, might even find a kind of beauty in their skeletal caterpillar symmetry. Traherne could find beauty in most things.

Did Syd ever go to Traherne's church?

She felt uneasy. She was on army ground. Had no doubts where Syd's loyalties would lie. While Merrily was locking the Volvo, Fiona was already walking towards the front door, between bare brown bushes, and then she stopped. Glanced over her shoulder towards Merrily, who moved towards her.

Fiona nodded at the white door. It was half open.

'Oh,' Merrily said. 'He's back, then.'

No sooner were the words out than she knew how wrong she was.

Fiona didn't move as they were surrounded. It happened very quickly, as if this was a surprise party, but all the guests were men, and none of them expressed a greeting. After what seemed a long time, one of them turned to Merrily.

'Mrs Spicer?'

She saw an older man, standing between the brown bushes, shaking his head.

'I'm sorry,' the first man said, and the older man approached Fiona, quite slowly.

'Mrs Spicer, we met once before, briefly. My name's William.'

He wasn't in uniform. None of them were. Fiona nodded.

'Yes, I remember.'

William was solidly built and had a full grey moustache. He wore walking boots.

He said, 'Should we go inside?'

'No,' Fiona said. 'I'd rather not.'

Her face had gone grey, like fresh plaster. Merrily took in three other men, one of whom she recognized: stubble and broken veins. Not military. It was Terry Stagg, detective sergeant.

William said, 'Who is this woman, please?'

Fiona half-turned, as if she'd forgotten Merrily was there.

'She's a friend of Sam's. In the Church. A priest.' She stood before William, her head tilted up to stare him in the eyes. 'You'd better tell me.'

'Mrs Spicer, I think—'

'Where's my husband?'

'Mrs Spicer,' William said, 'I'm afraid I have some… distressing news. I… very bad news.'

It was Merrily who nearly cried out. Fiona's lips were tight. She still hadn't moved, yet she seemed far away from here, as if replaying a scene which had occurred in her midnight thoughts so many times that emotions could be dispensed with.

25

A Lovely Thing

JANE USED TO know kids who loved messing with dead things, but she'd never been one of them, so she'd been dreading this all day.

At this stage of your school career, if you didn't have any particular classes, you had the choice of coming home, to work on revision. *Yeah, right.*

When she got off the bus, there was no sign of the Volvo outside the vicarage, so she went directly round the back to the garden shed. At least there'd been no blood on the path this morning.

Not yet four p.m., the sun still high, but weak. The shed was just a lean-to against the highest part of the wall. Wasn't kept locked and it had been the only place she could think of last night.

Needed some help with this, really. Even Mum who, as a kid, had wanted to be a vet and knew a bit about injured pets and livestock. Mum would have an idea how the bird had died.

Could hardly take it to Mum, though, who knew nothing about the earlier incident with Cornel and the beer. Tangled web. Jane began to part the garden tools, remembering pushing the sack behind them. She threw the door wide, pulled out the spade and the hoe and the rake and the hedge loppers, tossing them onto the lawn behind her, but…

Oh, God, *no…*

This could only be Mum. Now she'd have to explain

everything, which would lead to a chain of explanations, and that would get Lol in bother, too, for not disclosing what had happened on the night of the storm. She was in deep trouble and hadn't even dealt with the no-university situation yet.

Jane closed the shed door, walked away to the end of the garden, leaned against the churchyard wall, staring over at the old graves. Considering the worst options: could *Cornel* have pinched it back? Would he have gone to that kind of trouble?

He couldn't have seen her last night, could he? Couldn't, surely, have been in a fit state after the kicking he'd had and throwing up in Barry's yard. Last night, Jane had awoken twice, with the gritty ghosts of dead flies in her mouth and shuddery memories of the quick, efficient way in which Cornel had been damaged, that almost feminine cry of pain. Big, tall Cornel, *breast-fed for months and months.* Cornel, the winner who could do anything he wanted because the bank was paying. Cornel had been very afraid, had done as he'd been told, had taken the sack away. Except he'd been told to bury it and he'd only buried it in the bin on the square.

But what about the other guy? Who had just disappeared. Who hadn't seemed like the kind of guy who *would* just disappear.

Oh Christ. The very worst option: what if *he'd* seen her?

Jane began to sweat. Went over the whole garden, frantic now, looking behind all the apple trees, into the long grass under the church wall, leaning over the wall to see into the churchyard. Why the hell had she taken it? What was it sup-posed to prove?

She ran back around the vicarage, out of the front gate and down Church Street towards the river, pulling out her phone. She'd call Eirion. Hadn't called him back last night, just dropped him a quick text promising to explain tomorrow. She'd tell Eirion everything.

But his damn phone was switched off. Jane leaned over the bridge, watching the slow water making dark, languid circles around the pillars and buttresses. After the psychotic nights around Christmas, the river was back to its old torpid self, and there was no sign of a bin sack down there.

"Ow're you, Janey?'

'Oh!'

He was leaning over the bridge next to her, teeth clamped on an unlit ciggy, pale sunlight swimming in his specs. Hadn't even heard him approaching. Jane looked down at his feet.

'Gomer… you're wearing trainers.'

'Hay 'n' Brecon Farmers. Two for the price o' one.'

'That's, erm… normal in footwear, isn't it?'

'Two *pair*, girl. Don't worry, you en't gonner see me doing no joggying.'

'You don't fool me, Gomer.' Jane found a smile. 'I bet you've got a hoodie and a baseball cap in the back of the JCB.'

'En't even seen the bloody ole thing for nigh on two days. Danny's got him, workin' over by Walton, makin' a pond. Been fillin' my time with a bit o' spring maintenance in the church-yard. Found some bloody ole briars muster got missed last autumn, so…' Gomer eyeing Jane, head on one side '… took up the vicar's offer of borrowin' the ole loppers.'

He put the ciggy back in his mouth, stood with his hands behind his back, rocking slightly.

'Oh,' Jane said. 'Erm… from the shed.'

'Exackly. From the ole shed, back o' the vicarage.'

'Right. Wooh. So, you, erm…' Jane looked into Gomer's glasses: opaque white discs, relief enfolding her like an old bath robe. 'You probably found a black bin sack.'

'Sure t'be.' Gomer extracted his ciggy. 'Bit of a story to this, is there, Janey?'

Jane felt her shoulders slump.

'Got him back at my place. You wanner…?'

She nodded and followed him, down from the bridge. They walked up to the bungalow with the fading buttermilk walls, where Gomer had lived alone since Minnie's death.

Gomer. Sometimes, crap situations just rearranged

themselves for the best. With divorce and death and stuff, Jane had never really had a grandad. Her worst recurrent nightmare was probably the one in which Gomer had died.

Gomer didn't judge. Well, not Jane, anyway, so she told him virtually everything, in the sure knowledge that it would go no further.

He leaned against his wall, listening, chewing on his unlit ciggy. When she'd finished, he opened his garden gate.

'Dull buggers, some o' these fellers,' he said. 'For all their college papers.'

'He was really scared, Gomer. And probably shocked. That the guy could, you know, do whatever he did. He obviously knew who it was.'

'You sure it wasn't Barry?'

'I heard his voice.'

'Only Barry, see, he's had his times.'

'Oh, I know Barry *could* have done it, but he didn't. Definitely not him.'

Signs of springtime action in Gomer's garden – a rake and a hoe leaning against the wall, with a stainless steel spade, its blade worn thin and sharp.

'En't much into gardenin', see, Janey, 'cept for the ole veg, but Minnie... her always liked her daffs. These is in memory, kind o' thing.'

'They're nice, Gomer. Erm...?'

Gomer nodded towards the garden table. The black bag was underneath it, tied up with orange baler twine. He went over and dragged it out, placed it on the table, undid the twine.

Jane looked around nervously. The bungalow was raised up behind substantial hedging, tightly cut, obviously. You could see over it back to the river bridge and, in the other direction, the Church Street pitch, all the way up to the market square. But nobody could see into Gomer's garden.

'Shot it,' Jane said quickly. 'I think they shot it. Cornel, he was going, Oh, I'll have a blast at anything that moves.'

'Was he now?'

'He said it was all OK, as long as you *cleaned up* afterwards. Scumbags, Gomer. They went onto someone's property and shot it. I was going to put it back in the litter bin, but then I thought, no, it's evidence.'

'Shot, eh? That's what you reckons?'

Gomer brought it out and laid it on the iron tabletop. It was pretty battered, but you could tell it had been a lovely thing, with like a lion's mane, all golden. Jane swallowed. Dismay set in.

'I know this doesn't really prove anything. They could just say it was an accident. They're just—'

'Haccident?' Gomer ran a hand over the feathers. 'This don't happen by haccident.'

'Huh?'

'Janey...' Gomer sighed and brought out his ciggy tin. 'This boy en't been shot.'

'Well, I didn't really look. It was dark and...'

'See that?'

Jane saw there were spots of blood around the beak. She didn't understand.

'That en't good, girl,' Gomer said.

26

Bergen

'IT'S NOT YOUR fault, of course,' Huw said.

In the scullery, the red light was still blinking on the answering machine, the air swollen with its bleeps. Merrily sank down at the desk.

'You're a hypocritical bastard, you know that?'

Holding the big, Bakelite phone with both hands. Her stomach felt like a crumpled paper bag. About four hours' sleep last night, and she hadn't eaten since breakfast. Barely remembered driving home, very slowly. Ignoring the answering machine, taking two paracetamols with a glass of water.

She fingered a cigarette, drew a hard breath.

'You as good as told me something was coming. You were afraid for him.'

She felt momentarily dizzy.

'Merrily?'

The old black Bakelite phone, a present from Jane, felt like some kind of barbell in her left hand. Everything was heavy, even the waning sunlight. She slid her dog collar off.

'Sorry...'

'I said. How did he actually die? Where was he found?'

'On the side of the hill. He was in a shallow ditch. A depression near the foot of some steps.'

'You saw his body?'

'No... God, no. I just remembered the spot when they told

me. Earthen steps, the soil held in by boards. Walked up there once, Jane and me.'

'And is there any reason to think—?'

'They don't know. They're not sure. There's no suspicion of...'

Foul play. Why did they always say that? *Play.* Jesus.

'There'll be a post-mortem, obviously,' Huw said.

'Yes.'

Merrily was unbuttoning the top of her clerical shirt, wiping a hand across her throat. She was cold but sweating.

'They go running up there?' Huw said. 'The lads from the camp?'

'Bound to. There seems to be nothing to suggest it isn't natural causes. As if he'd just collapsed. Gone for a run, just like old times, but he wasn't up to it any more. Especially with all that weight. The big rucksack still on his back. The Bergen.'

The word had been used several times after they'd gone into the house. Syd had been found with his Bergen beside him. The big framed rucksack that the SAS carried their kit in. What they carried sometimes weighted with bricks, according to the legend – on exercises.

'Who found him?'

'I don't know. Walkers. A lot of people go walking up there. There's a car park and everything. He might've been lying there all night, or since early morning.'

'And they let you into the house, with his wife.'

'I think they were grateful to have another woman there.'

One of them had made tea. They'd sat Fiona down with her sugary brew and asked her some simple questions. When had she last seen Syd? What had been his state of health, state of mind?

She hadn't wept. She'd kept on her Gore-Tex jacket and her woollen hat and her scarf. The suppressed grief in the room had been like a still, white steam, Fiona's first word little more than a breath.

'How?'

A man who, in the course of his career, might have lost his life in a dozen different countries, and he'd gone out on a muddy hillside less than a mile from his kitchen, his kettle.

'We don't really know,' the man called William had said. 'He might have fallen and hit his head, he might have had a heart attack. Mrs Spicer, do you know if he had any health problems? Chest pains? Tightness of breath?'

'He had a medical before his appointment, didn't he?'

A silence, and then William had asked Fiona if she knew why the bedroom door was locked.

'Is it?' she'd said vaguely.

Putting her tea on one side, her expression saying it was too sweet. Merrily had gone into the kitchen to pour another. Feeling inadequate here. As a parish priest, you spent long hours in houses of bereavement, but not often surrounded by men whose experiences of death would always outweigh yours.

By the time she came back, William and the detective, Terry Stagg, had gone upstairs, the other two men outside to a police car.

Merrily had said to Fiona, 'Do you want to come back with me?'

'Where?'

'I've got spare rooms at the vicarage. Nobody should be alone at a time like this.'

'We don't really know each other, do we?' Fiona said.

They were alone in the living room. It had magnolia walls, a sofa, a small TV and a white melamine bookcase with a couple of dozen books in it. Merrily recognized the spines of the deliverance handbook and *A Time to Heal*, with its narrow black cross against sunburst red.

Fiona stood up and went to the window, where the view was over the camp, over the fields, over the River Wye to the Black Mountains and Wales.

'I don't particularly like the country,' Fiona said. 'I'll stay in Hereford tonight, then go home till... till I have to come back.'

'What about your daughter?'

'I'll phone her, when these people have finished with me.'

'Is there anybody *I* can phone?'

Fiona shook her head.

'Something kept telling me that the only way we'd stayed the course so far was by having long separations. Now we've got the big one.' Her mouth twitched. 'I don't like the country. It was no good for him.'

She'd turned away from the window, as if she never wanted to see that view again.

'She must have pre-lived Syd's death dozens of times. She starting doing practical things. Very methodical. She gave me her phone numbers.'

And the three books she'd found in Syd's car. Telling Merrily to put them in her bag before the men came back.

Merrily didn't tell Huw about the books, hadn't looked at them yet.

'Then they came back downstairs, this William and the CID man. And then some uniformed policemen came in, and a woman – I don't know if she was army or police family-liaison, but she was there for Fiona. While this guy, William, took the opportunity to get what he could out of me.'

'MoD?'

'You don't ask, do you?'

William had followed Merrily out into the front garden.

His heavy moustache was old-fashioned, a Lord Kitchener job. Authoritative back then, today it looked faintly comical, mock-solemn. William was stocky, built like a pit bull.

'Where've you come from, Mrs Watkins?'

'Ledwardine. That's a village, few miles over—'

'Yes, I know where it is. In fact, I've an old army friend living there. James Bull-Davies?'

'I know James.'

Knew him well enough to be sure he'd never been in the Special Air Service.

'I meant where've you come from… just now?' William said.

'From Hereford. Fiona's staying there. We… met at the Cathedral. Where I work, sometimes.'

'How well did you know Syd, Mrs Watkins?'

'We were… better than acquaintances. Worked together once.'

The motion of an eyebrow suggested that William had an idea what she was talking about, but he didn't follow it up. He'd gone to stand on the edge of the lawn, hands behind his back.

'Neighbour saw him leave here yesterday evening, Bergen on his back, as he apparently did most evenings. He was found lying by the side of his Bergen. He'd taken it off, as if to sit down for a rest. More or less full kit inside, and mint cake, water bottles. Over sixty pounds. Made weightier by a rather hefty and cumbersome addition. Not the apocryphal bricks.'

'Would it be a family Bible?'

William's eyes had widened fractionally.

'Fiona said he always kept a big family Bible in his bedroom,' Merrily said. 'On top of the wardrobe. She said it wasn't there any more.'

'I see. Yes, you're quite right. A Bible.'

Merrily followed William onto the front lawn, where the grass was still slippery from the winter. He jerked a gloved thumb back towards the long hump of Credenhill, the remains of its fort camouflaged in forestry.

'If he was *running* up that hill with a Bergen containing that kind of weight… we have youngsters, trained soldiers who think they're tough enough for the Regiment, collapse after a few miles carrying less than that. How old was Syd – fifty-two, fifty-three?'

'I don't know.'

Merrily had been thinking of the vivid green window in the Traherne chantry. The figure of the poet – or somebody – running along a path towards a wooded hill that was probably Credenhill.

'You all right, Mrs Watkins?'

'Sorry. Goose over my grave. Could I ask you something? Who lived here before Syd?'

William had looked at her sternly.

'There a reason for that question?'

'You'd probably think it was a fairly stupid one. Not another chaplain?'

'Here? No. The last chaplain had his own house nearby. I *believe* this was a sergeant, with a wife and a son. They were here, I'd guess, about seven years, until he retired. What exactly were you expecting?'

'Still, erm, alive?'

'And kicking. All over the world. He landed something of a plum job with a film production company, as a stunt adviser of some kind.'

'Oh. Well... thank you.'

Merrily had wondered if he'd mention the drawers pulled out, the mirror covered, the salt around the bed. He didn't, but she was convinced he now knew about her peculiar role in the diocese. Might even have rung James Bull-Davies while he and Stagg were upstairs. But he couldn't be sure if she knew what was behind the bedroom door.

'Why might Syd have a big heavy Bible with him, Mrs Watkins?'

'I'll need to think about it.'

'That's what you advised Syd to do, right? The drawers, the salt.'

'I told him what you did,' Huw said. 'Told him what you'd done in circumstances that might've been different. Giving him another opportunity to tell me exactly what was bothering him.'

Merrily sighed. Open the cupboard doors, take out the drawers, expose all dark places, leave nowhere for evil to hide. Maybe all symbolic, hooks for the mind, and maybe Syd had thought it was all crap, but he'd done it just the same. And then died.

'You think it's possible he killed himself?' Huw said. 'High suicide rate among ex-SAS men. They come out, can't adjust to normal life, and depression sets in.'

But Syd had come through. Like he said, things were looking up. Daughter getting married, grandchild on the way. Yet Merrily was remembering the sense of an optimism as synthetic as air-freshener.

'Why the procedure with the kit, though?' Huw said. 'His Bergen – part of his old identity, as a serving SAS man. And his Bible. His big Bible, representing the other half of him, but also, from what you say, a bit of a talisman. And he goes up the hill, carrying his whole identity, his memories, the weight of his religion. What's the significance of the hill? Would he have done exercises up there, when he was in the SAS?'

'They weren't based at Credenhill then. It's just a good place to run.'

'He was running away? Getting away from a house he thought might be contaminated? Not a word from this feller about his bedroom?'

'Not to me.'

'They'll want to keep that out of the inquest. Brush it under the carpet. It'll be natural causes or accidental death or, at worst, Spicer taking his own life while the balance of his mind were disturbed. Drawing a line we don't have to draw. And happen won't.'

'Because we failed him?'

'Talk about it tomorrow, eh?' Huw said.

Silence, except for the answering machine, bleeping away like a life-support system.

Merrily's bag was hanging over the back of the chair. She pulled out the three paperback books, laid them out on the desk, one by one: *Deliverance* – new edition, scuffed and tatty, well-thumbed, pages turned down but nothing under-lined, no margin notes. Only the Ledwardine Vicarage number.

And then there was *Wordsworth's Britain: a little itinerary*. This one was also quite tatty, dark green, far from new. Merrily flipped through it. Nothing was marked.

The third book was a larger paperback. On the cover, a

Roman soldier had his short sword raised over a cowering man in rags against a background of fire. Fiction. It had a blurb.

They came, they saw, they slaughtered...

It was called *Caradog* and it was by someone called Byron Jones.

Merrily turned it over. The price was $10.50. A US edition. The lurid cover, the language and the print size all suggested this was a book for children. Well, older children or young adults – although it had probably been published before that term was in use.

Caradog? Another name for Caractacus, the British leader who held out against the Romans and whose last stand was once supposed, probably wrongly, to have been on Herefordshire Beacon, overlooking Syd's last parish in the Malverns.

So no big mystery there. *Caradog* carried a very brief biographical note on the author.

Byron Jones was a Special Forces soldier in the British Army. He is now an expert on Roman and Ancient British warfare.

Ex-SAS, then. A book written by a former comrade? If there'd been time to examine Syd's bookshelves at length, Merrily might well have found Andy McNab, Chris Ryan, all the others.

She flipped through the pages to be absolutely sure that none of them had been marked, then gathered the books into a neat pile, leaned across the scullery desk and pressed the green piano key on the answering machine.

Fiona Spicer's voice. Very dry, very firm.

'Merrily, I'm sorry, could I— Could you do something for me? I'm not sure about the army protocol here. But could you bury him?'

She pushed her chair back, sat with space all around her.

A sign like a pointing finger from the clouds. The ultimate responsibility.

27

The Loser

THE COCK WAS a tumble of feathers, his neck coppery and gold in the late sunlight.

'En't a fox done this, neither,' Gomer said. 'Fox goes for the neck, and he don't leave much behind.'

'Maybe he was disturbed.'

Jane stepped back from the garden table as Gomer lifted up the bird's head. She wasn't squeamish, but an image from last night had stayed with her from when she'd first opened the sack under one of the lamps on the square: the ruined eye peeping up. The body was battered, feathers broken, maybe from the kicking Cornel had given the bin sack.

'See the blood on his beak? That's the real giveaway, ennit?' Gomer turned to her. 'You all right there, Janey?'

'He's beautiful, Gomer. That golden… like a lion's mane.'

'His hackle. Aye, nice bird, he is. You don't see the ole breeds too often n'more.'

'I mean, I don't know much about chickens and things, but it didn't seem like his neck had been wrung or anything. And the way they were talking about shooting anything in front of their guns…'

Gomer struck a match, ignited his roll-up.

'Janey, I'd 'ave to say no man done this. Goin' by the injuries. And the breed.'

'I'm not following you.'

Gomer took a drag on his ciggy.

'Gamecock, he is.'

'Game—' Jane sprang back from the table like it was electrified. 'But that's—'

'Died in the ring, sure to.'

'A *cockfight*? But that… It's like bear-baiting and stuff. History. *Illegal.*'

'Been illegal for over a century. But that don't mean it don't go on, see, on the quiet.'

'Where?'

'Few farmyards, gypsy camps.'

Jane stared at the dead cock, her fists and chest tightening.

'Big money in it, see,' Gomer said. 'Betting. Lot of it about when I was a boy. Some folks then, they couldn't figure why it was banned. Cocks fight – what they does.'

'But they don't kill—'

'I'm just tellin' you what the cockers say. All about mating. Like stags. Sure, once they seed the other cock off, it's over. But you puts the buggers in a pit what they can't get out of… the losin' cock, he en't got nowhere to go, do he? Far's the other bird's concerned, he's still a contender. So it don't stop. Specially with all the money ridin' on it, and…'

Gomer looked uncertain.

'Go on…' Jane said.

'Well, they got these… spurs, ennit? Metal spikes, couple inches long on their legs. See where this leg yere's—'

'That makes it more fun, does it?' Jane took one look, jerked herself away. 'More blood, more feathers ripped out?'

'Most of 'em dies from head wounds… or eyes. Like this boy, I reckon.'

'I just don't believe this, Gomer. When's the last you heard of it?'

'By yere? Thirty year ago, sure t'be. Used to be a reg'lar cocking fraternity, kind o' thing. Don't mean it en't been goin' on ever since, on and off. Just means it's more underground, kind o' thing. Under cover of gamefowl breeders' clubs.' Gomer nodded at the dead bird. 'Weren't so terrible bright o' that feller, just dumpin' him in a bin.'

'He offered him to Barry. For the kitchen.'

'That *weren't* bright.'

'He was drunk.'

Jane turned away from the table, her eyes filling up. She heard Gomer putting the cock back into the bin liner, and felt suddenly heartsick.

'You seem to know… like… a lot about it, Gomer.' She turned back as he tied up the sack. 'What does that mean?'

'Uncle,' Gomer said. 'When I was a boy, I had this uncle bred gamecocks. He'd've died when I was mabbe eight or nine. I remember goin' with my ma to clean out his house, and we finds all these photies. One's the ole feller with his prize bird and another cock, dead, what the prize cock killed. And here's my Uncle Gwyn, great big beam all over his face.'

Gomer shrugged.

'Thing is, he never seen it as cruel, do he? Gamecocks, they had a real good life, long as it lasted. Spoonful of porridge, spoonful of treacle… eggs, barley… nothin' but the best 'fore a big fight. And when you thinks of all these poor bloody battery chickens, fattened on drugs, never loosed out in the fresh air and then they dies on a conveyor belt…'

'Yeah, that *totally* stinks, but it doesn't…'

'No,' Gomer said. 'It don't. A cock don't even have to die in the ring, see, but it's like with them ole… what you calls them ole Roman fellers?'

'Gladiators?'

'One o' them, he gets the thumbs-down – curtains, ennit? Specially if he en't put up much of a fight. En't the same for the crowd, see, if both of 'em struts out at the end.'

'It's sick.'

Gomer puffed awhile, watching the sun.

'This that Savitch?'

'Cornel was one of his clients… guests. I mean it's bad enough they think they can go round just shooting anything, but… You think Savitch is actually staging cockfights?'

Gomer lowered the sack to the grass.

'He can't be that daft, can he? What you wanner do with this ole boy?'

'Isn't it evidence?'

'You gonner be a witness, girl?'

'I don't mind.'

'In court? Against the kind o' lawyer this banker feller's gonner hire? That's even if it went that far. One dead cock is all you got. We don't really know where he died or how. En't nothin' there for certain to say he went in the ring. Hell, Janey, I might be *wrong*…'

'You wouldn't've told me if you thought for one minute you were wrong. What about Barry? He saw it.'

'All he seen was a dead fowl in a bin bag. He's been around, that boy, but it don't mean he's ever seen a cockfight.'

'Yeah.' Jane shook her head gloomily. 'And like is he going to want to tear up his meal ticket? And the cops couldn't give a toss about rural petty crime. Apparently.' She looked up. 'There just has to be a connection with Savitch. It's the kind of thing he'd do, give the city guys a little extra thrill. Show them how hard people are in the sticks.'

'This banker feller… don't seem likely he owned the cock, do it?'

'He said it was rubbish.'

'Mabbe he had money on it.'

'Brought him back… the loser… to eat? Because it had let him down?'

'This other feller…'

Twin brownish suns in Gomer's bottle glasses. Pretty savvy for an old guy who, Mum reckoned, had rarely been north of Leominster or south of Ross the whole of his life.

'I didn't really see him and I didn't recognize his voice.'

'You figure they was both at the cockfight, Janey?'

'Sounded like it. He was sneering at Cornel. This was before he hit him. He said it was about manhood. He said Cornel wasn't ready. I have no idea what he meant. What do we do, Gomer? How about the RSPCA, the League Against Cruel Sports?'

'Mabbe I'll talk to a few folks,' Gomer said. 'See what I can find out.'

'You know people who might be involved?'

'Gotter get their fowls from somewhere. Mating season now, ennit? Cocks is well up for a fight.'

Gomer tapped the sack with the edge of his trainer, looked at Jane.

'Bury him, proper?'

Jane nodded. The sun had sunk terminally into cloud, and the air smelled sour. She watched Gomer pick up the black bin sack with its sad bundle of feathers. Her fingers were curling tight.

28

Like the Poet

WITH JANE, IT was always more than body language. She could give off fury like smoke.

When Merrily ran into her, where Church Street met the square, she was still in the school clothes she normally couldn't wait to shed, and she looked starkly monochrome against the vivid pink sky.

Or maybe everyone would look like that tonight. Merrily shook herself.

'Sorry, flower, had to go to Jim's. We were clean out of bread. You weren't looking for me, were you?'

'No, I… yeah.'

No, there *was* something wrong. But Jane turned it around.

'What's happened? You OK?'

'Bit of a shock, that's all. Syd Spicer, who was vicar of Wychehill, in the Malverns?'

'OK.'

'He's dead. He was found this afternoon on the side of Credenhill. Where the earth-steps are. Where we walked that time. Apparently he'd gone for a run on the hill. Might've fallen, hit his head. I don't know.'

'I'm sorry. That's awful. Was he still a mate?'

'Kind of.'

They walked out onto the square under a brushing of rain.

'Life's very often crap,' Jane said. 'Have you noticed?'

And she might well have gone on to explain if Barry, in his

black suit, with his polished shoes, hadn't come briskly down the steps of the Swan, striding across the cobbles, asking Merrily if she could spare him a minute.

If you could call that *asking*.

Barry's office was behind the reception desk, a small, woody, windowless space with nothing at all to say about the Swan's Jacobean origins. It had a strip light that turned Barry's face blue-white.

'Now I'm nervous.' He shut the door, pointed Merrily to his leather chair. 'You come in here last night, asking me what might frighten a man trained not to be frightened of anything, and next day he's bleedin' topped himself.'

'Barry, nobody's saying *that*. Probably natural causes, maybe an accident.'

'Accidents like that don't happen to men like Syd. Besides, that would hardly've caused what you might call a small tremor in the ranks.'

'What's that mean?'

Merrily instinctively pulled the cigarettes from her bag, then shoved the packet back. Barry waved a hand.

'Nah, light one, you want. This ain't public space.'

'It's OK.' She closed her bag. 'Who told you?'

'These things get round. You were with Fiona?'

'Yes.'

'One in a million, that woman. She understands. Better than both mine did, anyway.'

He stood over her, waiting. Merrily lowered her bag to the floor.

'All right, what happened, I was asked to talk to a group of clergy on a deliverance training course last Friday night, and Syd turned up, with something on his mind. Which he wouldn't talk about. Not to us, so we assumed it was SAS-related.'

'Who's us?'

'Huw Owen. My spiritual director.' Looking steadily up at

him. 'You knew Syd well, didn't you? Well enough to know his wife, obviously.'

'I served with him.'

'He was a friend?'

'For a time, yeah.'

'For a time?'

'We didn't fall out or nothing. I saw him a couple of years ago. He seemed OK. You can usually tell when they're not. I heard he was in full kit when they found him.'

'He had a Bergen, that's all. A lot of weight in there, including a very big family Bible. This... has kind of knocked me sideways, Barry.'

Merrily's right hand was shaking and she placed her left hand over it. Barry pulled out the other chair, sat down opposite her.

'I'm sorry. Didn't mean to sound like I was interrogating you.'

'Huw was convinced Syd needed help.'

'Kind of help?'

'He didn't *tell* us, did he? Some people are embarrassed by the... anomalous. Especially the clergy. He sat in the shadows and he listened to what we had to say in the chapel. Like he had to deal with it himself, get it out of the way.'

'You had dealings with him before though.'

'Yeah. He consulted me about something he either didn't believe or wanted nothing to do with. He told me, more than once, that he didn't like that kind of thing. He wanted *me* to deal with it. This time... I can only assume this was something he *did* believe in, however reluctantly. Or that it was personal.'

Even in here, you could hear the *plink, plink* of the pool table in the public bar. No voices, no laughter, just cue on ball. It sounded random, directionless. Lonely, somehow.

'Frank Collins,' Barry said, 'not long before he died, he became chaplain to twenty-three SAS – the reservists. So not as close as Syd. Only, when his book came out, it hadn't been cleared by the MoD, and he had to resign. Got very depressed about that. Looking at it from the other side, maybe it was the Church what done for Frank Collins.'

'It's true that when things get difficult you don't always get the support you might expect from the Church. The Church can be… strangely cold.'

'Could be none of this applies. Regiment suicides are mainly blokes who only ever went inside a church for a mate's funeral. Some of it's post-traumatic stress, some of it's because you get altered, and normal life don't seem like life at all and ain't worth holding on to.'

Merrily thought for a moment, listening to the pool game.

'Barry, can I hang a name on you?' And then, before he could reply, she came out with it. 'Byron Jones?'

His eyes went blank.

'Like the poet,' he said.

Merrily had quickly Googled Byron Jones before she came out. Not much at all, really. He was certainly an author, but not exactly a best-seller. Or not any more – the most recent reference was 2007.

'Actually,' Barry said, 'he *was* a poet.'

He sat waiting for a reason to continue.

'Syd had one of his books on the shelf,' Merrily said. '*Caradog*, a novel for older kids about the Roman invasion of Britain.'

'Yeah. I did hear he was writing books. A number of them have a go at that, as you may've noticed. But there was only one *Bravo Two Zero*. Not many millionaires among the rest.'

'*You* ever read anything by Byron Jones, Barry?'

'Lost interest when I heard they weren't about the Regiment. Anything about the Regiment we tend to collect, for various reasons. It was for kids, anyway.'

'Most of them are written under pseudonyms… Andy McNab, et cetera. Is he…?'

'His name *is* Jones. Byron – I was actually there the night he got that. We were due to fly out to… somewhere or other. About a dozen of us in the Paludrin.'

'Sorry?'

'The social club at the camp. Valentine's Day coming up and

one of the boys, he's got a card for his girlfriend what he's leaving for a mate to post, and he's trying to compose a verse to write in it. We're all helping. As you do. He's sitting there, this boy, with his notepad, getting nowhere – specially with our suggestions. "Some men sniff their armpits, others tubes of glue"… I won't go on, but you get the level. Then this person we're discussing…'

'Byron.'

'He looks up from his *Sun*, and he goes – never forgotten this, it was so unexpected. He looks up, very slowly, and he goes, in this dreamy sort of voice, "*Some men win at snooker and some at poker, too… but only one who dares can really win a girl like you*".'

Merrily smiled.

'Get it?' Barry said. 'Who Dares Wins? Big cheer goes up, and somebody goes, This lad's a regular Byron. And so, for ever after… He still didn't look the type, but how many of us did?'

'What type *was* he?'

'Spare one for me?' Barry nodding at Merrily's bag. 'Fag?'

She pulled the bag onto her knees, found the packet and the Zippo. Barry extracted a Silk Cut and lit up.

'So Syd was back in touch with Byron, was he?'

'I don't know. I'm just telling you his book was on the shelf.'

'And you just happened to notice it.'

She said nothing.

'Byron Jones.' Barry blew out smoke, thoughtful. 'I dunno about this, Merrily.'

'Is he a real writer? I mean, some of these guys, they have somebody to do it for them. But I suppose he'd need to be famous for that.'

'He's not famous.'

'And the poetry…'

'Like I said, that was a joke.'

'I mean was he *interested* in poetry? Or was Syd? Wordsworth, that kind of thing? Byron Jones's book was next to a book of Wordsworth's poetry.'

'Not that I know of. Byron was into history. He joined a local history club, and they'd do these field trips.'

'What… with local people?'

'Maybe. I dunno.'

'What did they do?'

'You know, just… poking round. Looking for bits of history. Archaeological remains. In the countryside. Around Stirling Lines back then, in Hereford.'

'Was Syd in this history club?'

'Probably.'

'So he and Byron *were* mates.'

'*Mates*…' Barry's smile was tight '… I have to say is not a word you'd readily apply to Byron.'

'He wasn't friendly?'

'Not being funny…' Barry straightened his black tie, folded his arms. 'Look, I never knew him well enough to say too much. He was very single-minded. On exercises, very competitive. I put this down to him being a bit nearer the end of his army career than the rest of us and no promotion. Like he had something to prove. I… I really don't know about this.'

'Not going to be filing a report on it, Barry. It's just I can't help feeling I let Syd down. Even though he didn't want to talk to me.'

Barry inspected his cigarette like he couldn't believe he'd already smoked half of it.

'Byron was… I mean, *ruthless* was not a word we used, seeing as how we all needed to live there sometimes. But Byron was less inclined to take prisoners, you know what I mean? You're aware that I'm telling you this…'

'In total confidence.'

'And if there *are* defence issues?'

'Doesn't worry me a lot.'

'Blimey.'

'You think, if I get too close to something embarrassing, I might get waterboarded?'

'I think you should not take the piss out of these people, frankly. And you didn't just see Byron's book on the shelf, did you?'

'It… was pointed out to me. But no explanation was given. I didn't know anything about Byron Jones until now. Is he still around? I mean here?'

'He was. I know where he *was*, 'cause his wife's there. Ex-wife. Ran into her on a tourist-board beano last year. She's doing B and B in the Golden Valley.'

'Another failed marriage, then.'

'Actually, the marriage survived quite a long time. Mostly through absence, I suspect. Yeah, OK, that's not a bad idea. If you want to know about Byron, you should to talk to Liz. Big Liz. I expect there's things she could tell you. If she was minded to. And I never said that.'

'Why wouldn't I just talk to Byron himself?'

'Not advisable.'

Merrily raised her eyebrows. Barry leaned back.

'I could give her a call, if you like, tell her you're all right.'

'That sounds like you *want* me to talk to her.'

'I don't *want* you to talk to anybody, but if you're determined to open this can of worms…'

'I'm trying to work this out. You think there's something I should know, but you don't think you should be the one to tell me? Or you *can't* tell me?'

Barry looked worried. He didn't often look worried.

'I wasn't expecting you to toss Byron Jones into the mix. If you get an approach from anybody, we haven't had this chat and it wasn't me put you on to Liz. All right?'

'Sure.'

'And Byron, I might've made him sound funny – the poetry and everything. He wasn't, do you know what I mean? He isn't.'

Merrily searched for anything in Barry's eyes, but it was like they'd been switched off, and she wondered if the evil from Syd's past finally had a name.

29

Impaler

THERE WERE SECURITY lights on stockade poles at either side of the entrance. The sign had a Roman helmet on it.

Karen Dowell was sitting in the passenger seat, arms folded over her seat belt. Apprehensive.

'You haven't told her, have you?'

'No reason to,' Bliss said. 'This is my inquiry.'

'Which just happens to overlap *her* inquiry.'

'Norra problem.'

Occasionally, he wished he could come clean to Karen about him and Annie. She'd be shocked rigid, but no way would she blab. And if she ever found out some other way she'd never trust him again, and that would be *very* bad. But he couldn't. There wasn't anybody in or outside of Gaol Street he could tell, and it was hard to imagine a situation where there ever would be.

'Was there really a Roman town here, Karen?'

'I think the actual site's about half a mile away. I remember we had this school outing there once. Of course, absolutely nothing to see but empty fields. One kid burst into tears. He was expecting something like the Colosseum. Always remember that.'

Bliss drove between the lights. Almost immediately, you could see newly covered polytunnels, like big white worms. Nobody about at all. In summer the tunnels would be like wasp nests.

'I'm not even on overtime for this, am I?' Karen said.

'I'll make it up to you, kid. One day.'

Needed her local knowledge, this was what it came down to.

There were details he might miss on his own. He parked near the top of a low hill, in front of a long shed with a poorly lit glass porch.

'We should really be in town,' Karen said. 'If even Rich Ford is predicting trouble...'

'Rich Ford's an old woman.'

'Been around a long time, boss, and he's got a nose for under-currents. If there's some underlying migrant issue here we know nothing about... I think he could be right – spot the retaliation and you're there.'

'Yeh, well, this won't take long.'

The manager, Roger Hitchin, was waiting for them. A vague-looking feller who said straight off that he was no use to them. Didn't deal much with the migrant workers, not being much of a linguist, just a man who knew about the business of growing strawberries. Which was why he wanted to introduce them to the firm's Personnel Liaison Officer.

Vasile Bocean. A Romanian whose halfway-good English had apparently lifted him out of the ranks, putting him into a permanent caravan with electricity. Vasile told them that, proud of his caravan. Couldn't be more than twenty-four. Spiky hair with gold highlights.

Hitchin left them alone with Vasile and they talked outside the office, under a metal awning. Vasile seemed to be a permanent resident now, going out with a local girl and, yes, he certainly remembered the Marinescu sisters.

He beamed.

'From village near Sighişoara.'

Bliss nodded. He knew that much. Confirmation had come in late this afternoon from the Romanian police. The parents already contacted, photos exchanged, talk of family members coming over to take the girls' bodies home. Elly Clatter had finally put out the sisters' names in time for the six o'clock news.

'Sighişoara!' A short laugh from Vasile Bocean. 'Is very famous town. Very small but very famous.'

Vasile was grinning, as though Bliss and Karen ought to recognize the significance. 'Sighişoara, *Transylvania*? Famous tourist place. Old-fashioned buildings, like Middle Ages. But *most* famous...' Vasile raising his hands, making his fingers into claws '... as birthplace of *Mr Dracula*.'

'Really.'

'Vlad Tepes. Impaler.'

Bliss let Vasile enjoy himself explaining how this English writer had borrowed this notorious serial killer's name and his castle and his reputation, turning the already uncuddly Vlad into an eternal emblem of the Undead.

'These were country girls, then,' Bliss said when it was over. 'Unsophisticated.'

'Huh?'

'Simple. Simple girls.'

'People there is all very weird, detective. Everything, they believe. Curses. Evil... omens? Spirits of the dead? Mr Dracula! Woowoo!'

'I'm sure.'

'These girls... full of all that.' Vasile waggling his fingers. 'Spooky stuff.'

Bliss exchanged glances with Karen, bulky in a blue fleece, looking like she wanted to be anywhere but here.

'Simple country girls, Vasile... can get preyed on. Like Dracula preyed on girls?'

Karen gave him a look. Bliss heard the rattling of a breeze on polythene, glanced down the valley, where no lights were visible, probably because of dense woodland.

'Who preyed on the Marinescu sisters, Vasile? You know, don't you?'

Karen barely spoke to him until they were back on the outskirts of the city. It had started to rain.

'I *had* to push him,' Bliss said. 'His English wasn't that good. He needed direction.'

'He was upset,' Karen said. 'He was shocked. His grasp of

English wasn't great. He was very distressed when you told him what was done to them. And you capitalized on that. He didn't *know*... He didn't even know they were dead.'

'Yeh, it occurred to me, when he was having a laugh about Dracula, that Hitchin hadn't bothered to tell him about the girls. The firm's way of distancing itself. Saying, we just employ them, whatever they get up to in their own time... nothing to do with us.'

Bliss wondered what Vasile was paid as *personnel liaison officer*. He figured about fifty pence an hour more than the pickers.

'At least we've planted the idea, Karen. He'll be thinking about it. And then we go back and talk to him again.'

Sex, Vasile. I'm talking about sex. Don't tell me it doesn't go on – and not necessarily always with consent. Women get raped on these farms, Vasile, you know that. It's just that they don't come and tell us about it, because of the possible repercussions.

Vasile had said, *Cushions?*

Because they're afraid of it coming back on them. People get beaten up on farms like this, too. Injured. Hurt. Isn't that right, Vasile?

I never!

Our information, Vasile, is that these girls, they were having a bit of trouble while they were here. No, no, I'm not saying it was anything to do with you, but if you don't tell us what you know, there might be repercussions when we eventually find out. You know what I'm saying?

Cushions?

Cushions, yeh.

'It's not as if he'd ever make a witness,' Karen said as they came up to the Westgate traffic island. 'Is it?'

'I don't expect that to be necessary, Karen.'

Listen to me, Vasile. Suppose the Marinescu sisters had been the victims of sexual harassment – men asking for sex in return for favours, easier work?

That never happen here! Vasile backing off, shaking his head, hands going like windscreen wipers on fast mode. *I swear to you—*

Vasile, a few people are known to have taken their own lives because of intimidation, bullying. Not here, maybe, but other farms. We know what goes on, and maybe we haven't asked as many questions as we ought to have. But murder, this is very, very different. Two young women beaten to death in the city, right under our noses? Anybody who withholds information about that, doesn't tell us what they know, we're gonna take a very dim view of it. Maybe they'll go to prison, these people who conceal information, maybe they'll get deported?

Listen, detective, please, I tell you everything I know. These girls, all they talk about... is about how this place is bad.

In what way, Vasile?

With ghostmen! Mr Dracula!

Ghostmen.

Come in the night... I dunno...

Of course you dunno, because...

I'm telling you—

Because what came in the night, Vasile, was ordinary *men. No, listen to what I'm saying. I'm talking about men from outside. You understand? I'm not trying to blame your people – your workers – for things they didn't do. Which happens sometimes, doesn't it? Sometimes they get the blame for bad things done by local men. Bosses. I know there was a boss who was very interested in some of the girls. And somehow... I think you know that, too.*

'The name Bull,' Karen said. 'All the name Bull meant to that boy was the murdered man on the farm. Who he felt he had to keep saying he didn't know in case you were trying to hang that one on him as well.'

'He knows more than he's saying. He thinks he's gorra good job, with prospects, and the future's rosy, and no way he's going to jeopardize that by grassing up somebody important. You notice how his English seemed to get gradually worse the more we pressed him?'

Bliss felt Karen's wobble of rage.

'We? *We* pressed him? This blind obsession with nailing Sollers Bull to the wall, it's turning you into a—'

'What?'

'Something I never thought you were.'

'Mother of God, this is nothing to do with what Sollers thinks about me, or how well he knows me father-in-law. Sollers finds a source of uncomplicated sex with women he doesn't even have to talk to. Vasile is the... intermediary, shall we say?'

'Pimp.'

'Whatever. All this spooky girls, Transylvania shit – he thinks we're that thick? This is an old-fashioned gut feeling, Karen. Remember them?'

'Sure, and you're an old-fashioned detective, Frannie. Which is no longer a compliment.'

'The blokes those kids saw in the pub,' Bliss said. 'Who's to say they weren't paid to do it? One job, big money. They're probably on their way home now.'

'Pulling two murders together – one knife, one blunt-force – because they both have connections to a man you don't like?'

'It was you who—'

'Yeah, and I said tell the DCI. Leave it to a senior officer who hasn't got a very visible axe to grind.'

Bliss drove slowly down towards the turn-off for Gaol Street. Traffic was light. The higher than usual percentage of police cars was very evident. He wasn't expecting to see Annie tonight, though a late-night phone call couldn't be ruled out.

Karen was right. It was best. He needed Annie to get Sollers.

Needed Annie to *want* to get Sollers.

30

Share

BACK HOME, MERRILY went directly through to the scullery, called Fiona's mobile.

Answering service. She thought of leaving a message, wasn't sure what she wanted to say. She sat looking at the American paperback, with the Roman soldier and the fire. *They came, they saw...*

The book fell open at page 35.

Caradog was a warrior, born to it. From childhood he had been taught that fighting was something to be relished and, when necessary, he killed without much thought. But he was learning that there was something different about the way the Romans fought and killed. He wanted to know what it was. What had made them the finest fighting force in the world... so that he might use it against them.

Who was he *really*? Where was he? Barry had avoided telling her Byron's real first name. There were ten million Joneses in the phone book.

Ethel was slaloming between Merrily's ankles, and she got up to put out some Felix. She could hear the sound of the TV from the parlour. A chance here of discovering what was on Jane's mind. Take some hot chocolate in. Meanwhile, she rang Lol to explain the situation. It was important to keep him in the loop. Start sharing more. Guard against slippage.

'It was on the news,' Lol said. 'About the body on Credenhill.

No name. God… Syd Spicer?' A silence, then he said, 'Don't even think of shouldering any—'

'It's not about blame,' Merrily said quickly. 'It's about finding out what was damaging him and making sure nobody else is affected. This is supposed to be my manor. If he was keeping something from us because it involved national so-called security… well, that's not my problem, either.'

'You need to be careful with those guys.'

'Me? A harmless lunatic? A medieval throwback? Oh… I've been asked to do his funeral.'

'Oh, no,' Lol said. 'Not *that*.'

And then there was someone at the door. An efficient tapping, as if with the tip of a walking stick or an umbrella. Or an army officer's baton.

Merrily watched James Bull-Davies shaking out his umbrella, shuffling on the doormat, angled like a tower crane.

'Not, ah, keeping you up, am I?'

'It's not yet nine o'clock, James. Coffee?'

'Bit late for caffeine.' James stood his umbrella under the *Light of the World* print. 'No, hell, might as well. Thank you.'

Merrily led him into the stone-flagged kitchen. Chilly in here in these days of post-Aga economic restraint.

'I'm sorry, I was meaning to call in, after…'

'Mansel? Second cousin, twice removed, something like that. Hadn't spoken to him in years. Nothing wrong, just never that close.'

'Still a hell of a shock, though.'

'Rather admired him for his refusal to give up the family home, the way we did ours. Otherwise, lived within his means. Which both his wives seem to have seen as being tight with money, but… shocking, as you say. Shouldn't happen. Country going down the lavatory.'

James pulled out a chair at the refectory table and spread himself over it in his ungainly way. He was wearing an old tweed jacket, grey woollen tie.

'Reason for disturbance… you met a friend of mine earlier. Lockley. William. Never Bill. Despises Bill, don't know why.'

'He said you were friends.'

'Shipped orf to the same school, for our sins. Christ Col, Brecon. Also served Her Maj together as young chaps, briefly, before he… took a slightly different path. Now. This man Spicer…'

'What does William *do?* With the Regiment?'

'Nothing too active now. Had his time in the sandpit. They keep him on. Chaps like him have their uses, if it's only a long memory.' James coughed. 'This is me talking to you, by the way. Not him. Not them. Fairly clear, that, I suppose?'

'You know I'd never suspect you of making covert inquiries on behalf of the Ministry of Defence.'

Army county, this. Someone's fingers snapped and men who were never quite retired came out of civilian limbo. James cleared his throat.

'Here – far as I'm aware – purely on behalf of my old friend Lockley.'

'As far as you're aware.'

'Or could ever expect to be aware.'

'James, my head's starting to ache.'

James shifted in his chair, like a minor rockfall.

'Didn't just drop out of the cot, Merrily. Fully aware of the degree of suspect politics which may appear to be lurking behind anything involving the military. *Fully* aware of that.'

'Good. Go on.'

'Having him as stand-in chaplain… not universally applauded.' James sighed irritably. 'Hate this kind of thing. Poor chap's gorn, that should be an end to it. However, one or two things still leave cause for concern.'

The atmosphere had altered, the banter was over. The coffee pot began to burble. Merrily went to it. James cleared his throat again.

'Probably know what they found in Spicer's bedroom?'

'I didn't go in. Wasn't invited.'

James was silent.

'All right,' Merrily said. 'I may have an idea what was in there.'

'I, ah… made it clear to Lockley that I had considerable respect for you, as a person. Wouldn't like you to be buggered about. However, they… that is, we… *I*… were wondering how far you'd be prepared to share.'

She turned to face James, a mug in each hand.

'Share?'

'Things are sensitive. We're in wars, could be for some time. Not made easier by the nation being in two minds about the need for it. Though, with all the loss of life, there's a lot of sympathy, at present, for the chaps who have to fight. Anything which might *affect* that sympathy or the morale of the fighting man, which, between ourselves, is getting bloody close to rock bottom… PTSD, combat-stress… obviously needs to be watched.'

Rain skittered like moths on the high window. Merrily frowned.

'I know how hard this is for you, James, but you're going to have to spell this out.'

'Merrily, this… hell's bells, they don't understand this stuff. Not their field of combat. Lockley's job's to ensure that whatever was bothering Spicer could not, if it ever emerged, be damaging to the reputation of the Regiment. Might've been the onset of mental illness. Might've been something personal or foolish. Or…'

'What do they think it might be?'

James didn't reply.

'Share means share, James. Two-way street?'

Merrily waited. James sat there for some moments, concrete-jawed. She guessed he often wondered where he'd be now if he hadn't been dragged out of the army after the sudden death of his father, to pull what remained of the estate together. Not too successfully, as it had turned out. Savitch was the squire now.

She began to lose patience.

'Maybe I need to consult my boss. Before this goes any further.'

James looked up sharply.

'Who are we talking about?'

'The Bishop?'

'Oh.' He looked relieved. 'Dunmore. Well, yes, of course. Absolutely fine. Apparently.'

You could only take *that* one way. Small county with a long history of cooperation between Church and Military. It felt like the walls were closing in on her with a sinister splintering of old, brittle wattle.

'Though we'd rather you said nothing to the other chap,' James said. 'Owen.'

Merrily let the mugs come down, *clunk*, on the table. James smiled ruefully, chin sinking into his tie.

'Complicated times, Mrs Watkins. Even in our own little world. Savitch bidding to buy the Swan, heart of the community?' He coughed. 'Apart from the church of course.'

'No, you were right the first time.'

'Should talk again.' James stood up, looking sorrowfully down at the spillage on the table. 'But I think you understand where we're coming from, broadly speaking. And, ah, perhaps it *is* a little late for coffee.'

After James had gone, Jane was still in the parlour, sitting on the sofa. But the TV sound was off, and she was talking into her mobile.

'Yeah,' she was saying, 'I'll consider it.'

When she came off the phone and didn't ask who'd been here... well, absence of curiosity was often a sign that Jane had something of her own to conceal. And when it was weighted with a muted fury which couldn't have been more apparent if the kid had been slashing the sofa...

'That was Eirion,' Jane said.

Tossing the phone onto a cushion, as *CSI Miami* played

silently on the TV: shiny, flawless techno-puppets moving in digitized choreography against glass walls and orange skies.

'How is he?' Merrily said.

'Bit bored.'

'With university?'

'He isn't *doing* anything. Just learning stuff, most of which he isn't going to need. His *fifteenth year* of learning. Weird, when you think about it, the whole university thing. Like, your mental energy levels are about as high as they're ever going to be, and it just gets poured down the system.'

Was *that* what the rage was about? Some acrimony with Eirion?

'And then you come out in serious financial debt,' Jane said. 'To *them*. With no guarantee of meaningful work. It's a scam. Eirion reckons if they can get a stack of foreign students paying an arm and a leg they're more than happy.'

On the box, a beautiful pathologist with uncovered glossy hair and perfect make-up wielded an electric handsaw, and a dead man's brainpan was eased away like the top of a soft-boiled egg. Without appearing to notice what was on the screen, Jane switched it off.

'I might get an early night.'

Merrily sat up in bed. The rain had stopped. No vehicles on the streets, only the occasional flattened notes of footfalls on the cobbles, the claw-patter of a dog on a lead. Townies talked about escaping to the country, but there was no escape out here. Everybody knew where to find you.

Too much had happened today, none of it good, but there was still work to do. Under the bedside lamp, she read Mother Julian's account of changing skin colours on the dead Christ, half his face coated in dried blood.

Merrily marked the place with a Post-It sticker. There had to be a logical sequence for this meditation and it should be stored in her head. No sitting at the top of the nave with a clipboard.

Just a low and steady voice, minimal inflection, not a preacher's voice. Julian's voice.

She worked with the book for an hour, until around midnight, applying more Post-Its. Syd hadn't used them. Pages of his Deliverance handbook had been folded seemingly at random, as if simply to mark his place. The book was uncared-for, as though he'd carried it around in his pockets.

And then thrown it at the wall because he couldn't find what he needed. You picked it up and you could almost feel the frustration. She'd left it downstairs. With Julian of Norwich, she'd been thinking, there would at least be distance.

Of course, there wasn't. After six centuries, Mother Julian was up-close and breathing, resisting impulses to look away from the horror because she knew that while she gazed on the cross her soul was safe. Apart from the cross she had no assurance. Interesting.

Merrily stopped work, went to the window and prayed for the capacity to interpret and to understand what had driven Syd Spicer on that final exercise. Then the bedside phone rang.

'Merrily. Me.'

'Barry.'

'You ain't gone to bed or nothing? Only, I phoned Big Liz. She'll be happy to talk to you on the understanding it's off the record.'

'Wasn't planning to use it in a sermon, Barry. You, er… haven't spoken to James Bull-Davies, by any chance?'

'No. Not for a couple of days, anyway. Look, you'll need to make it earlyish tomorrow. Liz's got her first Easter guests arriving after lunch. Start of the season. Can you do nine prompt? And wear the vicar kit – that'll impress her.'

Merrily dreamed of having to watch a post-mortem on Jesus Christ. Several of them in a gallery overlooking the table: James Bull-Davies, stooped and solemn, William Lockley behind his Lord Kitchener moustache and, in the darkest corner, Syd Spicer with his steady, soft-toy's gaze.

She kept walking away from the metal table and out of the door, then finding herself walking back into the morgue through a different door. Watching and worrying because the wounds of Jesus Christ, as listed in the New Testament, did not include a circle of black stitches between the eyes and the halo, where the top of his skull had been sewn back on.

31

Blue Sparks

WHEN THE MOBILE whined, Bliss was camped in front of the massed ranks of CCTV monitors in the Big Telly room.

'You talk?'

'Yeh, give me five minutes.'

Annie Howe said, 'If it's not a good time...'

'Good as any tonight.'

Looked like Rich Ford's reasoning had been well off-beam. In the aftermath of the carnage, it was unnaturally quiet on the night streets of Hereford. They'd spotted a handful of blokes who roughly fitted the inexact descriptions given by Carly Horne and Joss Singleton but nobody worth more than a mild tug. Bliss signalled to Vaynor to keep tabs and went downstairs and out to the car park and called Annie back.

'I was gonna give it another half-hour and then stagger off home. What's your day been like?'

'We've set up a phone line specifically for reporting rural crime – anything suspicious – *anything*. Which we may live to regret, as we pursue fly-tippers and kids stealing apples. On the positive side, we may actually have a response to the coded appeal for the guy who saw the man covered with blood. *And* I had to let Stagg go for a while, when this SAS chaplain was found.'

'Anything in that?'

'Looked borderline suspicious at first, but it doesn't seem to be. Nothing much for us to do. They look after their own.'

It was spitting again. Bliss moved under the awning by the door.

'Where are you?'

'Home. Thought about staying with Dad, decided that wasn't a good idea. Ah… the TV I saw, you handled it well.'

Bliss had done six TV interviews, including satellite. Only one reporter had slipped in a rogue question: *You feeling more comfortable on an urban case, Inspector?*

'They didn't use it, far as I know. Maybe they'll save it for if the rural-cops issue comes up again.'

'Ah, yes,' Annie said. 'Which it well might, I'm afraid.'

Here it comes. Bliss moved out into the rain.

Annie said, 'The Chief Constable's had an e-mail document, copied to both MPs, from Countryside Defiance. Containing what purports to be a list of over two hundred unsolved rural crimes in this division over the past year.'

'Like *what*?'

'Theft of equipment and vehicles. Arson. Damage to property – a rural bus company having seats repeatedly slashed…'

'Yeh, by a rival bus firm, if it's the one I'm thinking of. Point of honour for some of these redneck bastards to settle their own scores. Half your rural crimes, it's stuff they keep to themselves. Feud-linked, neighbours with a grudge. Leaving each other's gates open, cutting fences…'

'According to Countryside Defiance,' Annie said, 'some farmers apparently have given up reporting crimes because they're tired of wasting hours of the working day—'

'Balls!'

'—on worthless interviews and statements when in the end no one is ever arrested and they never get their property back.'

'Most thefts from farms are twats in vans, cruising the lanes, seeing what's unlocked. Chancers from the West Midlands, South Wales. It's not *organized*. What are we supposed to do about that? Put all the dozens of friggin' patrol cars we haven't got into hundreds of miles of twisty little lanes? Stop and search? You imagine how well that'd go down?'

'And there's something else,' Annie said.

***

At some point, Bliss forgot where he was. Finding himself the other side of the main road, by the steps to the magistrates' court, some drunk staring at him from under a street lamp. It was pissing down now, reminding him of the night during the floods when he'd doorstepped Annie's dad, and come off worst.

Go home boy. Charlie's finest sneer. *Go back to Liverpool or wherever it was you crawled from. Long outstayed your welcome down yere.*

Ex-Detective Chief Superintendent Charlie Howe, former head of Hereford CID. It was all different now, the organization, more remote. Bliss had met the Chief Constable just the once. He recalled a mild-mannered bloke, not a big sense of humour, but that had never been a qualification.

'The fucker wants me *out*?'

'Essentially... yes.'

'He told you on the Bluetooth this morning, didn't he? On your way to East Street.'

'I didn't say anything then because I didn't really think he was serious. And it... didn't seem a good time to discuss it.'

'The cowardly twat.'

'Francis, they're all the same. It's a difficult job at a difficult time.'

'"Difficult time"—'

The drunk was still staring at him. Bliss lowered the phone, advanced on him.

'Will you *piss off*!'

A sardonic, rubbery grin and a finger, and the drunk moon-walked away.

'I'm sorry,' Annie said. 'It's knee-jerk and it's probably unjust. And it's...'

'A small county?'

'Not quite set in stone. Not yet.'

'If he's told you, Annie, it's as friggin' good as.'

'He's told me because he's heard there's a long-standing hostility between us. He's told me, because he's hoping I'll expedite it. I imagine he thinks I'll quite *enjoy* expediting it.'

'He say how he expects it done?'

'The usual. It's to be made clear to you, quietly, that DI is very much as far as you're going if you stay here. Other opportunities will be aimed in your direction.'

Bliss stood with his face tilted into the rain, letting it come.

'Francis...?'

'I'm going home. I'm switching off.'

'No, listen, that...' Annie sounded tired and distressed. 'That's... not the half of it.'

Bliss sat in his kitchen until getting on three a.m. Under the naked bulb, from which Kirsty had taken the lampshade. One of the clutch of low-energy bulbs that came free from the lecky company, coiled white tubes like frozen intestine.

He'd been picturing Annie's incident room. Her little outpost at Mansel's yard. A message to the farmers: we're here for you. And we're local people. Maybe you remember my father. *Maybe you were in his Lodge.*

Bliss stood up, took his mug to the sink and held it under the tap with both hands for too long, numbingly cold water cascading over his wrists. Remembering something else Charlie had said that night in the rain.

You never deserved Kirsty. Nice girl. Good sensible head on her shoulders. Well rid of you, boy. Well rid.

Small county.

He turned away from the sink, hands dripping, staring at the bright, new brass lock on the back door. The locks had been changed now, front and back. Kirsty would never again get in to sniff the sheets, check the bathroom cabinet for cosmetic anomalies, the kitchen cabinet where the Brazilian decaff was, the only bit of exotica that Annie had ever introduced.

It was now entirely possible that Annie would never come here again, with her overnight bag and her expensive Brazilian decaff.

Bliss dried his hands, switched off the coiled bulb and went and sat down at the table in the dark. In his head, he was joining the wires. They ran from his father-in-law, Chris Symonds, would-be gentleman farmer, to Sollers Bull, who knew the family. To Charlie Howe, who knew the family.

And what about Lord Walford, Sollers's father-in-law and former member of the police authority? *Former?* Made no odds, he'd still have the contacts.

Chris Symonds says you consistently neglected your wife, Mr Bliss.

Had it actually come from Kirsty? No stranger to False Memory Syndrome, his wife. *Of course I won't be doing anything about it. He's not worth it. I'll just be glad never to have to see him again.*

Bliss could still hear Annie's voice in the mobile as he was standing in the rain outside the mags' court. The words still tight in his head like a migraine.

Abuse. Physical.

Confused at first. *I'm not getting this, Annie.* Hadn't realized who she was talking about.

They're saying… that your abuse of your wife also had a physical dimension.

And then, *Who? Who, who, who…?* he'd been screaming into the phone, until he realized that might make him sound like someone who easily lost it and…

… lashed out at his wife.

'*There* was *no abuse. Do you understand, Annie?* Making his voice very calm. *Physical or otherwise. Or, if there was, it was one-sided. She knows that all too well.*

Well, of course she knew it, but that didn't matter. Didn't matter whether he had or he hadn't. Didn't *matter.* In a small county.

Bliss sat there in the dark, head in his hands, remembering, as he often did, the first time he'd seen the DCI as a woman. Opening her front door to him on a December night, wearing the jeans and the loose stripy top. Hair down, glasses on the end of her nose. Those little blue sparks of static electricity. Maybe he should've seen the way this would go.

Sometimes I *don't like you.*

Just last night. And then this morning, in her car, after her Bluetooth discussion with the Chief: *I'm adapting to instructions, Francis. It's what I do. Adapt. Known for it.*

Thing was, he *had* seen the way it might go. His eyes had been open the whole way. He knew what Annie was and what he wasn't. After that unexpected, glorious compatibility on the night they'd nailed Steve Furneaux, together, he'd been fully prepared for a slow descent into the old brittle, viper-tongued, day-to-day disparaging. A relationship as workable as a frozen toilet.

And – here was the *really* sad bit – had even been willing to endure it for those brief moments of defrosting, the hair-down, glasses-on-the-end-of-the-nose moments, the blue sparks.

Bliss parted his hands and let his forehead come down on the tabletop, again and again and again.

Part Four

Yet in all this I wanted (as far as I dared)
to get a real sight of hell and purgatory...

Julian of Norwich
Revelations of Divine Love

32

A Soul in Camouflage

Abruptly, Big Liz rose, went over to a sprawling oak sideboard and came back with a green cardboard folder which she handed to Merrily.

'Just in case you thought we were never happy.'

Liz had wide grey eyes and copious white hair pulled back into more of a cob than a bun. And she *was* big. Tall, wide-shouldered, wearing a long sheepskin waistcoat.

In the wedding picture, she looked bashful in a complicated white veiled headdress, and the man she'd married was all smouldering hero in his morning suit and winged collar, with his thick dark hair.

'He could be very charming,' Liz said. 'Always good with my parents. That was half the battle, then.'

They were sitting near a bay window in a high-ceilinged, mauvey, chintzy sitting room with a wide stone fireplace and a view across the Golden Valley to the Black Mountains.

'My father – before I got married, he said, Elizabeth, you're going to have to be very strong – stronger than an ordinary wife – and very discreet, for the rest of your life. And you'll have to make allowances, because these are not ordinary men.'

'Your father was in the army?'

'No, just very patriotic, and Colin, being a career soldier in an elite regiment, he could do no wrong. I'm not very good at people. I just go along with things.'

Colin Jones. Right.

'How long have you lived here?'

The stone farmhouse, at Allensmore, south of Hereford, was Victorian and lofty. Big bones, like Liz. There was a small crenellated tower in the roof, aligned to the front porch with its double doors.

'It was my parents' house. My mother started the bed-and-breakfast side. I grew up here, and they always said that when Colin came out of the Regiment they'd sell the grounds, retire and move into a cottage and let us take over the house. At the time, Colin seemed delighted but...' Liz gave a small, helpless shrug '... I didn't realize then that was only because it would give me something to do. Keep me occupied while he did other work.'

'What kind of other work?'

'He took a job with one of the private-security companies in Hereford. Went abroad for weeks at a time, as a bodyguard to various businessmen. It was a bit on and off, and then it stopped. That was when he started to write his books. Non-stop, once he'd started one, early morning till late at night. He had a lot of energy. Too much for ordinary things.'

'He didn't get involved with your business here?'

'Wanted nothing to do with it. We had separate lives, almost. Well, except for sex, and that was...' Liz looked away, out of the bay window '... never very loving, but I made allowances. Anyway.' She placed her hands primly in her lap. 'There we are. I suppose I thought they were all like that. Oh dear.'

She blew out a short, startled breath, then sat back, looking a little surprised, as if she'd let herself be tricked into saying too much. Merrily looked around at the nests of chairs and coffee tables and saw why Byron Jones might have found it hard to settle here. Even the bookshelves had ornaments on them – little wooden boxes and china figurines and what might have been golf trophies, widely spaced. Liz's second husband was out playing golf, apparently. It seemed likely she'd arranged this meeting for early in the day not, as Barry had said, because she was expecting guests after lunch but because she knew that this morning they'd be alone.

Big Liz owed Barry. She'd met him on a tourism course. When Byron left, Barry had helped her keep the business afloat, attract some grants. Leading you to think that Barry had been sorry for her and maybe knew more about Byron than he'd revealed last night.

As for Liz… she was oddly incurious, hadn't once asked why a vicar might want to know about her first marriage. It seemed enough that Merrily had been sent by Barry.

'I'd begun to think it was all history. Then Barry rang and told me about Syd.' Liz's face became glum. 'Oh dear. You never know what you should or shouldn't say. I'm still a bit of a patriot, like my dad.'

'Where did you meet Colin?'

'Disco. In Hereford. I didn't go very often, but my cousin was staying with us and she was all for that kind of thing. It wasn't very long after the Iranian Embassy siege in London, when the Regiment rescued the hostages, and they were national heroes, and all the girls in Hereford… do you remember that? Perhaps you'd be too young.'

'Well, I wasn't living here then, but I can imagine what it was like.'

'Madness. They were like pop stars. It was when young men started pretending they were in the Regiment just to get the girls. Colin, though… I didn't even find out that he was one of them, not for a while.'

'He was actually one of the team who got into the embassy?'

'No, no. Just in the Regiment. Though he never made a thing out of it, never. In fact, not long after we got engaged he said he was thinking of leaving, he'd had enough. But… he didn't go until he had to. And by then he didn't want to.'

'You mentioned something being *history*. What was that?'

Clouds were lowering like a big gloved hand over the southern Black Mountains and the air was occasionally ripped by the screams of duelling chainsaws from middle-distant woodland.

'Yes,' Liz said eventually. 'The trouble between Colin and Syd. I may have mentioned it to Barry, once.'

'I'm trying to clear up a few things. Syd and I worked together… in the…'

Merrily lifted a hand to her dog collar. Liz nodded as if she understood, said she thought Colin and Syd had been quite close friends in the Regiment. So she was pleased – at first – when Syd had turned up one afternoon, not long after the publication of the first book.

Just passing through, Syd had said. Colin had been out when he arrived, and he said he'd wait and they had a pot of tea, Syd and Liz, and quite a long chat. Syd had not long been ordained as a minister, and Liz remembered he'd said it was as if his innocence had been restored.

'I think it was something he'd been building up to. Coming to see Colin. Not *just passing* at all.'

'Did they meet in the end?'

'It was a Sunday. Colin had been out shooting. As soon as he walked in, I sensed… It was like an encounter between two hostile wild animals. Colin still had his shotgun and a bag with what he'd shot – wood pigeons, I think. Standing there with his gun under his arm. I said, Well, I'm sure you two have a lot to catch up on. I was uncomfortable. The whole atmosphere had changed, and I realized there was something badly wrong between them. I don't think they even noticed me go out.'

'So you didn't hear what they talked about.'

'I didn't *want* to.' Liz looked agitated. 'I shut myself in the kitchen and put the radio on, loud. Classic FM. If there'd been guests in, I don't know what I'd've done, but it was out of season. I heard Syd shout, in quite an anguished voice, "They're dead! They're *all* dead now!" Didn't see him leave.'

'Who might he have meant? All dead.'

Liz looked out of the window. There was a long view over pastureland, channelled by woodland, to the foothills of the Black Mountains and then the smoky shelf of the mountains themselves.

'I don't know, my dear. Colin never mentioned it afterwards. I do know that resolving a dispute with Colin was never easy.

He didn't forgive anyone quickly, if at all. And, of course, he always seemed to despise the Church, even though we were married in one. I didn't like to mention that before, with you being... He once said Christianity was... *not a man's religion. Certainly not a soldier's religion.*'

'So could the antagonism between Colin and Syd have been anything to do with the fact that Syd had taken up a religion that Colin had no time for?'

Merrily shifted in the squashy chair. For a moment there, she'd felt something of Syd Spicer in the place. The quietness of him, almost an absence, a soul in camouflage.

'Possibly... I don't know,' Liz said. 'I thought... this sounds silly, but I kept thinking it was something to do with the books.'

The books had started not long before Byron had left the private-security company in Hereford. When the foreign jobs had become fewer. He'd begun talking about all the money that guys like the man known as Andy McNab were making from SAS memoirs and spin-off novels.

Liz took Merrily upstairs, where there were five bedrooms off the landing, the doors of all of them hanging open. A scent of fresh linen and a light musk from a dish of pot-pourri on a window sill.

Five doors open, one closed: narrow, Gothic-shaped, midway along the landing. The tower room, where Byron had written his books.

'A lot of controversy at the time about SAS memoirs. The Ministry of Defence didn't like it and Colin thought they were right. When some new regulations were imposed to make it harder for them, he thought that was good. He always said that what *he* was doing wouldn't affect national security in the least. Because his books weren't about the SAS. Well, not directly.'

'This is the ancient Britons, the Celts against the Romans?'

'He said all he was doing was using his experience of close combat to show what it was really like. He was going to be the first writer to really get inside the heads of the old warriors. He used to go running up the hill, where there's a Celtic fort.'

'Credenhill? But I thought—'

'No, the other one. Dinedor. The old Stirling Lines was close to it.'

That was interesting. The SAS had moved its headquarters from the shadow of one Iron Age fortified hill to a site directly below another.

'I think some Roman remains were also found around the camp itself, and he was very interested in that. He joined a local history group. In fact...' Liz's forehead furrowed '... I'm not sure they didn't actually form it themselves.'

'While still in the Regiment?'

'He'd read a lot of books. By the time he left, he knew all about the Celts and the Romans. And he had this idea about Caractacus, who he called Caradog, the Welsh name. Colin's family was from Wales, although he was born in London. The later books were written in the first person – as if *he* was Caradog, you know?'

'I've only seen the first one.'

'He was furious when publishers kept turning him down. One of them said it had all been done before, and Colin rang the man up and raged at him – no, this has *never* been done before, you... effing idiot.'

'Was it always going to be for children?'

'Oh, no. No, it wasn't. It made him furious when the only publisher who was interested said it should be written for children. He said he was going to forget the whole thing. Then the publisher came to see him. A woman. I think she'd persuaded him it was going to make a lot of money.'

'How many has he written?'

'Five. He'd stopped by the time we parted. He was quite bitter. Used to say they'd led him on with lies about selling the books all over the world. But they only ever sold one – to America, and the Americans demanded all kinds of changes which made him angry. His publishers kept saying it would build a readership when it became a series, but it never really happened. It was always going to be the next one.'

Liz unlocked the door of the tower room, and the pot-pourri scent followed them up four steps from the landing. The room was west-facing, white-painted walls, one small window. No furniture, only cleaning utensils, bathroom sprays and bumper packs of toilet tissue.

'He'd shut himself in here for whole days… He could go a long time without meals. I was glad at first when the publishers wanted him to go to schools and talk to children, to promote the books. But he hated that. He didn't particularly like children. Or pets. An encumbrance. He didn't like encumbrances.'

Liz looked down at the boarded floor. Had she wanted children and Byron hadn't?

'Wouldn't make any concessions in the books, to young people. I tried to read them, but I had to skip some of it. Scenes where people are garrotted and… worse. There was a lot of bad feeling with the publishers, in the end. His editor… she rang one day, when he was out, very upset. He didn't like having a woman edit his books. She sounded quite frightened, actually. Very shrill. He didn't write another one after that. Broke his contract, but they didn't try to stop him or get any money back. I think they were worried about antagonizing him any more.'

'Were *you* frightened, Liz?'

'I'd learned to keep out of his way when he was angry. I kept thinking of what my father said. The pressure he must've been under, the things he'd had to do. He certainly never touched me… in anger. When things became too much, he'd go out walking a lot. And shooting. Sometimes he'd stay out all night. I got used to it. Well, you have to, don't you?'

Liz had left the door of the tower room wide open, pushed back against the wall. She was standing against the frame, her hair coming loose.

'Some nights he wouldn't come home, and there'd be no explanation. I never once thought about other women. He didn't *like* women enough. I knew he went to Hereford, drinking with his mates, and I just assumed he was unfit to drive and sleeping on someone's sofa. Seems everyone knew except me. But then, I'm not very bright. He used to say that.'

Merrily sighed. Liz tried vainly to pile her hair back.

'Stella, who helps here, told me in the end. I think she was embarrassed on my behalf. Not like it was just one woman. He was playing the field. As if he was in his twenties again. In the pubs and the clubs. He was... you know, *walking out* with them. Stella's brother's a minicab driver in town, and he picked Colin up twice with different women. Drunk and all over one another in the back. I was sick to my stomach, and it took me a long time to ask him about it. When I did, he admitted it at once. Apologized and offered to find me a good lawyer. All very businesslike.'

'How long ago was this?'

'We've been divorced exactly two and a half years. Married Paul last year – known each other since we were kids. It's fine. It's all right. Quieter now. I was glad when Colin took his books away – all the second-hand books he'd bought for research. Not the kind of books you wanted guests to see. Pagan religions and the occult. I was always worried he'd leave this door unlocked and someone would come in and... Don't like this room.'

You could see the marks where bookshelves had been taken out. Liz's hair had come free now, like a cloud of white steam. She swivelled her head, looking from wall to wall, as if there might be blood oozing out of the plaster.

'When he left, I cleaned it out and put a bed in here. A woman came to stay for two nights. An older woman. The outspoken type you could imagine as a magistrate. Miss Pleston. Came down to breakfast next morning, and straight out with it: how often do you *clean* your rooms? Insisting there was a... *a men's stench*. It kept waking her up, and she'd had to open the window.'

'Oh.' Merrily had gone still inside. The weird excitement of the unthinkable. 'And could *you* smell anything?'

'I... no. Didn't charge her for the room. You can't afford that kind of talk. Perhaps she was making it up, I don't know.'

Merrily half-turned, had a discreet sniff: only Jeyes Fluid.

'Where's he now, Liz?'

'Brinsop. Near Credenhill. Do you know it?'

'I know *of* it.'

Passed the signpost hundreds of times. Never actually been, though the church was apparently worth a visit – couldn't remember why.

'He took aerial photos. He'd been on a course in the army so he could take pictures from helicopters for surveill— Should I be talking about this?'

'What was in the pictures?'

'Well, there isn't much there, at Brinsop. Just a few houses and farms and things and an old manor house on the outskirts. And a church, of course. And lines. On the more distant aerial photos he'd drawn lines and marked things with crosses.'

'Did he explain that?'

'Kept showing me the pictures and saying what a terrific place it was and how we should live somewhere like that. I didn't think he was serious. Then suddenly he'd bought some ground. He had a separate bank account for his earnings from the books, and he'd bought this ground before I knew anything about it. About twenty acres, part of a farm where they'd sold the house separately. He said he could get planning permission for a bungalow or something there and convert the outbuildings for accommodation.'

'He wanted you to move to Brinsop? Sell this house?'

Liz shook her head vaguely, still baffled.

'My father had died and my mother had gone to live with her sister in Pembrokeshire, and Colin said there was nothing to stay here for now. He said I could still do B and B. Well... I didn't often say no to him, but this house means a lot to me, and it was in my name!'

'Was this before he... went off the rails?'

'About the same time, I suppose. After we separated, he just moved over there. He was in a mobile home, apparently. Like a big caravan.'

'Do you know why he wanted to live there? To be back near the SAS?'

'I don't really understand it. They don't talk to you after you've gone – the ones left in. Well, they do... but they don't tell you anything. You're not part of the family any more. He was quite bitter about that, too. Bitter about a lot of things.'

'What does he do? Farm? Still write?'

'I think he's a consultant to one of these firms that runs these survival courses, self-sufficiency and... I don't really know.'

Merrily nodded. Picked up her bag, then put it down again.

'Liz... erm... please say no if you think it's silly or offensive, but would it help at all if I did a little blessing thing... in here?'

Huw Owen's primary rules: never leave the premises without dropping a blessing, or a prayer. Never leave anyone agitated or stressed. Never leave a vacuum.

Liz looked as if she didn't quite understand and perhaps didn't want to.

'Yes, all right,' she said. 'Thank you.'

33

Colleagues

KAREN DOWELL WAS on the phone when Bliss got into Gaol Street, just after half-nine, but still managed to flick him a warning look, glancing at his office door. Which was shut. Someone sitting in there.

Bliss decided that if, by some serendipitous anomaly, it was the Chief Constable, he'd smash the bastard before he could get up. Partly because the Chief was bigger than him and partly because he felt like shit this morning – shivery and light-headed, like when some hovering virus was figuring out if you were worth taking down. And partly because it might just be the finest thing he'd ever do in his life.

He nodded to Karen, opened the office door, walked in with his aching head held high, and it was Annie Howe.

The old Annie. The dark trouser suit, the ice-maiden white shirt. The no make-up, the no jewellery. Sitting behind his desk, marking the homework.

Bliss shut the door behind him.

Might have slept last night, but he didn't think so. He remembered the sun coming up before his wide-open eyes, before the clouds had smothered it. He'd got up, drunk a whole pot of tea, hoping that Annie might call him from Malvern before either of them left for work. Nothing.

'If you've gorra screwdriver on you, Annie, I'll take me name off the door.'

'I'm meeting a witness at ten.' Annie stacked the reports,

looked up at him. 'Why I'm here rather than Oldcastle. I thought you might like to sit in.'

'Witness to what?'

'A man in a field? Covered in blood?'

'Oh.'

'Agreed to meet in town, if we can protect his identity. Actually, it was the girlfriend who rang in, from a mobile. I'm meeting them at Gilbey's. Told her I might be accompanied, but that wouldn't change anything.'

They walked up towards High Town, well apart on the pavement. Annie was wearing a grey double-breasted jacket, a long white woollen scarf.

'I do hope the Chief realizes this won't be bloodless,' Bliss said.

'Don't do anything stupid. There may be room for manoeuvre.'

'Rather be out than have this shite. Chuck in me papers.'

'You're being ridiculous.' Annie quickened her pace. 'Nobody wants you out of the *job*. Might even simply be a case of staying in West Mercia, just leaving the division?'

'No. No, no, *no*.' Rage ripping into Bliss as he caught her up on the corner, near the zebra crossing. 'You don't understand, do you? I've only gorra close me eyes and I can *see* them... Kairsty and her old man... Sollers Bull and his friggin' father-in-law from the House of friggin' Lords. All the foreign hunters behind Countryside Defiance and the tweedy twats who like to think they still control this county, and—'

'The Chief's just watching his back. It's how they survive.'

'—and right there in the middle... your old man. Charlie Howe with one hand held out for the money and the other making some Masonic sign. Corruption's embedded in this county, Annie, like... like the blue bits in Danish friggin' Blue. Try and cut yourself a slice that isn't riddled with it.'

'You could say that of just about anywhere.'

'Yeh, well, I don't live just about anywhere. And one thing I've noticed is that when they go down, the bad guys… when they go down in Hereford, it's always the outsiders.'

They turned along the narrow passage leading to Gilbey's bar, where the city's movers and shakers occasionally moved and shook. In its own secluded little space up against the back of St Peter's Church.

'We have to sit outside.' Annie headed for the farthest table, under a tree and in the shadow of the steeple. 'You go and order some coffee. I'll wait here, in case he's early.'

'Do we need pink carnations?'

Inside, Bliss scanned the clientele. A few faces that he vaguely recognized. Fortunately, nobody he actually knew. He'd thought maybe Annie had asked him along because she had something encouraging to say to him about how they'd fight this thing together, but that evidently was not going to happen.

When he came out, there was a woman sitting with Annie. Mid-thirties, pale-skinned, wind-straggled blonde hair tucked into the collar of her red leather jacket.

'This is my colleague, Francis Bliss,' Annie said. 'Francis, this is… Janette.'

'Jan,' the woman said.

Bliss sat down the other side of Jan.

'And when will your friend be joining us?'

'She won't,' Jan said.

Bliss looked at Annie, who smiled colourlessly.

'Jan is our witness, Francis.'

It took a moment.

'Ah,' Bliss said.

Jan told them she was taking up an appointment after Easter, as head teacher at a local primary school.

Bliss said, 'You mean, out there, in the sticks?'

'Out there, yes.'

Jan said the person she'd been with in the car on the night of Mansel Bull's murder was married, but wouldn't be for long. They'd been at college together, found one another again after fifteen years. She was the reason Jan had come looking for work in the Hereford area.

'There might *not* be complications with either parents or governors, but there just might. It's necessary to be discreet and take things slowly. This is, after all, a rural area.'

'You're quite right there, Jan,' Bliss said. 'It very much is.'

He wondered if her girlfriend was fairly well known in the area. And if the husband had any inkling. Jan still looked nervous.

'You won't get me to give evidence in court. You do accept that?'

Annie said, 'We can talk about that later.'

'There won't *be* a later if I don't get an assurance.'

Annie Howe nodded.

At least they got an accurate location, a good half-mile from where they'd stopped searching for blood traces in the fields. Covered some ground, this guy. The access involved several unmarked single-track lanes. There was a derelict barn you couldn't miss, Jan said, and the ungated field entrance was about fifty yards after that.

Bliss made notes. Asked her if she'd seen any other vehicles on the way there, and Jan shook her head, said nobody lived up there any more.

'I've walked that whole area. I'm staying in a guest house at Tillington, about three miles away, looking for a cottage, so I've done a lot of exploring around. Essential preparation for taking over a local school. Kids can be evil wee sods if they think you're an innocent abroad.'

'And your friend? She's local?'

'Do we have to go into that?'

Bliss shrugged.

'Credenhill,' Jan said. 'Though not originally.'

Bliss didn't react. Was it possible that Jan was snuggling up to some SAS man's missus while he was in foreign parts? That'd make anybody nervous.

'In your letter,' Annie said, 'you called Mansel "Farmer Bull". Was that how your girlfriend knew him?'

'It's what they called him in the local shop.'

Bliss said, 'When you saw this man in the field, did you also see any sign of a vehicle? Off-road, perhaps? Or any other people?'

'We didn't hang around, if I'm honest. Out there in the middle of nowhere, it was pretty frightening. We'd only just arrived, so we still had the engine running and the headlights on when he came rushing out of the dark. As if he'd been blown out by the wind.'

'You say you couldn't see his face – what about his hair?'

'I think he *had* hair... I mean, I don't recall him as bald or anything, but... it could've been slicked back with the... with the blood. I don't know.'

'Tall, short, thin, fat?'

'He certainly *seemed* tall. And well-built, I suppose. And quite fit, I'd imagine, the way he was moving. I go to the gym twice a week, but you wouldn't get me out running in those conditions.'

'Let me play devil's advocate here,' Annie said. 'How do you know it was blood? How do you know he wasn't simply plastered with mud? Red Herefordshire mud.'

'And then I heard about the murder afterwards, you mean, and put two and two together and made eleven?'

'You wouldn't be the first to make that kind of mistake in a situation like that.'

'Chief Inspector, I spent many hours agonizing over whether to send you that letter, knowing that if it got out that a respectable married woman was having a relationship with a gay woman who was about to become head teacher at the school attended by her *children*...'

'Yeh, OK,' Bliss said. 'What did he do, this feller, when he saw you?'

'Stopped. I mean, he had to, or he'd've run into the front of the car. Then he turned away and ran off. Almost casually. As if he was an athlete running for pleasure, and he was full of endorphins, you know?'

'What was his… you know, his mood? You gerra sense of that?'

'It was – this is going to sound crazy – but it was as if he was loving it. Despite all the blood. Obviously, we thought it must be his own blood, and you think… even as you're backing the car away, you're thinking, does he need help? And yet that really wasn't…'

'Like he was *relishing* the blood?' Bliss said. 'I'm thinking the way a new huntsman – a fox-hunter – when it's his first time, they splatter him with the fox's blood?'

Bliss's eyes met Annie's, saw a flickering warning there. He smiled.

'I'm afraid I've had nothing to do with blood sports,' Jan said.

Annie asked her, 'Do you think he saw you?'

'I don't know.'

'He must've seen what kind of a car you had.'

'And if you backed up and accelerated out of there, he must have known you'd seen him,' Bliss said.

He watched Jan playing nervously with a stray blonde curl. Women of a Sapphic persuasion, it wasn't as easy to identify them any more. In a few ways, she was more girlie than Annie.

'I did think of that, yes,' Jan said. 'Another very good reason not to want to be identified, wouldn't you say?'

Bliss said, 'If we were to show you some piccies…?'

Felt Annie Howe's head coming round on him with the weight of a gun turret.

'It would be very unlikely that I'd recognize anybody from a photograph,' Jan said. 'As I say, it was all terribly fast and rather blurred.'

Bliss saw the waitress leaving the doorway of the bar with their coffee and cups on a tray.

'What about your friend?'

'She saw less than I did. Screaming her poor wee head off by then.'

***

'I firmly trust you weren't actually going to do that,' Annie said. 'That you were saying it just to annoy me.'

Jan had left. They knew where to find her. Bliss licked his spoon.

'Why not? It'd be with a selection of other photos.'

'Planting the idea that West Mercia Police suspect Sollers Bull of killing his brother?'

'Got that twat's prints all over it.'

Telling her about his and Karen's visit to Magnis Berries last night and the reason. Annie scowled. Bliss shrugged.

'Don't tell me you wouldn't've done the same.'

'As it happens, I did know about Mansel selling the land to Magnis.'

'Done behind Sollers's back?'

'According to Sollers, it was a decision made without much forethought. Mansel was using those top fields for training his sheepdogs. And then simply decided he'd had enough. The offer came, and he took it. Shortly before he was killed, he'd arranged to sell all his dogs to Berrows, from Kington, who you'll know.'

'Jeremy?'

'He's taken them all. Five dogs.'

'That's a bit odd, isn't it?'

'What's so odd about it, apart from the timing? Mansel pre-sumably didn't *know* he was going to be murdered. He'd lost the patience for it, according to Sollers. Not winning trophies any more. That's all it is.'

Bliss said nothing. Sat and looked at Annie, sitting with her jacket open, her long woollen scarf hanging loose. The slender neck, the carelessly brushed pale hair.

'Right,' Annie said. 'We'd better get back. I'll send Slim Fiddler to find that field, and I'll make sure he goes over every last blade of grass.'

'Good luck.'

Bliss contemplated the oval miniature of his own face wizened into the sugar spoon. Spent a couple of cliff-edge seconds reconsidering his decision not to tell Annie about Kirsty's first little bombshell: *...when it all comes out, won't one of you have to move to another division? Isn't that how it works?*

Annie said, 'Presumably you didn't get anything useful from Magnis Berries?'

'Nothing of immediate significance, no.'

Annie stood up, buttoning her jacket, the tower and steeple of St Peter's in the wedge of white sky behind her. For a moment Bliss thought she was smiling as she looked down at him.

Then she said, 'Don't.'

'Don't what?'

'Don't assure me again that you never hit your wife. I believe you. However, for the foreseeable future...' she tucked a two-pound coin under the coffee pot '... I think we need to be colleagues.'

'What?'

'Colleagues,' Annie said. 'People who work together.'

34

Burned

HALFWAY ALONG THE Golden Valley, a green hill bounced up on the right, its summit shaped by the earthen ramparts of another British camp. Tiny compared with Credenhill, but they were everywhere, a whole layer of landscape sculpted by ancient Britons. Still here, still dominant.

Merrily was driving slowly, under clouds like the rolling smoke from a grass fire. She'd brought a flask of holy water up from the car and done the blessing, with Liz. An appeal for calm and light in an oppressed place. Most times you were uncertain: an unaccountable man-stench in the tower-room – wishful thinking, Miss Pleston?

And yet a faint sensation of something resistant had come back at her, and she'd walked downstairs feeling unexpectedly drained. Maybe she was just overtired and underfed, or affected by the mind-altering properties of Jeyes Fluid.

No, Barry had been right. Byron Jones was not funny.

It would've been interesting to see the books he'd kept in the tower. *Old pagan religions and the occult.* Merrily thought about the people of the hilltop camps, whose priests had been Druids. Talk to Jane, and they were kindly nature-worshippers and all they ever used a sickle for was cutting down mistletoe. Read the Roman accounts, and you got blood-drenched savages, well into human sacrifice. They probably didn't smell too good, either.

In the straggling village of Peterchurch, she pulled into the parking area opposite the Norman church, called home to check the machine and found just the one message:

'*Merrily, this is Fiona Spicer. I think we have loose ends.*'

A voice still perfectly contained, wholly together. A widow of one day. Merrily sat staring across the parking area at a children's playground which looked like a small power station. Lit a cigarette and called Fiona.

Lol had been in Danny Thomas's barn since eight. Danny was walking up and down in the straw, rehearsing a verse of 'Trackway Man', talking it into the mic.

'"Among the hills where shepherds watch, we'll march towards the skyline notch. From tump to twt we'll mark the route..." What the hell's a *twt*, Lol?'

'I thought you were Welsh.'

'I'm from Radnorshire, it en't quite the same.'

'I thought it was a Radnorshire word. I dunno, maybe a burial mound, a small tump. Rhymes with *route*, anyway, that's all that matters.'

'This don't seem like your kind o' song, somehow,' Danny said. 'Them Biblical quotes at the start. "Set me up waymarks, writes Jeremiah"?'

Lol explained how Alfred Watkins had collected bits from the Bible which seemed to support the idea of ley lines. He was thinking it would be quite good to use them with a kind of monastic echo. Resonant.

'Just trying to connect, Danny. You were born here, I'm just... don't know.'

Passing through?

'Just 'cause you lives yere, it don't necessarily mean you connects.' Danny squatted down in the straw between a vintage Marshall amp and Jimi the sheepdog. 'Did once, mind. Had what you might call a spiritual experience where I seen the poetic truth of ley lines. Looked at the veins in my wrist and seen the arteries of the countryside. Magic, that was.'

'I thought it was acid.'

'Well, aye, it was, but a vision's a vision, ennit? Bloody hell, what a long time ago that was. I was only a kid. Thirteen, fourteen?'

'You were dropping acid at thirteen?'

'Very progressive area, Radnorshire, in the ole days, boy. 'Sides, nobody knowed, back then, what it could do to your brain.'

'Radnorshire?'

Danny grinned. Then, abruptly, his face was solemn.

'Seen much of young Jane, past day or so?'

'Uh… not really.'

'That business in the Swan, where she poured that feller's beer… Got a bit overshadowed, that did, when the word come in about Mansel Bull.'

'An ill wind.'

'Never seen her like that before. Serious. The changes round yere – gettin' to her. Savitch.'

'Getting to all of us, one way or another.'

'Only, Gomer and me, we got a problem,' Danny said.

Fiona said, 'No commiserations. Sympathy cards, I won't even open. Don't want to be treated like an invalid. When you've lived with a vicar, you know all the bereavement rituals. '

Merrily thought naked grief was easier to handle.

'You're not still on your own, are you?'

'Emily's on the way up to Hereford, with her boyfriend. And I have things to organize. Better than thinking. I'm sorry we didn't get a chance to talk last night, and I'm grateful for what you did. And what you might have done if we… if we'd been in time. You *will* take the funeral?'

'Well, if you… I don't do quickies, Fiona.'

'What's that mean?'

'Well, it doesn't mean endless eulogies. But there are things *I* need to understand. Whatever he wouldn't tell me, it's not going to rebound on him now. Which… is one reason I've just been over to Allensmore. To talk to Byron Jones's ex-wife.'

'That was quick.'

'When you were talking about the books that Syd was reading, back in the Cathedral, I don't recall you mentioned Byron Jones. So when I found that book, with the others...'

'I was certainly surprised to see a copy of that book on the desk.' A pause. 'OK, the last time I saw one was when we were at Wychehill. A parcel arrived one day with a copy of *Caradog* inside. Newly published.'

'This was when they were still friends?'

'I thought they were. A short time afterwards, I opened the wood stove, because it seemed to be nearly out and... you know how you can tell something used to be a book, for just a second, before the ashes collapse?'

'Syd burned the book? Without even reading it?'

'He never explained. Though he now seems to have acquired another copy. They were good friends, once. Byron was a bit older than Sam. He came out of the army first, but they stayed in touch.'

'Was Syd in Byron's local-history group?'

'His *what*?'

'Liz says Byron was in – or might even have set up – a society to study the history around Stirling Lines. Romano-British history. The inference being that this was where he got much of the background for his fiction.'

'I know nothing about that. Though it's hardly something you'd need to keep secret.'

'Liz said Byron despised Christianity.'

'Not sure if he despised it quite so much before Sam got into it. Sam was hyper at that time. His ground-to-air missile period.'

Merrily shifted in her seat, looked over towards Peterchurch's Norman church with its fibreglass steeple. It was called The St. Peter's Centre now, and it had a café and a library. Was this what Uncle Ted had in mind for Ledwardine? Which reminded her there was a parish council meeting tonight to discuss it. *Bugger.*

She said, 'You *do* know about Syd going to visit Byron at Liz's place?'

'When was this?'

'Liz said two or three years after Byron left the Regiment. Possibly around the time *Caradog* was published. Would that have been *after* the burning of the book?'

'I didn't know that Sam had ever visited Byron,' Fiona said. 'Or imagined he'd want to. What did Liz say about it?'

Merrily told her. Everything, including the shotgun, which provoked a short, sour laugh.

'Perhaps he felt he needed it as protection. Turning the other cheek was the one Christian premise I always felt Sam could never quite swallow.'

'You've met Liz?'

'One or twice. At funerals. Walking – metaphorically – half a pace behind Byron. They're often the ones who get hurt in the end. Wholesale philandering goes with the territory. Like Vikings.'

'But not Sam.'

'Sam was a misfit who didn't know what he wanted or where he wanted to be. The army straightened him out for a while, religion messed him up again.'

'Did he ever mention Brinsop?'

'Who?'

'It's a hamlet near Credenhill. Where Byron lives. Where, according to Liz, he seems to think it's very important for him to live. Syd ever mention it?'

'No. And if you were thinking of going to visit him I'd urge you not to. Some of these guys, there's another side to them which is great in warfare but, in ordinary life, relatively... antisocial.'

'Fiona... do you have any idea what all this is about? You must've given me those books for a reason.'

'Knee-jerk reaction. Probably a mistake. I don't know anything about deliverance, and Wordsworth – no idea what that's about either. Merrily, I have to go. Have people to see... solicitors... and whoever you see to register a death. I'm sorry.'

***

Danny pulled down a squared bale of straw and sat on it.

'Likely you don't know much about cockfighting. Well, me neither. Us ole hippies, we never done that stuff. Foreign to our nature. But it went on.'

'Round here?'

'Part o' country life. Country folks was cruel, too.' Danny reached over and turned off the amp. 'Gomer found a dead gamecock in the vicar's shed. Turns out young Jane put it there. Told Gomer a feller dumped the sack in a bin on the square. Feller was this Cornel.'

'Oh...' Lol closed his eyes '...*God.*'

'You en't lookin' as surprised as I figured you might be.'

'No.'

Lol pulled the Boswell across his knees and told Danny about what he and Merrily had watched in the Swan, the night before last.

'Only we got the impression from Barry that it was a pheasant.'

'He still stayin' at the Swan, this Cornel?'

'I think he just comes in for meals now. I don't know where he's staying. How did Jane know it was a fighting cock?'

'Her didn't. Gomer knowed straight off.'

'Gomer's on the case?'

'En't nothin' Gomer wouldn't do for Jane, is there? Jeez, why they gotter—' Danny pulled off his baseball cap, sent it spinning to the straw. 'Cockfights! They tells us we're in recession, so we gotter degrade ourselves by stagin' cockfights for the freakin' tourists?'

'Who?'

'Who d'you think?'

'You really think Savitch would risk his reputation by supporting something illegal and... universally condemned?'

'Gomer phoned around. Farmers, dealers. Drew a blank. Wherever it's happenin' it en't at no farms round yere. Gotter be some bastard from Off. Now... where was the ole Ledwardine cockpit?'

Lol shook his head.

'I'll tell you,' Danny said. 'Up by the top bridge, where the river come through in the floods? Used to be a pub there, knocked down seventy, eighty year ago. You can still see the outline, they reckons. Like a depression, middle of a copse, now. Cockpit was back o' that pub.'

'So that...' Lol stroked a sinister E-minor on the Boswell '... would be on the ground...'

'Bought up by The Court last summer – when wassname, Wickhams, sold up?'

'You're saying that whatever remains of the old Ledwardine cockpit is now owned by Ward Savitch.'

Suddenly, Lol could see why this just might be Savitch. *All for traditions.* The first man to stage a cockfight in Ledwardine for a century or whatever. Even if he only did it once or twice, for selected guests.

'Jane know about the cockpit?'

'Not yet, boy. See the problem?'

'Case closed, far as Jane's concerned. And it looks very likely, doesn't it? I mean, how else would Cornel've been to a cockfight?'

'Exackly.' Danny stood up, strapping on his Telecaster. 'So what's Gomer do now, boy? Do he tell her... or don't he? Bein' as how her's likely to go off like a rocket.'

'Even if Savitch wasn't charged with anything,' Lol said, thinking hard, 'it would makc him a figurc of hatc.'

'Sure to.'

'Would *you* be able to tell, if you saw the pit, whether it had been used recently?'

'Gomer might. But... private land now. Big fences.'

'Not this weekend. It's open to the public on Easter Monday.'

'Still be restricted access. Public won't get near an active cockpit.'

Lol said, 'Tomorrow, however...'

Laying down the Boswell in a manger full of last year's straw, he told Danny about Savitch's visit and the offer of a site for an open-air music event. Half afraid that Danny, whose musical aspirations had been frustrated for so long, would see it as a once-in-a-lifetime opportunity to stage some kind of Welsh Border Woodstock. Danny sniffed and smiled.

'En't life a bitch?'

'So I've got these two tickets for the press launch and reception for invited guests. Be far more informal. Fewer stewards, not much security.'

'Right.'

'If I gave the tickets to you and Gomer, would you be able to maybe find out one way or another?'

A short, worried whine came out of Jimi the sheepdog as Danny stood up, gripped the Telecaster around the bottom of its neck, pulling it hard to his gut.

'What time?'

35

Comper's Bling

AT ONE STAGE, the narrow lane to Brinsop pointed you directly at a wooded flank of Credenhill. You felt that if it didn't veer off soon you'd vanish into a green mouth.

The first time, Merrily missed the turning to the church, then spotted in the rear-view mirror what might be a bell tower. At approaching midday, a pale blue hole in the clouds was broadening into a small lagoon. She reversed into the next track, and the long hill fell away to the side. Nobody about. No other vehicles.

No village. Plenty of fields, woodland, a few dwellings, and a church, on its own, set apart.

Merrily's stomach was hurting. Really needed something to eat. Maybe she should go home. Only twenty minutes away. Three warnings about Byron Jones – secretive, embittered, obsessive. She didn't want to find him, not yet. Just to get a hint of what, in Brinsop, had caught his eye.

The church was at the end of a private track with weeds growing up the middle. A sprinkling of homes, old and newish, barns and sheds, and then the Volvo was up against a fenced field of ewes and lambs. A dead end with the churchyard along-side, raised up. Jane maintained that an elevated churchyard always indicated a former pagan ritual site. But then, for Jane, signs of paganism were everywhere.

OK. Merrily stayed in the car and leaned back, easing the pressure on her stomach. Do this properly. She pulled her bag onto her knees and consulted her contacts book.

Dick Willis, priest in charge of the Credenhill cluster of churches. A cautious guy, not far off retirement. The signal here wasn't good, but she got him.

'Ah, Brinsop,' he said. 'The jewel in my crown.'

'I'm afraid I've never been before.'

'Then I mustn't spoil it for you, Merrily. Is there a problem there? I certainly haven't heard of one, but when one hears, out of the blue, from your good self...'

'Do you know a guy called Byron Jones? Colin Jones?'

'Ah, now, that would be the man with the private army base?'

'Say that again.'

'I exaggerate. He calls it The Compound. Once a pig farm, a mile or so out of what used to be the village. The farm became derelict, the house was sold off and this chap bought the land. Lived there in a caravan, then suddenly built this rather lavish bungalow, as if he'd come into money.'

'What did you mean by private army?'

'Not an army, a base. He has a training area with an assault course and all that sort of thing. He run courses for military enthusiasts, and the place is done out like a real army base with high wire fencing and authentic warning signs. Part of the mystique, I suppose. Looks more secret and exciting than the actual SAS place down the road. Boys will always be boys, Merrily.'

'He had planning permission for all this?'

'Not always needed. And some of the objectors were appeased when, at his own expense, he planted extensive woodland to conceal the site. That was about a year ago.'

'Mr Jones is ex-SAS, I believe.'

'Well, yes, that always helps, doesn't it? Especially in this area.'

'Does he come to church?'

'If he does, it's not when there's a service on,' Dick Willis said.

The sun was just visible through the cloud, like a pound coin in a handkerchief, as Merrily got out and locked the car. She shook herself, felt a little better.

The site was fairly remote, but the churchyard was well looked after. Nothing overgrown here, and most of the uncrowded gravestones were upright. A huge sentinel evergreen stood beyond the wooden gate, looking taller than the church which sat behind it, under the hill. A compact greystone church with a conical bell-tower. More central Wales than Herefordshire, but comfortable in its lusher ground.

And the site… Jane might well be interested. Different levels, perhaps a suggestion of earthworks and, across the lowest field beyond the church, a small, dark-green lake. Or a big reeded pond. Or, possibly, a moat, all wooded-in.

A lovely spot, really. This was one of those churches that had *had* to be here, Jane would say. Had to be *here*. Sacred ground long before Christianity.

Merrily walked past the church porch towards the water and was pulled up by a name on a gravestone, directly in front. Not ornate, but tall and prominently sited and making an instant connection with one of the paperbacks on Syd Spicer's desk.

SACRED
TO THE MEMORY OF
JANE WINDER
WHO WAS BORN AT *KESWICK*, CUMBERLAND
AND DIED AT *BRINSOP COURT*,
IN THIS PARISH OCTOBER 16, 1843
IN THE 43 YEAR OF HER AGE.

This Stone is erected by WILLIAM and
MARY WORDSWORTH, of Rydal Mount
Westmoreland in affectionate and grateful
remembrance of her faithful services conti-
nued through fifteen years.

Good *God*. Merrily began to tingle. That sense of the preordained. A piece of an unknown jigsaw. The piece that slotted in to tell you there *was* a jigsaw.

William and Mary. Rydal Mount. Westmoreland. The Wordsworths – *the* Wordsworths – were here?

She walked back to the porch, went in. Always the same when you approached an unknown church, that frisson of mild apprehension, as you turned the ring handle. Some resistance, but the door wasn't locked. It gave, and she went in, and whatever she was expecting – perhaps, given the location, something frugal, cold, drab, rudimentary – it wasn't.

No smell of stone or damp. She made out lurking colours, and not only in the windows. Much metallic glistening from the chancel.

Merrily waited at the bottom of the nave. Waited for something to happen, something to move, shadows to part.

'Blimey,' she said, to nobody she could see.

This was all strongly medieval. Medieval like in the actual Middle Ages. A concave golden canopy was shining over the altar, like the reflector on a lamp. There were three gilded angels, wings aggressively spread, brandishing candles.

A treasure house. Out here in the deep sticks it was all so entirely unexpected as to be approaching the surreal. Merrily picked up a leaflet from the pile and took a seat at the back. Chairs, light-coloured wood, not pews. A lot of money had been spent since medieval times, enhancing what was here. The angels were confidently balanced on the top edge of the chancel screen, guarding a Christ on the cross. A chess-piece kingly Christ in a golden crown. Not suffering, but proud and triumphant. In control.

And when you looked more carefully, you began to see all the dragons. Merrily came back to her feet.

Everywhere, dragons were dying.

There he was, red-crossed, in a window. And here he was again, more modern and explicit, on a pedestal, in full armour with his foot on the dragon's neck, his spear down its throat.

Merrily opened the leaflet. *St George.* Brinsop Church was dedicated to the dragon-slaying patron saint of England. The leaflet said the church had been saved from 'certain ruin' in the mid-nineteenth century, old windows rediscovered and restored. It had never looked back since, acquiring much sympathetic embellishment by Sir Ninian Comper, ecclesiastical architect and Gothic revivalist, in the early twentieth century. His work included the angels on the wooden screen. And yet, for all Comper's bling, it still felt like a country church, small enough to be welcoming. Some bright, modern stained glass: a St Francis window with birds. A First World War window with crucifixion symbolism. And one...

In memory of Wm Wordsworth, poet laureate.
A frequent sojourner in this parish.

Back to the leaflet. Wordsworth's wife, Mary, had been a sister of Thomas Hutchinson, who was leasing the twelfth-century Brinsop Court, the poet often spending holidays here, with his wife and his sister, Dorothy.

Merrily stood up, feeling ignorant... parochial. Why hadn't she known about this? The next church to Traherne's, at Credenhill. Traherne and Wordsworth... separated by more than a century, but two poets with a lot in common. Lovers of landscape, solitude. Nature mystics.

Odd. *Was* it odd? She walked into the chancel, looked back to where the far window was halved by the bar of the screen, split by the shaft of the cross. This was very much a theme church, St George the principal one. Why did you always feel sorry for the dragon, instantly disliking the smug bastard with the spear? The charitable view was that – lance, deep throat – it was a piece of early sexual symbolism.

She padded across the nave. As usual, alone in a church, Merrily didn't *feel* alone, but this time it wasn't just about God. That little green book of Wordsworth poems suggested that Syd Spicer had been here.

Byron *and* Syd? Byron who despised Christianity... *not a man's religion, not a soldier's religion.* She felt Syd pondering this, lighting up. He'd want to smoke in here. Too rich for Syd, this place. Wouldn't have liked the golden angels. *Phoney High Church iconography,* he'd said of what had been inflicted on his own church at Wychehill. *Grotesque.*

Syd, you just knew, preferred drab, damp and frugal.

Merrily moved on to a small lady chapel with more Wordsworth memorials. A medieval stone coffin lid in the floor reminded her of the Knights Templar church at Garway. Stories everywhere, written in glass and stone, many of them modern and literal but no less effective for that.

And then she came to what, unmistakably, was the real thing. Out of place, isolated, but probably pre-dating the wall into which it was set.

A stone slab. Carved images. St George again, an early depiction. George in dragon-slaying mode, but on a horse this time. She consulted the leaflet: originally a tympanum, a piece of ornate masonry between the top of a door and the arch. Herefordshire Romanesque. She knew a bit about that – early medieval. The leaflet said that a stone in an adjacent field was believed to mark the actual spot where St George had killed the dragon.

Sure. The St George who apparently was Turkish, the dragon whose legend was set in the Middle East. Merrily imagined Syd tapping his ash on the saint's helmet, knowing he could've taken George, unarmed, any day of the week.

Never quite understood how saints like George fitted into the fabric of Christianity. A medieval thing, probably, an excuse for crusades, brutality masquerading as valour... *a frenzy of pure excitement.*

There was a whiff of cigarette smoke. Syd Spicer was back.

The Syd of an overheated confessional afternoon in the church at Wychehill, when he'd used those exact words, recalling the lethal focus you acquired in the Regiment.

...a frenzy of pure excitement... I understand the rush you get when you convince yourself that, in the great scheme of things, it's not only justified but necessary. When you know that a difficult

situation can only be resolved by an act of swift, efficient, intense and quite colossal violence.

God…

Merrily was jerked back against the stone by a shuddering in a pocket of her jeans. She fumbled out the mobile.

There was no sound for a couple of seconds, wonky signal, then Fiona's voice.

'You're there, aren't you?'

'Brinsop. At the church.'

'Alone?'

'Yes.'

'I'd better tell you,' Fiona said.

36

The Having Done It

MERRILY TOOK THE phone outside and stood by the grave of the Wordsworths' faithful servant Jane Winder. Looking across to the possible moat, the clutch of trees on what might be an island, the viridian march of conifers up the flank of Credenhill.

'There was a party,' Fiona said. 'A publication party. Not for Byron: one of the other better-known SAS authors, a friend of Sam's, so although he didn't like parties much he thought we should go. And there were a lot of people there that Sam hadn't seen in years, so he was doing a fair bit of catching up. Are you still there?'

'I'll try and improve the signal.'

Merrily moved up to the high ground behind the church, overlooking lumped and tiered fields where a village might once have stood. The signal had moved up to two stars.

'When was this?'

'About a month after the book was burned. I hadn't been feeling well that night, and Sam was talking to his old mates, so I slid away and sat down at a table on my own. And then Byron was there. Not Liz, just Byron. Sam was conspicuously avoiding him, but he came up to me. Very charming and attentive. Very smooth and elegant in his Heathcliff way. Got me a brandy and sat down. Said he didn't know what he was doing here, he'd never particularly liked… the author we were supposed to be celebrating, and his book was rubbish.'

'This was in London?'

'No, it was a country-house hotel, in Buckinghamshire. We'd decided to stay there, so Sam could have a few drinks. All free – the publishers were spending a lot of money on this guy at the time. A lot more than had ever been spent on Byron, anyway, and he seemed to be taking it as a personal slight. But he was very nice to me. Coming out with all sorts of bullshit. How he wished he had a wife like me, who understood.'

'Understood what?'

'Oh, you know, what it was like leaving the Regiment. Having to slow down your metabolism… all this. His metabolism didn't seem to have slowed at all. He was very intense, whatever he was talking about, very *concentrated*. Much, I suppose, as you'd imagine he'd be on some operation behind enemy lines. In fact, I remember thinking perhaps that was how he saw this party. Someone else's wealthy publisher, someone else's inferior book. As though he was at war with other writers who'd been in the Regiment. The underdog, because his was a kids' book.'

'This was before Harry Potter, I presume.'

'Probably. There was a tremendous… frustration there. Pretty soon, he's pouring out his troubles, and I'm trying to be sympathetic.'

'Wife didn't understand him?'

'Wife didn't understand anything. Wife was completely bovine. After a while, I was starting to find it repellent. Self-pity I can handle – it was the venom I didn't like.'

'Against Liz?'

'Against *life*. Anyway… as I said, I really wasn't feeling terribly well that night. Eventually I excused myself and went to the loo and then went out for a breath of air. In the grounds, which were extensive, though not remote like you get round here. You could always hear traffic. And he was there.'

'Where?'

'Emerging from the bushes, as though he was on an exercise. The exercise being… *I* was the exercise, I— God, I can't believe I'm telling somebody about this with Sam lying in a mortuary. It makes me feel sick. I feel sick now, and I felt sick then.'

'He was drunk?'

'No, I don't actually think he was. I don't think he needed to be. I wish I could explain what I mean by that. It was as though the... the night had released something in him. Sorry, that sounds stupid.'

'Not to me. Go on.'

'When I said I wasn't feeling well, he put an arm around me and said some air might help, and he walked me away from the terrace. Down across the lawns, away from the floodlit area. What could I do? He'd been a friend. He said he wanted to talk to me. Seriously. Very focused. He told me Sam was making a terrible mistake in going into the church, that he was throwing away his life and damaging his country, and if I didn't want a life of misery I should stop him. Or leave him.'

'Bloody hell, Fiona...'

'He said Sam was an idiot who didn't deserve me. And a coward. He actually said Sam was a *coward*. And when I opened my mouth to protest, he... his lips were there. And he started to touch me. Fondle me. As if it was the most natural thing in the world? And I'm going, No, thank you, Byron, let's go back now. I was pretty terrified, naturally. Also terrified that Sam would find us.'

A pause. Merrily moved back towards the car.

'That's not... how it seems,' Fiona said. 'I knew that if Sam had found us, what would've happened... it would've ended in some appalling violence.'

'But Sam was becoming a priest...'

'He was *trying* to become a priest. He'd had long talks with other priests. Used to say there were aspects of himself he'd have to... alter if it was going to work. There'd've been no turning of cheeks here, would there?'

'What did you—?'

'I mean, it wouldn't've mattered who came to the rescue,

would it? The result would be the same. Do you know what I mean? Sooner or later it would involve Sam in violence. These guys, that was the only way it could ever be resolved. I'm not saying it's the only language they understand, or that they're stupid and mindless, but Byron…'

Fiona broke off, as if she was trying to rethink this, to see if there was any other way it might be viewed.

'Byron, the way he was that night… it seemed to me, in those moments, that that was what he wanted. He wanted Sam to come for him. He wanted an excuse to release some kind of animalistic rage.'

'You mean at Syd, or just…?'

'I mean that he wasn't attracted to *me*, as such… it was because I was Sam's wife.'

'Jesus.'

'There was a real kind of… a real evil about it, I suppose. That is, an emptiness – a hole where love and humanity should be? Is that evil?'

'Oh, yes.'

The clouds had gulped up the sun. Merrily, starting to shiver, walked down through the little gate and stepped down towards the car. The fields looked raw and winter-stripped.

'So… what happened?'

Convinced that Fiona, unprompted, would simply not have finished the story.

'I didn't resist him. He had me against the side of a garage block, and I didn't resist.'

'He raped you.'

'It was over very quickly. It was, for him, I think, not so much the doing it as the *having done it*. What I remember most was the sound of his breath. A hollow sound. As though he was drawing breath from somewhere else. Afterwards, he just said goodnight. I don't think he even remembered my name.'

'You've never told anyone?'

'You're the first.'

One in a million.
Barry had said that.

Merrily smoked half a cigarette, put on her coat and went back into the church.

Byron's church.

Up to the glittery chancel, but it didn't feel right. She walked back down the nave and across to the Romanesque stone tympanum. St George spearing a snake-like dragon. An untypical St George in a kind of pleated skirt. *Essential violence.*

Fiona had said she'd gone back into the hotel through another door. Gone upstairs to their room and locked herself in and showered for a long time and put on fresh make-up and a different dress. Syd had been looking for her. She told him she hadn't been well. She said she'd been sick and had had to change.

All that night, her skin had felt greasy and she'd had a filthy taste at the back of her throat.

Merrily thought about Denzil Joy, found she was breathing far too fast and became aware that on the wall opposite her, above the church door, another act of violence was evoked in smoke.

She stood staring at it, uncomprehending for a few moments, taking several long breaths before approaching it across the space at the back of the nave.

It was not smoke. Nor was it imagination. She stopped, flipping feverishly through the leaflet.

The 13th century wall painting above the door is of The Crucifixion.

Like most wall paintings, there wasn't much left. Could have been a dampness stain, like the grey monk in Huw's chapel.

Two pains... the first wrought to the drying while his body was moist, and that other slow, with blowing of wind from without...

All the colours gone. The cross gone. He was a corpse or very nearly, drained of all resistance. His head, dead weight, had collapsed into an elbow. His body was brittle as a chrysalis, flaking into the wall.

37

Loaded

FOUR-THIRTY. TOO QUIET in the CID room. An air of getting nowhere.

'Boss, you're dead on your feet,' Karen said. 'Go home, eh?'

'I'm all right. Just sick of drawing blanks. Not even as if it's a wall of silence.'

Bliss quite liked a wall of silence. Justified the use of a wrecking ball. Problem here was that once you were over the language barriers the Bulgarians, Romanians, Lithuanians, Poles would tell you anything you wanted. All of them shattered by the East Street atrocity. Not an enemy in the world, these girls. Clean-living, religious. Just wanted to make some money to send home.

Men? Of course not. They were inseparable, anyway. The prevailing opinion now was that they'd somehow, perhaps innocently, offended one of the criminal gangs. That the men seen by Carly and Joss in the Monk's Head were hard-core. Following the sisters out, pretending to fancy them, that was just an act.

'Something will give,' Karen said. 'On the third day, something always gives. Now, please, will you go home? Me and Darth can hold it together till the morning. Have a big glass of whisky and go to bed. Anything breaks, we'll send a car for you?'

'Yeah,' Bliss said.

'Now, boss? Straight home?'

'I'm gonna make a call first. I'll be in my office.'

In the office he didn't quite shut the door and stood by the gap, out of sight, listening. But nobody seemed to be talking about the DI beating up his wife and nobody's expression changed when he walked back in, claiming he'd left his chewy behind.

Bliss sat down and put in a call to Jeremy Berrows, who farmed beyond Kington, where Herefordshire met the paler hills of Radnorshire. Jeremy lived with a lot of sheep and a lot of sheep-dogs. Also with a beautiful woman called Natalie, who was known to the police from way, way back, but it was all right now.

'You sounds a bit on edge, Mr Bliss,' Jeremy said.

He was what people called an *old-fashioned* kind of farmer, open to superstitions and signs and portents. A haloed moon, three magpies, the ash out before the oak, all that. Jeremy thought his land confided in him.

Bliss said, 'You've got Mansel Bull's dogs, I believe. All of them.'

'They're a gang. He didn't wanner split them up. Problem with that?'

'We're talking to everybody who'd had dealings with Mansel.'

'Wasn't exactly a deal. Bit of an agreement, that's all, between two blokes as knew a bit about dogs and sheep. Not everybody got along with Mansel, but he looked after his dogs.'

'And you came and took them after he died.'

'Before. Just as well. His brother woulder stopped it. Trained dog's worth money. Or mabbe he'd've had the whole bunch shot.'

'What?'

'Mabbe that's unfair,' Jeremy said.

'See, apart from the inhumanity of that, Jeremy, it would indicate a fairly strong element of not exactly honouring his brother's memory.'

Jeremy didn't reply. Bliss liked the sound of the silence. He'd once listened to the lovely Natalie at the right time, and whilst Jeremy didn't exactly *owe* him...

'Word is,' Bliss said, 'that Sollers wasn't too pleased when Mansel sold that ground. Any whispers about that?'

'Don't go much on whispers. Too many of 'em round yere's been about me and Nat. As you know.'

'How is she?'

'Good.'

How many local people knew about Natalie's time in detention was debatable. The probability was that the gossip was just about how a little woolly-haired farmer held on to a serious beauty from Off. But it was unlikely either of them would ever be able to relax.

'Jeremy, you're a straight sort of bloke, as farmers go, so I'll be straight with you. I think there's quite a lot Sollers Bull hasn't told us. I accept you don't listen much to gossip, but how did you *feel* things were between Mansel and Sollers?'

'Different generations, different attitudes. Mansel was a businessman in the ole sense. Tight as a duck's arse, but you knowed where you was. Sollers is all for the image. Puttin' hisself around. Prize cattle at the Royal Welsh, diversifyin', farm shops and cafés. Huntin'. I was at school with him for a few years. Lady Hawkins.'

'And what was he like at school?'

'Head boy.'

'Figures. See, I'm guessing Mansel would *realize* Sollers wouldn't be too keen on him flogging that ground to the fruit farm. So why'd Mansel do it? Bit of pique, maybe?'

'No, no, that wasn't it at all, he...'

Jeremy sounded uncertain again, like he was worried about breaking a confidence.

'He's dead, Jeremy. He was killed. It was *mairder*. Remember?'

'Wasn't going well, that's all. The dogs. Mansel thought mabbe he was losin' it.'

'What, his marbles?'

'His skill. Had three shelves full of awards. Come close to winning *One Man and His Dog* on the box, once. Then it wasn't workin' n'more. Used to train his dogs down by the river, but

Sollers wanted more ground for his cattle, and he had to move up to the top field. Not used much for stock, usually they just had the hay off it. And it wasn't the same. Seemed obvious to me it wasn't the dogs, but he was losin' heart. Mansel, either he was on top or he didn't wanner know – got that much in common with Sollers, at least.'

'I'm not sure what you're saying, Jeremy.'

'Couldn't hack it. Dogs was all over the place some days. He'd give a command, dog'd go for it real slow. Or run off, back down to the river. Couldn't count on 'em. He was gettin' real depressed. Thought it was his age. Got so he didn't wanner take the dogs out n'more.'

'So you got all these valuable dogs for nothing from a man who's known for being tight as a duck's arse?'

'Too many dogs is more of a burden than anything, Mr Bliss. We agreed mabbe he'd have 'em back one day. I told him I reckoned it wasn't about him and it wasn't about his dogs. They works fine yere. Poetry.'

'I'm not getting this.'

'You're a copper, Mr Bliss. Nobody 'spects you to get it. Had to be a reason them top fields wasn't used much – and that was how it was for years. Generations, mabbe. I had a walk over it when I went to fetch the dogs. Some places, the air feels loaded. A place looks quiet, but it en't. A lot of ravens, too, for some reason.'

'Ravens.' Bliss thought about this, and it was Vasile Bocean all over again. 'You know what, Jeremy?' he said. 'I'm tired.'

He sat at his desk for several minutes. All right, raised a Catholic and, whatever anybody said, you never lost that and all the baggage. And what Jeremy had been hinting at – feelings, atmosphere – he wouldn't entirely rubbish any of it. Privately. In the midnight hour. It was just nothing to do with police work. It didn't help.

He got up and stood by his window. The sky was like the inside of an orange peel. The light nights were coming. Didn't like them any more, dark was best, watching the lights going out across the road, on the hill above Great Malvern.

Colleagues only. The way those words had been pinballing round his head all day. Telling himself she didn't mean it, she'd come round. He'd find some way of bringing her round. Have to. Couldn't lose this. Couldn't let it just come apart like a cheap supermarket bag.

Somehow, he had to get Kirsty to refute any suggestion that he'd ever abused her physically. She could call him any kind of shit as long as she told the truth about that, sent it back up the line.

Bliss pulled out his iPhone, checked his incomings. No e-mails of any consequence, just the one phone message.

Annie Howe. Thank Christ. Bliss clicked on it. Annie's voice was very low, but not so low the words weren't metallically distinct.

'Didn't think I could be surprised any more at the level of your blind stupidity.'

Bliss clapped the phone tight to his ear, both hands around it in case anybody came in.

'Don't know how you could have thought for one minute that I wouldn't find out. Your wife. Your own bloody wife.'

Deadness for several seconds.

'Anyway,' Annie said, *'That's it.'*

End of message.

Bliss wrenched the phone away from his ear, stabbed at the screen to call her back. All right, no, he *couldn't* explain why he hadn't told her about Kirsty's suspicions, except to say that he hadn't believed the bitch, couldn't imagine how she could possibly know about Annie. *Still* didn't know.

Annie's phone was switched off.

Bliss stared at the iPhone, all the little symbols, the ten thousand useless friggin' apps. Rubbed the cold sweat from his forehead.

So who had the bitch told?

He strode out of the office, through the CID room without

speaking to anybody, down the stairs and out of the building, his face and the back of his neck feeling like they were badly sunburned.

38

The Energy of Sorrow

LOL WATCHED MERRILY collapse back into his sofa. Late sun honeying the room, red veins pulsing among the ashes at the bottom of the woodstove. As so often these days, Merrily looked vacant, wiped-out.

'So where do I go from here?'

Lol was thinking maybe a new career. It was a crap job, the clergy, and no indication it would ever get better. So much open contempt now. The Church, God, the afterlife – all delusion. Thinking it and getting a buzz out of saying it, loudly, in public, on TV, and the only people who shouted back were the crazy fundamentalists like his late parents who'd cut him out of their lives.

Merrily had come home this afternoon to find the answering machine going, Uncle Ted, the churchwarden, trying to lean on her, before tonight's parish meeting, about his plans to turn the church into a greasy spoon. It was about paying bills.

The bleeping of the answering machine had chased her out of the house and across the road in search of sanctuary. *I think I need help*, she'd said, and they'd talked for an hour, sharing an omelette and toast. She'd told him about last night's visit from James Bull-Davies and everything she'd learned about a man called Byron Jones. From Barry, from Jones's ex-wife and, finally, Syd's wife, Fiona.

'You believe this man raped her?'

'You think it's something she'd invent?'

'But she didn't go to the police. Or to anyone.'

'Syd would've killed him.'

'And now he's dead, does Mrs Spicer want you to *do* something about this?'

'I'm not sure.'

Lol sat down next to Merrily.

'How would she feel about you simply dumping it all on Bull-Davies? Who asked you to share.'

'She wouldn't like that. I'm only telling you because I know it won't go out of this house. I mean, who *is* William Lockley? Why does he want the information? Does he want to use it or suppress it? Who am I working for?'

'So tell Bull-Davies what you've heard about Jones without naming names. And then back off.'

'Can't now. Not with Syd's funeral.'

'That,' Lol said, 'was a mistake.'

He slid off the sofa, gathered up two logs from the hearth, opened the stove and put them in. Watching the fire seizing one, thinking of the insatiable furnace in a crematorium, where quickie funerals were conducted by a duty vicar who'd never met the customer.

And this... *this* was the summation of a life, Merrily would protest. Where was the electricity, the surge of transition, the smoothing of the final earthly path by the subtle energy of sorrow? No wonder some of them didn't rest. She didn't do quickies. A properly conducted funeral needed the history. Bottom line: if she'd felt an obligation to Syd before, now it was cast in bronze.

'What was I supposed to say? No, thanks, best to find somebody who doesn't give a toss? Lol, it's like he's haunting me. The way he showed up at the chapel. I keep hearing that flat voice in my head when I'm not expecting it. "Samuel Dennis Spicer, Church of England". Smell his cigarette smoke in church.'

'Isn't there a term for that?'

'Psychological projection?'

'Arising from guilt. Self-recrimination,' Lol said. 'Misplaced.'

'No, this is something else.' Merrily stood up, walked to the window, looked across the cobbles at the vicarage. 'He was taking steps to protect himself against something he considered evil. He goes out on Credenhill with a Bergen full of Bible, as if he knows he isn't coming back. And he leaves these books behind like clues to something. One pointing directly at a man who went from good friend to bitter enemy.'

'Just do a meaningful funeral. Pray for both their souls or something.'

'Sure.' She smiled. 'Walk away. Credenhill's twenty minutes down the road.'

'And always go the other way to Hereford.'

Lol had planned to tell her, finally, about Jane and Cornel and the cockfighting, but that would be too much for her to handle. Needed to deal with that himself. At least with Danny and Gomer on the case he felt better about it. Get the evidence, share it with Jane, then take it to the RSPCA and the police. Let Jane take the credit if it worked out; shield her from repercussions if it didn't.

He sat down on the hearthrug, looking up at Merrily on the sofa. She looked small, vulnerable, and there must be something he could do.

'OK,' he said. 'Why don't we try and work this out?'

'Don't have much time. Parish meeting at seven. Maundy service tomorrow. Chrism mass at the Cathedral – I'm not going to make that this year. Why does Easter always come at the wrong time?'

'Does Barry know anything about this?'

'I don't think Barry's told me everything he knows. I don't think he knows about the rape, but he does think Byron's a dangerous man. Warned me not to try and talk to him.'

'But you still went to find him.'

'No… I just went to the church because there was clearly something there that fascinated him. He must've spent virtually everything he had buying that land.'

'Where he now stages war games behind barbed wire?' Lol leaned back against an inglenook wall. 'The rift between him and Syd – what was that about?'

'All we know for sure is that he hated Syd becoming an ordained priest. Byron's own religious beliefs, if he had any, appear to have been pagan. Saw himself as a Celt, like his hero Caradog. Locked away in his tower room, turning himself into Caradog. Leaving Caradog's... ambience.'

'If I've got this right,' Lol said, 'Caradog held out against the Romans until he was betrayed and captured and taken to Rome. Where his oratory made him a celeb. A hero.'

'But Byron's fictional story seems to deviate. He's not inter-ested in oratory. His Caradog has to impress the Romans with his military skills. Which are obviously akin to SAS methods. I called in at the bookshop to see what the chances were of getting his other books, but Amanda says they're out of print.'

'And Caradog was a druid?'

'He worked *with* druids. According to the stories.'

'What might Jones have been doing, then, in that tower room?'

'Maybe meditation, visualization. To focus his mind for the writing.'

'And the smell?'

'I don't even want to think about the smell.'

'Did Syd know Byron was at Brinsop, when he took on the job?'

'That's the interesting question. I'd say he did. My feeling is that he always knew where Byron was, at any given time. When Byron was at Allensmore, Syd went to see him, maybe to try and sort something out... but maybe not. "They're all dead," he's saying. "All dead now." Who did he mean?'

Merrily spread her hands in defeat.

Lol said, 'Would Syd have known, do you think, the reason Byron wanted to live at Brinsop? Or at least have an idea?'

'Let's assume he did. Let's also assume there a connection with this very unusual church, which Byron kept photographing from the air.'

'How would he *do* that?'

'Not a problem in this area. He'd know people with private planes. Helicopters. A lot of the SAS had contacts with Shobdon airfield. Recreational. Parachute clubs, all this.'

'It's just that aerial photography might suggest the site of the church is more important than the church itself,' Lol said.

'And lines. He'd drawn lines across the aerial photos.'

'Woooh… leys?'

'Possibly. Not saying a word to Jane. I don't want her within five miles of Byron Jones.'

'Leys, if they exist, are pre-Celtic,' Lol said. 'Bronze Age or earlier.'

'I'm just telling you what Liz said.'

'I'd quite like to look at Byron's book sometime.'

'It's in my bag.' Merrily gathered it up from the floor and stood. 'In fact, they're all here. I'll leave you the Wordsworth, too. Any perceptions, flashes of inspiration… would be very welcome.'

'Merrily…' Just inside the door, he grabbed hold of her, hugged her, hard. 'I'm *sorry*…'

'What for, exactly?'

She kissed him and he felt a quiver in her.

'Been letting things slide,' he murmured. 'When something's finally paying the mortgage, you tend to go at it round the clock in case it doesn't last. And you forget what's really important.'

'At least you don't have God on your back. Swan later?'

Lol opened the front door. Up the street, at the Eight Till Late, Jim Prosser was taking in his paper rack. A news bill said: HEREFORD HORROR.

Lol watched Merrily walking back to the vicarage. The voice in his head sang, *Do something*. But he didn't know where to start.

39

Seer Takes Fire

THE BLOOD ON the book cover was embossed, glossy-bubbled against the background's matt black and greys and the white title.

CARADOG

They came, they saw...

Lol took it over to the desk in the window, flipping through for any local place names. Nothing he recognized immediately, but it was, after all, fiction.

> *He took the legionnaire from behind. A thrust to the spine and then, as the man fell back, moved around and hacked off his head from the front, a practised upward stroke. They were easy meat, most of them, mercenaries who'd never seen Rome. They obeyed orders and understood discipline – he'd give them that. But they lacked the ability to think for themselves or operate in small units. And, as lowly foot soldiers, they were not attuned to the higher energies known to the elite and now, at last, known to Caradog, who felt them rising like fire from the pit of his gut. A fire kindled from the sun itself.*

Cartoon violence. Kids loved this stuff, but they'd probably turn off at the first mention of *higher energies*. Lol scanned several chapters, finding two more references to Caradog drawing energy from the sun, at one stage holding up his sword to catch the light before going calmly into battle and efficiently slaying a large number of Romans.

Druids worshipped the sun.

It was a start. Lol opened up his laptop, put Google on the case. There was modern druidry, the religious arm of Greenpeace, and there was the kind the Romans had known, altogether darker, with animal and possibly human sacrifice. But the Roman accounts might have been propaganda.

He Googled Wordsworth and Brinsop. Quite a lot. Wordsworth had been Poet Laureate when he was holidaying at Brinsop Court.

And then the Net, as occasionally happened, threw up an unexpected link – not to Brinsop but somewhere not far away – which sent Lol back to the small green book: *Wordsworth's Britain: a little itinerary.*

He found it tucked in after 'Tintern Abbey'. A poem commemorating:

ROMAN ANTIQUITIES DISCOVERED
AT BISHOPSTONE, HEREFORDSHIRE

WHILE poring Antiquarians search the ground
Upturned with curious pains, the Bard, a Seer,
Takes fire:—The men that have been reappear;
Romans for travel girt, for business gowned;
And some recline on couches, myrtle-crowned,
In festal glee: why not...

The poem was dated 1835 and carried a note from Wordsworth describing its inspiration: a Roman pavement discovered only yards from the front door of Bishopstone parsonage:

in full view of several hills upon which there had formerly been Roman encampments

Doubtless including Credenhill, with its Iron Age fort. In Wordsworth's day, any kind of camp might be considered Roman.

Lol put a block of ash on the stove and dug into the shelves for an OS map: *Hereford, Leominster and surrounding area.* Cleared his desk and opened out the map to the area west of Hereford.

It brought an invisible landscape into existence in various archaic fonts and symbols.

ROMAN ROAD (course of)

Again and again: Roman roads either side of the Wye. One skirting Credenhill. Under the hill was Brinsop, the church marked only by a small + but earthworks and moat nearby signifying an area of extreme antiquity.

Bishopstone, a hamlet with a church, was no distance from Brinsop. Directly east of it, two more Roman roads made a kind of V-formation into the point of which was tucked something identified on the map as RAF Hereford. Which could only be the SAS camp. Just before the Roman roads converged on

MAGNIS (ROMAN TOWN)

the ruins of which, according to several Internet sites, had still been visible in recorded memory. Much of the masonry had gone into the foundations of Hereford. By 1772, the antiquarian William Stukely was discussing a fine mosaic floor unearthed at Kenchester and the remains of a temple, and also noting that one Colonel Dantsey had paved his cellar with Roman bricks.

Around the original Roman army camp there had been evidence of streets and shops. The remains of a shrine had been uncovered near the Wye, part of a villa found in the river itself.

Lol went through to his kitchen for a glass of water, digesting the key point: the SAS, quite recently, had moved its head-quarters from Hereford itself to a former RAF base at the convergence of two Roman roads serving a Roman military base.

Back to the roots.

Brinsop Church, however, was part of a different story. He remembered it now. Remembered a wet Sunday when he and Jane had been enthusiastically defacing another copy of this same map, circling every stone, mound, cross and old church, marking up every conceivable alignment of prehistoric sites and then checking them out to see if they'd found anything that Alfred Watkins had missed. Alfred Watkins of Hereford, the original Simple Trackway Man on whom Lol and Danny had based the song. Whom Jane claimed for an ancestor.

Lol pulled down his copy of *The Old Straight Track*, Watkins's masterpiece, the book which, long after his death, had sent generations of Brits – young hippies, old hippies, pre-hippies, post-hippies like Lol, *post* post-hippies like Jane out into the countryside, to find the stones and mounds and mysterious church formations that lit up an alternative Britain.

OK, most archaeologists rubbished the idea, but it was still exciting to think of being surrounded by ancient landscape patterns, which also drew in churches because so many of them had been built on sites of prehistoric pagan worship. You saw church towers and steeples, you saw four thousand years of ritual.

And, in the middle, the Romans.

Alfred Watkins had suggested that the Roman roads had often followed the old straight tracks – in his view more by design than accident, as if the Romans had merely widened existing prehistoric routes. Lol felt a twitch of connection. He'd known that, of course. Even worked it into 'The Simple Trackway Man'.

From moat to mound we'll mark the ground
From barrow to camp we'll carry the lamp
From Roman road to trader's track
And over the pitch and all the way back.

Interesting to think this guy Byron, a man who could rape a friend's wife, might have been on the same trail, fascinated by the same magic landscape.

He'd drawn lines across the aerial photos.

Lol found a pencil and, using the edge of *The Old Straight Track* as a ruler, drew in three of the lines that he and Jane had found radiating from Brinsop Church, one linking it with four other medieval churches.

Brinsop Church was on a site of some significance and, although it was only a few miles away, he'd never even seen it.

The sun was low in the sky over Ledwardine, but there were a good two hours of daylight left to find what could be found. Lol picked up his car keys, went out to his truck.

Two hours.

40

Magic Dragon

BRINSOP CHURCH WAS locked now. Maybe the smoking ghost of Syd Spicer was inside, waiting there in motionless, crampless silence, the way the SAS could. Waiting for a signal.

Lol moved among the graves through the soft light. The bell tower was crisp against the cooling sky, the giant conifer black, like a knobbly monolith.

It didn't matter that the church was locked. Outside, the landscape had revealed itself. The Ordnance Survey map was opened out in his head, the lines drawn in.

At the end of the short grass, before the woodland began its march up Credenhill, you could see, like an entrance to the underworld, what the OS map identified as moat. Alfred Watkins thought some moats might have been dug not for protection but to mark the tracks by reflecting sunlight or beacon fire or lamplight.

Lol had looked across the dark stain of the moat to the wooded thigh of Credenhill, imagining the pale essences of long-gone villagers walking the spirit paths that intersected here. Syd Spicer following some distance behind, cautiously adjusting to being dead.

In the adjacent field, a stile gave access to a squat monolith on top of a circular stone slab with a metal drain cover set into it. On the stone it said *The Dragon Well*. As it was unlikely that a dragon had died here, what did it actually mean?

Half an hour ago, standing at the side of the lane somewhere around Kenchester, Lol had gazed out over the fields which enclosed the ghost of the Roman town. He'd seen isolated farms and, further away, on the higher ground, the frames of this year's polytunnels spreading like worm-casts.

He'd driven past the SAS camp with its armed guards. A military base built close to, maybe even on top of, the buried remains of another. What could *that* mean? What could it mean to Byron Jones?

A cyclist was bobbing along the lane, dipping periodically behind the hedge, heading this way. Lol waited. The man wheeled the bike to the dead end of the track. He was thin and bearded, maybe in his early sixties, wearing a scarf and a flat cap.

'Nice truck,' he said. 'Animal or Warrior?'

'Animal.'

A match flared. The guy applied it to a roll-up.

'Used to have one meself. Comfy, for a truck.'

He looked like an archetypal peasant, therefore obviously from Off.

'On your own, mate?'

'It's what country churchyards are for,' Lol said. 'Being alone.'

'Not so much these days. One of the finest St George churches in England, this, but who bovvers now?'

The guy checked him out again, then took a step back.

'Hang about... I fink... stone me! I was at your gig. In the floods? At Ledwardine? Hey... how cool is this?'

Lol smiled, a bit bashful. This never used to happen at all, but it had occurred a dozen or so times since Christmas. Local recognition: a mixed blessing.

'Forget what I said,' the guy said. 'This is *exactly* the right setting for you, Lol. There should be a soundtrack. *Sunny Days*?'

The edges of his Londonish accent were rounded off, as if he'd been living here a good while.

'Well, you know, that was a long time ago,' Lol said.

'Well, I had it first time around, I'm proud to say. Hazey Jane. First album I ever bought by a band a good bit younger than me. Big fing, that, when you first accept younger guys can get it right. Seventeen, was you?'

'Another lifetime,' Lol said.

The guy put out a hand.

'Arthur Baxter. Bax. I live a mile or so back there, over the pitch. Still come here most nights, on me bike. Meet the dragon.'

'Uh-huh.'

'You feel his breath?'

'Like a blow-heater?'

'Exactly.' Bax grinned. 'You know the story?'

'Um… no. You got time?'

'Got all night, mate – the missus is rehearsing a community play, down the leisure centre at Credenhill. Dragon's drinking at the well, right? George comes down off of Credenhill, lookin' for trouble. Slash, slash, spear downa froat, all over.' Bax took a meditative drag. 'You out here looking for inspiration, Lol? If you're not, don't spoil it for me. I wanna point to a song one day and go, *I was there when he got that one.*' Bax drew deeply on his cigarette, offered it to Lol. 'Try this? It ain't bad.'

A certain sweetness drifting up. More than one kind of dragon. Lol smiled, shook his head, nodded at the truck. Bax assured Lol that he'd been biking these lanes, pleasantly stoned, for the best part of two decades, never once been stopped.

'Tell you how far back this all goes,' Bax said. 'If we could get into the church you'd see this old stone slab with a picture carved on it of St George and the dragon. Only George is wearing like a skirt? Which means somebody seen him either as a cross-dresser or a Roman soldier – you know the little whatsits they had, wiv the belt?'

'St George is portrayed as a Roman?'

'Well, that's the answer, innit? That's what it's about. It's the Romans slaughtering the Celts. You really here for inspiration?'

Lol told Bax about 'The Simple Trackway Man'. Which could use another verse. Bax was delighted, clapped his hands.

'A lot of Roman stuff around here, too,' Lol said. 'Or there used to be. I was reading this poem by Wordsworth. "The men that have been reappear".'

'Yeah, yeah, I know it. Often wonder… did he *see* them?' Bax waved his spliff. 'Bigger than they know, that Roman town. Me and the missus found maybe a dozen coins down the years.'

'And the men who reappear?'

Bax shuffled around, prodded a tyre on his bike.

'I live in hope.'

Lol said, 'Ever come across a bloke called Byron Jones?'

'Round here? Should I have?'

'I think he lives in a caravan. Or he did.'

'Oh…' Bax blew out smoke. 'You mean *Colin* Jones?'

'Probably do.'

'He don't live in the caravan no more. Got permission for a bungalow on the edge of his land. The Compound. Nice, too. Swimming pool.'

'Compound?'

'That's what it looks like. All that high barbed-wire fencing. Don't *know* him, exactly. We are *acquainted*. He does intensive fitness training. Got a gym in there and an assault course where you swing over a pond on a rope, that kinda caper. You know him?'

'Know *of* him.'

'Ex-Sass. And then he was a minder. Quite well fought of, in these parts.' Bax sniffed. 'As they are, the Sass.'

'People like you… ever go on these courses?'

'Me? Nah. Wouldn't be able to afford it. Though occasionally Mr Jones offers a one-day crash-course sort of thing to local boys, for nothing. Excellent for local relations.' Bax took a long, noisy pull on his spliff, now down to a fragment. 'Blimey, that din't last long, did it?'

Lol smiled.

'I was wondering if that wasn't the dragon you came here to meet.'

'The Magic Dragon. Poor ole thing, he ain't too welcome at home no more, not since the missus joined the WI. When we first come here and she wore cheesecloth, we grew it in the dingle. Gotta pay for it now, in town. But, tell you one thing, Mr Lol… it ain't slowed my brain enough that I can't tell you're fishing for som'ink? Nah, nah…' Bax held up his hands like saucers. 'I don't wanna *know*, mate. You wanted me to know, you'd tell me, wou'n'cha?'

Lol didn't know what to say. It was an odd, dreamlike encounter, Brinsop Church snuggling into its shadows behind them, only its bell tower showing like a periscope.

'To be honest,' he said, 'I'm not quite sure what I'm looking for. But a new verse for the song would make it worthwhile.'

Bax said, 'What about the fings what reappear?'

'I thought you hadn't seen them.'

'I know a bloke who has,' Bax said. 'You interested?'

41

Pain

IT WAS STILL fully light when Bliss reached the entrance to Chris Symonds's farm, so he drove past, crawled around the lanes for a while. Needed to be sure the kids were in bed.

He drove out towards Moreton-on-Lugg, through the flatlands, towards the western horizon.

Saw no way round this any more but to take her on. How the hell she'd found out about Annie he still had no idea, but if she knew, then she knew, and he was tired of playing games. He'd let her know that, yes, he was prepared to leave the division. He'd go on the transfer list directly after Easter. With the single proviso that the shit-stirring stopped.

As from now, as from tonight, any more lies about physical abuse, any whispers about him and Annie Howe... *anything*... and he'd flog his car and give his last penny to the flashest lawyer he could find to trash her through the courts and anywhere else she showed her devious little face.

Tell her now. On the doorstep. No discussion, no explanations, no attempts at self-justification. Then piss off back home, get the best night's sleep he could manage and throw himself into nailing the killers of the poor bloody Marinescu Sisters before he left Hereford.

Credenhill, rising like a crusty loaf across the shadowed fields, told him he was only a few miles from Magnis Berries, and he felt a pang of guilt about his behaviour there, the way he'd leaned on Vasile Bocean.

And yet…

Why did they leave, Vasile?

I told you. They always seeing dead men, ghostmen.

They were fired? Dismissed… for that?

They was causing upset. Bad vibes. Praying out loud. Lighting candles. Is fire risk! Health and Safety!

Vasile had said he thought they were, in the end, happy to take some money to go. Maybe they took the ghosts with them. Or maybe they didn't, all the murmurings that went on afterwards.

Bliss could hear Jeremy Berrows telling him about places where the air was *loaded* and Mansel's sheepdogs had become uncontrollable. He'd thought of going back, alone, to talk to Vasile again, man to man. But the problem was that when people's testimony bordered on the unlikely it negated everything else they'd told you, making them useless as witnesses. Guaranteed to get you laughed out of court.

He turned the car at the next junction and headed back to his father-in-law's farm.

Jane lit a candle on the altar and sat down in the choirmaster's chair.

She was alone, hadn't seen much of Mum tonight – parish meeting at the village hall, Uncle Ted, usual trivial crap, but at least it kept her out of the church.

The full preparation now, systematic relaxation.

Sitting upright, hands on knees, slowly sensing the body from the toes to the top of the head. It was getting a lot easier. Practice. Jane was finding she could almost slide into a relaxed state these days, without the tedious preliminaries.

Meditation: probably the only procedure which actually transcended all the halfway-workable religions. Of course, Jane only did this in here when she was sure she wouldn't be disturbed by Uncle Ted or some other tosser. Didn't want anyone to think she'd found Mum's God.

The Easter holiday had begun tonight. Tomorrow would be the first day of what was, in effect, the last school holiday she'd ever have. When the big summer holiday began, it wouldn't count because she'd have left school. Not a break, but a springboard into adult life. Whatever that was about.

Jane listened to her breathing. She'd brought along the copy of *Revelations of Divine Love* from Mum's desk. Mum had marked a section where Mother Julian was welcoming the sickness she'd contracted at the age of thirty, wanting it to bring her as close as possible to death. To know the reality of dying, in the hope this would cleanse her and bring about a spiritual rebirth. OK, a touch masochistic but this was not a woman who messed around. Maybe knowing there were some secrets you could only learn through pain. Jane went into some chakra breathing, a kind of energy conveyor belt, but soon lost the cycle. The body was still, but the mind wouldn't switch off.

She'd seen Cornel again tonight. He'd parked his Porsche on the square but, instead of going into the Swan, he'd followed his jutting chin down Church Street, like some zombie on the prowl, and she'd watched him enter the Ox, where the serious drinkers went. She'd almost gone after him – Mum would be in the village hall for at least two hours – but wasn't sure she was ready to handle it.

Had to be done right.

Getting off the school bus, she'd run into Gomer outside the Eight Till Late. He'd looked embarrassed. Admitting, as they walked down Church Street together, that he was getting nowhere. Talked to everybody he could think of, either side of the border, and, while some could remember when there *were* illegal cockfights, nobody knew of any happening hereabouts at present. Gamecocks were still being bred, but for collectors, poultry buffs, not for fights.

En't gived up, mind, Gomer had said. Jane didn't think he was optimistic. But, look, that was OK. That was actually good. It meant local people weren't involved. Now the finger of suspicion could only be pointing one way.

She knew a lot about cockfighting, now. Not something she'd ever wanted to study, but this was not a responsibility she could walk away from. She'd sat down in her apartment and spent nearly two hours on the Internet, downloading everything except the cockfight videos. Fights had been staged for over two thousand years and were still happening, mainly in the Far East, South America. Less publicly in the UK, where they'd first been introduced by Roman invaders.

Bastards. She couldn't stop thinking about the bird with the lion's mane.

But mainly she couldn't stop replaying what she'd heard last night, outside the kitchen door.

James Bull-Davies.

Complicated times, Mrs Watkins... what, with Savitch bidding to buy the Swan...

Dear God, the final insult. The oak-panelled Jacobean core of the community. How many people knew? Mum had obviously known already and taken a decision not to tell the kid. Hey, let's not have Jane doing something stupid. But she wasn't a bloody kid any more and whatever she did wouldn't be stupid.

Jane concentrated on her breathing, taking the air down to the solar-plexus chakra.

Preparation.

Curved bars of blackening cloud made the western sky look like an old ribcage as Bliss turned, like he had hundreds of times, along Chris Symonds's farm track.

In a glow of excitement, once upon a time, at the thought of seeing Kirsty, in tight black jeans and a straining top, waiting for him where the track forked by an ancient oak tree with a trunk wider than his car.

A dirt track in those days. Now it was tarmac. The real thing, not one of your itinerant-gang jobs that cracked up in weeks; this one was in better nick than the county roads. Possibly even quietly laid by a few of the same fellers, Bliss had heard. The word was that Chris was putting himself up for the council next time.

He turned left at the fork, driving slowly without lights, following the track leading to the stone outbuildings converted into classy stone holiday cottages, one of them currently occupied by Kirsty and the kids. Bliss slowed, did a tight three-point turn and parked on the grass verge a good distance away. Didn't want her looking out and recognizing his Honda and not answering the door.

Just as well. When he got out of the car, not fully closing the door to avoid the noise, he saw another vehicle, a light-coloured Discovery, half hidden on the edge of the pair of fat leylandii which separated the holiday cottages from the farmhouse and threw their front doors into evening shade.

No sign of Kirsty's Ka. Chris Symonds drove a Discovery; maybe she'd borrowed it to cart stuff around. Worst scenario would be that Chris and Pat were in there, in which case a mere exchange of bitter words would be the least he'd get away with.

Bliss was about four paces from the door when there was muffled click and then he was standing like a social-club compère in overlapping circles of garish lemon light.

He backed off sharpish. Who the hell had installed security spots?

A shadow crossed the upstairs window and he heard a muffled biffing – the heel of a hand repeatedly hitting a jammed window frame. And then, as it gave way, a voice from up there.

'... bloody thing. See, told you it was nobody. Not even the paparazzi.'

...trailed by a sound he hadn't heard in a good long while: Kirsty's little shocked-but-thrilled, plumped-out giggle.

Bliss crouched in the damp grass at the edge of the track until the security lights reached the end of their cycle and went out, and he could see the figure in the window, out of shadow up there.

The shock and the pain came sudden and vicious, like a knife-thrust in some clammy alleyway, as the setting sun showed him that the parts of Sollers Bull visible above the window frame were unclothed.

42

Don't Go There

It took a while to come out – it always did around here. The two brothers had been introduced by Bax as Percy and Walter. They lived in a small red-brick cottage, nineteenth-century, at the end of a row of modern houses and bungalows near Kenchester. They travelled in the slow lane. The silent Walter, who was probably over ninety, wore an apron and made the tea. Percy had never heard of anybody called Lol before.

'Short for Laurence,' Lol said.

He'd crawled up from Brinsop in the truck, behind a man on a bike.

'Well, well,' Percy said.

Walter handed Lol tea in a china cup. A low-wattage bulb, its brown flex hanging over a blackened beam, had probably been on all day. Coal was burning in an iron range. There was a TV set that had to be fifty years old and probably didn't work any more. The room smelled of… well, it smelled of old blokes.

'Lol writes songs,' Bax told Percy.

'Too many bloody songs, now. All sounds the same.'

Percy was a few years younger than Walter. His hair was white and curly.

'No, *proper* songs,' Bax said. 'Folk songs. Songs about life. And songs about things what goes on…' he winked at Lol '… that people don't talk about much no more.'

'Talk? They wanted me to give a talk, look,' Percy said.

'Women's Institute. Some woman comes round, asks me to give a *talk*.'

'That was my missus, Percy.'

'Wasn't gonner talk to a load o' women. They spreads stuff all over, women does. *And* they gets it wrong.'

'Always a problem with women,' Bax admitted.

'En't I don't *like* to talk.' Percy nodded at Walter. '*He* don't like to talk much, never has, look. I likes to talk, long as folks gets it right, what I tells 'em. Half the buggers, they don't listen proper, n'more.'

Bax nodded.

'Talks back, don't listen,' Percy said.

After a while he seemed to notice Lol, sitting on a stool by the door. Lol was listening. Percy nodded approvingly.

'Tell Lol what you seen in the long field that night,' Bax said.

In the feeble light, the already muted colours in the room had died back into a sombre sepia. Percy did some thinking.

'Wouldn't 'appen to 'ave any more o' that scenty baccy, would you, boy?' he said eventually.

Halfway down Church Street, Jane began to feel cold and a little stupid in the sawn-off white hoodie that she'd worn in the Swan the night she'd met Cornel. But he'd been pissed then and she needed him to recognize her.

Ready for this now. Knew exactly how she'd handle him. Sure he'd come out of the Ox at some point. Maybe he was here with his cockfighting mates. Eventually she went in and had a glance around.

Mistake.

'Watkins!'

Slobby Dean Wall at one of the gaming machines.

'Don't get excited, Wall,' Jane said calmly. 'I'm only looking for somebody.'

'Yeah.' Wall looked at her bare bits, sucking in his breath. 'It looks like you bloody are, too.'

Jane took a couple of steps inside. Stink of stale beer. Only the

Ox could sell beer that smelled stale when it was fresh out of the pump. Men's eyes were flickering her way from all corners of the cramped bar with its tobacco beams and stained flags. A barmaid was clearing glasses from a table. Six pint glasses in two hands, fingers down in the dregs, clinking. She looked up, and it was Lori Jenkin, who worked part-time in the Eight Till Late. Jane leaned over, lowered her voice.

'I'm looking for Cornel.'

'Your mum know about this, Jane?'

'Got a message for him, that's all. Somebody said he was in here.'

This was going all wrong. She needed to just, like, bump into him.

'I think he's in his room,' Lori said. 'I'm not sure.'

'He's *staying* here?'

The Ox had two spare bedrooms, which Jane understood were used mainly by sad downmarket commercial travellers too pissed to go back on the road. A guy with a Porsche staying here… that did not sound right.

Lori said, 'I'll get somebody to give him a knock, if you like.'

'*No…* No, it's OK. It's not urgent, I'll catch him again.'

Jane got out of the Ox under Dean Wall's soiled, beery gaze and stood there feeling like a prostitute, shivering. They always underdressed, apparently. This wasn't working. Give up for tonight, go home.

Rapid footsteps across the street and, oh jeez, it was Mum walking up from the village hall. Jane hung back, keeping close to the shadowed cottages. But, after a few paces, inevitably tonight, Mum looked back and saw her.

Jane walked up, hands jammed in her pockets to pull the hoodie down over the bare bits. How was she going to explain this?

'Meeting's over already?'

'Uncle Ted couldn't make it, so we had a fairly restricted agenda, thank God. Apparently, he, erm… tried to ring me earlier.' Mum glancing sideways at Jane, as they walked up to the empty square, taking in the skimpy apparel and then glancing away. 'Jane, look, I know it's none of my—'

'I needed to walk and think and stuff. Didn't realize how cold it was.'

They reached the square, with its tumble of black and white buildings, the weary lanterns coming on outside the Swan, soon to be owned by...

Jane's fists tightened.

'So,' Mum said, 'you were thinking. And stuff.'

'Last day of term. Last school holiday. The future.'

Everybody had been demob happy at school. Those facing A levels probably less so, but nobody quite as messed-up as she was.

Mum said, 'I'm not so old I don't remember what that's like. You've made a decision that could determine the rest of your life and you're thinking, God, have I done the right thing?'

'Oh.' Jane went to stand with her back to the open-sided, oak-pillared market hall. 'Like... most of the guys at school, they just can't wait to get the hell out of here and go to London. Or Paris or New York?'

'Sure.'

'Me, I don't even want to go to university.'

There. It was out.

'Ah,' Mum said. 'So that's it.'

'Three years? That's like...'

'Flower, compared with the rest of—'

'The rest of my life, yeah. It *is* actually about more than that, though, isn't it? And, like, for what? A degree means nothing any more. There's guys out there with PhDs who can't spell. Coops is Dr Cooper, and he just works for the council. And the... the forces of darkness are gathering. Hereford's already as good as gone. All crap superstores and charity shops and women getting murdered in the back streets...'

'Jane—'

'And if I leave... if I *go*... I'll come back and it'll all be shit here, too.' Jane felt the pressure of tears; hadn't intended to go this far. 'That sounds bonkers, doesn't it? So why do I keep waking up depressed and frightened?'

'Frightened, how?'

'Frightened that like in ten years or something I'm going to be looking back with this awful self-hatred because I didn't do what I should've done at the time.'

'Flower—'

'Yeah, I know, teenage angst. A phase. It's always a *phase*, isn't it? Well, how do you know for sure when it's a *phase*, Mum? Is it after you like walk away, live in a city, get a mortgage, get pregnant... *grow up*?'

'I don't know,' Mum said.

They were alone on the square. Only a faint wisp of the woodsmoke which used to scent the whole village. Jane felt like they were both enclosed in a cold vapour. Mum looked young and waiflike tonight, in her dark jeans and woolly, no dog collar, not even a pectoral cross. Like somebody who hadn't grown up after all. Who still knew nothing. It made Jane want to cry with despair.

'What about you? What about you and Lol? If Bernie Dunmore retires, and you get a bunch of extra parishes dumped on you... and Lol has to go back on the road because nobody's making money out of CDs any more... how long are you going to last as an item then?'

Actually crying now, couldn't help it.

'Let's go to the pub,' Mum said.

'What?'

'Let's go to the Swan and get a drink.'

Men who *had been* reappearing? Oh aye, Percy knowed about *them*. He sat in the ochre glow of the firelight and the haze of scenty baccy, and he talked and giggled as the small windows grew dim.

Walter had gone off somewhere. He'd doubtless heard it all before, these tales of the people who came up the fields in the river mist, no faces, no feet. Maybe Bax had, too, but he didn't seem to mind. He was an incomer, and the fact that someone like Percy would talk to him at all about such matters, even after thirty years, was clearly a source of pride to him.

Lol was thinking this was Percy's routine – his act, his gig, his repertoire, the tales told, rebored, remoulded over many years. What was interesting was the way the anomalies were mingled, some otherworldly and some just odd in an ordinary way. To Percy, there seemed to be no difference. The people who came up from the river, all he could say was that they were greyish and one had a bird's head, and sometimes you could see through them to the winter trees behind. Oh aye, he'd seen them on three occasions in his life, only for a few seconds, mind, each time. It was when you *didn't* see them that they were dangerous. When they got inside your tractor and fiddled about. That was how Harold Wilding had lost a leg, and he was lying there, a new furrow filling up with his blood and he reckoned he could hear them laughing.

Then Percy talked of lightless vans and trucks on the lanes after midnight. Men driven like sheep along the paths, over stiles. They had no faces either. And there were other things Percy had seen but couldn't talk about.

'Give him time,' Bax had murmured.

But there hadn't been time tonight. Bax had looked at the clock, coming up to half past ten, and said he needed to be off before his wife came back from her rehearsal. He left Percy a couple of baggies, on the sideboard, behind the clock, and they said goodnight.

'Course, he'll deny to the end of his days that he's the least bit superstitious,' Bax said. 'He was born here, like his old man, worked hard all his life on this ground, and these things were what happened now and then. Like gales and flooding. Nobody wrote to the papers about it.'

They were leaning on a fence behind Bax's cottage, looking out towards the darkening fields where villas had stood, with mosaic floors and perhaps bathhouses. And the rows of wooden barracks where the Roman squaddies slept – probably a bit like some of the huts occupied today by migrant workers on the fruit farms, Bax said, only with better facilities.

'The vehicles with no lights,' Lol said, 'and some of the men with no faces...'

'That's the Sass, innit? Anyfink odd happens round here, folks exchange glances, nod to one another... and say noffing. They don't question it. They're patriots. Whatever fings those boys get up to, it's done for Queen and country, for the security of us all, so that's all right, innit?'

'What sort of things?'

'Not entirely unknown for them to help themselves to a farmer's stock, is it, on an exercise? Dropped in the wilderness with no food, and you got to exist for whole days on what you can find in the hedgerows or trap and kill? Been known for them to lift the odd sheep, or a chicken from a farm. Some of the farmers, if they know where they are they give 'em a big fry-up in the barn. Makes sense.'

'But not round here, surely? This isn't the wilderness.'

Bax said nothing. Lol gazed over the fields. It felt like they were standing at a sea wall overlooking dark waters, the distant Black Mountains like the far arm of a wide bay.

'Jones's place,' he heard himself say. 'Can you see it from the road?'

'Not any more.'

'No signs to it? I didn't see any.'

'Secrecy's part of the image. The punters like that. So I'm told.'

Lol had the map from the truck.

'Could you show me where it is? On here?'

Bax sighed, fishing out a spectacle case and holding up the map to the last of the light.

'What's these marks all over it?'

'It's a ley map we made. Four or five going through Brinsop Church. Don't know how you feel about leys?'

'Maybe somefing to it. Lol, look—'

'Do any of these lines go through Byron's land?'

'Lol, mate...' Bax bent and rubbed his knees then straightened up. 'I don't know what to say at this point. You listen to a geezer's music over the years and you fink you know him. Don't get me wrong, I've very much enjoyed our evening, and I got a great respect for what you do. But we don't talk about our neighbours.'

'To strangers.'

'That's right.'

'One day I'll explain.'

Bax pulled a pen from his jacket.

'Can I deface this map a bit more?'

'Feel free.' Lol held the torch, while Bax worked out some distances then drew a small cross. 'That's the farm, is it?'

'Wiv your line going right frew the top corner, near his boundary, where he had his... excavation. That what this is about? They have a digger, him and his partner from Hardkit. Geezer who owns the land overlooking it reckoned there was archaeologists involved. Dunno what was found. Nothing was ever made public. Then Jones had conifers planted inside his boundary fence.'

'Hardkit?' Lol said. 'You did say Hardkit?'

'Kenny Mostyn. He owns the Hardkit shops.'

'He's Jones's partner?'

'You din't know?'

'No. No, I didn't.'

Kenny Mostyn of Hardkit. Byron Jones's partner, Ward Savitch's partner, kind of.

'Do you know of any ancient monument on Jones's land? Anything they might want to excavate?'

'No. And he's... trust me, he's not the kind of bloke you ask.'

Lol nodded, looking up at the sky, figuring there was a good half-hour of daylight left.

'Well, I'd better go,' he said. 'You've been very helpful, Bax. I'll send you a copy of the album when it's out.'

43

Brazilian Decaff

Seeing the female silhouette through the frosted door-panel in the dusk, Bliss thought, *Annie.*

Almost wept. It had come to this. Memories of winter nights when she'd parked around the corner, walked briskly, all muffled up, down the icy drive to the back entrance. The sweet, old-fashioned romance of it.

What a twat he'd become. Bliss unlocked the door, thinking he hadn't even made the bed.

'I thought I'd better come round,' Karen Dowell said. 'Two reasons. One, I really didn't like the sound of your voice on the machine.'

Bliss started to laugh and went into a coughing fit.

'And obviously didn't get that wrong,' Karen said.

He'd called her on his mobile from the car, having tried Annie twice – switched off, and he hadn't left a message. But he'd left one for Karen.

How long have you known?

Because this had so explained Karen's attitude. Advising him to back off, pass the information about Sollers and the fruit-farm girls to Annie Howe.

You want to be a bit careful, boss, that's all. Under the circumstances.

Bliss backed up the narrow hallway, switching on lights.

'Sorry, I was…'

'Not drinking, I hope.' Karen stepped into the living room,

pulling off her baseball cap, looking around. 'God. You into minimalism now, Frannie, or is this all she left you?'

'You want some coffee?'

'Show me where the stuff is, I'll make it. I had your coffee once before.'

'Look.' He felt stupid now. 'I didn't expect you to come over.'

'I told Craig it was work.'

'I feel like a twat.'

'You *are* a twat. God, Frannie, I thought you *knew*. I just didn't see how you could *not know*.'

'Well, I didn't. That's the kind of shite detective I am.'

Karen stood there, shaking her head. Bulky, uncrushable. Farming stock.

'And then I thought about it, and I was thinking, well, if by any chance he doesn't know all the *history...*'

'What are you saying, Karen?'

'Oh my God, you don't know *any* of the history, do you?' Karen tossed her cap on the sofa, from which all the cushions had been stolen. 'He hasn't always been a rural pin-up, Frannie. There *was* a time when being seen around with Kirsty Symonds was serious kudos for a guy like Sollers.'

Bliss stared at her.

'You're saying that my wife and Sollers Bull were an item... before?'

'Sorry to spring that on you.'

'When?'

'Quite a while back, actually. Couple of years before you showed your face in Hereford, anyway.'

Bliss collapsed onto the naked sofa. Karen wrinkled her nose.

'Actually, thinking about it, she can't've been all that long out of school at the time.'

'Mother of God...'

'Sorry. Must be a lot to take in.'

'She used to tell me she always went out with farmers. She said I was the first feller who wasn't a farmer and didn't go on about sheep prices all the time. We used to laugh about it. How do you feel about discussing sheep prices? It became a euphemism for... you know... back in the days when we made up euphemisms for it. When we were both laughing at the same time.'

'You never her asked which farmers she went out with?'

'Karen, why would I care? They all look the friggin' same to me. Industrial woollen shirts and hairy arms.'

'Not Sollers, however.'

'No.' Bliss looked down into his hands. 'Not Sollers.'

Karen sat down opposite him, in the chair by the cold grate. Looked across at him, a bit apprehensive, as though she still wasn't sure how much to say.

'When did it end, Karen? Or when was it *suspended*?'

'Just fizzled out, I suppose. Sollers was at college, and mixing more in... you know, hunting circles... with the nobs. I suppose that was how he met Charlotte, Walford's daughter. Walford was a hunt master, I think. And then one thing led to another. That is... did Charlotte get pregnant? I think maybe that was it. My mum reckons it was never destined to last. They pretty much lead separate lives now, since the kids went to boarding school. I wouldn't imagine Lord Walford knows about him picking up again with Kirsty, but – like, from what you've told me – it's pretty clear Chris Symonds does.'

Sollers's big 4x4 shoved among the trees, just the other side of the farmhouse porch.

'Symonds never liked me. Despised how I earned me crust. And now, coming up to forty, and still not behind a big desk at headquarters. Who else knows?'

Karen looked glum.

'All right, tell me.'

'Stagg.'

'*Fuck... no!*'

'Actually, it was Stagg who got the whisper, on his travels. From the inevitable nosy neighbour. Probably made his year. Couldn't wait to go blabbing to the DCI. As you can imagine.'

'When was this?'

'This afternoon.'

Bliss closed his eyes. Total explanation of Annie's phone message. Him thinking she'd somehow found out that Kirsty knew about them.

'Has it got out to the press?'

'I think, on balance, it wouldn't be too much in Sollers's interests for it to be in the papers that there was a private issue between you and him.'

'Maybe not.'

What was evident was that Kirsty must've made it clear to Sollers that her husband didn't know about them. That she'd never told him. And if he had found out, Kirsty had him and Annie in her back pocket for bargaining purposes.

How long had Kirsty and Sollers been meeting quietly? Months? Years? Bliss thought of how she'd looked the last time he'd taken the kids back. The short skirt, the classy make-up. Thinking she'd done that for him, to let him know what he was missing. He felt… not so much humiliated as ashamed.

And afraid. Afraid of the implications for the future. His kids. And also… 'You know what this means? It means I can't touch him, Karen. It means I can't nail the cun—' He straightened up. 'Sorry, sorry. If I sound like I'm coming apart, it's because I am. The friggin' twisted irony of it…'

'Have you even *got* anything on him? *Anything?*'

'You know how much I've got.'

'Then it's nothing. And no legitimate reason to connect Mansel's murder with the Marinescus. I'll make that coffee.'

Bliss followed Karen into the kitchen.

'They've been stirring it for me. Did you hear that? Did you get that from Stagg, too? How it got back to the Chief Constable that me and Kirsty were splitting up? That it was down to physical abuse?'

Karen turned slowly.

'Who's saying that?'

Bliss shrugged.

Karen said. 'Sollers? Chris Symonds? Kirsty herself?'

'Hardly matters now – it's done its job. Persuaded the Chief to take steps to remove me from the division.'

'You're not just *accepting* that?'

'No. Obviously not. But even taking on the Chief, through the Federation or whatever, means I'm out of here, one way or another.'

'A few of us won't stand by and watch it happen. Where's the coffee?'

'I've had it with this place, anyway. Cupboard over the sink.'

'Vaynor.' Karen reached up to the cupboard. 'Me. Rich Ford, even. What's this?'

Karen was holding up the last jar of Brazilian decaff.

'Kirsty must've left it,' Bliss said quickly.

'No wonder you were doomed – this is what the DCI drinks.'

'Is it?'

'You've not got anything else?'

'I don't spend much time at home these days. Out of interest, do you think Kirsty knows Sollers was shagging a Polish kid from Magnis Berries?'

'That was a while back. Do you want some more bad news?'

'Yeh, I'd love that, Karen. It's what keeps me alive.'

'It doesn't…' Karen opened the coffee jar. 'This is the other reason I'm here. Doesn't look like Sollers Bull killed the Marinescus.'

'*Had* them killed. I never said he did it himself.'

'No.' Karen shook her head. 'I haven't given this to Brian Wilton yet. I met a woman earlier tonight.'

'One of the toms?'

'Middle-aged lady who sings in the Cathedral choir.'

'Takes all sorts.'

'No, *not* one of the toms, boss. She's manageress of Harriet's of Bridge Street, clothing emporium for the maturer lady?'

Bliss shook his head.

'Two young women came in, looking at clothes a bit too old for them. There were three elderly customers in at the time, and

319

the girls were being very solicitous to the one *not* being served. Like, *What about this one? Really suits you. You try it on, I look after your bag,* kind of thing.'

'How do you know it was the Marinescus?'

'Showed her the pictures.'

'How disappointing,' Bliss said. 'Come to something when you can't even trust a girl with an icon of the Holy Mother any more.'

He started to laugh before he could cry. Another curtain closing.

'Anyway,' Karen said, 'Harriet's is a small enough shop for the staff to notice these things, and some tops had been nicked the previous week. When she offered to take care of the bag herself, the two girls were out the door in a flash.'

'Doesn't surprise me a great deal,' Bliss said. 'Also ties in with the new gear in the wardrobe at Goldie's. Is there a word for a female Fagin? The Marinescus were hard up.'

'It's not the first,' Karen said. 'Last time, they got away with it. This was a much bigger store than the mail-order surplus place up on the Holmer.'

Bliss waited. Karen spooned coffee into mugs.

'This was another old lady, right? Eighty-three. They took her bag, containing her purse, photos of the grandchildren... all the usual. She was very, *very* upset. They called the police and then they had to take her home. Remember it now?'

Bliss nodded vaguely. Karen stood with her back to the cooker.

'The proprietor rang up the old lady next day. She wasn't there. She'd been rushed to hospital the previous night.'

'Did we know about that?'

'No, we didn't. She had a long history of strokes, and anyway she made a brief recovery. The family agreed to keep quiet, didn't want her getting fussed. The shop woman told me that when I rang her. Three weeks later – that would be a week or so ago – the old girl had another stroke and died in hospital.'

'I see. Handbag.'

Bliss was thinking of the Marinescus, the way one handbag had been emptied out at the scene, the other and its contents trailed all the way to the river.

'I think you should get to bed, boss,' Karen said. 'An early start might be advisable.'

44

From the Killing House

NO MORE THAN a third of the tables in the lounge bar were taken. Merrily had followed Jane to the one under the smallest leaded window, its old glass thick and fogged like frogspawn.

'Cider?'

'Please.' Jane slid into the short bench under the window. Merrily bought two medium-sweet ciders from Barry, looking around for Lol. No sign. Barry gave her a mildly inquiring look; she leaned across the bar, voice lowered.

'Liz was quite forthcoming, in the end. Though why I should tell you any of it, considering how much you *didn't* tell me...'

One side of Barry's mouth twitched. Merrily carried the ciders back to the table. Shadows hung shiftily either side of the mullion.

'So archaeology is, erm, history.'

Jane didn't smile.

'It's a joke, anyway. Archaeologists can't get to grips with anything much any more, unless the council wants to do something crass with the land. And whatever they find, it still gets built over. I'd just keep getting annoyed.'

'You'll still keep getting annoyed if you don't have any qualifications. The only difference is, you'll be regarded as an annoying crank. No one will have to listen to you.'

Jane shrugged. Merrily sipped cautiously at her cider.

'Or maybe you're worried that the world of archaeology isn't yet sufficiently attuned to the concepts of Bronze Age geomancy and earth energies.'

'*You* accept all that.'

'Some of it. But I'm not an academic, just a jobbing C of E shaman in the ruins of Christianity.'

'And you don't believe *that* for one—'

'Still wake up in the night in a cold sweat, watching a ghostly Dawkins coming through the wall.'

Jane's smile was a long way behind.

'You won't have to keep me. I'll get some kind of job.'

'Yes. I'm sure you will.' Merrily thinking, don't push it. Don't get into an argument. Plenty of time yet. Well, there wasn't, but... 'Actually, I was going to ask you something. As you know more about the ancient world than I do. Though maybe Roman archaeology is not your thing.'

'Prehistory, my thing. We know too much about the Romans. Anyway, Coops is your man, he's well into the Romans. What were you going to ask me?'

'Credenhill?'

'Not Roman.'

'No, but there was a Roman town below it.'

'Magnis.'

'All under farmland now, right?'

'Yeah, but probably more extensive than they imagined. Credenhill? Is this something to do with Syd Spicer?'

'Possibly.'

Merrily gazed into the inglenook, where the fire was in, just, the logs smoky grey and not apple. OK, here they were, mother and daughter, in the pub. Adults. Not much, if anything, she couldn't discuss with Jane any more.

'Syd was at Huw's chapel last week, genning himself up on aspects of deliverance. We never found out what he was looking for. I need to find out whether that had any relevance to his death.'

'Need to?'

'Don't ask.'

Jane shook her head.

'You lead a very weird life, Mum.'

'I know.'

'What's up with Barry? Why's he keep looking at you?'

'I think he wants to talk.'

'But not with me here, right?'

'He can wait.'

'No, it's OK.' Jane sank the last of her cider, slid to the end of the bench. 'I need to call Eirion again. He's coming over at the weekend. Staying tonight with his dad and his step-mum and then coming over to Hereford to see some mates from school, and then...'

'He wants to stay with us?'

'If that's OK. I said I'd meet him in Hereford tomorrow afternoon.'

'It's always OK. But are *you* OK?'

'Yeah, I'm OK. I'm glad we...'

'Always remember we're on the same side,' Merrily said. 'You know that.'

'Yeah. I do. Thanks for the drink, Mum. And like... thanks for... you know... not biting my head off.'

And she was gone, leaving Merrily deeply unsettled. *Thanks for not biting my head off?* Had she really said that? Jane?

A new glass and a bottle of Brecon spring water arrived on the table. Barry slipped into Jane's seat.

'Didn't think you'd want another cider, but I can go back.'

'No, that's fine. Thank you. How much do I—?'

'On the house.' Barry nodded towards the fire door, through which Jane had left. 'Problems there?'

'Jane's a bit... overwrought about proposals for the village. Can't help thinking she's heard something about Savitch and the Swan. Not from me.'

'Nice when a kid bothers about heritage.'

'Yes. I suppose it is. Never felt part of anywhere before, and so if she thinks anyone's trying to damage it...' Merrily poured out some water. 'I suppose you want to know how I got on with Liz.

Put it this way, I've learned more than enough in the course of the day to support your opinion that Byron Jones is a man to be avoided if at all possible.'

'Good.'

'Unfortunately, it may *not* be possible, so I'd quite like you to tell me everything you were keeping quiet about last night. "They're dead," Barry. "All dead now." What's that mean?'

Barry wasn't drinking tonight. He glanced over his shoulder.

'Could mean a lot of things.'

'I could go and ask James Bull-Davies, and he'd ask William Lockley, and Lockley would feed it back up the line.'

'And five weeks later James would come back and tell you your question was *inappropriate*.' Barry looked down into his cupped hands on the tabletop. 'Remind me which of us started all this, Merrily, and then tell me how necessary it is to go on with it.'

Merrily moistened her lips with spring water.

'Can we go back to when you said Byron had changed. Last night, you suggested he'd become abnormally ruthless. When did that happen?'

Barry looked around again. Nobody was close.

'I'd say there was a change in him after the Iranian Embassy operation.'

'But I thought he wasn't—'

'I know he wasn't. But he thought he *should*'ve been. Missed out on all the acclaim. No kiss from Maggie Thatcher.' Barry shrugged. 'Luck of the draw, but he didn't see it that way.'

Merrily remembered watching it live on TV. A sunny early evening in London, a very public operation. Normal TV programmes cancelled for the final act of the big news story of the week. Half the nation gathered round the box as cameras tracked the masked men abseiling down from the roof, into the embassy where six terrorists were holding twenty-six hostages. Smoke bombs going off. All but one of the hostages rescued, all but one of the terrorists killed. Shot dead, with practised efficiency, by the boys from Hereford, some of whom, even now, were only ever filmed in silhouette. James Bond for real, and it had turned soldiers into superstars.

'When you say the luck of the draw…?'

'They just pulled the boys from the Killing House. It's all in the public domain now. There's this training building they call the Killing House, where we practised how not to shoot the good guys by mistake. Word comes through there's a job in London, they pick the boys who've just completed that aspect of their counter-terrorism training. Driven out of Hereford, down to London in the white Range Rovers.'

'Frank Collins was one, wasn't he?'

'Did the smoke bombs.'

'Why did Byron think he'd been passed over?'

'Because maybe he was. I don't know what happened, I wasn't there, but he might've made some small error of judgement in the Killing House or elsewhere. Situation like that, you can't afford the smallest mistake. A guy who was closer to him than me, he reckoned Byron was convinced he'd been dropped because they thought he didn't have the bottle for it. That was how he seemed to have translated it.'

'I thought you weren't even selected for the SAS unless your courage—'

'He's the kind of guy gets fixations. Even the Regiment can't alter your personality. Something drove him further into himself and into his training. Personal training. He never stopped. No more social life for Byron. When he got married, we're thinking, where'd *she* come from?'

'Syd wasn't in the embassy operation, was he? Even peripherally?'

'No, he wasn't. And, before you ask, most of the embassy boys are still alive.'

'Can you think why Byron might have wanted to live near Credenhill?'

'Don't make much sense to me. He never served there.'

Merrily poured out more spring water.

'Barry, what are you not telling me?'

'Blimey, vicar… Look… all right… it would be silly to say no psycho ever got into the Regiment… although selection does weed them out.'

'You think he's psychotic?'

'I'm not qualified to make a mental-health assessment. It's my understanding – and for Christ's sake, keep this *totally* to yourself – he was later seen by army psychiatrists.'

'You know why?'

'Um… yeah, I do, more or less. Same rules?'

'Of course.'

'I wasn't there when this happened, either, but it was an exercise in the Beacons, where you're divided into two opposing sides. It's about fitness and tactics and ingenuity – thinking on your feet. In reality you're on the same side. You know where it stops. Or you should do.'

'What did he do?'

'Nothing. That was the point. Thick fog. Young guy falls some distance down a slope, bangs his head on a rock, dies a week or so later in hospital. Byron was lying in the bracken, watching, when it happened. It was suggested he could've warned the boy he was close to the edge. He didn't.'

'They were on opposite sides?'

'For the day. And it would've drawn attention to his position.'

'Byron didn't know when to stop?'

'It was… according to what we heard, it was like he'd forgotten you *had* to stop. Couldn't understand why anybody was even questioning his attitude. I believe there were other occasions when his… common humanity was called into question.'

'How?'

'Not going any further down that road. The guys on the end of it, they're mainly still around. And it wasn't like he was the only one.'

'Can you explain that a bit more?'

'I can't explain it at all, Merrily.'

'You said before that even the Regiment couldn't alter a man's personality. Something did.'

'Yeah,' Barry said. 'Something did. What it meant, of course, was that nobody in his right mind wanted to be in Byron's gang any more. Which was causing a bit of upset so, in the end, he had to go. He was given an admin post. And then he went.'

'Where did Syd come into this?'

'He didn't. Syd had gone before it got tense.'

'Because I'm wondering if this could be a reason for the rift between Syd and Byron. Liz and Fiona both think it was some-thing to do with Syd getting ordained, but they could be wrong.'

'All I can tell you, Merrily, is Byron wasn't popular, the last years.'

A wary stillness around him now. Merrily had the feeling that while he'd been talking he'd worked something out. Something he was still unsure about. It was becoming clear that anything she pulled from this was going to have to be worked for. She looked around the bar. James Bull-Davies had come in, with Alison. Amanda Rubens and her partner, Gus. Still no sign of Lol.

'In view of all this,' she said, 'it seems more than a bit odd that Byron should want to come back and live near the new camp at Credenhill.'

'You asking me if he had a grievance to work out? No way. That don't happen. More likely it's just business. If he's running an adventure centre for SAS-fantasists, nowhere better to put it than near the SAS.'

Merrily shook her head, had a drink of water.

'He seems to have virtually cleaned out his bank account just buying the land.'

'Well, it's paid off if he's bringing in the punters.'

'Syd was in this history club that Byron started, right?'

'Was he?'

'Do you know any of the others – who might be prepared to talk to me?'

'No.'

Too quick, too casual.

'But you must know a bit about the history club, Barry, because it was you who first told me about it.'

'Yeah.'

'So you know who was in it – at least some of them.'

Barry took a long resigned breath.

'I knew them, yeah.'

'*Knew* them.'

'Yeah,' Barry said. '*Knew.* You satisfied now?'

45

The Thorny Night

THE CLOUDS HAD sunk to the horizon in layers of brown, like the sediment in cough mixture. An early yellow moon was floating free, very close to full. The night was saying, *just do it.*

Lol had driven slowly along what the map had identified as a Roman road, right through the centre of Magnis, where you turned right for Kenchester and then back towards Brinsop Common. He'd reversed the truck tight up against a field gate, the kind of place you'd never leave a vehicle in the daytime, but at least it was out of sight.

Bax was right, you couldn't see the place from the road, only the recently planted woodland, a black cake of conifers at the top of a slow rise, Credenhill hard behind it like a prison wall.

There was an entrance with a cattle grid but no barrier except, about thirty paces in, a galvanized gate, ordinary farm-issue, closed, with a padlock hanging loose. Nothing to suggest private land.

Except the sign. Quite a modest sign, black on white, mud around the edges.

THE COMPOUND TRAINING CENTRE
TRESPASSERS UNWELCOME

The night that had said *just do it* went quiet.
Lol stood and looked around.
He'd put on his walking boots. He had the mini-Maglite in his

jeans, but there was still enough light to see where you were going, so he left it there. He didn't have a jacket. His sweatshirt was worn thin; he had to push up the sleeves because he could feel the cold through a hole in one elbow.

He climbed over the gate, but left the track, stepping into a thicket of low spruce. There was a caravan at the side of the track. Derelict, long abandoned, a coating of mould, rags at the windows. Further along, an old cattle trailer, its tyres long gone, was held up on concrete blocks.

A little scared? Maybe. But fear wasn't the worst of emotions. Fear could be a stimulant, while shame and regret could destroy you. Letting things slide, forgetting what was important.

Lol walked close to the hedge. Couldn't see far ahead now, and then something splintered under his boot. He patted his pockets in case he'd dropped the torch, but no, it was there. He turned the top to switch it on, shielding the beam with a hand. Something made of grey metal lay between his boots. He bent down. A grey panel, the words *Digital Interface* printed along it.

Part of a CCTV camera, smashed. He looked up and saw a pole from which it might have fallen. He picked up the camera. Metal. Sturdy, professional. Industrial-quality. No need to worry about showing up on a monitor in Byron Jones's study, then. Lol carried on up the side of the track. Wasn't going to be stupid about this. He'd go as far the wire fence and just…

'*Uh…!*'

The pain had come from several places almost simultaneously.

It ripped up through both legs, and Lol stumbled to his knees, then lost his balance, fell over, threw out a hand to push himself up, and it was snatched and stabbed all over.

He tried to roll away, and dragged his hand free and made it to his pocket and the Maglite. Its light showed rusting metal tendrils wound around his lower legs like a manacle of thorns. Oh God, this *was* the fence.

Had been. He looked up and saw double strands of barbed

wire stretched between poles like arched lamp-posts. Between the strands he could see where a hole, man-sized, had been cut. Where he'd walked into the wire cuttings coiled on the ground, brutal metal brambles.

Someone had done this. Someone had been and smashed the CCTV cameras and then taken wire-cutters to the fence. Someone had broken into Jones's training facility.

Breathing through his teeth, Lol began to unwind the wire, barb by barb, until he could stand up. He stayed there for a while, as though if he moved it would go for him again. Slowly, he pushed his hands down his legs: damp jeans fused to the skin by warm blood and cold dew. His hands hurt: he found three more deep cuts on fingers that wouldn't be holding down a chord for a while. Danny would be furious.

He found a ragged tear in the wrist. A dark cord of blood unravelling into his palm. As he stepped away from the barbed wire, a severed strand whipped past his eyes and he realised that, without wanting to be, he was now inside Byron Jones's compound, bleeding all over it.

Lol crouched behind a bush. Everything here seemed to come with spikes and barbs and thorns, and the metal had seemed more alive than the winter-brittle foliage. A filmy moonlight exposed a space surrounded by conifer woodland, like the exercise yard in some old POW camp. Half-cindered, huts around the perimeter, an oil tank on concrete blocks. Close to the centre, a barn-sized building of galvanized metal with no windows. Nearest to him, a Nissen hut, half buried in bushes and brambles.

When a small, tight creak came from the hut, Lol almost threw himself back into the wire.

One of the doors. One of the doors had moved. He sank down again, breath slamming into him like a punch. He waited… must've been five minutes. Nothing happened, nobody came out. But he knew the doors were open. Someone had left the doors open.

Out. This is not good. Get out.

Not that it was going to be easy driving home with this hand. He touched it tentatively with the other one. The blood was coming faster. His palm was full of blood.

Lol felt his wrist, and the flap of skin that came up under his probing thumb was the size of a plectrum. He made a shameful, strangled noise, turned away towards the hole in the wire. Into a hot, white, blinding blaze and the quiet shadowy movement of men all around him in the thorny night.

46

Crucible

MERRILY WENT DIRECTLY round to Lol's, but the lights were out. She fumbled in her bag for the key, went inside. The door to the living room hung open, the Boswell guitar on its stand, the draught sending shivers through the strings. If Lol had gone over to Kinnerton to rehearse with Danny, wouldn't he have taken the Boswell?

She would have called him on his mobile but – this happened all too often – there it was on the table under the window.

Bugger. She came out into the usual sensation of being watched – neighbours at their windows just happening to notice the vicar slipping round to her boyfriend's cottage, her boy-friend's bed, under cover of darkness. She felt a rush of angry despair, wishing, hardly for the first time, that she was living here with Lol. Wishing she was normal. Thinking about what she might do if she left the Church to choke to death on its own tangled politics.

Walking across the corner of the square to the vicarage, Merrily wondered what she actually *could* do?

Sod all. There was nothing else here for her, just as there'd be nothing for Lol – nothing he could live with – if Savitch was in virtual control of a bijou tourist village. What if they were both to get out? Would he want her to go with him?

Leaving Jane, who wanted to go nowhere else.

When she got home, Jane had gone to bed. She evidently did not want to talk any more. Merrily fed Ethel, then went into the scullery and sat down under the anglepoise lamp and switched on the laptop.

Dead. All dead now.

Barry could remember three of the other members of the history club. Merrily pulled over the sermon pad and wrote down the names before she forgot them. Mostly nicknames.

Jocko: killed in a car crash near Bristol. He'd been drunk.

Greg: kicked to death in a fight outside a bar in Madrid. He'd been on holiday.

The third one, known as Nasal, Merrily easily found on the Net by Googling *Nasal, SAS, murder.*

Sunday Times, April 11, 2004.

A former SAS man serving a life sentence for the murder of his girlfriend has been found hanged in his prison cell. Rhys Harran, 43, was said by friends yesterday to have been unable to cope with incarceration. He had been involved in several fights with other inmates of London's Pentonville prison. Harran, known as 'Nasal' because of a sinus abnormality, was jailed two years ago, after being convicted of strangling his long-term girlfriend Cassie Welsh at their home in Fulham. The court heard he had been suffering from post-traumatic stress syndrome after service in Western Iraq and had failed to adjust to civilian life. Harran, who left the SAS in 2002, was described by a former colleague last night as 'a real tiger of a bloke'. His army career included operations in the Falklands, Afghanistan and Northern Ireland.

Abruptly, Merrily switched off the computer and rang Big Liz at Allensmore.

Liz said. 'I went into the tower room tonight. Alone. In the dark.'

'Was that a good idea?'

'I don't know. In some ways, Colin feels closer now than he did before you came, but perhaps that's because I was forced to go over old ground. I'm starting to see the bad things I'd turned a blind eye to. Just, you know, small things, intimate things that I didn't realize weren't... I was a virgin, you see. I didn't *know...* some things.'

'Where's your husband?'

'Paul? I haven't told him. He doesn't even know you've been.'

'I think you should tell him everything,' Merrily said. 'You've kept it to yourself too long. And, Liz, when you next go into the tower room – humour me – say the Lord's Prayer, if you can remember it. And discuss it with your husband. All of it. Tell him I'm a crank. Listen, could I check something? When Syd came to see Byron, what year was that?'

'Oh... dear. I'm not good on...'

'Same year as the first publication of *Caradog*? That would be 2004?'

'I expect. Are you all right?'

'I'm fine. Liz, one more thing. You remember you told me about Byron's publisher coming on the phone once? A woman? Do you remember her name?'

'Ah. I do know this one. Alexandra... Alexandra... *Bell*. I remember it put me in mind of Alexander Graham Bell.'

'Same publisher still?'

'I'm not sure. You want to speak to her? I'll try and find the number, if you can hang on...'

'It'll do tomorrow. But if I could mention your name to her that would be useful.'

'She might not even remember me.'

'I suspect she will, Liz.'

All one-time members of Syd's team, his gang. Working together in Bosnia and operations during the Colombian cocaine war, over twenty years ago. Then the history club.

Barry had said stubbornly, *Car crash, bar-fight, hanged in prison. There's no connection. It don't mean anything. Three ex-Regiment dead, not of natural causes. All their deaths are different. It means nothing. How could it?*

He was right, of course. These were men for whom violence had been a way of life, who found it hard to adjust when they came out of the army, who were often emotionally damaged. It was no big deal, except that they were all mates.

Syd's mates. Assume that his visit to Byron at Allensmore *had* coincided with Nasal's death. Maybe he'd even read this same account in the *Sunday Times*. Gone to tell Byron that another member of the club was history.

Merrily began to make notes on the sermon pad, under the anglepoise, but she was too tired to construct a logical framework. And, anyway, there was something missing. Something which almost certainly related to Byron's reasons for coming to Brinsop, where the church, with its celebration of *necessary violence*, was a kind of spiritual crucible.

She sprinkled some dried cat-food in Ethel's bowl, put out the lights and crawled off to bed, pausing to look out from the landing window where she could see, across Church Street through the wintry trees, Lol's house, still in darkness.

She awoke at two. Back to the landing window. Still dark at Lol's, but perhaps he'd come in, gone to bed. A vehicle crossed the square, but it was a light-coloured van. She'd rung Lol's landline twice, finally leaving a message, just asking him to ring her back, whatever time he got in. Now she wanted to ring Danny, but it was far too late; Greta at least would be in bed, and Greta had to work in the morning and…

…oh God, the Maundy service.

The next time she awoke she was in a corridor.

Sporadically lit, lumpy with pipes and the smell was of antiseptic and bleach, and there were double doors and an old leathered bench, and the need for a cigarette.

I'm afraid you can't smoke in here.

Breathing. The uneven respiration of the chronically sick. A dim and wobbly light. Grey-white sleepers.

We've always had him in a side ward.

An iron bed. Tubes.

Brace yourself…

Lowering herself into a clammy vinyl-covered bedside chair, summoning reserves of compassion as she peered below the hair dyed black, into the reptilian eye-slits. Green tubes curling up either side of the nose like a smile. Hands out of the sheets, rubbery snaking hands, and the smell…

Don't wake up, don't wake up, see it through, don't wake up, and Jesus, don't let him touch Jane with his…

Curling nail on yellowed finger. *Scritch, scratch…*

The air rushed through the corridor like a hollow scream, trailing an awakening into half-light and… exhaust.

Merrily sat up to find the dawn gleaming like raw meat in the bedroom window.

Part Five

...they're all mad in one way or another. There's Kev, who knows he's a reincarnated Viking. There's Si, who only reads books about the para- normal... Only a few of the boys are normal, but they're so normal that they're weird. What a bunch of crazies we are. And we go out with our lethal weapons every day.

Frank Collins
Baptism of Fire (*1997*)

47

Fizz

IT WAS NEARLY light but not quite, the sun still below the Tesco clock turret, when Bliss raided the Plascarreg Hilton.

DC Vaynor with him and three of Rich Ford's uniforms, two of them women. No enforcer, they just rang the bell, and a worried-looking Asian lady let them in, and then Goldie was there, halfway up the reduced baronial stairway in a yellow kimono with pink dragons on it and matching turban.

'Wassis, wassis? You won't find no drugs yere, Mr Francis, and that's a damn fact! We en't never had no drugs, and anybody yere who says we 'ave—'

'Norra problem, Goldie.' Bliss opening out his arms with transparent generosity. 'We find any dope, you can keep it for those quiet nights in.' Turning now to his team. 'Colleen, ground floor with Darth. Kath and I will accompany you to your bou-doir, Goldie, while PC Timlin will hang around the hall in case any of the guests try to leave without settling the bill.'

Goldie stood her ground, arms folded like a very mature geisha, as Bliss mounted the stairs.

'Come on now, Goldie, how much more considerate could Her Majesty's filth *be* to a respected senior citizen?'

'What *is* this? What's it about?'

'Clothing and fancy goods, Goldie. We're collecting for Oxfam.'

'Gotter warrant, have you?'

'Has Stevie Hawking gorra GCSE in physics? Now, *back off*, you old witch.'

Within half an hour they had quite a little boutique going in the hallway: designer tops, silk scarves, perfume, odds and ends of jewellery. Much of it still in the wrapping, labels intact: River Island, M & S, Fat Face. Harriet's, of course, and a couple of quality shoeshops. Bliss was made up, the Mersey going tidal in his vocals.

'Just like me bairthday all over again, Goldie.'

'All paid for, Mr Francis. I got all the receipts. Somewhere.'

'How much did they owe you?'

'Who?'

'The *gairls*! How many weeks' rent for that nasty little room?'

'I don't remember.'

'Yeh.' Bliss smiling kindly down at the old girl. 'You're well known for having no head for business.'

They were sitting in extravagant peacock wicker chairs in what Goldie called the breakfast room. Just the two of them. Nobody breakfasting yet. It was just gone half-seven. Bliss was due to meet Karen at Gaol Street at nine. He'd had four hours' intermittent sleep. Flying on blind rage – so much cheaper than crystal meth.

'All right,' Goldie said, 'a few weeks, thassall, swearder God, and I never pushed hard for it. Some weeks I let them off it, I did!'

'Yeh, that's why, the morning they were missing, you were all over the estate after them because it was rent day.'

'I never—'

'Shurrup. You know what I think? I think – and it just kind of came to me in a flash, the way these things do – *I* think that you told them ways they could *pay in kind*.'

'If people wants to give me presents...'

Goldie had shrivelled herself into the wings of her wicker throne, hair like brass curtain-rings escaping from the pink and yellow turban. Bliss shook his head sadly.

'An' I never had them on no streets!' Goldie said.

'Only 'cause they wouldn't bloody do it, as decent icon-carrying Russian Orthodox— Oh, the shame of it, Goldie.' Bliss leaned towards her, sniffing at the perfume she evidently wore in bed. 'Oh, the ignominy of one of Hereford's leading hoteliers nicked for fencing leggings and camisoles.'

'What you want?'

'... and all the extra menial offences which might come to light.'

'What you want off me?'

'All right.' Bliss lifted a calming hand. 'Let's stand back a little from this. Allow me to bring you up to speed on West Mercia's investigation of the murder of the Marinescu sisters.'

Leaning back into the silly chair, Bliss talked very simply and with compassion about an old lady whose handbag had been stolen by two young women in a mail-order surplus store and who'd been so upset that she'd subsequently passed away.

'This old lady,' Bliss said, 'her name was Cynthia Wise, from Bobblestock. She had five children and, I think, sixteen or seventeen grandchildren?'

All this background had been waiting for him when he'd arrived at Gaol Street, well before dawn. A little fizz in the air at a normally cheerless hour.

'I never knowed her, Mr Francis. I never goes near Bobblestock.'

'Yeh, but what a tragic story, eh, Goldie? Could be you, couldn't it? In a year or two. Y'know, if that was *my* gran, God rest her little old soul, I'd feel more than a bit aggrieved at these people coming from the fringes of the Euro-heap, as good as murdering innocent pensioners for a cheap handbag and a couple of twenties. Cause the death of a decent, much-loved old lady and what happens to them if they get nicked? First offence. *Bugger all!* What kind of justice is that, Goldie?'

'I still don't know...' Goldie's cold eyes jittering just enough for him to know he was in '... what you wants.'

'Well, I haven't actually made up me mind, yet, but I'm… you know, I'm *wairkin'* on it.'

'Always helped you out, Mr Francis, you knows that.' Goldie folding her arms, hands vanishing into the opposite sleeves. 'I do's everythin' in my powers to help the police.'

Bliss sniffed.

'Not done much at all, the more I think about it. Nor'enough to melt me stony heart on this one.'

'Well, I don't know about no handbags.' Goldie so far back in the chair now that you could hear its fibres twisting. 'You won't find no handbags yere, thass a damn fact.'

'Well, no, the only place I'd expect to find a stolen handbag is at the bottom of the Wye with a brick inside.' *Oh yes… closing in.* 'I suppose you *could* try talking to me. Maybe a few anecdotes you've heard from your clientele and the gentlefolk around the Plas. Bearing in mind that I don't care where it comes from if it's sufficiently entertaining and contains an element of verifiable truth, and… You've gone quiet, Goldie.'

'I needs time.'

'No, you don't, not really. But go on, I'll give yer five minutes. During which you can tell me why the girls left Magnis Berries. Was one of them raped? Threatened with rape or a beating if they didn't do what they were told? Or was it simply just an unhappy love affair with a man who wasn't what he seemed? What did they disclose to you over the cocoa and the tarot?'

'Now listen, Mr Francis, I don't know about none of that. You gotter believe me.'

'No cocoa?'

'No tarot, neither. I brings out the cards one night, they was near to crossing theirselves. Them ole villages in Romania, it's like nothin' changed in centuries. I says, right you are, loveys, I understands. '

'What we talking about?'

'The dead.' Goldie looked up, defiant. 'That's why they was told to leave.'

Bliss was silent. Oh fuck, was this contagious?

'Dead people all around in the mornin' mist. The cold comin' off of 'em. Dead men. Got so nobody would work with them, so they was told to leave.'

'And that's it, is it?'

'I knowed you wouldn't understand.'

Bliss felt his mood darken.

'Goldie, that earns you no points at all. And you're out of time, so let's go back to the old lady. Here's the bottom line. If the killing of Maria and Ileana Marinescu *is* linked to what happened to Granny Wise, and the killers were to find out exactly why—'

'You're bloody mad, you are!'

'... *why* those girls were forced to target old ladies in a hitherto safe city... *if*, by some unfortunate leakage of investigative data, they were to find who was running the Marinescus... they – or their mates – might think there was unfinished business, Goldie. You know what I mean?'

Goldie's wicker chair creaked in a fragile way.

'You're an damned evil bastard, you are, Mr Francis.'

'Yeh,' Bliss said. 'And the *wairst* of it is, from your point of view... I might soon be departing this division, so I have absolutely no reason to look after you any more.'

18

Aggressor

THE LIGHT IN the church was dusty brown, a muffled sunglow in the chancel. This early, it always felt like some ornate derelict cinema.

Merrily had washed and dressed, very basically. A couple of hours before she'd need to get ready for the Maundy service. No sign of Jane yet, so she'd fed Ethel and run across the road to Lol's house. The early light had hung a grey pall on the empty living room where the wood stove was dead. She'd tried the knocker, pointlessly, and then she was walking back across the empty pink-lit square, panting, dazed and wide-eyed with panic.

Could she ring Danny at Kinnerton this early? She was not *possessive*, didn't pressure, didn't chase. Not a *worrier*.

She sat on the edge of the chancel, the church keys lying on a stone flag at her feet. She'd prayed, then let her fears lie for a while, unexamined, as flesh-coloured light through the high plain-glass windows laid a greasy sheen on the pew ends.

Been letting things slide, Lol had said.

You and me both. Merrily picked up the keys and stood. She already had her mobile out.

'Not at all, Mrs Watkins!' Greta Thomas, a woman who'd spent half a lifetime competing with amplifiers. 'I been up hours.'

Merrily waited in the dewy churchyard until Danny came on and said no. No, Lol wasn't there. No, he hadn't been last night, neither.

'When you seen him last, Merrily?'

'About five-thirty last night. I had a parish council meeting, and I thought we'd arranged to meet in the Swan, but he didn't show up, and he's not been home.'

'He don't go many places, do he? His truck—?'

'It's not like him, is it? I'd ring the police, but it's just a few hours and he's a grown man. They'd probably just laugh at me.'

'You got any idea at all?'

'Only a worst-case scenario.'

'I better come over now,' Danny said.

On the refectory table, there was a note written in dying biro.

Mum... sorry... totally forgot E's birthday.
Need to get the early bus into town. I'll
call you.
Love, J

Jane needed to get a birthday present for Eirion before she met him in Hereford this afternoon. Eirion's birthday again, so soon? Was he nineteen... twenty even?

Feeling half-relieved at not having to tell Jane about Lol, Merrily started making tea and toast which she didn't want, just giving her hands things to do while waiting for the news on Radio Hereford and Worcester. Like if there was nothing on the news, everything would be OK.

The only local item was Ward Savitch talking about opening up The Court to the public over Easter *to thank the delightful people of Ledwardine for being so welcoming.*

When the phone rang in the scullery, Merrily abandoned both the toast and Savitch.

It should have cleared her head like a bucket of water from a deep, cold well.

Any other time.

'Liz said a colleague of yours died, leaving unresolved issues relating to a man I had dealings with.'

'Yes.'

'I no longer publish him, of course,' Alexandra Bell said. 'Nor, I imagine, does anyone. It was the worst three years of my career, so I feel under no obligation *at all* to protect whatever remains of his reputation. Heartening to hear that Liz finally got away.'

A faint Australian accent. An editor of children's books, you expected circumspection, a touch of the fastidious, but this was a woman who wasn't holding back, who had clearly waited a long time to let all this out to the right person. Merrily sat down and lit a cigarette. Maybe she was the right person, but this really wasn't the right time.

'Erm, I didn't want to... my original intention was to try and find out the substance of the other two books in his *Caradog* series, which now seem to be out of print.'

'Don't know how much you know about publishing, Reverend Watkins, but first-novelists are normally easy to work with. You want changes made, they're so grateful to be getting into print they seldom argue.'

'He argued?'

'He simply ignored all my suggestions and refused to answer my questions. If I asked about the historical basis for something, he wouldn't tell me. *Need to know,* was one of his phrases. Have you met him?'

'No.'

'As a writer, he wasn't arrogant, he wasn't boastful, had no pretensions to be any kind of stylist. He simply thought that if he came up with good enough stories – and they *were* good stories, no question – it didn't matter where they came from. But children's fiction requires, if anything, more attention to history. So...'

'Well, yes.' Merrily watched the sunlight gobbling up the dusty panes in the scullery window, the day racing. 'Look, if could—'

'So, in the end, I went up there to see him.'

'Oh.'

'I'd been before, when we first signed him, to persuade him that *Caradog* would work better as a children's book - a boys' book. He was charming. A very attractive man. I think he thought I was just a girl with a chequebook, I don't think he realised I'd be his editor. The second time, he was *very* different.'

'When was this?'

'Probably six months later, around 2003. This was when a number of issues had arisen about his manuscript. Sexism. Extreme violence.'

'A lot of that?'

'Oh, Christ, yes. Lot of kids' books involve mega-violence, but not – how can I put this? – not delivered with the relish, the *exultance*, that Byron displayed. I'm no wilting lily, I come from a part of Australia not widely known for being ultra-PC, but to me it was unsuitable for young readers without major surgery. In the end, we got away with reducing it to the bald facts – as in, *he cut the man's head off*. He rarely minded us toning down his prose, no prima donna stuff there. What I found most iffy - and I'm not what you'd call a person of faith - was the way the violence was equated with religion.'

'In what way?' Merrily pulled over the sermon pad and a pen. 'In the first book, Caradog's faith doesn't seem to be defined. We assume he's a pagan, but what kind?'

'I did some research of my own. There's a story that Caradog was converted to Christianity while in Rome, after his capture. Now, that might be a myth, but it's an *accepted* myth. In Byron's book, however – in the second book – he's already been converted, here in Britain.'

'By whom?'

'By himself.'

'I'm sorry?'

'Caradog's first battles with the Romans are in the east, in Kent, and they're largely defensive. But at some stage he travels west to attack Roman settlements. And he becomes the aggressor.'

'Would this be at Credenhill?'

'Don't remember. What I do recall, the reason Caradog is able to inflict such wholesale carnage is that he and his men are beating the Romans at their own game. They've studied and adapted and *developed* the Romans' own tactics... which are strengthened by certain religious practices.'

'He explain what these were?'

'In gratuitous detail, which was one of the reasons I came to see him. Came down this day on the train, and we went out to lunch. In his Land Rover. It was winter. *Really* winter. When I asked if we might have the heating on, he said it didn't work. Plus, the Land Rover was open at the back, and it was absolutely flaming perishing. When we got out at the pub, I could hardly speak for the cold.'

'Didn't he notice?'

'If he did, he certainly didn't comment on it. Afterwards... I'd foolishly asked if we could visit some of the locations, not realising I'd be expected to follow him on foot to the top of a very steep hill. Not wearing the most suitable footwear. When I stumbled, he... stepped in to stop me falling'

'Good of him.'

'By seizing my left breast?'

'Oh God.'

'I was pretty scared. But he didn't try to kiss me, and he didn't touch me again. It was as if it had never happened. He pointed out aspects of the view, which I don't remember *at all*, and then we went down and he dropped me off at Hereford station, and that was that.'

Merrily thought, *Afterwards, he just said goodnight. I don't think he even remembered my name.*

'He touched you as...' She heard a vehicle drawing up in front of the vicarage drive. *Please God...*'I'm sorry... are you saying he touched you as he might have touched, say, a man?'

'Oh, no. It was done in an explicitly sexual way, but without... in some way, it was done without emotion. With *firmness*, rather than... what you might expect. With dispassion. I really don't think I imagined that.'

'Presumably, Liz doesn't know about it?'

'God, no. I told her later how difficult he was as an author and if it hadn't been a three-book deal we'd've dumped him. I doubt she passed the message on.'

'Did you see him again?'

'I did *not*. I reverted to emails. The fact that the second book in the series was rejected by his American publisher I think convinced him to soft-pedal. They were far more sensitive about the religious aspects than we were – Bible Belt and all that.'

'I'm still not quite getting this.'

'The books seem to be suggesting a violent, merciless type of Christianity which makes men into pitiless killers. They slaughter everything – women, children – in their path without an atom of remorse. And the training for this militarised savagery is described in exhaustive detail. I'd email you copies of the original manuscripts if I hadn't binned them years ago. Is that what you wanted to hear?'

'It's not what anyone *wants* to hear.'

'I don't want to know what he's done but, if you do have to see him, best you don't go alone.'

'Can I call you back, if…?'

So many more things she needed to ask, but the possibility that the vehicle outside might be Lol…

'Have to be tomorrow,' Alexandra Bell said. 'I have meetings all day. Why I called you so early.'

'It was good of you.'

'Yeah, well, no worries.'

Only a floating dread. When Merrily made it back into the kitchen, clawing her way through a fog of anxiety, all of it now involving Lol, the sun had come out and the refectory table was lightly dappled. Suddenly, perversely, it was a lovely spring day, the first of the year.

And it wasn't Lol at the door, it was Danny Thomas and Gomer Parry.

Gomer had an unlit roll-up between his teeth. He was wearing one of his own GP Plant Hire sweatshirts under his old tweed jacket.

'We been round the lanes,' Danny said. 'Talkin' to folks we knows. One feller, he seen a truck like Lol's gettin' some attention. Then it was took away.'

'I don't— Where?'

Merrily looked from one to the other. Gomer with his cap rolled up in both hands like an overstuffed brown baguette. Danny's pitted, bearded face expressionless, his mobile in one hand.

Danny said, 'And then I just had a call... Merrily, this en't good.'

49

Spout

'NO, ALL RIGHT,' Bliss said, 'we won't bring anyone in just yet. We need to gerrit all neat before we make a move.'

Karen Dowell was with him in his office in Gaol Street. Also Darth Vaynor, newly promoted to Position of Trust. On his desk, in white sunlight, a file. Victoria Buckland, aged twenty-five, a woman of violence. Eighteen drink-related convictions, four for assault.

The latest of these included violent assault on a teenage girl during a brawl outside a dance-music venue off Widemarsh Street. The most interesting was the attack on a man she'd been living with. One snappish, hungover Sunday morning, Victoria had stabbed him in the right eye with the broken-off spout of a teapot.

Oh, she was a celeb, Victoria, and cultivating it. The tattoo on her left arm said *I DO THE FUCKING*.

Karen said, 'You remember Nerys Edwards, DC at Leominster?'

'Vaguely.'

'Bit her on the face.'

'Victoria?' Bliss nodded. 'I do remember her now. I remember the scar. But if that was down to Victoria, she could only've been... what...?'

'Nine.'

'Mother of God.'

'Passenger in a car nicked by a couple of kids not much older.

It crashed into a lamp-post and Victoria had some bruising and abrasions, so Nerys bends down and lifts her up. Bad mistake.'

'Not one anybody could feasibly make now, is it?' Bliss looked down at the picture, winced. 'I take it we have her on the streets at the right time?'

'We have her in…' Darth Vaynor consulted a printout '… four or five pubs so far, including the Monk's Head. We also have her twice in High Town in the early hours. At 1.45, she was depositing a lager bottle tidily in a litter bin.'

'That's gorra be a first.'

'Hard to believe even Goldie Andrews grassed her up,' Vaynor said.

'All the way to the hossie,' Bliss recalled, 'the lad with the spout, who could've died, was still insisting he stuck it in his own eye. Goldie, however, I'm pleased to say, spotted the writing spray-painted in gold on the wall at the top of her naff Hollywood stairs.'

'You have a way, boss,' Karen said.

'Victoria is just the icing, Karen. You baked the cake.'

She'd done some exemplary work on this, must've been in long before dawn, on the phone then slipping over to Bobblestock, soon as he'd rung in from Goldie's, to see Granny Wise's family. All right, it wasn't exactly the result he'd wanted. But maybe that was partly why she'd worked so hard on it. Bliss felt grateful and a little ashamed.

'So we're gonna do this right, and we're gonna bring them all in at once. Background again, Karen?'

She had this little family tree drawn on the pad, demonstrating how easily even the most respectable units could become polluted.

'The late Cynthia Wise, former primary school teacher. Two daughters. One of whom, Lynne, was originally married to a Peter Singleton, a public-health officer with the council.'

She'd got all this from the other daughter, who lived a few doors away from her late mother's house up in Bobblestock.

'Lynne and Peter get divorced. There's one child, Josceline – custody to Lynne, of course. Lynne is then remarried to a widower, Gerald Buckland, father of three, of whom Victoria is the eldest.'

'Mr Buckland got form?'

'One conviction for drink-driving, boss. Seventeen years ago. People like Victoria… sometimes they just happen.'

'What about Joss?'

'Not known to us in any respect until she and Carly Horne volunteered as witnesses, which somehow always looked a bit iffy to me. A quiet kid, according to her aunt. Possibly *too* quiet. Still waters kind of thing. After her parents' divorce, she seems to have blamed them both, withdrawn into herself. Not happy in the Buckland home. Only person she was really close to is her gran.'

'Grannie Wise.'

Karen smiled sadly.

'We gorra statement from Auntie, Karen?'

'No, and we're not likely to get one. Families, boss. Especially extended families containing Victoria Buckland. But at least I'm confident she won't be tipping Victoria off.'

'How close is Joss to Victoria?'

'The aunt thinks not very, but… Joss is not the most communicative kid, as we know.'

Bliss nodded.

'Never mind. We'll get there. DCI know about this yet?'

'DCI has one or two things to deal with this morning,' Karen said. 'You probably haven't heard, have you?'

Full morning assembly, the whole gang. A strong buzz. Five numbers on the Lotto, everybody waiting for the bonus.

Bliss said, 'This should be fairly straightforward. DS Dowell will bring in Josceline Singleton and Carly Horne. Arresting both, if necessary. DC Vaynor and a few other biggish lads will pull Victoria Buckland. She's probably still in bed, so we'll need a couple of women. Volunteers? Anybody?'

He was coming down now, feeling a bit queasy. Probably just needed more coffee. Rich Ford stood up.

'I'll put Family Liaison on standby. Just the three of them, you reckon, Francis?'

'I'd be inclined to say not, wouldn't you? We're looking at Victoria's known associates. CCTV tells us she was with different groups at different times. Whichever permutation of them killed the sisters would split up afterwards.'

'Women on women, Francis?'

'I'm not ruling out this being an all-female attack, no. *But…*'

'What about the signs of sexual assault?'

'Well, yeh, but, Rich, they weren't *big* signs were they? It was comparatively superficial, like an afterthought. I'm thinking of damage inflicted by a woman or women to maybe *suggest* it was sexual?'

'Revenge, you reckon, rather than racial?'

'That's how it looks. In the wake of a fairly despicable robbery and the tragic consequences, a little girl – emotionally insecure – loses her beloved granny. The only relative she's close to.'

'Except her big, notorious stepsister?'

'Yeh, well…'

Bliss had been remembering Joss Singleton, the quiet one with the citrus hair, her mate Carly Horne doing all the talking, casual, nonchalant. *Got us an afternoon off college, anyway.*

Although you couldn't help being knocked back by how unshockable kids were these days, he was inclined to think these two hadn't been around for the final act. They couldn't have been so cool if they'd watched two women die like that… could they?

'Still some basic questions to be answered, like how did they know it was the Marinescus who'd robbed Joss's gran? Now, I'm thinking that was most likely down to Victoria herself, who has wide contacts. This is still a small city, and there aren't that many double acts on the street at any one time.'

The fact that Goldie knew this was down to Victoria… well, no surprise at all there. You could fill Yellow Pages with all Goldie's contacts. How long had she known it was Victoria, though? At some point he'd have to go back, on his own, for a bit of a heart-to-heart, but not till Victoria was safely banged up.

'OK,' he said. 'Let's all do this quietly. Let me know as soon as you have them.'

As the room emptied, he looked up – and there was Annie Howe. In all the excitement he hadn't even noticed her come in. Annie was wearing her coat, no make-up, and she had her rimless glasses on. Must've left very early.

'You sound sure about this, Francis.'

'I think we can send the interpreters home,' Bliss said. 'Scary, isn't it? Little girls. What've we come to?'

'These girls actually came in here?'

'Fingering some blokes they claimed were eyeing up the Marinescus. Very cool.'

'You think that was Buckland's idea?'

Bliss shrugged. Annie nodded across the room.

'Your office?'

Annie said, 'I've never known you not want to be in on a round-up.'

Bliss shrugged.

'Not gonna be a siege, is it? Not even Victoria. She'll scream and threaten, look around for a bottle. Accuse the cops of feeling her up, especially the women. I don't need to see that again.' He sat down, hands behind his head. 'Anyway, it's Karen's collar. She's been up half the night.'

'Haven't we all.'

'I don't know the details about that, yet.'

Annie sat down opposite Bliss. He stared at her, tingling with emotion and caffeine-rush, impressed at the way she could separate her private and professional lives.

'Seemed promising at first,' Annie said. 'Now it's slightly silly. But still odd. A call to the Rural Crime Line. Person seen acting suspiciously, couple of miles from Oldcastle. In a truck?'

'Worth a punt.'

'It stood up, too. Secure compound, with warehouses. CCTV cameras smashed, hole cut in a wire fence. And, of course, the offender still on the premises.'

'You've got him, then?'

'He's downstairs. Stagg brought him in last night. By all accounts, Stagg was practically wetting himself with excitement, thinking he was on the verge of cracking Oldcastle. It was apparently two hours before somebody persuaded him to call me.'

'This feller in the cells, this is someone we know, right?'

Annie sighed.

'Laurence Robinson, musician. Of sorts. Also known for his association with your friend, the vicar of—'

'Fuck's sake, Annie, you've gorra be *kidding*...'

Bliss sat up, hands dropping away from the chair arms.

'I don't do kidding, as you know. Robinson denies it. Denies breaking in, but he had injuries requiring stitches. We're still looking for the wire-cutters in the woods, and his truck's been brought back – being gone over as we speak.'

'Annie, this is... I mean, I know you don't like Mrs Watkins or her God, but this—'

'Yes, it seems faintly ridiculous, but the faintly ridiculous often turns out to make perverse sense. And he *does* have psychiatric history.'

'That was twenty years ago, and—'

'All right, what am I supposed to do, Francis? You tell me. He was caught on the premises.'

'What's he saying?'

'When Stagg finally got him into an interview room, he was saying very little. Refusing a lawyer, not helping himself at all. According to Stagg, he sounded guilty. By the time I got here he'd been formally arrested and binned for the night. It wouldn't be the first time Stagg's overreacted. On the other hand...'

'Who owns the premises?'

'Guy called Colin Jones. A co-director of Hardkit. They have a warehouse there, and a gym. Run survival-type courses, rent out equipment. Jones is ex-SAS. He's coming in later to make a statement, but he's confirmed that the fence was intact and the cameras functioning at least until early yesterday evening.'

'They don't have a nightwatchman?'

'Apparently not. And they've never had any trouble before.'

'You want me to talk to Robinson?'

'No, I do not.'

Annie was staring at him. Her coat had fallen open. Underneath she was wearing the stripy sweater she'd had on the night last December when he'd gone to her flat, and…

Annie stood up.

'You have what seems like a result. Run with it.'

'And keep on running?' Bliss said.

Annie looked away.

Tap on the door. Terry Stagg leaned in.

'Ma'am?'

Annie went out. Bliss stared at his desk. A result, yeh, but hardly the result anybody wanted, and not his result. All he'd done was put the squeeze on a semi-literate woman of seventy-plus. Karen had pulled his chestnuts out of the fire, and he'd get the credit, do the talking-head, the radio soundbite. *We've now arrested several people in connection with the Marinescu murders and we expect there to be charges. Nothing else I can tell you at this moment, thank you…*

… unless of course you want to give me something on Sollers Bull…

Bliss smashed his fist into the desk. It hurt; he was glad.

Annie came back to the door. Her angular face was unreadable. They were so *not* an item any more. This time she didn't come in.

'Actually, Francis, there is one thing you could do while you're waiting. Talk to Robinson's… partner. She's in reception. And then get rid of her, would you?'

50

Girlie Returns

EITHER IT WOULD happen or it wouldn't. As the morning wore on, Jane was beginning to hope there'd be a get-out.

There were three buses to Hereford today, and she'd missed one. Watched it coming as she was waiting down the street from the Ox. It gave her an hour before the next and then, like, another four hours before the one after that.

OK, this was the decider. If the bus came before there was any sign of Cornel, then fate had decreed she should be on it. That would be fate lifting it out of her hands.

She'd been down to the Ox earlier. 'Mr Cornel?' Whizz Williams, the lugubrious licensee, morosely scrubbing the bar down. 'Dunno where he is, but he en't paid his bill yet, and them's his bags, so I reckon he'll be back.'

Leather cases in front of the bar, airline stickers on them.

Jane had hung around for ten minutes, then walked back up to the square, wandering quietly around, being anonymous. No sexy stuff today; she was in the high-necked black Bench jacket, fully zipped up, jeans and trainers, an old red beret of Mum's.

This was business. A handful of people had gathered to wait for the second bus. She hadn't joined them, but stayed within range, looking into the bookshop window where two copies of Mother Julian's *Revelations of Divine Love* were displayed. On impulse, she went in and bought one from Amanda Rubens.

'You're joining the meditation tomorrow, Jane?'

'Maybe. Think it'll work? Into the valley of pain and death? An Easter miracle?'

'That'll be £6.99,' Amanda said.

As Jane left the shop, the book jammed into a jacket pocket, the bus was coming round the corner, the morning sun bursting in its windows. Chariot of fire. Jane felt a certain half-guilty relief and stepped out across the cobbles.

Then a dark grey shadow glided in front.

'Girlie returns,' Cornel said from inside the Porsche.

Jane looked up, blinked and then walked slowly over like she didn't know who this might be but was intrigued. A few people moved around her, some giving her a glance before getting on the bus.

'Remind me,' Cornel murmured over his raunchy little engine growl. 'Do I owe you an apology?'

'Could be me.' Going automatically into the voice she'd used on him that night in the Swan. 'I was, like, a bit pissed?'

'Very charitable of you,' Cornel said. 'But I was a lot pissed.'

He was wearing this kind of dated short chamois-leather blouson jacket over a khaki shirt with camouflage patches on it, and sunglasses. He didn't look cool, maybe a little sad.

'Look, do you need a lift?'

'I was getting the bus into Hereford, actually, but if you want to get a cup of coffee somewhere, you could park on the square?'

'With you? You'll miss the bus.'

'I, like, wanted to ask you something?'

'I'm not going in the Swan, girlie. Not too popular, you know?'

The bus was up against the Boxter's back bumper. The driver jerked his thumb.

'Cornel, you're, like, blocking the bus stop?'

'So hop in. Stone me, girlie, it's a Porsche! Mass-rapists don't drive cars this conspicuous.'

Jane's scenario had them on foot or in the back room at the Ox, lots of people around. But she supposed he was right.

Never been in a Porsche before. The passenger seat moulded itself around her. She hardly heard the door close.

'There you go. That wasn't too hard, was it? Where we going?'

'I was going to Hereford,' Jane said.

'I could go that way, I suppose.'

Cornel drove off into Old Barn Lane, speeded up. Jane looked over her shoulder at the diminishing square.

'OK, look,' she said, 'I was pissed and you said something about shooting cats. I've got a cat.'

'I didn't shoot your cat, did I?'

'Well, no, but…'

'I was *legless.*'

Cornel came out of Old Barn Lane, hit the bypass with a satisfying tyre-bounce and shot her a glance.

'What's your name, again?'

'Jane.'

'And what did you want to ask me?'

'I…' She floundered, hadn't expected things to escalate, was still talking in girlie's voice. 'Like… what you said about Paris?'

'Ah… Paris, France.'

Cornel began to smile, the skin over his face stretched so tight that when he opened his wide mouth it was as if you could see his skull. The sun was behind them now, the fresh countryside opening up all the way to the Black Mountains, but that wasn't the way they were going, and it didn't seem to be towards Hereford either. Cornel had the top down now, flooring the Porsche's accelerator on the bypass.

'Oh, and I didn't go out killing sheep and chickens either, OK? Mr Savitch needs the support of all the farmers and landowners he can schmooze.'

Jane looked across at him. Hint of cynicism there, in relation to Savitch?

'Besides,' he said, 'chickens are too easy. Even for me.'

It was like a gift. OK, go for it.

Jane took a breath.

'They, like, kill one another, anyway, don't they? Maybe that's more fun?' Concentrating on not looking at Cornel, even when she felt the flicker of his glance. 'Well, cocks, anyway. This time of year.'

Feeling the pull as his foot came off the accelerator. Cornel slowing down very gradually, saying nothing, coming off the bypass at the smallest exit lane, which was just there for the sake of a couple of farms. The road surface was full of potholes from the winter. There was no other traffic. When they hit a straight stretch, Cornel just stopped in the middle of the road.

'It was you, wasn't it?'

'Me?'

'Nicked a sack from a litter bin?'

His lips were stretched, his big chin thrust out. The Porsche's engine was muttering. She could, of course, get out now if she wanted to. Just climb out and walk off. He could hardly leave his Porsche in the middle of the road. Jane watched him warily.

'What did you see, Jane?'

'I… saw you put a sack in a bin. That's… that's it. I just… wanted to see what was in it.'

'And then you took it.'

'I just wanted to show it to somebody? My grandad?'

'What for?'

'He breeds them.' She had this bit all worked out. 'And he's always—'

'Breeds what?'

'You know…'

'I don't!'

'Gamecocks!' Jane backed hard against the car's door. 'And like he's always going on about how great it was in the old days? With all the betting and how they used to feed the cocks special diets and like it wasn't really cruel because they had a good life, and he… he still breeds them.'

'What's he do with them?'

Cornel released the handbrake, let the Porsche creep along the lane like a hunting cat.

'Well, that's it,' Jane said. 'Nothing. He just breeds them and he's like, Oh, I wish it was still going on. Like, Oh I'd give anything to put one of my birds in the ring again.'

'So you told him, did you, where it came from?'

'No. Like, I told him where I found it but not how it got there. And he had a good look at it, and he's, like, yeah that's been fighting.'

'So what did you see before you took the sack?'

'What *was* there to see?' Could blow it all if he thought she'd listened to him getting humiliated by the Brummy-sounding guy. 'I'm just coming up Church Street and I seen you toss the sack in the bin and walk off. I was, like, curious?'

'Curious.'

'When I seen it, I thought it was, like, one of his? My grandad?'

Inspired. She was cruising. Just don't sound too glib.

'So, like, that's why I took it to him. Thinking maybe somebody shot one of his birds? But it wasn't one of his. But when he seen it he got all excited. And, like, it's his birthday next week, he's, like, seventy-eight? And I was thinking if I could like arrange for him to go to a cockfight one last time?'

'Oh, I *see.*'

'It was probably stupid.'

'That's why you came to the Ox last night, is it? Because your grandad wants to go to one last cockfight before he dies? What did you do with the bird?'

'Got rid of it. In the river.'

Cornel nodded. He let the Porsche pick up speed. The next time he spoke, it was kind of sadly.

'Lies.'

'Huh?'

'They just come pouring out of you, don't they, girlie?'

51

Criminal Damage

MERRILY WAS READY to scream at Bliss until she saw the state he was in. Coming through the door from the stairs, his jacket trailed over a shoulder, out of breath, a harsh pallor on his face. He looked older and he looked barely in control, like a man feeling his life running away from him.

'Frannie—'

'No!' Wiping his hands in the air, his voice sharp and shiny. 'Where's your car?'

He followed her out and they sat in the Volvo on the Bath Street car park. He had his iPhone in one hand. She hadn't seen him since Christmas. His face was damp and his eyes looked far back. He shut them for a moment.

'I was gonna come round and see yer.'

'When was that?'

'A few times.'

'But you were busy.' Merrily was trying to hold on to that sense of twisted relief she'd felt when Danny had told her that Lol had been arrested for damaging a wire fence. 'Where is he?'

'He's in a cell, of course.'

'Frannie, this is *Lol*...'

'It's not my case, Merrily, but if you can throw any light on the situation I'll pass it on.'

Bliss turned to her, head on one side. She sank back into the patched seat. She'd called Sophie at home, asking if she could find an emergency stand-in for the Maundy Service. It had happened before, never exactly endearing her to Uncle Ted. Maybe it was *her* life that was spinning away.

'I don't know what it's about. Lol tried to ring me but I was on the phone. Probably a situation where he was only allowed one call, so he rang Danny Thomas instead, you know the guy—?'

'Merrily, I've got till this phone goes off, which could be four or five minutes. We've suspects being brought in for questioning about the Marinescu murders.'

'You're getting somewhere on that?'

'Yes. Tell me about Lol.'

'There were things he probably couldn't say to Danny in the time he had, so I really don't know what he was doing at Brinsop.'

'I'm sorry,' Bliss said, 'I know me memory isn't what it was, but did I mention Brinsop?'

'Frannie, for God's sake, you *know* him—'

'All I *know* is there are two smashed CCTV cameras and a hole cut in a wire fence. Nothing stolen, so it could just be criminal damage or—'

'That's insane!'

'No, hang on… my guess is, unless they've found a big pair of wire-cutters in his truck, with Lol's prints all over them, he'll get police bail and he'll be out within an hour. And if the owner of the property doesn't wanna take it any further it'll disappear.'

'Who's in charge?'

'Be Annie Howe.'

'Oh.'

'And I think the owner's coming in himself later. We'll have to see if he wants to press charges.'

'Colin Jones?'

Bliss looked up. Merrily watched curiosity pushing through the weariness like a baby bird's head in an old nest. Then the phone in his hand began to bleep, and he shouldered the car door open.

'Merrily, this conversation may not be over.'

When Bliss was back in the station, Merrily stood on her own at the edge of the police forecourt, across the road from the red-brick magistrates' court. How many other women had waited here for their boyfriends to be bailed? How many vicars?

She started to laugh. It sounded discordant, a bit manic. She left a message on Danny's phone, saying the situation now seemed less fraught. Lol would probably be bailed. Dear God. When the mobile chimed and she brought it to her ear, she found that her cheek was wet.

'Danny?'

'Neil Cooper, Mrs Watkins. County Archaeologist's Department? Jane said you might want to talk to me about Magnis. Do I have that right?'

'Magnis, yeah. Sorry, Neil, you've caught me on the—'

Merrily sat down on the car-park wall.

'Military base, on the Welsh border road from Caerleon,' Neil said. 'Built in the late first century, in the time of Claudius, when the occupying army was having trouble with rebellious Celts. Anything specific you're looking for?'

'Well… religion, I suppose. A warrior's religion? Nothing meek and mild. Something that might put the Celts, if they'd adopted it, in a state of mind to beat the Roman army on its own terms.'

'You're talking about Caradog here?'

'Probably.'

A door under the police awning had opened and Lol was coming out quite slowly, the way a discharged patient walked out of hospital.

'You see, if you're talking about this area,' Neil said, 'most of the soldiers defending Roman Britain were probably not Romans at all, just a ragbag of recruits from all over Europe. They'd been absorbed into this great disciplined military structure and taught the basics. So Caradog's success isn't that extraordinary. He wouldn't exactly have been taking on the cream of Rome. Where did this religion idea come from?'

'A novel, actually. So it didn't exist.'

Merrily stood up, and Lol saw her, the sun finding the first strands of silver in his hair. He stood facing her, as if slightly bewildered by the fresh air and the traffic. It felt as though the whole city was watching them, as she walked across, the phone at her ear.

'Well, of course it existed,' Neil Cooper said. 'It's a Roman religion favoured by the military elite. It's Mithraism.'

'Neil... can I call you back? I have to... go.'

52

Grassed

THE EDGES OF the bandage were pink. Lol pulled his sweatshirt sleeve back over it.

'Five stitches. The cops took me straight to the hospital.'

Merrily had pulled off the road a few miles out of the city, where the suburbs leaked into the countryside. She let go of Lol's hand, relief and compassion turning to an irritation she didn't want to feel.

'I still don't see why you did it… what you expected to find.'

'I know. It was stupid. I can see that now. It just seemed like I was being pointed at something. If I went there something significant would jump out.'

'Like half the Hereford police?'

'Five of them,' Lol said. 'All because of the truck, apparently. There were sightings of a pickup truck near Oldcastle the night Mansel Bull was killed.'

He told her how, after his wrist had been stitched, they'd put him in a cell in Gaol Street. Banged up. Instant flashback: eighteen again, slammed into the system. Fear had flared inside him. He *knew* how easy it was to get yourself convicted of something you hadn't done, through being in the wrong place. The wrong vehicle.

They'd put him into a little grey interview room that stank of guilt. He'd kept telling them exactly where he was the night Mansel Bull was murdered, giving them a list of people they could call – Danny Thomas, Barry, James Bull-Davies. DS Stagg didn't seem to be interested. Lol had met him before and he'd seemed OK, but now he was a predatory stranger, a schoolyard bully swollen with ignorance and conceit.

'He kept looking at my hands and the stains on my sleeves. He said, did I like that – the feel of blood all over me? He asked me that twice, like he'd thought of something really clever. Still...' Lol leaned his head back over the top of the seat, where the headrest had broken off. 'The other cops, in general, were OK. One went out and brought me some chips.'

'What did you tell them?'

'I said I'd been working on some songs, went out to soak up some atmosphere. It sounded bonkers, even to me, but then they found the ley map in the truck, so obviously I *was* bonkers. They still took a swab for DNA.'

'You see Annie Howe?'

'No.'

'Right. Let's just get back home.' Merrily started up the car. 'You need sleep.'

'Uh...' Lol shook himself. 'I need – if you've got time, I need to get something sorted.'

'Where?'

'Brinsop.'

The wide fields were opening out before them into what remained of Magnis, which was nothing you could see.

Merrily switched off the engine.

'Aren't we both too tired for humour?'

This wasn't good. They were parked where a rutted mud track finished inside a wood, near the top of a hill which Jane didn't know, except that it was nearer Leominster than Hereford and therefore not where she wanted to be. Trees, mostly conifers, were dense on three sides, a mesh of branches overhead.

Jane's left hand was already behind her, groping for whatever passed for a door handle.

'For a start,' Cornel said, 'how about you drop the hokey

accent? Your mother's the vicar of Ledwardine, and you haven't lived here that long.'

Jane thumped back against the door. Which of them had betrayed her: Lori from the Ox or Dean Wall, who hated her from way back?

Cornel's tongue tickled his top lip.

'You want to take a walk, Jane?'

'No, I don't.'

Maybe she could manage to get out, and maybe she could run. But Cornel's legs were a lot longer than hers and he was clearly a fit guy, despite all the drink. There were things you couldn't easily do in a Porsche, if one party was unwilling, that would be so much easier on a lonely wooded hillside, so best not to move.

'What *do* you want?' Cornel said.

Half-turned towards her, one hand on his thigh. Jane looked him in the eyes.

'Like I'm supposed to feel threatened up here? It's a small county. All I have to do is scream.'

'What *are* you like?' Cornel shook his narrow head, then tipped it back and let out a roar. 'Help! Help! This girl keeps grabbing my cock!'

A crow replied from somewhere. Flashes of hard white sunlight were splintered by the still-wintry trees.

Jane was shocked into silence.

'What do you *want*?' Cornel said.

She didn't feel scared any more, just stupid.

'If you're this big, successful banker, why are you staying at the Ox?'

Even to her, it sounded sulky, a bit childish.

'I like the Ox,' Cornel said. 'It's full of sad oafs who live with their mothers and wear wide wellies. To stick the sheep's hooves down while they're…?'

'We all knows that one,' Jane said in a small voice. 'Round yere.'

'Where you really from?'

'All over. Cheltenham, Liverpool... but this is where I belong.'

'Where's your dad?'

'Dead. Car crash, years ago.'

'My dad lives in LA now,' Cornel said. 'Got out while he could. My stepfather's a maths teacher at a comp in Middlesex. Last year his entire salary came to *so* much less than my bonus. Pretended he was pleased for me, but anybody could see how totally pissed off he was really.'

'Right.'

'It's moments like that make it all worthwhile – the day you watch your pompous little stepfather eat shit.' Cornel leaned back, hands behind his head. 'There's my confession. Now it's your turn. Why were you looking for me? And don't say you weren't, you were in the Ox twice.'

'Cockfighting. I told you.'

'Uh-huh.' Cornel's head shaking. 'That was girlie's reason.'

'Yeah, well it's *my—*'

'Seems to me girlie wouldn't've come near me again after that distressing incident in the Swan.'

'No... no, listen, I'm telling you the truth. If Savitch is running cockfights, I want him exposed. I want it in all the papers, so he can never hold his head up here again and has to... leave.'

'Savitch? The vicar's daughter takes on Ward Savitch?'

'You don't know me. This used to be a good place – I mean Ledwardine. Seeing it become the New Cotswolds was bad enough, all these women hugging each other in the street, *How are yoooo, mwah, mwah...* but having it turned into some bloody hunting resort for bastards who think you can get away with anything if you can afford to pay people to look the other way...'

'I see.' Cornel tapped his fingers on the steering wheel. 'I *see.*'

'You see what?'

'Where you're coming from.'

'You did go to a cockfight?'

'Oh yeah. It's one of those things they make you do. Prove how hard you are.'

'Savitch?'

'Let's get some lunch,' Cornel said.

Lol seemed to know exactly where he wanted to go. Merrily was wary, experiencing a fleeting fear that he might have lost it and he was actually taking them to Byron Jones's place. The fields looked wide and bright and open. Sporadic woodland, isolated dwellings, a clear grey border of small mountains. The fox-brown soil and the bones of Magnis.

Over a rise, a small timber-framed farmworker's cottage had appeared. A ramshackle porch, peeling render. A man on his knees inside a circle of spanners and a spilled socket set, tinkering with a quad bike. When Lol got out of the Volvo, he came to his feet, wiping oily hands on his jeans.

'Fawt you might come back.'

'If only to find out why you grassed me up,' Lol said.

53

Sideshow

A BRASS OIL lamp, obviously still in use, hung low over the table. The underside of the central beam was blackened. Two chocolate Labradors prowled around, watched by a ginger cat on the window sill, but only the Rayburn growled.

'Yeah, I heard he was friends with a lady vicar,' Bax said. 'That's nice.'

Just the three of them around the table, in chairs painted in primary colours. Bax's wife was at work, at the farm shop owned by Sollers Bull.

'I'm sorry,' Bax said, 'but anybody could see that no way was this boy going home till he'd had a peek over Mr Jones's fence. Didn't want him hurt, was all. What else can I say?'

'You could've told me,' Lol said.

'Told you what?'

'Whatever you didn't tell me that made you think I might get hurt.'

Bax shook his head slowly.

'Don't do that, mate. Even if you fink you know a guy from his music.'

Merrily understood. Bax belonged to an established sub-cat-egory of incomer: the old hippie good-lifer who'd made a go of it, eventually winning the respect of the native farmers but knowing, all the same, that if he put a foot wrong they'd turn on him: bloody Londoner, give them an acre of ground and a few sheep and they think they know it all.

He'd learned the rural virtues of caution, circumspection and some other word beginning with c that meant you kept your head down and didn't spread gossip if you wanted to survive.

'To actually get somebody arrested,' Merrily said, 'you'd have to be very worried about what might happen to them.'

'Yeah, well.' Bax nodded at Lol's bandage. 'What happened there?'

'Barbed wire.' Lol pulled his sleeve down. 'Wire which had already been snipped. Presumably by the same person who brought down the CCTV camera?'

'Can't tell you noffing about that, mate. That's a mystery, that is.'

'One of several, apparently,' Merrily said.

'Yeah.' Bax massaged his whiskers. 'I had a good long chat with Percy one night. A lot of the old funny baccy getting smoked, and he really opened up. All the other stories come out. The ones he still feels a bit aggrieved over, as a farmer.'

He fell silent.

'Percy had dealings with Byron Jones?' Lol asked.

'Dear oh dear,' Bax said.

It seemed that Percy and Walter had sold off the family farm and the buildings, for conversion. They were well-off now but still kept bits of ground, a few acres here, a few there. Mostly rented out for stock and grasskeep. But periodically Percy would invest in cattle and sheep again, just to keep his hand in.

At least, he used to, until the night when somebody stole a young bull from his herd of Herefords.

'Percy's about to report it to the police when this package appears in the back porch. Brown-paper parcel, 'bout this size...' Bax opened his hands out, shoebox length. 'Containing what you might call a considerable sum of money. No note, just the money.'

'Compensation?'

'*Good* compensation, but no compensation at all, far as Percy was concerned. But what could he do?'

'I don't get it,' Lol said.

'I fink we talked about the Sass helping themselves to stock?'

'A *bull*?'

'Whatever they do,' Bax said, 'it don't get questioned too hard. Everybody supports them. You get used to their little ways.'

'Except this probably wasn't the SAS, was it?' Lol said.

'*I* wouldn't fink so, no.'

'Any idea what happened to the bull?' Merrily asked.

'Unlikely to've been nicked for breeding purposes.'

'Mr Baxter, what *did* you think might have happened to Lol if you hadn't called the rural crime line?'

Bax leaned forward in his spindly chair, inspecting a burn mark on the tabletop.

'Two travellers show up one night in a van. This ain't gossip, this is fact. Be not long after Jones moved in, so they didn't know who he was. Looking for scrap, you know?' Bax looked up warily. 'Bear in mind this never come out, no cops involved. This geezer got systematically done over. While his mate's still squirming around in the barbed wire. Fair play, they never fingered Jones. Too much to hide, 'spect. But, there you go... no police, no defence lawyers. Done and dusted.'

'Jones beat up the guy?'

'Maybe they was used for practice.' Bax might have smiled. '*This is how it's done, boys.*'

'What boys?'

'I dunno – whatever boys was on the training course at the time. These courses, they say it's all a bit unorthodox. Blokes arrive like soldiers, back of a truck, back of a van. Posh blokes, usually. City blokes living the SAS life for a few days. Don't ask me what that means. Folks make allowances. But the travellers, that was a bit of a sideshow.'

'This widely known?'

'Not widely known at all. Had it from a mate of mine in Hereford, scrap dealer who saw the state of them when they was back in business. Bad guys, in general, avoid the area. Don't know whose place they might be breaking into. Who needs cops, all them rules and paperwork, when you got Mr Jones?'

'What's it like up there?' Merrily asked him. 'What's there?'

'Bit like a golf course. Manufactured landscape, pond size of small lake wiv a rope bridge across. Quite a few sheds. Jones's new bungalow's halfway up the hill, wiv a pool. 'Bout four wooden chalets, parking area. But you can tell it's not your ordinary holiday place. No flowers, and most of the trees are pine and fir, so it's screened off all year round. Functional.'

'No women?'

'Nah. They say Jones is seen around town wiv women, but he don't bring them back. Look, I'm sorry. You mind if I ask what your interest is here?'

'It's the SAS chaplain who died on Credenhill. He was a friend, and… he had some past involvement with Byron. Sorry I can't be more explicit.'

'Only I'd rather you didn't say noffing about me, wiv regard to Jones. The spooky stuff, that's different. Percy always says he don't like talking about it, but he loves it really. Some of it he exaggerates, some he don't.'

Lol said, 'So those figures in the mist that Percy saw…?'

'I'm not sure it's all as easily explained as like, Oh it's only Mr Jones and his course students. Odd fings happen, don't they?'

'Percy says he's seen… figures,' Lol said to Merrily. 'Where the Roman town was. In the river mist. One had a bird's head.'

'He ain't the only one, neither,' Bax said. 'But that's neither here nor there. Less you got a weak heart, *they* ain't gonna harm you. But you *can* get harmed. Which is why I set the cops on you. I'm sorry, squire.'

***

As they drove away, they could see the afforested hill from end to end, a rambling natural mansion with great wooded halls and conifered corridors and the earthen back-stairs where Syd Spicer had died.

'Mithraism,' Lol said, 'I don't know anything about that. Do you?'

'Not much. It was mentioned once at college, by a visiting lecturer. Pagan religion curiously similar to Christianity. Neil

Cooper recognized it immediately when I mentioned Byron Jones's soldiers' religion. I don't think there's ever been a suggestion that Caradog adopted a Roman god to improve his fighting prowess, but it obviously worked for Byron.'

'He was practising it?'

'It would answer a few questions. Why he was getting careless with other people's lives. It might also explain the rift with Syd, who went into Christianity with the wimps and the women.'

Not a man's religion, Byron Jones had told his wife. *Certainly not a soldier's religion.*

'What do I do with this, Lol?'

'I keep saying this... perhaps you take it and dump it, in its entirety, on James Bull-Davies.'

'James is not the most imaginative of men.'

'Really, *really* not your problem.'

Merrily turned onto the Brecon Road, past fields scrubbed raw by winter, a landscape seldom noticed. No villages, no church towers, just a road that started on the edge of the city of Hereford and finished in Wales.

'On the other hand,' Lol said, more than a bit hesitantly, 'Hardwicke's... what... fifteen minutes away?' He jerked a thumb over his shoulder. 'In that direction.'

'I knew you were going to say that.'

'If anybody can put a kind of perspective on this...'

'Dear God. Do we need that kind of perspective?'

'Of course, she might not be there any more,' Lol said. 'She might even be...'

'We'd've heard,' Merrily said tightly. 'We'd *know.*'

'OK,' Lol said. 'I didn't want to say anything about this. I'm just a dreamy, whimsical songwriter, looking to pull tunes and textures and things out of the air. I don't know why I went to that place last night. I just did. And it was a bloody awful place.'

Merrily slowed.

'Awful how?'

'I'm probably being subjective.'

'Doesn't matter. Tell me.'

'It just… I don't want to use emotive words, it just sounds like a cliché.'

'This is no time for songwriter-pride, Lol.'

'It was like it didn't want to let me go. Like even the barbed wire was alive and hungry. Yeah, I know.' Lol put up his hands in defence. 'I know what that sounds like.'

'Go on.'

'So when the lights… when I found out it was only the police, I was so relieved I would've confessed to murder just to get the hell out of there.'

Merrily took the next left and turned the Volvo round clumsily in the mouth of the junction.

'Hardwicke, then.'

54

Hell's Kitten

IT WAS A shock, really. She was in a wheelchair.

Brenda Cardelow, proprietor of The Glades Residential Home, pushed her into a big lounge freshly painted in magnolia. Bright red cushions on four cream sofas, like big jammy-dodgers.

A bulky cardigan around her tiny shoulders, a blue woollen rug over her knees.

'Of course, Cardelow's *entirely* to blame for this,' Miss White said in her little-girl voice. 'Tries several times a week to kill me. *Utterly* psychotic.'

Mrs Cardelow, a large woman with bobbed white hair, said nothing, apparently still trying for dignity. It was never going to work.

'But how little she knows.' Miss White smiled, crinkling her malevolent mascaraed eyes. 'The poor cow has no comprehension of what I shall do to this place when I'm dead.'

Mrs Cardelow sighed, stepping away from the wheelchair. Miss White turned her sooty smile on Merrily.

'How charming you look, my dear. And Robinson, with a bandage to hide the needle marks. Hadn't realized you people put it into the wrist nowadays. *So* long since I used to watch Crowley shooting up.'

Lol, smiling patiently, had wandered over to the window, which had a long view down the garden, over the Wye to the Radnorshire hills, pale as old mould. Lol had a jittery rapport, which Merrily found unsettling, with Anthea White, she who insisted on Athena.

'You don't mind if I leave you,' Mrs Cardelow said. 'One can only stand so much of this. She gives the other residents tarot readings and tells them when their friends are going to die.'

Miss White didn't react, sat gazing placidly into the coal fire behind its guard, not looking up until there was the click of a closing door.

'Has she gone?'

'She's gone,' Merrily said.

Miss White tapped the arm of the wheelchair. 'I keep a cyanide capsule in here, you know, to be used if ever I see a doctor approaching with a catheter.'

Lol said, 'For him?'

'Ah, how well you know me, Robinson.'

Miss White giggled, a sound like the chinking of old bones in an ossuary. Merrily coughed.

'What, erm…?'

'Hip. Common or garden. I'm apparently in the queue for a stretch in some frightful NHS hellhole where, if they don't like your face, they slip you a fatal infection. Somewhere else to haunt. In the interim, I do rather like this chair – it allows one to move around in a perpetual meditative state. Would you like me to describe your aura?'

'Not really.'

'Jaundiced.'

'What?'

'A worrying amount of yellow. You're afraid of losing control. In fear of your immortal soul again. *Oh, dear God, keep her out, keep her out!*'

Merrily moistened her lips, recalling the first time she'd been to The Glades, when there'd been reports of a presence on the third floor and the then proprietors had wanted an exorcist to calm the residents. Underestimating Miss White's propensity for playfulness, like the elderly kitten she so resembled. A kitten with over fifty years' experience of the techniques for personal growth circulating in the ruins of the Hermetic Order of the Golden Dawn. Hell's kitten.

'But how strange to see the two of you in the same room at last. An *item*.'

Her eyes twitching from Merrily to Lol and back again.

'Flitting in and out of one another's energy fields, like neurotic damsel flies. Delightful in its way, but… it must not go on much longer, *do you hear me*?'

Arching suddenly out of her chair, expanding into so much more of a presence.

'Sort yourselves out at once. You don't have long to decide before something makes the decision for you. And that may not be the one you hope for.'

'Thank you, Miss White,' Merrily said lightly.

A constriction in the throat. *Dear God, how stupid was it to have come here?*

'Now, remind me, Watkins, what was the name of the detritus that became briefly attached to you?'

Merrily hesitated, just like she had the first time. There were clergy she could name who'd have her defrocked for even talking to this woman.

'No, don't tell me,' Miss White said. 'How could I forget? It was delightfully appropriate. *Joy.* Yes?'

'Yes.'

'*Joie de vivre… Joie de morte.* He's back, is he?'

'He isn't back. It isn't me, this time. It's someone else.'

'Someone who can't come in person?'

'Due to being dead.'

'But not at rest.'

'Athena, I don't know.'

The Glades had a lift, and they went up in it to the exotic room on the third floor. Not much had altered. The same Afghan rugs on the walls, the same book cupboards, the same radiogram, although the whisky bottles inside would be several generations down the line.

Miss White sent her chair whining softly to the uncurtained sash window and turned her back on the view of Hardwicke Church, which was greystone, Welsh-looking like Brinsop, a small bell tower with the bell on show. *Your church*, she'd said that first night, *is like some repressive totalitarian regime. Everyone has a perfectly good radio set, but you try to make sure they can only tune in to state broadcasts.*

Signalling Merrily to the Parker Knoll armchair and Lol to the bed, her face became momentarily serious.

'So it's Mithras, is it?'

'If you'd be so good,' Merrily said.

'Which one? The original Persian lord of light, who pre-dates Zoroastrianism… or his very much darker Roman descendant? Who may just spoil your day. Do you mind awfully?'

Merrily sat down.

'We had a one-off lecture at theological college. It was about dealing with the smart-arses who'll tell you Jesus was just another permutation of the pagan archetype. Wasn't Mithras born on December 25th?'

'Indeed. And his mother was a virgin, and he never had sex. His crib was visited by adoring shepherds. His followers were baptized and worshipped on a Sunday. They represented holy blood with wine and, at this time of year, ate hot cross buns.'

'And all this half a millennium before the birth of Jesus,' Merrily said. 'What's left to spoil?'

Miss White frowned. Always encouraging.

'They're just patterns, Athena. Death and rebirth, all that. Early Christianity slipped into the time-honoured seasonal rituals so people could begin to see them in a new light – now that the world was finally ready to learn about the unifying chemistry of love. There you are – a quiet revolution and no blood shed but His. How's that?'

'Glib.'

'I prefer *succinct*,' Merrily said.

Never entirely comfortable with all this, though. The candles of faith flickering feebly under the arc lights of history and scholarship. The nights when you couldn't get to sleep and doubts hovered in the shadowed corners, challenging you to snap on the bedroom lights and discover there was really nothing there... nothing at all...

Except Athena White showing her little teeth.

'If you *know* all this, Watkins, what do you want from me?'

'Well... that's *all* I know about Mithras and Mithraism. Although I think I recall old pictures of him in one of those caps like a beanie.'

'The Phrygian cap. I'll accept that the little chap was less handsome than Christ, with that... perpetual petulance. But then, the Roman Mithras was all about finding spiritual fulfilment through killing. An ancient sun god adopted by Roman emperors, hailed as the protector of soldiers. A sun god *worshipped in darkness*... in underground chambers stinking of blood. Now, what exactly are you looking for?'

'Don't know how it works, basically. Only that it was eventually supplanted by Christianity.'

'Supplanted. That's what you think, is it?'

'Well, it certainly came off second best. Even at the time.'

'Did it?'

Miss White hunched herself up, coquettishly, like a venomous bushbaby in the fork of a tree.

'I imagine you're familiar with the missives of St Paul? Who instructed the Ephesians to put on the whole armour of God... the breastplate of righteousness... the helmet of salvation... the sword of the Spirit...'

'What a thug that guy was,' Merrily said uncertainly.

'And where did he get it? Where did all that military imagery come from? His home town, of course. Tarsus. A veritable hotbed of Mithraism. *Onward, Christian Soldiers.* Mithraism wasn't supplanted by Christianity at all – they existed side by side for centuries and one fed the other. Scholars ask why Mithraism suddenly disappeared. It didn't, of course.'

Merrily sat shaking her head. Whatever you got from Athena White you had to pay for, big time.

'Consider, Watkins. It's not merely the military imagery that's seeped into the churches, it's the whole ethos. Think of the Crusades, the Spanish Inquisition… the ghastly Bush and that grinning shit Blair who took us to war and then had the audacity to turn Catholic.' Miss White's eyes lit up. 'Now *there* was an interesting coincidence! The bloody thread of the *true* Roman religion. Does he even know, do you think?'

'Not for me to say.'

'Hold up your bloodied cross, and what do you see? The handle of the sword of Mithras. The sword which now forms what some might think of as the spine of Christianity.'

'Well, that's not quite—'

'Tell me this, Watkins… how do you know that you yourself are not, to some degree, a child of Mithraism?'

Merrily smiled.

'Because, Athena… I'm a woman.'

Miss White clapped her tiny hands.

'*Excellent* reply. Now we can begin.'

55

Cutting Edge

DANNY LOOKED UP at the black iron gates which would've replaced a standard wooden five-bar, the wall of dressed stone where it used to be chicken wire.

'What we gonner be looking for, then, Gomer? Blood? Feathers? Empty lager cans?'

He had his new phone with him. Supposed to be a decent camera in there with a shedload of pixels. Should do the job. Shading his eyes, he looked out over the shining roofs of all the cars to the high ground behind the Court.

'It's all changed.'

'Can't change the countryside, boy,' Gomer said.

'You reckon?'

'The ole Unicorn was up by the top bridge, and the cockpit was in the field behind the yard, so I reckon it's gotter be up by that stand o' pine.'

'Well fenced off,' Danny said. 'So we gotter do it the hard way?'

He'd been hoping they could get what they'd come for without having to go in with the media and the gentry and the dickheads in chains of office. Far as he could judge from the number of parked cars, there was likely two hundred people here: press, radio and telly and a bunch of bored freeloaders helping themselves to a rich bastard's hospitality.

Halfway up The Court's new gravel driveway they were stopped by a stocky woman, short bleached hair, a warning finger on her lips. Regional BBC were interviewing Savitch with his house in the background. The reporter, Mandy Patel, smiling up at him and nodding hard, the way TV reporters did but nobody ever did in real life.

'Oh, dear me, *no*,' Savitch was going. 'Not the New Cotswolds, this is absolutely *not* about the so-called New Cotswolds. This is about the *Old Marches!*'

Lifting a fist, like he'd just coined a new slogan. What a *dick*. A phoney cheer went up from behind him, from folks Danny had never seen before, whose idea of the Old Marches would be around 1998.

Gomer turned away, fishing out his ciggy tin. In his old tweed cap, yellow muffler, red and green trainers from Hay and Brecon Farmers, he looked like part of the stage dressing.

'Now, it's a fact,' Savitch was saying, 'that last year, by far the highest percentage of British incomers t'this area was from London itself. However—'

'You included, of course,' Mandy Patel said.

'Indeed. Yes, of course, Mandy, but what's seldom understood is that most of us don't want t'bring London out here, we want t'sustain and fortify the essential character of the *Old Marches*. Everything we do here comes out of the area. Local skills, local tradition. I want to win the respect and trust of the *real* people.'

Jesus wept. This was how the Americans used to talk in Iraq, while all the corpses got shovelled off the streets. *Hearts and minds.*

Gomer sniffed, rolling his ciggy. Got a few hard looks but nobody was gonner challenge a man who looked more *Old Marches* than any bugger here. Danny looked beyond the TV people at the tarted-up farmhouse, its reblackened timbers bulging like black Botox lips around the white plaster. He saw men in old-fashioned leather jerkins, women dressed as serving wenches with trays of fizzy wine. He saw a load of phoney shite.

There wasn't much more to Savitch than spreadsheets and flow-charts, but a few folks would clock the muted tweedy jacket and what looked like working men's boots and go, *Gotter hand it to him, at least he's making an effort to fit in.* Some country folks, when it came down to basics, were no wiser than town folks.

Mandy Patel lifted a finger, then the cameraman straightened up from his tripod and Savitch shook hands with both of them and moved on along the drive, people patting him on the back.

'OK, thanks,' the woman with the short bleached hair said to Danny. 'You can go through now. Thank you for your patience.'

Looking down her nose at Gomer's ciggy, then turning away, talking to a woman with a name-tag that said *Country Pride magazine*. Danny hung around, listening.

'… going to ask you about Countryside Defiance, Rachel,' the magazine woman said. 'I see you've a stand over there.'

'Well, sure,' this Rachel said, and Danny recognized her now, from the TV. 'Country-dwellers are still seen either as dinosaur gentry, old hippies or retired roses-round-the-door types. If we *don't* start appealing to younger people with money we're going to be dead in the water, darling.'

Danny turned away, feeling like he was drowning in liquid shit. Saw the TV woman and the cameraman, tripod over one shoulder, head across the lawns past the Green displays – solar panels, domestic wind-turbines, geo-thermal heating and other expensive kit that never quite worked.

'Smiffy Gill doesn't come cheap,' Rachel said, 'but he's certainly good value if you're trying to show how *cutting-edge* the country is.'

'He's not here, is he?'

The magazine woman looking hopefully around, Rachel frowning.

'Might come later. Meantime, talk to Ward. Talk to Kenny, who's an absolute treasure, frighteningly macho. Talk to the local councillor, Pierce, who's youngish and *local.*'

'And bent as a bloody ole fork-end,' Gomer said before Danny towed him off.

'Gomer, we don't draw *attention*, right?'

Danny had nearly suggested that they call it off when he'd heard about Lol being in the slammer, but Gomer had said it could be even more important now to nail Savitch on the cocking, and mabbe he was right.

They moved on down past a white van with *Oldcastle Catering* on the side, Danny beginning to see folks he and Gomer had worked for, digging new soakaways, wildlife ponds. Also, the usual Ledwardine notables – James Bull-Davies tapping the green-oak frame of a new barn that was never gonner be used for hay, swimming pool more like. Poor ole James likely figuring out that it had cost more than his entire stable-block *and* his new roof. Realizing he was part of history, but mabbe not the kind Savitch was looking to restore.

Between two buildings not yet converted was a dark green marquee with HARDKIT HARDKIT HARDKIT stencilled in black all over it and these display boards with photos of men covered in muck. Alongside, a track ended at a stile, an empty field on the other side, stubbled with the dead stems of last year's docks and stumps of trees and piles of branches gathered for burning.

'That it, Gomer? Up there?'

Colder now, mucky-looking clouds converging as Gomer and Danny scaled the stile and walked up the field. The sound of a medieval band floating up behind them, drums and possibly a crumhorn. *Merrie Englande.* As they moved up the rise, Danny looked around, from landmark to landmark: the church steeple, Cole Hill, The Court itself, in its own green nest.

Then he saw they were standing on the edge of what surely had been the cockpit behind the long-demolished Unicorn pub.

You wouldn't be able to tell in summer, but the grass hadn't really started growing yet and the shallow bowl was obvious. Not many trees left around it, and only a few scrubby bushes in the middle, so it *had* been preserved at one time, sure to've been.

And that was the point, wasn't it?

One time.

'Shit,' Danny said.

No blood, no feathers, no beer cans. The ole Ledwardine cockpit was wilderness. Disappointment plunged deep into Danny's gut.

'I'm sorry, Gomer.'

Gomer didn't move.

'Mabbe we was a bit dull to think they was doin' it yere,' Danny said. 'Most likely it moves around, farm to farm, like a circus.'

'Where?' Gomer's fists clenching in the air like mini digger-buckets. 'They was moving round, we'd know about it.'

He was right. They likely would.

'It...' Danny hesitated. 'Gomer... it possible you was wrong about that cock?'

Gomer didn't even answer. They climbed back over the stile, to the sound of some audio-visual presentation going on in the Hardkit tent, the voice of Smiffy Gill, mad-bastard presenter of *The Octane Show*, which Danny had watched just once when it'd been about Jeeps.

'*... just had an amazing time on the quad bike, Kenny, mate, but I would, wouldn't I?*'

Smiffy's haw-haw laugh. Danny couldn't stand no more of this. Figured he'd forgo the free champagne lunch guaranteed by Lol's tickets, unless Gomer...

'You all right, Gomer?'

'Bloody let her down this time, ennit?'

'Jane? Gomer, you done everything a man could do. Mabbe we was wrong about Savitch. Mabbe *her* was wrong.'

'No. Gotter be folks from Off. It was local folks, I'd *know*.'

Danny felt suddenly choked up. Things were changing yereabouts. Things were happening that even Gomer Parry didn't know about. Because Gomer Parry's era was nearly over.

He looked at the Hardkit tent. Had their catalogues through the post, same as most country folk, only now they were inviting him to spend £250-plus on a waterproof jacket. Three year ago they was just this one tiny little run-down shop with the window all blacked-out, looked on the verge of closing down. Now a bloody chain with jackets at two-fifty.

'*Listen…*'

Gomer was standing by the half-open flap of the framed porch at the front of the tent. His ciggy was out, his face looked flushed. He'd taken off his glasses, like this improved his hearing.

'*For us, the quad bike is just for getting to the location.*' Another voice, not Smiffy. '*After that, yow got to rely on your own power, look.*'

Now Danny got it. He walked over, stood in the entrance. A flickering darkness inside; he could just make out rows of chairs, about twenty people watching a video on a big-screen TV, stereo sound turned up loud.

Danny stepped inside. On the screen, two men were bawling at each other across a moonscape: Smiffy Gill, with his kooky grin, and a wiry guy with a shaven head and a kind of circular beard like a big O around his lips.

Smiffy said, 'So, Kenny, I'm guessing this is where the men get separated from the boys?'

A picture came up of a landscape that was nothing but rocks and shale, sloping down near-vertically to a roaring, spitting river. Two men in crash helmets were crossing the gorge on this unstable-looking rope bridge.

'Give the lad a coconut,' Kenny said.

Then heavy-metal music was coming up under the crashing of the river and Smiffy Gill's laughter, and the temperature in Danny's gut dropped a few degrees as he walked out to Gomer.

'Shit,' Danny said.

In his ears, the whoops of Smiffy Gill getting into his harness for his river crossing. In his head, the metallic rumble of a new JCB tractor with a snowplough attached. Gomer going:

This a hexercise, pal?

Then the long, cold silence. Then the short laugh, then:

Give the ole man a coconut.

56

The Beast Within

No more kitten.

'So you think it's happening now, do you?' Athena White said. 'And you think it's happening here.'

'In a way,' Merrily said. 'On some level. Yes, I do.'

Miss White had directed Lol to one of the book cupboards, a repository of information rather than a bibliophile store, with many books stacked horizontally to get more on the shelves. *Shelf four, sixth from the bottom, flaking cover. Yes, that one... and the one below it.*

She leafed through one of the stained tomes. It smelled of whisky.

'Mithraism is still quite widely practised by pagans. Remind me of any ancient cult, I'll show you its modern counterpart. Most of the contemporary groups, of course, are harking back to the original Persian *Mithra* – the sun god. The Lord of the Wide Pastures as he's referred to in a cobbled-together but rather pretty ritual. All very green and comparatively bloodless. Some groups even let women in now.'

'I don't think that's what we're looking at,' Merrily said. 'How did it come to be a Roman religion?'

'I don't think anyone knows. Senior Romans, to begin with – emperors, generals, then spreading to lower officers, if not the ranks. The chaps most interested in promoting a state of mind conducive to warfare. Mithraists called one another *brother*. Fusing themselves together as supremely efficient fighting units.'

'Like the SAS.'

'I suppose. If it's any small comfort, Watkins, one writer comments that the Roman cult of Mithras adopts the paganism of the original Persian cult *without* its apparent tolerance of other religions… and the harshness of Christianity without its redeeming qualities of love and mercy. A combination, therefore, of the least humane aspects of both Christianity and the original Mithraism.'

'Does that suggest the Roman religion was, to an extent, manufactured?'

'I'm sure it does. The Romans were such pragmatists, even the Vikings seem soppy in comparison. Even as magic, it's considered to be a lower form, happy to trade with elementals and demons rather than with what you might call a spiritual source. Make of that what you will. But gosh, frightfully useful in a scrap.'

'How widely did it spread in Britain?'

'It's not ubiquitous, but far from invisible. A very good example of a mithraeum – one of their temples – was found in London. Also a famous one at Hadrian's Wall in Northumbria.'

'What about this area?'

'That's what I was…' Miss White lifted an old brown book, *The Mithraic World* '… attempting to discover. I don't think so, actually. I think the nearest evidence of Mithraic worship is at Caerleon – which *was* linked to Hereford by a Roman road. But there's probably a tremendous amount of Roman archaeology as yet undiscovered in the Credenhill area.'

'So it wouldn't be surprising if there was?'

'It wouldn't surprise *me*. The Romans often built shrines and temples in the shadow of Iron Age hill forts.'

With a pile of books accumulating at the side of her wheelchair, Miss White talked for some time of what little was known of Mithraic theology and a concept of the afterlife.

'Nothing quite comparable to the risible Islamic promise of an unlimited supply of virgins for chaps martyred in the cause – that's the stuff of men's magazines. And yet there *are* similarities in the way it must have been used by the Romans. Those who died in battle were expected to have an untroubled afterlife, as a result of the rituals they'd practised and the degree of attainment.'

'And the rituals were...?'

'Well... following a baptism, you would have a series of grades or degrees. Spiritual ranks – raven, lion, soldier, and so on, each with an appropriate face-mask. Each an initiation to a higher level, through tests involving danger and suffering. We read of the "twelve tortures of Mithraism" – ordeals which might bring the candidate to the very brink of death. From which, obviously, they would emerge much strengthened. A universal concept. If you consider *your* chap's forty days and forty nights in the wilderness, constantly exposed to psychic attack...'

'Bit different, *really*...'

'Not so different from the ordeals where recruits were made to sleep on frozen ground or in snow, or were branded and buried alive. Though I suppose the less savoury ones – like being compelled to eat animals which are still alive...'

Merrily was immediately reminded of one of the more repellent anecdotes in the late Frank Collins's book. Where Collins, in North Africa or somewhere, was urged by a senior officer to carry out an ethnic custom involving biting the heads off live poisonous snakes and eating the still-threshing remains.

'And they would be taken to the very edge of extinction,' Miss White said gleefully, 'in the sure belief that they *are* going to die. Pushed to the absolute limits of human endurance.'

Very SAS. It was all starting to make sense – how Byron Jones married Mithraic ritual to his own experiences in the Regiment. But how far had he practised it for real, in a ritual context?

Miss White was talking about *haoma*, a herbal drink, ingredients unknown, named after a pre-Mithraic Persian god but probably also adopted by the Romans because it stimulated the senses and induced an unstoppable aggression. A drug of war.

'Athena...' Lol had his OS map opened out on the Aztec

bedcover. 'Where might we be looking for a temple of Mithras?' Tapping the putative ley lines issuing from Brinsop Church. 'Have any been found under churches, in the same way you sometimes find a crypt built around a Neolithic burial chamber?'

'Not unknown, Robinson, according to this book. The odd mithraeum *has* been found under a church – one in Rome, for example – but, again, I'm not aware of any inside British churches. But, you see, one could be anywhere. This whole area has been a military playground for two millennia. Interesting how it continues to attract the army and the MoD to this day. A landscape quietly dedicated to war.'

Miss White was pointing to a spot a few miles south of Brinsop, where it said *Satellite Earth Station*.

'Satellite dishes collecting intelligence surveillance from all over the world and feeding it to GCHQ at Cheltenham – where, as it happens, I worked for a period in my civil-service years. Bloody place leaked like a sieve.'

'*Athena* – you were a spook?'

'Don't be cheap, Robinson. And what *did* you do to your wrist?'

'It got entangled in the barbed wire around a private military playground.'

'Not sure I like the sound of that.'

Merrily sat back and thought about some implications.

'What does a mithraeum look like?'

'Like a public toilet,' Miss White said. 'Rectangular. Fairly basic and utilitarian, apart from a few astrological symbols and a representation of Mithras himself. And, of course, partly or entirely underground, to simulate a cave. Certainly no windows. And a channel down the middle, for the sacrificial blood.'

'Oh.'

'What did you expect?'

'Are we talking about human sacrifice, or—?'

'Bulls,' Miss White said. 'All the pictures of Mithras show him slitting the throat of a bull.'

***

Leaning across, a knee in the bull's back, a hand hauling back its head, fingers in its nostrils – or so it seemed. Carnage where the sword or long knife went in.

The act performed dismissively. The perpetrator gazing away. Directly, as it were, into camera.

It was known as the *Tauroctony*. Athena White displayed a double-page illustration, sitting the big brown book on the blue blanket across her knees. 'In all the sculptures and carvings and bas-reliefs, Mithras always looks away. In much the same way as the Greek hero Perseus, as he prepares to cut off the head of the Gorgon, averts his gaze.'

Merrily would rather have averted hers but kept on looking, frozen, registering all the detail, hearing Arthur Baxter at his kitchen table.

Unlikely to've been nicked for breeding purposes.

Lol was the first to find his voice.

'They still *do* this? The modern followers of Mithras.'

'If they do, it's hardly mainstream. All a psychological exercise now. In the Roman myth, the slaying of the bull in the cave is seen as a creative act, releasing all manner of good things, positive energy, along with the blood. To the modern Mithraist, the bull tends to represent the ego which must be overcome – the beast within us. Cut him down – sacrifice that side of your essence – and don't look back.'

'But the Romans did it for real.'

'Their temples clearly were designed for it. The bull might have been sedated before being butchered, torn apart, so that the initiate would be covered from head to foot with the blood.'

'So it would be like an abattoir.'

Lol, sitting on a corner of the bed, looked unhappy. Unlike Miss White, who seemed stimulated by thoughts of blood-spatter.

'One wonders precisely when blood sacrifice – that staple of the Old Testament – was brushed under the Christian carpet. For a while, certainly, Christianity and Mithraism were rivals, and then Christ appeared to have triumphed while Mithras simply disappeared – up the arse of Christianity. So who *really* triumphed? Did they take it this far at your college, Watkins?'

Merrily looked into Lol's eyes. The room was awash with bland spring sunlight, bringing up the richness in the Afghan rugs.

'So this is the summit,' she said. 'The final act. The last step to attain the highest grade, when the initiate takes on the persona of the god.'

Miss White put her hands together as if in prayer, although you never liked to think what she might be praying to.

'What might it do to a person now, Athena? We have a man hardened up by lying in the snow, made braver by coming close to death. Where does he go next?'

'Ah, Watkins, so much for you to *dwell* upon. That dark seam of masculine aggression, the spinal fluid of the Church. What might it represent? This insidious flaw in the very foundations of your poorly fabricated faith.'

'I'm not talking about the Church, I'm talking about an individual practising a religion created in the days when he'd be expected to stroll through a village, torching dwellings and hacking the limbs off babies. Where would that level of aggression take him now? What kind of training would he need to control it?'

Down in the bowels of The Glades, a gong was banged.

'Heavens,' Miss White said. 'Lunchtime already?'

Before the lift doors opened on the ground floor, she said, 'Radical corruption of a religion… there's always fall-out. It's corrosive. A maxim worth remembering is *if the worse can happen, the worst will.*'

In the gilded opulence of Brinsop Church, they confronted the early-medieval sandstone tympanum. The mounted St George with his Roman soldier's skirt, thrusting his spear between the dragon's jaws.

'More like a big snake than most dragons.' Merrily stepped back. 'But no way is it a bull.'

'No, but…' Lol pointed, with his good hand, to the frieze at the top of the slab '… *that* looks like a bull, doesn't it?' He bent, feeling the sandstone with both hands. 'And these are definitely lions. Another of Athena's degrees of Mithraism? Also the crow, raven…?'

'Yes.' There was also astrological symbolism here and there in the fabric of the church. 'Are we suggesting there's an element of Mithras embedded in this landscape?'

'Maybe literally. It could be simply that the early-medieval artisans who made this slab copied images from Roman artwork that they'd found in the ground – in the remains of Magnis. Must've been quite a lot left in the eleventh and twelfth centuries.'

That made sense. Unfortunately, what also made sense was that if you wanted an aspect of Mithras acceptable to the Church, you might look no further than St George.

That was the trouble with churches. Full of Green Men and Sheela-na-gigs and all the wall-eyed mutants in the pagan directory. And now maybe a killer in saint's armour.

Merrily watched Lol's gaze panning slowly around the stained-glass light show. George was everywhere, even though much of it was down to Sir Ninian Comper working as recently as the 1920s. A window in memory of the ornithologist Herbert Astley, of Brinsop Court, had been signed by Comper with his emblem.

'A strawberry plant,' Lol said. 'How prescient of him.'

'Huh?'

'Polytunnels?'

'Oh… right.'

How much more of this? Merrily sat down in a chair at the end of the back row, feeling as though she'd been mugged. Fragments of faith scattered like credit cards in the gutter.

57

Arena

EARLY AFTERNOON, CORNEL found a slot for the Porsche on Corn Square in Leominster, and Jane followed him down the street and across to the Blue Note café bar. All period jazz and blues posters. Cellar-club darkness all day long, except it wasn't in a cellar.

The wood where they'd parked was no more than four miles from the town and they'd come most of the way in silence, just one word stopping Jane from walking off to the bus station and never looking back.

The word was *Savitch*.

'I thought everybody loved him in these parts.' Cornel sugared his coffee. 'Thought he was the village's salvation. Brought the dump alive. Fairy godfather.'

'Grim reaper's closer.'

'But then, I also thought you fancied me a little bit,' Cornel said.

'I have a boyfriend.'

Who, in a couple of hours, would be waiting for her in Hereford, under the clock in High Town. Actually, the last time she'd been in the Blue Note was with Eirion and they'd sat under a vintage Blind Lemon Jefferson poster, killing themselves laughing making up tasteless names for damaged old British blues singers, like Quadriplegic Cyril Hewlett and Morbidly-obese Dilwyn Lloyd-Williams. It was like a different lifetime, when she was young and free, and now she was thinking she might never get back to that.

'I find it quite distressing, actually,' Cornel said, 'that you actually thought I might be planning to rape you.'

'You were trying to take me upstairs the other night!'

'Jane, I was legless… and you played along. We all thought you were up for it. Anybody would. They were taking bets on it, for—'

'*Bets?*'

'Men out on a jolly tend to get childish.'

'Cockfighting's a jolly, is it?'

'There was no cockfight that night. And anyway, if you don't enjoy a good cockfight you're hardly going to be up for the rest of it.'

'The rest of what?'

'Don't totally trust you yet, Jane. Would you really expect me to?'

Even though Cornel's face looked grey and creased in the dimness, she realized for the first time that he actually wasn't that much older than her. Maybe twenty-four? She felt a rush of determination. For some reason he was no longer a supporter of Savitch, and she needed to roll with that. She brought her coffee cup to her lips, then put it down again.

'OK, I told you a bunch of lies. My grandad… I lied about that. My grandads, one lives abroad, I don't hear from the other. Neither of them breed gamecocks, far as I know. I got all that from a mate I took the cock to and he told me how he thought it had died. I hate cruelty, OK?'

He sat looking at her with… not respect, obviously, but he was probably more comfortable with this admission. In Cornel's world, women would always have to be a bit shocked at what men did.

Jane picked up the coffee cup again, took a long, slow sip, considering the evidence: he was no longer staying either at Savitch's place or the Swan. No longer hanging out with his mates – maybe they'd gone back to London. But he'd stayed. On his own. And he wasn't happy. Look at the mindless way he'd been driving, like he didn't care if he crashed. He peered at her in the gloom.

'So you think I'm going to tell you about the cockfights. And help you tie Ward Savitch into it.'

'Somebody's got to stop him, before he buys up the entire village.'

'And you'd expose him *how*? Being as how Savitch is ring-fenced and lawyered to the gills.'

'My boyfriend,' Jane said. 'He's a journalist?'

'Is he really.'

'He can get the story out. All we need to know is where it's happening, where he's doing it.'

Cornel had started to laugh.

'You don't know me,' Jane said. 'I can *do* this.'

'And you think I'm going to tell you what I know?'

'You don't have to be implicated. We don't have to name you.'

A silence. Holding her hands together under the table.

'Which paper's your boyfriend work for, then?'

'He freelances for the *Sunday Times*. You might've seen his name. Eirion Lewis?'

She was on safe ground here. A big fat paper, and nobody ever remembered reporters' names, only columnists.

'So what's in it for me?' Cornel said.

She didn't know what to say.

'Jane, you just don't know who you're messing with, do you? You just don't fuck with these guys for the sake of a few bloody chickens and some flea-riddled badgers.'

'Badgers?'

Jane stared at him.

'Badgers are vermin,' Cornel said. 'They cause TB in cattle.'

'That's… debatable. You're saying they go after badgers as well? With dogs? Where you dig out the badgers and set dogs on them, and the dogs and the badgers both get ripped to—'

'Keep your *voice* down.'

'Like hell I will!'

'Not me, all right?' Cornel looked up to where three women were sitting down, a couple of tables away. 'Not me personally. I don't like to get my hands dirty.'

'You only don't dig out badgers for hygiene reasons?'

'*Shut up.*'

'But that's something else Savitch organizes for bored rich bastards, right?'

'Jane, drop it. You're a kid. Go away. Have fun.'

'Anybody,' Jane said through her teeth, '*anybody* who expects me to go away and *have fun* while this obscene shit— Just give me something on Savitch, Cornel. Why can't you do that?'

A silence between them. You could hear everything, every gush and tinkle from behind the counter, every scrape of a chair leg. One of the three women at the next-but-one table was talking about how she'd only take some guy back if he promised to cut down on the booze.

'You told anybody about this?'

'No.'

Instinct saying *lie, think about it later.*

One of the women at the other table told the first woman she was making a big mistake because they never cut down on the booze, whatever they told you, unless some quack told them their lives were on the line.

Cornel said, 'So you didn't tell your mother, for instance?'

'*God,* no. Why would I? She's in a difficult enough position, as vicar. Anybody gets the shit on Savitch, it's better it's me. I'm just a pagan.'

'Yes,' Cornel said. 'They were laughing about that in the Ox.'

'Yeah, well, they would, those morons.'

'Some of them found it rather titillating.'

'Yeah, Dean Wall. Moronic slob. Like I go out dancing naked. It's just native religion. It's my central interest. Ancient sites and stuff. Studied it for years.'

Cornel had his smartphone out, flicking through some stuff on the screen, then he handed it across.

'What's this, then?'

'Huh?'

'Look at it. If you know so much about paganism, tell me what this is.'

The picture blinked up at Jane, very clear in the dim light. You were looking down this weird kind of stone vault, like the crypt of a church with a fairly primitive plinth at the end. A tablet of stone with a carved face on it with like a Mohican haircut. Primitive, but not prehistoric, and definitely not Celtic.

'Is it Roman?'

'You tell me.'

'Well, where is it?'

Cornel didn't reply. Jane had another look. You could see stone blocks, like seating, stepped up from a closed-in area, like an arena. She'd seen arenas like this on the Net. Well, not *exactly* like this, but the same size, a small, closed-in area, impossible to escape from.

If you were poultry.

Holy shit.

'Cornel…'

'What?'

'Is this where it happens? The cockfights?'

Thinking back to the Web sites she'd forced herself to read. It was starting to make sense. The *sport* which had apparently been introduced to Britain by the Roman invaders.

Was this some little purpose-built Roman arena, a cockfight colosseum?

'You going to tell me where this is, Cornel?'

Cornel smiled.

'Why should I?'

'Then why are you showing me this?'

'Just thought you might know what it is. Obviously you don't know as much as you—'

Jane put the smartphone down again, looked Cornel in the eyes.

'They do badger-baiting here too?'

You could just imagine that, the squeals, the yipping and the ripping in this claustrophobic vault, blood all over its walls

It had Savitch written all over it. The way he was always going on about reviving old traditions.

'Cornel… please.'

'Jane, I'm a stranger here. I don't even know what the place is called. Guys who go there… what usually happens is they're taken at night. Sometimes blindfolded.'

'But you know where to find it?'

'You're asking me to take you?'

Jane read the car number plates over the bar again, right to left.

'I'd keep you out of it. I'd just take some pictures on my phone, and that would be it.'

'I hate to be boring.' Cornel looked at her, and not just at her face. 'But what's in it for me?'

'Cornel, I've got a *boyfriend*.'

'And even if you hadn't, you wouldn't fancy me, would you?'

Jane said, 'Please…?'

58

Poultry Contest

IF DANNY HAD ever seen Gomer this mad before, he didn't know when it was.

'Hangin' offence, sure t'be.' The ole feller was flattened against the back end of a stone ex-pigsty, firing up another ciggy like it was a little stick of gelignite. 'Passing theirselves off as Her Majesty's Special Forces. Wartime, that'd be a bloody capital offence. Treason, see. Treason, boy!'

'Gomer,' Danny said. 'There's boys all over Hereford pretends to be Sass, to get their end away with the local talent. This en't—'

'This is bloody different!'

'It was common land. It was under a foot of snow. No different to… to kids goin' out with sledges.'

Knowing, even as he was saying it, that this *was* different. Remembering the tone of voice, the sense of threat. The feeling he'd had at the time that they were gonner get done over at the very least. And a man naked in the snow. Laughing, but serious. The whole thing serious.

'You know another thing?' Gomer said, quieter, more sober now. 'What happened that night all but destroyed my bit o' faith in the Sass. The Sass is hard bastards, sure t'be, but I always had 'em down as polite, kind o' thing.'

Ah, so that was it. Danny stared out over the field with dead docks and no stock. *Put your lights out, then fuck off.* Gomer Parry Plant Hire dissed.

'Kenny bloody Mostyn,' Gomer said.

'You knows him?'

'Knowed his ole man, Eugene Mostyn. Inherited a tidy farm from an uncle and pissed it all away. Goes off to Birmingham weekends, nobody lookin' after the stock. Ewes caught in the wire, cattle left out in freezin' conditions.'

'I hates that kind,' Danny admitted.

'Gets a Brummie girl up the stick, right? Seventeen years later, this boy Kenny turns up from Brum, lookin' for his ole man. Eugene's gamekeeper now for ole Glenda Morgan – and her was three sheets by then, else her'd never've employed the useless bastard. Boy gets took on by Glenda, to help his ole man, which means doin' Eugene's job while Eugene's down the bettin' shop. Best thing happened to Kenny was when Eugene comes out the pub on a dark afternoon, goes for a slash in the road and gets flattened by a timber lorry.'

'Kenny collect much?'

'No, but ole Glenda seen him right, and when her's gone he rents a shop in Hereford, and that's how Hardkit was born. Right, then.' Gomer peeled himself off the wall in a blast of ciggy smoke. 'I'm goin' back in there. Gonner find that boy, have a word.'

'No, listen…' Danny stepping in front of him. 'Mostyn en't there. I looked around. It's just a promotional video. Fellers in there's just punters and a few blokes as done it before, spreadin' the word.'

'Where is he?

'I don't *know*, Gomer.'

'Ah, this is nasty, boy.' Gomer's ciggy hand was shaking, and that didn't happen often. 'Like goin' back to the days when you got all kinds o' scum lurkin' in the hedges after dark.'

'Only difference being,' Danny said, 'that this is rich scum payin' for the privilege of crawlin' through shit and brambles an' freezin' their nuts off in the snow. And freezin' your nuts off en't a crime.'

He watched a few blokes leaving the Hardkit tent with leaflets, some shaking hands with a bulky bloke he figured he'd seen before.

'Cockfights is a crime,' Gomer said.

'Who said this got anything to do with bloody cockfights?'

'I never thought, see. Must be goin' bloody senile, boy.'

'What – this Eugene was a cocker?'

'Eugene, he wouldn't have the patience to feed up a cock for the ring, but he *let it go on*, see. Glenda Morgan had a fair few spells in hospital, them last years, and Eugene let all sorts go on when her's out the way. Few quid yere, few quid there. Bad blood, Danny boy. Kenny Mostyn's a rich man now, and still out on the hills, middle of a blizzard, callin' the shots. Why's he need to do that?'

Danny had no answer. Unless that was how Mostyn got his rocks off.

Inside the dark green tent, the Hardkit DVD was starting up again, with a blast of metal and commentary: '*You know me. I'm Smiffy Gill. I'm a bloke likes to grab life by the balls.*'

'All right,' Danny said. 'You stay there, Gomer, you'll only send your blood pressure through the roof. I'll go back, see what I can do.'

The guy was outside the Hardkit tent and he'd been joined by another feller Danny recalled from the night of the storm.

Danny reckoned if he was right, one of them would have a bit of a Scottish accent. He strolled over.

''Ow're you?'

They just looked at him. Danny nodded at the Hardkit sign.

'Seems like good stuff.'

'It's very good stuff, ma friend,' the bulky guy said.

Thickset, couple of days' stubble. A big-money bloke on his day off. Danny put on a rueful smile.

'Too bloody costly for me, I reckons.'

The other guy – sharp-faced and wary-eyed – said, 'There *are* shorter, more economical courses that don't involve staying here. But we're not the best people to talk to about them. Sorry.'

'Weeell,' Danny said slowly, 'thing is, I en't that interested in the shootin' weekends and all that. Just I was told to ask in yere about… other events.'

The Scots guy eyed him.

'In connection with what?'

'Poultry,' Danny said. 'Poultry contests. Kind o' thing.'

'Oh…' The Scots guy grinned. 'Right.' Turned to his mate. 'This gentleman's looking for a poultry contest.'

'I usually talks to Kenny, see. I was told he'd be yere, but he en't.'

'That's quite true, ma rustic friend. He isn't.'

'I'd ring him,' Danny said 'but phones, you never knows who you're talkin' to, do you?'

'You do not.'

'See, I'd arranged to bring a bird. Kenny, he was gonner let me know when and where, kind o' thing.'

Starting to sweat a bit now. If Kenny Mostyn was to walk in now, he'd be stuffed.

'You're a breeder yourself, then?'

'Of many years standin'.'

Putting a bit of menace under his voice now. If you looked like a bit of a hard bastard, why not play to it?

'Good for you,' the Scots guy said.

Danny looked him in the eyes.

'If this is a problem for you fellers, just forget you seen me. I'll call by the shop tomorrow. If I can find the time.'

The two guys looked at each other.

'Ah, well,' the Scots guy said. 'That possibly could be a wee bit too late, you know?'

'Bloody *is* tonight, is it?' Danny slapped his thigh. 'Fuck.'

The bald guy gave the Scots guy a look, and the Scots guy looked at Danny with no fear at all but definitely a measure of respect.

'Y'know how it is, pal. Busy guy, Kenny. But if you want to stick around, I believe he's due to call in later.'

'Sure to.'

Danny nodded, a bit curt, walked away without looking behind him, to find Gomer. They went back to the Jeep on the parking area, where they unwrapped the sandwiches that Danny's wife Greta had put up for him, sat there eating them very slowly, not saying much, Danny pretty unsure how he felt about this.

It was around four-thirty before a battleship-grey BMW four-by-four pulled in. HARDKIT in a neat curve across the bonnet. They watched a man jump down. He had on a shiny suit and a bow tie and carried an overnight bag.

'Wassis about?' Gomer said.

Danny moaned.

'Bloody dinner, ennit? It's on the tickets Lol give me. This feller can't be goin' to no cocking tonight.'

'Mabbe afterwards,' Gomer said. 'Mabbe a few of 'em, sittin' with their cigars, watchin' the feathers fly.'

'Not yere. Savitch wouldn't risk it.'

'We better find out, then.'

'Aw, Gomer…'

'En't gonner get a better chance.' Gomer sat back, tilted his cap over his eyes. 'Mabbe a long night, boy.'

59

Cheated

DARTH VAYNOR AND Elly Clatter arrived in the CID room simultaneously, Bliss ejecting from his office, all caffeined-up.

'I'm not wearing this, son. Not like she can hide in a cupboard under the frigging sink.'

'Last her dad knew,' Darth said, 'she was living with a bloke in a flat in Belmont. We turn up there, front and back, only to find the guy in the sack with somebody else. Didn't know where Victoria had gone. Didn't seem too upset, mind.'

'Just grateful he'd still got both eyes. How long since she went?'

'Days. "Duh, whatever day this is" – that kind of guy, you know? Observant.'

'Right.' Bliss looked around. 'Where's Rich? I want this frigging city dismantled.'

Elly Clatter said, 'Francis, if I could just—'

'*What?*'

'BBC are here. They—'

'No! Tell them to piss off. Tell them we'll let them know soon as—'

'Francis.' Elly's hands on his shoulders. 'They *know*. It's all over the Net. Carly Horne was with some of her mates when Karen picked her up?'

Karen came over, nodding. Bliss moaned.

'Kid's a big social networker,' Elly said. 'There's now a *Friends of Carly* Facebook site, campaigning for her release?'

Bliss let out his breath in a slow rasp. If he *ever* came face to face with the little twat who invented Facebook…

'So what that means *is*?'

'Sky,' Elly said. 'And BBC *News 24*. So far.'

'What it also means,' Karen said, 'is that wherever Victoria is, she'd have to've gone blind and deaf not to know we're looking for her. Meanwhile, Carly's denying everything and Joss is saying very little. Time for you to have a go, boss?'

'Yeh,' Bliss said. 'I think it could be.'

Mentally sharpening a knife on a steel.

A mile or so before Ledwardine, Merrily's phone chimed and she pulled onto the verge.

'I don't know quite what you were expecting,' Fiona Spicer said, 'but I've just been given the results of the post-mortem.'

It was as though her voice was in a straitjacket.

'Natural causes.'

'Oh.'

'If he'd been younger,' Fiona said, 'they'd be using terms like… if I can say this… *Idiopathic Hypertrophic Cardiomyopathy*? I'm told it means a sudden, inexplicable heart attack. In an older man, even one as fit as Sam, it's… less inexplicable.'

'Had you… any reason to think he had a heart problem?'

'No, and if he had I'm not sure he would've told me. He liked to deal with his own problems. As you know.'

'Yes. How do you—?'

'Angry. Cheated. Angry that he won't see his daughter married.' Finally, fissures of a deep grief under her words. 'Cheated by his God. Nobody to blame but his damned God. Can you understand that?'

'Yes. I can understand it. Fiona—'

'I've a few other people to call. And Emily's arrived. Our daughter. And her fiancé. I suppose that means they'll release his body, so we can… Perhaps I could call you tomorrow, if that's convenient – I do remember what Good Friday involves for a vicar.'

'Whenever you like. If I'm in church, I'll call you back as soon—'

She'd gone. Would not share the sob. Merrily put the phone on the dash and told Lol. Felt like she'd been kicked.

'I realize people can go for years without knowing they have a heart condition, but this is… There may still be an inquest, but it'll be a quickie. No reason for anything to come out. Not now.'

She picked up Lol's hand, below the bandage. Since he'd told her about his minutes of fear inside Byron's compound, she'd felt they were together again, in a deeper sense. *Flitting in and out of one another's energy fields, like neurotic damsel flies. It must not go on.*

'I was thinking I could leave it for a while. Until after Easter. See if it made any more sense. Now… if I don't do something now.'

Lol squeezed her hand, as if to show he still could.

'Start by telling James.'

'About the possible re-emergence of an ancient Roman pagan cult and the possible involvement of a retired SAS trooper in the theft of a bull?'

'We both know what you can tell him.'

'Lol, I hardly like even to mention it out loud.'

'You mean bull?' Lol said. '*Mansel* Bull?'

Merrily put on her sunglasses and started up the car.

'Thanks for saying it first.'

'Watch much TV, Carly?'

Carly looked up, ebony hair still slanted defiantly across one eye.

Bliss said, 'Bet you've seen all them women's-prison reality shows. Could be worse inside, couldn't it? Get to wear your own clothes, have yer hair done, decorate the cell.'

'Think you're scaring me?' Carly said.

'Of course they're a *bit* misleading, them shows. They only talk to the mouthy prisoners, the ones who're a bit of a laugh. And speak English. No point in following one of the many smouldering, resentful East European ladies on Her Maj's guest list.'

'I fear you're sailing perilously close to racist shores, Inspector,' Mr Ryan Nye said.

Everyone's favourite duty solicitor, all glossy black hair and geek specs. Interesting how the smarmy twat was always first out of bed for something newsworthy.

Bliss shook his head.

'You know me better than that, Mr Nye. I'm just thinking how aggrieved certain migrant ladies in the slammer might feel at having to share a landing with someone who set up two of their innocent compatriots to get murdered.'

'Innocent, bollocks!'

Carly halfway out of her chair. Bliss smiled.

'Had it coming, did they? Look, Carly, I'm just giving yer a chance to make things easier all round. We'll have the DNA matches up soon, and that'll be that. Though I think it's only fair to tell you that poor little Joss has already seen the light.'

Ryan Nye looking at him, trying to work out if he was lying. Bliss just looked sad.

'It was that ugly scratch just below the left shoulder blade that did it. No wonder she was wearing a high-necked sweater. You got any scratches anywhere, Carly? We can get yer a plaster and a dab of Germolene. Should I summon a doctor and a nice police lady to hold your clothes?'

'I *never*…' Carly wrapped her arms around her chest. 'You listening? You won't find no DNA 'cause I never touched either of them women.'

'Could be you never did, Carly, but that doesn't make a lorra difference nowadays. Whether or not you struck any of the fatal blows, you still helped engineer a double murder. The courts draw few distinctions any more. You were *involved*, kid.'

Bliss paused, the flat of a forefinger angled thoughtfully under his bottom lip.

'Now, it *could* be you didn't realize it would get that far. If you were able to convince us of that, it might help you no end.

Though *pairsonally*, Carly, I'd find it hard to credit, 'cause your attitude so far has been unremittingly cocky with norra hint of remorse. The attitude, in fact, of someone who feels the world can only be a better place without the likes of Maria and Ileana Marinescu. Someone almost proud of her—'

'No!'

'*Yes.*'

Carly said nothing. Bliss was also silent for a while. Coming on like he was thinking something out. Giving it nearly half a minute before he said, 'How well do you know Victoria Buckland, Carly?'

Now was that a little shudder?

'See, we know Victoria of old, and she's gorra hell of a talent for self-preservation. The very last person to put both hands up and say, No, no, it's all down to me, officer, those kids had nothing to do with the actual violence, I'm a grown woman, me, and there's no way I'd let young girls take the rap for smashing anybody's—'

'Inspector…'

'Mr Nye?'

'Perhaps we could save some time. May I have a word in private with my client?'

'Absolutely, Mr Nye,' Bliss said. 'I'll be just outside, if required.'

60

Cult

THE TIN-ROOFED LEAN-TO that James Bull-Davies called his study overlooked the stable yard. They could see Alison out there forking sodden straw into a barrow. James's face was stretched, his washed-out eyes mottled with uncertainty.

'Normal way of things, this makes very little sense, even you must see that.'

'Normal way of things,' Merrily said.

She wouldn't sit down.

'Never your favourite word, is it, vicar? Normal.'

Out in the yard, Alison tossed the fork into the barrow. She looked tired.

'I should be doing that,' James said. 'Should've been done hours ago, but we had to go into town this morning, see a man about an overdraft. Or a woman, as it turned out.'

'Things are bad?'

'Recession, still. People don't want to burden themselves with extra horses, feed bills, vet bills…'

'It'll lift.'

'My lifetime, you think?' James frowned, watched Alison wheeling the barrow away. 'Should've made William Lockley clear out his own shit.'

'May not be his to clear,' Merrily said. 'Not all of it.'

She felt the ground becoming marshy. She'd left Lol on the square, in search of Danny and Gomer. Feeling obliged to come here alone.

'And I know my limitations, James.'

He sat down in the hard chair behind an old oak desk stained with cup marks. Drumming his fingers on a worn blotter.

'SAS are the finest in the world at what they do. Train, train and train again. And, the pressures being commensurate with the rewards of the job, there's little doubt that some chaps get drawn into odd byways. But the idea of a *cult*...'

'In fairness, much of it seems to have developed after they left the Regiment.'

James grimaced, drew in his chin.

'This Roman army business... you're suggesting that's actually in some way become central to the exercises devised by Jones and Mostyn for their clientele?'

'Think what people pay to go on Buddhist retreats and stay at ashrams. Add to that a powerful physical regime. And the almost mystical glow that surrounds the SAS.'

'And this includes the ritual slaughter of animals?'

'I... believe so. For some participants. The ones considered suitable. And discreet. And able to meet the fees.'

'An elite?'

'Belonging to an elite has always been very sexy.'

'And not really a swindle, I'd guess.'

'Only in that nobody should have to pay for spiritual knowledge. No, I... I think it almost certainly works. I think it alters them psychologically and in quite dramatic ways. I think there might even...'

'I'm sorry?'

'Doesn't matter. But you have to remember we're looking at something specifically shaped to the military two thousand years ago, when life was cheaper that we can imagine. Which, today, might have some questionable side effects. On some people.'

'Dangerous, you think.'

'Very. I think.'

James said. 'What about Savitch?'

'That's all circumstantial. The link is Hardkit, which supplies the equipment and know-how for Savitch's hunting and paint-balling weekends.'

'Was at his press launch today. Everything in place, all boxes ticked. Green energy, but also farmer-friendly.' James craned forward onto his elbows. 'No right at all to resent that man. My family, what's left of it, we can't do anything for the community any more – barely hold ourselves together. But Savitch is… Used to hear him sneering at anything that didn't fit his ludicrous concept of what country life should be about. Now he smiles tolerantly, witters on wistfully about tradition. Not a sham, as *such*, he just…'

'You can't stand him, can you?'

'Is it that obvious?' James looked pale with defeat. 'But he's such an *insubstantial* man that it's hard to see him getting down and dirty with the likes of Jones and Mostyn.'

'I don't think he does. I think that killing, for Savitch, is something done from a safe distance with a twelve-bore and nice gloves. I think he simply passes some clients on to Jones, probably via Mostyn, for a cut. And even then, I suppose, it's like SAS selection – many won't go all the way.'

'And the ones who don't slink quietly away? Don't like it, Merrily. Army turns out men. Danger of this creating…?'

'Monsters.'

'All right. What's the bottom line?'

'That's where it gets even more speculative.'

'Then speculate.'

'I'd much rather go and lie down in a dark room, but…' Merrily pulled out her cigarettes without the usual request for clearance '… it's just about conceivable, James, that, somewhere along the line, this takes in the killing of your cousin Mansel.'

She lit up, as the legs of James's wooden chair screeched on the stained flags.

William Lockley was back on the phone within half an hour of James's call. James just listened, his chin retracted, eyes half-closed.

'Have to remember Mrs Watkins is not actually in your employ, William,' he said after a while, then spent some more time listening and then barked, 'All right, will do,' and hung up. 'William conveys his respects, with a polite request for you to pop into Hereford.'

'Me? I'd've thought...' Merrily had her cigarettes out again. She shut the pack and pushed it back into her bag. 'Where in Hereford?'

'Seems Colin Jones is coming into police headquarters in about an hour. Seems that after the events of last night, the police thought it might be a good idea to visit his premises. Jones said he wouldn't be there today but, as he'd be in Hereford, he'd be happy to call in at Gaol Street. He says he won't be pressing charges against the man who broke into his premises.'

'Good to know,' Merrily said, guarded.

'Lockley thinks it would be a good idea to make the most of Jones's presence. In view of what you told me, they'd like you to be there when they talk to him. As a consultant.'

'They?'

'William himself and the Senior Investigating Officer. Howe.'

'Annie Howe asked for me? I don't think so, James.' She watched Alison leaning the barrow up against the house wall, then taking off her leather gloves. 'I expect I'm the one who'll look stupid if none of this stands up to scrutiny.'

'That bother you?'

'If it bothered me, I'd be in a different job.'

She called in at the vicarage to put out dried food for Ethel and check the answering machine. For once, no messages. On the way out, she noticed a brown Jiffy bag propped up against the wall and took it back inside.

The bag contained a large-format, lavishly illustrated hard-back book.

RISKING ALL
The SAS Experience

Another kill-and-tell Regiment memoir. By Trooper Z. There was a sheet of Black Swan headed notepaper, marking a page, Barry's scrawl across it: *More from the Public Sector.*

There were just pictures on the marked pages, in colour. One with a pencilled cross against it showed a bunch of smiling guys in T-shirts holding up white mugs. The caption said:

Teatime in Colombia for (L to R) Greg, Syd, Jocko and Nasal.

Various guns were laid out on the parched grass in front of them. Syd was only vaguely recognisable; his teddy bear's eyes were covered, like all their eyes, with a black rectangle. All dead. All dead now.

Except for Byron, of whom there was no sign.

61

Passed Away

CARLY SAID, 'VICTORIA... I reckon she thought Joss didn't like her. Well, nobody likes her that much, to be honest. And like most of them she don't care, but Joss was her little sister, you know?'

Little sister. Lemon hair and a frozen scowl. But you forgot; underneath, they were both little girls, citrus-haired Joss and Carly, with her black nails. Little girls who got the life beaten out of two women they didn't know.

Carly said, 'Victoria's, like, I'll find out who they are and we'll deal with them?'

Bliss nodded in an understanding kind of way, while wondering how he could make her cry.

'She explain exactly what she planned to do to them?'

'Just deal with them. We never thought. It's not like she's, you know, gone that far before, is it?'

'As far as we know, Carly. As far as we know. Tell me what you saw.'

'Didn't see nothing. I wasn't looking. I mean, it was cool at first, but then you thought, like, maybe it's not...'

'Not that cool, eh?' Bliss said. 'Killing people.'

Carly turned away. Bliss eyed her with dispassion.

'Let's go back. I'm talking about after Joss phoned Victoria to say the sisters had left the Monk's Head and were heading up towards the Cathedral. What happened then? What did Victoria do?'

'She's, like, in the middle of the street? The narrow street with the cobbles?'

'Church Street.'

Amazing how kids could be born and grow up in this city and didn't know the names of its streets.

'And she, like, she's got her arms folded – like this? And she's not moving. Like, if anybody tries to come past, they're gonner get... you know? And when these two seen her just standing there—'

'The Marinescu sisters?'

'Yeah. They, like cut off into this other street?'

'East Street.'

'Yeah.'

'And did you follow them?'

'We started to, but Vic walks over then, and she's with this guy?'

'Guy you knew?'

'No.'

'Joss know him?'

'Don't think so.'

'You know who he is now?'

'No.'

'I'll be asking you to describe him in a minute, and it better not be like the description you gave of the non-existent fellers who followed the Marinescus out. But let's not break the flow.'

'Uh?'

'Was there anybody else in East Street?'

'No.'

'What happens next?'

'Vic... she puts on these gloves.'

'Kind of gloves? Black suede? Woollen mittens?'

'Rubber gloves. Long. That, like, unroll up your arm?'

'And the guy? He put on gloves too?'

'I din't see, to be honest.'

Bliss glanced at Mr Ryan Nye, who was looking down into his hands. Not yet five o'clock, but the light seemed to be fading early today, as if something had sent the year into reverse. Up at the end of the table, Karen was watching the tape machine as if it was a lie detector.

Bliss said, 'Go on, Carly.'

'Vic catches up with the… you know, the women, and she's talking to them? We couldn't hear what they were saying. Then, it's like one of them… she just trips? Like, stumbles over? And the bloke's come out of, like, nowhere, and he catches her.'

'What was Victoria doing?'

'Laughing. Just starts laughing real loud, and going like *oops*, kind of thing. Like the woman was a bit pissed and she'd slipped. And then… they all, like, vanished. That's all we seen.'

'Vanished where?'

'Into this… where people park?'

'And what did you and Joss do then?'

Carly looked at Mr Nye. Mr Nye didn't even look up.

'I think, Inspector,' he said, 'that you can understand how intimidating my client must have found Victoria Buckland. Even though she had no reason to believe that Ms Buckland's intentions extended beyond, shall we say, putting the fear of God into the Marinescu sisters.'

'Apart from the gloves,' Bliss said.

Mr Nye said nothing.

'Carly,' Bliss said, 'didn't you or Joss feel tempted to have a little peep at what – or who – was going down on the car park?'

'No.'

'Really?'

'I don't wanner talk about this no more.'

'Where were you, exactly?'

'Just round the side of the building?'

'And you saw nothing. But you surely heard—'

'They weren't even *from* here!' Now Carly was jerking up and back like somebody had set light to her clothes. 'They were bad bitches! They robbed Joss's gran! The bitches robbed her handbag with all her personal stuff in it and she was so upset she died!'

'Is that why you took *their* handbags, Carly?'

'I never took nothing!'

'With the pictures of their parents, and the little dog?'

'Leave me alone.'

'Um, Carly,' Mr Nye said. 'You remember what we talked about.'

'I wish I was dead. I wish I was fucking *dead*!'

Bliss shook his head, settling back in his chair, watching stupid little Carly Horne come slowly to pieces for the tape.

It was one of those country garages that didn't sell petrol and didn't have a shop, looked like a semi-derelict chapel of rest. A bloke in brown overalls seemed to recognize Cornel's Porsche, came shambling round to his wound-down window.

'Wannit again, chief?'

'Same one as before?'

The bloke nodded. Cornel got out his wallet, turned to Jane.

'This is where we leave the car.'

'Why?'

'Because it just is.'

Cornel drove the Porsche round to the back of the garage where an old grey van was parked. When he got out, the garage guy handed him a ring of keys with a wooden tag on the end. Cornel gave him a small fold of notes, then leaned into the Porsche.

'For you, girlie, the luxury transport is history.'

The sun had gone in. Jane slid out of the Porsche, zipping up her jacket, beginning not to like this again. It had taken them a long time to get here, as if Cornel had been stalling. They'd walked around Leominster and he'd kept wanting to buy her things, like she was his girlfriend now, and she'd kept refusing, while feeling a bit sorry for him. And then they'd gone into a pub, where she'd had one cider and he'd swallowed two pints of bitter, which would probably put him over the limit. He didn't appear to care.

Now he was around the back of the Porsche, opening up the boot, pulling out a leather bag and a bulked-out rucksack, lugging them back to the van.

'Get in.'

'What's this about?'

'Just get *in*, eh, Jane? This is necessary.'

It was dark inside the van, which smelled of oil and rust. Cornel clanged the clutch pulling out into the lane. Jane fastened her seat belt. The strap was frayed and flaked with mud.

'That guy seemed to know you.'

'That's because I've hired this heap a couple of times before.'

'What for?'

'Because a Porsche can be a bit obvious?'

'Oh. Right.'

Jane supposed it would, at a cockfight.

'So we're going there now?'

'Wait till dark.'

'But...' *Oh God.* 'You mean we're actually going to a...?'

'That bother you?'

'I don't know.'

'Thought you wanted evidence.'

'Erm...'

OK, nailing Savitch would be the best thing she'd ever done in her life. And there might be a few other people there she could identify, maybe even sneak some pictures of them on the mobile, shot from the hip. But what if anybody recognized her? No secret in Ledwardine where she stood on these issues.

Jane watched Cornel wrestling with the steering. He was driving without a seat belt. She'd felt sorry for him a couple of times and, OK, she was grateful that he was actually going to help her, but that didn't mean she could actually like him. There were two sides to him: the ruthless and the kind of weak. And he'd done things, obviously. He'd shot things without a thought, and he'd been to a cockfight and wanted to eat a cock because he'd lost money on it.

'How do you get on these courses, anyway?'

'Sponsored by your firm. I was the first from my bank, as it happened. Heard about it on the grapevine.'

'Heard what?'

'How some other guys were so impressed that they kept coming back for more. You could see the effects, somehow. In their attitude. Well, not only that. Some guys, it was almost awesome, the difference.'

'So you got to come back?'

The van went rattling onto the main road, its suspension creaking. When Jane looked at Cornel to see why he wasn't answering his face seemed to have darkened.

'Lot of envy in my business, Jane. People whisper lies, and get believed. People who didn't want you going all the way.'

'All the way?'

'Because you just might go further than them, and that would never do because they went to Eton and you struggled through the system. And so the knife goes in.'

'Dead,' Carly said. 'He's, like, "She's dead."'

'This is the man?' Bliss leaned across the table. 'The man with Victoria?'

'And then he's, like, "All I done was push her." And then Victoria, she's a bit annoyed, she goes, "Oh, she fell on a kerb."'

'Kerb?'

'Kerbstone. That's what she said. She says, "Oh, she must've got a head like a…"' Carly jerked back, her raven's wing of hair flying up. 'I can't do this…'

Bliss said, 'Head like a…?'

'…eggshell.' Carly twisted away. 'And then she goes, "You're f—" Can't we do it later? Tomorrow? I might be able to remember better. I'm all—'

'Carly,' Bliss said. 'I want you to tell me *precisely* what Victoria said. The words exactly as you remember them.'

'She says, "You're fucking right. She's passed away."'

Something penetrated Bliss's spine. He leaned across the table.

'She used those actual words? "Passed away?"'

'Yeah.'

'And what did the other one say? The other sister?'

'I don't reckon she understood what they was on about. Then there was like a bit of a... like a scuffle? And then, like, Victoria...' Carly grabbed Mr Nye's arm. 'I can't say this stuff. Tell him I can't do this. *Tell him.*'

'You'll note my client's level of distress, Inspector. This was quite evidently something so abhorrent to her that she could hardly believe it was happening.'

'Point taken, Mr Nye. For the moment. Carly, what did Victoria say next?'

'I won't have to see her again, will I?'

'I'm guessing not for many years, if at all,' Bliss said softly. 'If you tell us the truth.'

'I can't go to prison.' Carly's cheeks all zebra-striped with damp mascara. 'You gotter promise me I won't go to no prison.'

'Out of my hands, Carly. I mean, you know, sometimes I get listened to. But you'd have to get me on your side first, and you've gorra *long* way to go before—'

'Where's my mum? Did you call my mum?'

'Carly, you refused to have your mum in with you.'

'Well, now I want her.'

Bliss thought about his own kids, how they might turn out after exposure to the influence of a rich, cocky farmer with hunting skills. Carly must've seen the darkening of his face. She seemed to throb.

'Gonner be sick.'

Bliss didn't move.

'What did Victoria say, after she noticed the lady had *passed away*? Come on, Carly.'

Carly sniffed hard, eyes filling up.

'What did Victoria *say*, Carly?'

Carly leaned back in her chair, face shining with teary snot.

'"That's..." She said, "that's a bugger." Then she said, "We're... gonner have to do the other one now."'

Bliss watched Karen Dowell's lips forming a distinct *o*.

'I think this might be a good time to take a break, Inspector,' Mr Nye said.

62

Blood Sugar

SHOULD HAVE SEEN this coming, from the first tap of James Bull-Davies's umbrella on the vicarage door. In this job, looking stupid was part of the package.

It was a rectangular room with pale yellow walls and a row of windows overlooking the east city. William Lockley accepted the padded chair at the top of the conference table. He wore a crumpled grey suit and a grey woollen tie, and his moustache screened his lips. An air of wariness. If Lockley looked less than comfortable, maybe that was something to do with women. Things you could discuss with them, things you couldn't.

And then there was Annie Howe, putting down her briefcase, taking the chair opposite Merrily, who was trying not to stare.

No rimless glasses, longer hair, hoop earrings. A soft, stripy woollen sweater. *Soft? Stripy?* You'd almost think there was a man in the background.

'We're here because Ms Watkins seems to have convinced Mr Lockley that I should be considering a possible connection between the death, due to heart failure, of Samuel Dennis Spicer, chaplain to the Special Air Service… and the murder of Mansel Bull. Is that correct?'

As if she was addressing a fourth person at the table. At least the voice hadn't changed. Still crunching ice cubes.

'And the link,' Howe said, 'would appear to be a third man, Colin Jones. A man in whom Mr Lockley's people seem to have been interested for a while.'

'Been felt...' Lockley cleared his throat '... that an eye should be kept on him, yes.'

'Although nothing was conveyed to *us*. Until now, when it might just be getting embarrassing.'

'Nothing to say until now, Annie.'

Howe leaned back, arms folded, a posture reflecting decades of resentment between the police and soft-shoed spooks who wrote their own rules.

'Who exactly did you have keeping an eye on Jones, Mr Lockley?'

'People we trust, mostly ex-army. And it's been *very* low-key. For example, we once booked a chap into a tourism course that Jones's ex-wife was attending. Which was quite productive.'

Merrily sat up. Those old contracting walls. Garrison Ledwardine.

Annie Howe bent to her briefcase and slid out a laptop, which she opened up on the table.

'And there's another man, in whom *we*'ve had a mild interest over the years – Kenneth Mostyn, Jones's business partner. Since establishing Hardkit he's been suspected of selling imported surveillance equipment – illegal at the time, though nowadays there's not much you can't obtain through the Internet.'

'Mostyn's very much a type,' Lockley said. 'More common in the US, where you find whole communities of them in cabins in the wilds, living out their fantasies of the collapse of civilization. Every man for himself, usually armed to the teeth.'

'He certainly sells a range of shotguns. How he became involved with Jones... can you throw some light there?'

'Simply convenient for them both. Mostyn had a side enterprise running adventure holidays – canoeing, rock climbing – but it didn't have the glamour that an SAS connection confers. The joint enterprise operates under a rather enticing cloak of secrecy – students brought in at night, sometimes blindfolded, or driven around to disorient them. Quite soon, through word of mouth, it became, you know, the thing to do. If you could afford it.'

'And perhaps we should also mention Ward Savitch.'

'Chap running champagne shooting weekends for corporate clients. High-level contacts in the City – venerable financial institutions putting their executives into an intensive course designed to make them leaner and fitter. Especially useful – and this is the ingenious part – after the recession and the huge backlash against the financial sector, particularly banks and bankers. The old killer instinct shrivelling under the public spotlight.'

'So the idea,' Howe said, 'is to get them believing in themselves again.'

'And not only in themselves.' Lockley looked at Merrily. 'Apparently.'

Merrily felt small and unprepared, like when you arrived in an exam room and your mind had been wiped.

Sometimes, when she looked up, the room would blur. Forgotten how tired she was. God knew what she must look like. She fingered the bulge of the cigarette packet through the fabric of her bag.

'Some of this is going to sound a bit… loony.'

'I'd expect nothing less from you, Ms Watkins,' Annie Howe said. Then lifted a placating palm. 'I apologize. Go on.'

'Building a case against people… not what I do, obviously. All I can give you is possibly enough background to shape some questions. Essentially, Mr Jones follows a pagan religion adopted by the Roman invaders of Britain two thousand years ago. A soldiers' religion, which—'

There was a tapping and a very tall young guy put his head around the door to say that, down in the canteen, Mr Jones was getting a little restive, making noises about having to attend a dinner.

'What do you want me to do, ma'am?'

Annie Howe lifted a finger.

'Perhaps I should have reminded you both that Colin Jones came in this afternoon in connection with last night's break-in at his premises. He's downstairs and apparently happy to answer any questions we might have for him.'

'Rather interesting in itself, that,' Lockley said. 'I'm guessing you wouldn't normally expect a man who's had a minor break-in to visit the police station just to say he doesn't want to press charges.'

'Well… says he was coming into town anyway, but my guess would be that he was disconcerted to find quite a large police presence in his backyard last night.' Annie Howe turned to Lockley. 'Get him up?'

'He knows what you want to talk to him about.'

'He knows it's about Spicer.' Howe looked at Merrily. 'Looks like you get to ask the questions yourself, Ms Watkins.'

Were those contact lenses magnifying an old malice, or what?

The mouthy ones like Carly, he could enjoy the scrap, so Bliss had left Joss to Karen and Darth. Never been as good with the deep and the silent. Karen had more patience, and she was local and so was Darth. They'd get there. Good as cracked, really.

Bliss sat on his own in a corner of the CID room. All falling into place, who'd done what: one sister killed *accidentally*, the second purely to keep the lid on it. In cold blood, pitiless. Head repeatedly banged on the bricks until she died. In Hereford. Made you shiver. Who'd suddenly cranked up the violence level in this county?

The sexual assault? Probably an afterthought, to make it look like a rapist attack, but who could say? Who was the bloke, how much of it was down to him? It would doubtless come out, when they brought Victoria Buckland in. Which, in theory, should not be difficult. But then, in theory, they should've had her already.

Bliss stood up and went to the window. The end of the rush hour, brake lights like snail trails under the purple sky. Maundy Thursday was always purple, Good Friday black. No matter how lapsed a Catholic you were, Good Friday would always be black.

A black Easter, too, this year, in both his professional and private lives. He might leave the city, find a copper's job on the other side of the country, but there would still be loose ends here, one of them forever sticking out like a fuse awaiting a lighted match.

His kids. The worst of all scenarios was his kids being brought up by *hunt hero Sollers Bull.*

Bliss wanted to smash a metal chair into the toughened glass, shatter the skyline.

And there was Annie. Images of Annie, his mind filling with one every few minutes. Tousled hair and a stripy sweater. A shadowy areola under a white nightdress.

The longer he left it, the harder it would be to tell her that he – a copper – hadn't known about Kirsty and Sollers Bull. Too late now. Maybe he'd write her a letter one day, from a bedsit in Gloucester or Swindon or wherever he wound up.

Bliss stood at the window, watching homebound traffic. Couldn't see himself going home tonight, not with Buckland out there.

He was no longer tired, anyway; his body was burning with blood sugar.

Here came the footsteps on the stairs. Light and unhurried.

Here was a man who kept quiet as a comrade plunged to his death in the Brecon Beacons. Here was a man who calmly dismantled his marriage. Here was a man who raped his friend's wife in the grounds of a hotel in Buckinghamshire and then said goodnight.

'Mr Jones, ma'am,' the tall detective said.

William Lockley did the introductions. Knowing him from the old days, brothers in arms, all that.

'Byron, this is Detective Chief Inspector Howe. Senior Investigating Officer in the Mansel Bull murder case.'

Byron Jones nodded. He wore a dark suit and a mid-blue silk tie to match his eyes. He was guided to the foot of the table, facing the door. The optimum no-threat comfort seat, Merrily thought, as Lockley moved to sit opposite her, next to Byron.

'And this is Mrs Merrily Watkins,' Lockley said, 'whom I think we could describe as an investigator with the Hereford Diocese.'

'Really.' Byron turned his bright blue eyes briefly on Merrily. 'What does the Diocese investigate?'

'Overdue books from the Chained Library,' Merrily said. 'That kind of thing.'

Byron didn't smile, by then looking away. He was not what she'd expected. But then, what *had* she expected? Cropped hair, multiple scars?

'Byron,' Lockley said, 'I think I should say at this point that this is just a discussion... a chat. Without prejudice. It will not be recorded, it will not be used in evidence. This began as a routine police inquiry, which seems to have crossed over into our territory, and, frankly, we're all a bit confused and hoping you can help us.'

Merrily wondered if this sounded as phoney and patronizing to Byron as it did to her. Byron said nothing.

'As you know,' Lockley said, 'the Regiment lost its new chaplain this week. You'll also know the circumstances. And that it was a bit of a shock for all of us who knew Syd.'

'Myself included,' Byron said.

'Though none of us, I'd guess, knew him quite as well as you did, Byron.'

'He was a mate.'

'But not recently.'

'No. Not recently.'

Another knock on the door. Two uniformed male cops came in, ostensibly with coffee, but possibly, Merrily was thinking, to familiarize themselves with the layout and seating positions of the people in the room. It had been William Lockley's idea that they should place Byron Jones near the door, where you'd never seat a suspect.

Annie Howe took the chair next to Merrily, opposite the two men. The first lights were coming on in the city below them. You could see the greying steeple of St Peter's, where the late Frank Collins had been a curate.

Byron shook his head at Annie Howe's offer of sugar for his coffee, turned to William Lockley.

'Is there any suggestion that Syd's death was suspicious?'

Before Lockley could reply, Howe said quickly that nothing had been ruled out, and Byron appraised her, thoughtful.

'You think somebody might have killed him, Chief Inspector?'

'We're still examining the evidence.'

'Or did he kill himself?'

Merrily said, 'If he *had* killed himself, would that be a surprise to you, Mr Jones?'

Byron looked at her properly for the first time, and she felt able to study him. Older than she'd imagined. Older than Syd, although Syd had been the first to retire so he actually might be a little younger. He looked like… maybe like a cathedral canon, ascetically lean, with thick white hair. He looked… above all, he looked calm and distinguished.

'Suicide's hardly unprecedented among men who served in my former regiment,' Byron said. 'Post-traumatic stress disorder is far from fully understood.'

His teeth, unexpectedly, were jagged, with thin black lines down the front ones as if they'd been scored by a pencil. It made him look as if he had more teeth, as if he was smiling when he wasn't. It made Merrily think of SAS men who were caught and tortured. Teeth and pliers.

She said, 'Can you think of any good reason why Syd would be particularly stressed?'

'How long you got?'

'I was thinking, since leaving the army.'

'We didn't see much of one another.'

'Any particular reason for that?'

'Mrs… I'm sorry…?'

'Watkins.'

'I may be wrong here,' Byron said, 'but I think when a clergyman rejoins the army he's no longer under the authority of the Diocese.'

'He was a mate, Byron,' Merrily said.

He turned his blue eyes on her again – *an emptiness – a hole where love and humanity should be* – and she fought against a blink. Instinctively putting a hand to her chest, where a pectoral cross would lie. Nothing; she'd left the vicarage too quickly this morning. She heard Annie Howe's voice, flat and formal.

'Mr Jones, perhaps you could tell us how you came to develop what we can only call a pagan sect inside the Special Air Service.'

63

Syd's Candle

BYRON SCOWLED.

'Then how would you describe it?' Annie Howe said.

'I would call it,' Byron said, 'a discipline.'

Of course he would. Merrily was feeling hollow with fatigue, yet nursing a need to smoke this man out.

'A discipline based on worship of a Roman god?' she said.

'I dislike the word worship,' Byron said. 'In the army we did not worship our officers.'

Merrily recalled that in the SAS only senior officers were addressed as *sir*. No lack of respect. The Regiment was informal; it was about mutual trust and reliance, practicalities.

'You saw Mithras as your mate?'

If Byron was surprised that she knew about Mithras, he wasn't showing it.

'I would call him a device.'

'Is it possible you could explain that for us?'

Byron said nothing. William Lockley pushed his chair back.

'Not as if paganism's against the law, Byron. We've moved on since witch-burning.'

'In that case, why's the Hereford Diocese here?'

Neat.

'She's here because neither Annie nor I would know what the hell you were talking about, Byron,' Lockley said.

'Oh, I think you would, William. I think you'd have a better idea, to be honest. This is my business. My living. I'm hardly the first veteran to use what he learned in the Regiment as the basis for a new career. But carry on, Mrs Watson.'

'Erm… all this started back at the old Stirling Lines in Hereford, I think. When some Roman remains were discovered within the precincts?'

'Coins, pottery. Not much.'

'But enough to get you thinking.'

'A few of us had an interest in military history. We'd be spotting things when we were out and about. Roman roads, Celtic forts. Having a bit of Welsh in the background, I thought I identified with the Celts. But the Celts were a bunch of drunken hooligans compared with the Romans. The Romans had a commitment which even today is unequalled.'

'Except possibly by you,' Merrily said. 'By the Regiment.'

'If you like.'

'The last all-male corner of the army.'

Byron leaned back, stretching his legs under the table so that Merrily instinctively moved hers out of the way.

'You know much about Mithraism, Mrs Watson? Or maybe think you do. Maybe you're someone who's looked at it from the Christian perspective, thinks she knows what it represents and misses the whole point.'

'Mithraism was a soldiers' religion. You could see parallels.'

'For a start, I dislike the word religion. But yeah, we were young men. Full of energy. You'd have to be dull not to recognize some of it.'

'You mean like initiation rites. Out of darkness into light. Through barriers. Skirting the boundaries of death.'

'Mind games. William knows.'

Lockley said, 'If I'm getting this right, I suppose the best and most widely known example would be the one where the chaps are taken up in a helicopter, blindfolded and ordered to jump out without a parachute. Not realizing the chopper's only a few metres above the ground. Is that what you mean?'

'Mind games. The Romans didn't have that kind of terminology, but they understood.'

'The twelve tortures?' Merrily said.

'Yeah, we found good parallels there. In physical and mental endurance of hardship. I could give you names of historians and psychologists that we consulted. The aim being to develop a progression of exercises, linked to the Mithraic grades, that would lead to a level of… resilience. Courage, essentially. Attributes of manhood which some people think have been allowed to lapse.'

Lockley was nodding, encouragingly.

'My students come out of this fundamentally *altered*,' Byron said. 'Better men. More successful men, in every respect. If they've got the balls to see it through.'

'And the money,' Lockley said. 'Presumably.'

'We're not a charity, William. It costs. A lot. But you ask the guys we've trained if they think it was worth it.'

'We? That's you and Mostyn?'

'He mainly provides and maintains the hardware.'

'And has he been initiated?' Merrily asked.

'Not one of my words. We don't even use the term Mithraism to the students. Not until they're able to understand what it means.'

'But Mr Mostyn would've been your first civilian… whatever the word is – neophyte?'

Byron winced.

'I'd also like to stress that the students choose how far to take it. Some will drop out. *Most* of them will drop out at some stage. But a small number will cross a threshold and begin to revel in it.'

'An elite.'

'I've no quarrel with that word. We encourage levels of excellence.' Byron looked up, narrowing his eyes. 'Do we need all these lights? It's not very green, is it? Also a bit like an interrogation. That what this is, William? An interrogation?'

An edge of impatience, now. William Lockley looked at Annie Howe. She stood up, went to the switches on the wall and killed all the lights except for two at the top of the room. The reflections of the conference table vanished from the window and the early glow of the city came up under the long beach of the evening sky.

'Thank you,' Byron said. 'I find light pollution offensive.'

Annie Howe sat down again, next to Merrily.

'You seem to be saying this is all pure psychology rather than religion.'

'Finally sinking in, is it?' Byron looked pained. 'I mean, do I look like a fantasist? We analysed Mithraism, took it apart, found out how it worked, then reconstructed it for our purposes. The Romans weren't hippy-dippy *spiritual* types. They were practical and pragmatic. This is a system for self-development. The only one of us who ever talked about religion was Syd Spicer.'

Merrily said, 'For confirmation, Syd was a member of the original history club?'

'Oh, yeah. You could say that.'

'Along with, erm… Jocko and Greg. And Nasal.'

Annie Howe pushed her chair back, curious. The names would mean nothing to her, but Lockley would know.

'All dead,' Merrily said. 'Like Syd.'

'What's your point?' Byron looked irritated, nothing more. 'What conclusion could you possibly be drawing from that?'

'What conclusions was Syd drawing?'

They were all looking at her now, Byron smiling, but not really.

'I wouldn't know.'

'You were presumably practising this form of self-development when you were still in the army.'

'To the extent of our knowledge. We were learning about the use of meditation and visualization to achieve focus.'

'And it carried on when Syd left.'

'Sure.'

'Sometime after you'd *both* left the army and gone your separate ways, Syd possibly had reason to think it had… escalated? And the other guys, Jocko, Greg… and finally Nasal… had all died. Which he thought—'

'You baffle me, Mrs Watson. One was a drink-driving smash, one a drunken brawl and the third topped himself in the wake of a distressing domestic incident. What's your point?'

'I think Syd was suggesting – to you – that the regime they'd been following had made them… reckless… prone to seeking out violent situations.'

Byron's expression conveyed an element of pity. Merrily struggled on.

'Maybe he felt they'd let in something they couldn't control. Nothing gained without sacrifice, and in this case the sacrifice was their humanity.'

Byron looked at Lockley. *How long do I have to suffer this shit?*

Merrily looked away and tried again.

'You never wondered why Syd left the Regiment and immediately threw himself into Christianity?'

'Syd was religious. He had to think that what we were doing was spiritual, and when he realized it wasn't he went cold on it.' Byron smiled. 'Or did he?' He sat looking at Merrily. The lines in his lean face were like hieroglyphics in sandstone.

'Syd was fascinated by all the places where Mithraism overlaps with Christianity. How you could appear to be practising one religion but it was really the other. And nobody would ever know. We used to talk about that.'

'Oh no.' Merrily shaking her head, too quickly. 'I don't think so.'

'You don't, eh? You claim to have known him. You never think there were times when his behaviour wasn't strictly priestlike? I heard he once beat the living shit out of a street dealer who sold his daughter pills.'

'I—'

Merrily was hit by a memory of what she'd once seen Syd do to a young guy in the Malverns, when they'd needed information in a hurry. His famous evocation of the SAS buzz. *The rush you get… when you convince yourself it's not only justified but necessary. When you know that a difficult situation can only be resolved by an act of swift, efficient, intense and quite colossal violence.*

'We were soldiers,' Byron said. 'We knew about immediate action. We didn't do turning the other cheek.'

Annie Howe stood up.

'You'll have to excuse me. I'm afraid I've been drinking too much coffee today. Ms Watkins?'

Howe looked at the door and back at Merrily.

'Oh.' Merrily rose out of a fugged image of Syd Spicer smoking in his church on a summer's day, knowing that his deity was entirely OK with that. 'I'll come with you.'

Byron leaned back, arms hanging down, limp as empty sleeves, so relaxed. The state of his teeth gave him a dark grin.

'Yeah,' he said. 'Mithras. He really lit Syd's candle.'

64

Control

'THIS ISN'T WORKING, is it?' Howe said. 'He's tying you in knots.'

'Sorry. Tired. Complicated day.' Merrily backed off towards the top of the stairs. A wreck in sweater and jeans, no make-up, a woman who'd left home too quickly, a long time ago. 'But I can certainly see why Byron agreed to be interviewed.'

'*Agreed?*'

Annie Howe moistened her lips, took a long breath, Merrily thinking that, despite the softening effects of early middle-age, they were never going to be friends. Too much rancid history.

'It's a set-up,' Howe said.

'I'm sorry?'

'You're here to look like a fool, I'm here to witness that. And Jones, quite clearly, is only here because it was suggested to him – presumably by Lockley – that it would be very much in his best interests to get his defence in first.'

'Defence against what?'

'With a view to pre-empting any possible police investigation of his activities. Damage limitation. And it's working, wouldn't you say?'

'Well, it…'

Out of Byron's presence, the flaws in his argument were beginning to show. Here was Fiona: *He told me Sam was making a terrible mistake in going into the church, that he was throwing away his life and damaging his country.* Was that coming from a man who knew that Syd hadn't forsaken Mithras?

But what the hell would any of that matter to Howe or Lockley? This wasn't about theology.

A door opened, and DI Frannie Bliss appeared, cradling a mug of coffee.

Annie Howe didn't quite look at him.

'No arrest yet, Francis?'

Bliss said, 'Good evening, Reverend.'

He looked worse than this morning. A sweat-sheen on his freckled cheeks, feverish eyes.

'We're covering all the nightclubs, I suppose?' Howe said.

'Young coppers looking faintly ridiculous in clubbing kit. We're also doorstepping all her so-called mates. As if anybody's ever grassed Victoria up.'

'Apart from your friend on the Plascarreg.'

Bliss came out of the doorway like he was about to say something smart, then he shrugged.

'Good point, actually. Increasingly, I'm wondering why Goldie Andrews did that.'

'I thought you had her over a barrel. Cleverly manoeuvring her into a corner.'

Howe's voice rinsed in acid. Nothing changed, did it?

'Maybe I was just too plain euphoric to ask some significant questions,' Bliss said. 'Think I'd better go back down the Plas, boss? On me own this time?'

'No. Take Vaynor.'

'He's going clubbing.'

'Then take care,' Howe said coldly. 'And be sure, when you eventually bring Buckland in, that she's undamaged.'

'That a joke, ma'am?'

Bliss stepped back through the doorway, not looking at Annie Howe, as if he'd been expecting something from her that she hadn't supplied. The atmosphere between them no sweeter than it had ever been.

All this in front of a civilian. Merrily had a sense of unreality, nothing quite what it seemed. Even Annie Howe looked, for a moment, almost vulnerable as she turned away from the closing door, the white-gold hair pushed back behind the ears, the woolly riding up the back of the creased black skirt.

She turned again to Merrily.

'Those three men you mentioned to Jones…'

'Nasal, you might remember him.'

'Killed his wife, yes. You're suggesting that whatever they and Jones and possibly Spicer had been doing had made them less in control of their aggression?'

'I certainly think Syd was thinking along those lines. On the day it was in the paper that Nasal had hanged himself, he went to see Byron at his wife's place in Allensmore. No violence on that occasion, just… harsh words.'

'Harsh words.' Howe shook her head. 'Jones looks to me, Ms Watkins, like a man with a huge chip on his shoulder. But basically nothing to hide. Nothing that would be of particular interest to me, anyway.'

'You reckon?'

Merrily took a step back.

No choice now.

'I need to tell you something. Purely for information. If you take it any further at this stage, I'll have to deny having said anything.'

Annie Howe steered Merrily into an unoccupied office, a room without lights, and shut the door.

'How sure are you of this?'

'Sure as I can be without forensic evidence.'

'Where's Spicer's wife now?'

'No, listen, I'm telling you for clarification only. If she didn't report it then, she isn't going to say anything now.'

'Why *didn't* she report it?'

'Because she knew how Syd would react and what that would do to his prospective career in the Church.'

'You're saying that, like all these other guys, Jones lost control?'

'No, that's the— He *didn't* lose control, that's the whole point. This was a rape in cold blood. I think Byron Jones raped Syd's wife as an act of violence against Syd himself.'

'And Spicer... did he know?'

'It's a good question.'

'All right,' Howe said, 'tell me the rest – very briefly, we've been away too long. Tell me about the taking of bulls. I really can't imagine that would be easy, unless the bull was sedated.'

'I'm told that even in Roman times it *would* be sedated. Maybe it was even done in the field, if it was remote enough, I don't know. Any kind of blood sacrifice is senseless and sickening to me, but it was done. And it looks like it still is.'

'Only one man wields the knife?'

'That would seem to be the idea. He emerges completely covered in the bull's— What?'

Annie Howe had the door held back, her eyes wide open to the lights.

'We'll go back.'

65

The God of the Regiment

THE CONFERENCE ROOM was still half-lit, with the city murmuring below. Byron Jones was telling Lockley about the archaeology. The pattern from the sky.

'How did you know?' Lockley asked.

'Discoloured ground. Paler grass in the shape of a rectangle. I kept very quiet about it, of course I did.'

'Individual skills are crucial in the Regiment,' Lockley said to Howe, 'and Byron went on a photography course.'

'Got the chopper pilot to go back over it,' Byron said, 'give us a closer look. Took some decent pictures, and later sent them to an archaeologist I knew – in Germany, as it happened – without identifying the location. He thought it was probable.'

'So that's why you went after the land. What did you use before that?'

'We improvised. Caves, a disused reservoir. But to have the remains of an actual mithraeum…'

'Exciting.'

'Took everything I'd got, but I knew I'd never get another chance like this. Put the digger to work initially, but most of it was done by hand. Spent three months on it. Sifted all the soil, kept everything in little trays. Didn't find much – bits of masonry, and a stone tablet, very worn. Handful of Roman coins. But that didn't matter. It was confirmation, of a kind. And there were other pointers I won't bore you with showing that this was part of a ritual landscape.'

'You mean Credenhill and Brinsop Church.' Merrily sat down. 'And the alignments with other churches and ancient monuments.'

'You *have* been doing your homework, Mrs Watson. I'm impressed. It's not a *Roman* ritual landscape, we're probably talking Neolithic. The Romans fitted in. In the way Christian churches would be built on Neolithic ritual sites. Pragmatic.'

'So where *is* this mithraeum?'

Byron tapped his nose.

'Need to know,' he said. 'You don't.'

'Was there much left?'

'Some reconstruction was required. Another good reason to keep quiet about it.'

Merrily glanced at Howe, who nodded.

'Is this where the bulls are sacrificed, then?' Merrily asked.

Byron laughed. Leaning back from the table, his jacket open. Merrily thinking that, however old he was, he was still very fit, no paunch under the leather belt. And relaxed. Too relaxed for this situation.

'Popular farmer murdered by former trooper off his trolley?' Byron said. 'How can we ever trust them again?'

'Excuse me,' Annie Howe said. 'Am I missing something here?'

'Byron's been putting two and two together,' Lockley said. 'And making seven.'

'That's your big inquiry, isn't it? Doesn't take a genius.'

'Perhaps,' Howe said, 'you could tell us about the bulls you took.'

'Rustling, too, eh?' Byron said. 'Is there no depth to which this scum won't sink? Tell me, do you have any evidence of that?'

'Do you deny ever taking a bull?'

'Absolutely. It's ridiculous.'

'But central to the practice of Mithraism,' Merrily said. 'Surely.'

'It *was*, two thousand years ago. In the days before the slaughter of livestock was subject to regulations. Even then, there'd have to be a compromise as, according to the legend, Mithras personally hauls the bull to his cave.'

'And how do you get over that problem?'

'Meditative visualization. Do I need to explain that? All right, I will. The candidate is summoned to the mithraeum. He travels from wherever he lives, books into humble accommodation – or brings a tent – and spends a day in contemplation of his role, during which he's permitted to drink water but must eat nothing. He bathes in a river, usually the Wye. He's brought, blindfolded, to the mithraeum, where his comrades are gathered. The ritual begins.'

'His comrades.' William flipping him a glance. 'Just so we know, anyone from the Lines involved in this?'

'Not any more. Like I said when these ladies were powdering their noses, none of this need concern you, William. It started in the Regiment, just a few of us, now it's moved on. I'm not saying it won't come back one day, as long as the camp sits on Magnis.'

Lockley glanced towards the window. He seemed unsettled, as though the world had skidded out of his mental grasp.

'What does that mean?' Merrily said. '"As long as the camp sits on Magnis"? When you were talking about a ritual land-scape... with its own god. The god of the Regiment?'

'By your rules, I'm an atheist.'

For a few seconds, nobody spoke. Down in the city, a car horn blared.

'It's about mindset,' Byron said. 'You don't know what I mean, do you? None of you. Not even you, William. Communism in your day, and the IRA. Now it's men driven by religion, who don't care what happens to them in this life or how they leave it. We could lose it this time, because we ain't got the mindset.'

'Byron,' Lockley said, 'we don't do holy wars any more.'

'You think the Crusades were holy, William? The Crusades served man's need for *extreme warfare*.'

'Mithras coming through,' Merrily said.

'Call it what you want.'

Merrily put her head on one side, holding Byron's electric blue gaze, hands clasped under the table.

'Do you ever think you might be dealing here with something so powerful that while experienced soldiers like you might be able to handle it, civilians—'

'Mrs Watson, you're in no position to make any kind of qualified assessment.'

'—might just become a little crazy?'

'Come back to me when you're better informed.'

'Can I just ask… when did you last see Syd? Did you see him again after he came to Credenhill as chaplain?'

No reply. Merrily thought she glimpsed a flaring rage in his eyes, blue lights in a ravaged landscape.

'I've been wondering if you were the main reason why Syd felt he had to come back. Mithras and you, the demons from his past that he had to deal with.' Merrily glanced at Howe. 'Maybe he thought something still lived in him. Something repugnant that was buried so deep inside himself that he couldn't reach it. Something he had to come back and deal with.'

Winging it now. She felt quite dizzy, the room tilting, a throbbing in her chest. Byron was still looking at her, his hands either side of the chair ready to launch himself out of it. And in his eyes…

He can enter you without moving, that man, one of the nurses had said.

And then it was gone.

Byron didn't move.

'Chief Inspector, why don't I just give you a DNA swab, so you can compare it with whatever you found in Mansel's yard?'

'I still haven't mentioned Mansel Bull,' Annie Howe said.

'Don't treat me like a clown.'

'You knew Mr Bull well?'

'I was acquainted with Mansel and his… family.' Byron blinked. '*Mansel Bull*. You're making something out of it because his name's Bull. That's all this is. Am I right?'

Howe said, 'Do you know who killed Mansel Bull?'

'How would I?'

'Am I right in thinking that in this… virtual ceremony of the slaughter of the bull, it's considered important that the candidate imagines himself covered in its blood?'

'You can find all this in books and on the Net. But if you really think I'd go out and carve up a neighbour—'

'Let's end it there.' Annie Howe began packing her laptop into her case. 'I'm glad you felt able to open up to us, Mr Jones.'

Byron didn't look at her, or at Merrily. At the door, he glanced back.

'I once thought of asking you to join us, William. When they package you off, maybe you should think about it. Bring you alive when you're least expecting it. Unimaginable, mate.'

'But purely a psychological thing,' Merrily said. 'Just a discipline.'

William Lockley rose to his feet, flexing his shoulders.

'Is there an offence of desecrating an historical monument, Annie? Because, as I see it, that's all you've got.'

'May not even be an ancient monument,' Howe said.

'He's not your killer. That's my opinion.'

'You're probably right.'

'It's an oddball thing, but if he's used it to turn around his fortunes, good luck to him. Though if he thinks it'll ever be embraced by the Credenhill boys…' At the door, Lockley turned, smiled. 'Worthwhile exercise, ladies, and I may be in touch to clarify a few points. Anything you want from me, you know where I am.'

Annie Howe strode across the room and shut the door firmly, stood with her back against it, her angular face unusually flushed.

'What would Spicer's reaction have been, do you think, on learning about the murder of Mansel Bull?'

'I doubt it would've helped him sleep.'

'All right, I'll tell you something else. We have a witness who saw a man in a field, on the night of the killing, drenched in blood and apparently high on the experience.'

'*High?*'

'Well, in a state of some apparent euphoria, according to our witness.'

'Oh.' Merrily stood up. 'Bloody hell.'

'Bit of a coincidence, isn't it? Jones said he knew Mansel Bull and his… at which point he hesitated and then said *family*.'

'I remember that, too.'

'Mansel Bull didn't have a family, as such,' Howe said. 'He had two ex-wives.'

'So I gather.'

'And a brother.'

'Yes.'

'Have you met Sollers Bull?'

'Never.'

'He's an ambitious man. Someone I suppose you'd call a member of the new countryside elite.'

'Elite.'

Annie Howe thought for moment.

'Would you mind coming to meet him, if he's available?'

'Well, I… '

'Give me half an hour,' Howe said. 'Get yourself a cup of tea and a sandwich.'

Merrily wound up crossing the street to the pizza place, grabbing a salad with hummus and couscous and a coffee. Sitting in the window with her phone, on which Neil Cooper had left a message with his home number.

'Sorry, Neil, I was going to call you back, wasn't I?'

'If you remember, we got as far as Mithras. Magnis is very much my ongoing project, but I've been wondering all day if it's conceivable that you know something I don't.'

'You can relax, I don't really know anything. I would have asked you if there were any Mithraic remains in this area.'

'Not… as far as we know. The fact is, although signs of Mithraic worship are common enough in Germany and Italy, evidence in the UK is rather sparser. You're looking at four suggested centres of worship – London, York, Chester and Caerleon. Now, as it happens, the principal Roman road linking Caerleon, in South Wales, and Chester, on the northern border, passes through Credenhill.'

'So it would've been used by soldiers travelling between two significant Mithraic centres. Through some fairly hostile country, I would have thought.'

'And as they built a base here which became – as we're gradually finding out – quite a substantial community, surviving into the fifth century… well, I've often wondered.'

'Why *did* they build a base here?'

'All to do with the Wye,' Neil said. 'They were probably using the ford at Hereford to get across. You see the reason I wondered if you might have heard something is that there's a rumour been going round for a while about something of this nature being found in Herefordshire.'

'Rumour?'

'Within archaeological circles. Stories of aerial photographs showing interesting linear patterns. I've never met anyone who's seen one, but we've been monitoring aerial surveys. Nothing found, so I was thinking it might be apocryphal. Unless you – or someone – know otherwise?'

'You checked, erm, the Brinsop area.'

'Actually, we have. Nothing obvious there that we didn't already know about.'

'I suppose if somebody wanted to keep quiet about it, they could just cover it up. With a temporary building or something.'

'It *is* a thought,' Neil Cooper said.

Part Six

Throughout the vision, I thought I was
being obliged to recognise that we are
sinners who commit many evil things that
ought not to be done and who omit many
good deeds that ought to be done. We
deserve to suffer pain...

Julian of Norwich
Revelations of Divine Love

66

Anything You Want

THE EVENING SKY was blotched with small clouds, like a field of late mushrooms, brown and rotting. Jane stood on the grass bank, watching Cornel taking the leather bag from the back of the van.

A mile or so out of Credenhill, he'd swung the van between some overhanging bushes, branches ripping at the side windows. When he'd hit the brakes, Jane had been thrown forward, the rotting seat belt snapping, her head bumping painfully into the windscreen as the mobile started vibrating in her hip pocket.

She slid it out now and checked it while Cornel was messing with his tool bag. All she could see were small fields keeping wedges of woodland apart and, ahead of them, a conifer screen at the top of a rise. The eastern horizon was formed by the great wooded bank of Credenhill itself, like a crouching bear.

A new text from Eirion – *J... whr t L r u?*

What she wouldn't give to be able to return the call. To be with Irene with his reticent smile and his solid body, just slightly overweight.

Other people would surely be missing her by now. OK, Mum would think she was with Eirion, but if Eirion rang Mum...

'Cornel,' Jane said, 'if you're worried about going to this place, maybe we could do it some other time?'

He'd become morose, his mood turning like the sky. It was getting cold, too, and the van's heater didn't work. This whole thing with the van… it showed a calculating side of Cornel, a secretive side.

A jangle of tools. What did he need tools for?

'I'm sorry,' he said, 'but wasn't it *you* that wanted to go?'

'Not in the dark.'

Jane glared up into the fungal sky, wondering now if she really *had* persuaded him, if it wasn't the other way round. He'd been all too ready for this, with the van and whatever was in the rucksack and the leather bag.

'It's always in the dark,' Cornel said.

And Jane imagined some squalid gathering in an underground chamber. It was going to be horrible, gruelling – she wasn't sure she could even watch.

'How far do we have to go?'

'Mile or so?'

'A *mile*? But it's all muddy!' She felt it was important to retain something of girlie. 'This is my best jacket. We're not all loaded like you.'

It seemed to disarm him.

'If you get messed up I'll buy you a new outfit.'

'What've you got in the bag?'

'Wire-cutters. Stuff like that.'

'You mean we're going in like… undercover or something?'

'It might help if you didn't ask too many questions.'

'Help who? Where are we going? Is it a farm?'

'Give me a minute.'

Cornel went crunching off into the woods. Gone to relieve himself. Jane gave him time to, like, get started and then pulled out her phone to send Eirion a text.

But Cornel was back before she could get more than a few words down. She stashed the phone. He seemed happier, a big, wide, sloppy grin across his face. He was breathing hard and fast.

'OK, let's do it.'

Jane followed him, his long legs spidering across the darkening grass and the nettles, until they came to a barbed-wire fence. Cornel unslung the bag, and then the wire-cutters were in his hands. They didn't look that big, but they went through the barbed wire like it was bailer twine, the ends springing away from the fence, Cornel still grinning like, for him, this was what the countryside was about.

What happens is anything you want...

Barry said, 'Got a job interview next week, Lol, did I say?'

Business in the Black Swan was slow. Barry had brought some drinks, pulled out a chair and sat down with Lol who'd been trying, not too successfully, to lay down some lyrics between pacing the square, waiting for Merrily to call, Danny to come in, anything.

'Where?'

'Wiltshire.'

'Oh.'

Lol didn't remember a Ledwardine without Barry. Originally the manager at the Cassidys' restaurant, then seamlessly taking over at the Swan. Wry, unflappable, trained killer in a black tie, balancing a loaded tray while helping old ladies with their cases.

'My second wife, she lives down near Swindon, and we're, you know, talking again. I had it in mind she'd come back up here, but maybe this is best.'

'Can't believe you're letting Savitch drive you out of the area.'

'Clean break, new start. Done it before, I can do it again. You can't live with resentment, Laurence.'

'No.'

'Mind you, it gets hard sometimes,' Barry said. 'Remember how you were accusing me of telling Savitch about the open-air concert thing?'

'Wasn't *accusing* you exactly—'

'It *was* my fault. Should've found it. Marion, it was, found it this morning. Women and dusters always get into places men don't even see. Anyway, there it was, nicely concealed in a picturesque crack... in that beam?'

'What are we talking about?'

'I just ripped it out. Before I'd really thought about it, I'd ripped it out and stamped on it, how bleedin' stupid was that? Little microphone and transmitter, Laurence. Size of your thumbnail. Maybe wouldn't work too well when the bar was crowded, but on a quiet day, just a few of us there...'

'A *bug*?'

'You stand and you think, who'd do a thing like that?'

'Savitch... *planted a bug*?'

'Don't *know* it was him. But... find out who you can win round, who you can buy, who's best avoided...'

Lol shut his lyrics pad, thinking of everything that had been said about Savitch in the Swan. Speculation about some corrupt alliance with Councillor Pierce. Barry remarking that if Savitch bought the Swan there was no way he'd be sticking around.

Now there was no way he could.

'Who do you think actually planted it?'

'He's got half a dozen staff at The Court. I know Hardkit used to market listening devices and spy-video toys, from their web-site. Could actually be Mostyn himself – he's been in a few times with his clients. Kind of thing he'd do for the sake of it. James Bond.'

'Barry, what is *happening* to this place?'

'I should've left it in place, fed him disinformation, but I just... lost it. Knee-jerk. Getting old and crusty.' Barry looked steadily at Lol. 'What you waiting for?'

It seemed like a good time to tell him some things.

They seemed to have been walking for ever, getting nowhere, when Jane tripped over something hard, twisting, and went down.

Sitting, almost tearful, in the damp grass, rubbing at her ankle and then angrily picking the thing up, whatever it was. Cold, wet metal. She held it up to the emerging moon as Cornel kept on walking up the rise, following his jaw, the way he did, before tossing what Jane took to be a grudging glance over his shoulder.

'Come on, come on, come on, it's just an old CCTV camera. Put it down.'

Jane looked up and saw a wooden pole in the trees with a boxy shape on top, wires spraying from it. Her ankle twinged. She tried to stand, and then went down again.

'Get up, Jane, you're not hurt,' Cornel said breezily. 'Hadda be done, hadda be done.'

'*You* did it?' Her bum felt damp, her new jacket was ripped. 'You broke somebody's security camera? Jesus, Cornel—'

'Bit of payback. Now will you—?'

'What's that mean?'

Jane squirmed to her knees, still holding the remains of the camera. CCTV? What kind of place *was* this? Cornel waited for her to reach him, then he grabbed the camera out of her hands, half-turned, drew back his arm and hurled it deep into the wood.

'Payback for what?' Jane said.

'Lower your voice, eh, Jane?'

'I'm not going any further till you explain.'

'What you gonna do then, girlie? Limp all the way home?'

He turned away. She hissed at his back.

'Payback to who?' And then, absurdly, 'Whom.'

He just kept on walking. Anger spurted inside Jane like a blowlamp, and it just came out.

'The bloke who filled you in at the back of the Swan?'

Cornel stopped.

Oh hell... mistake.

Jane slid back down, both hands grasping wet grass. She felt the tearing of a fingernail. Story of her life. Never thought things out.

'Cornel, look—'

He'd come shambling back, and now he was hanging over her, loose and lopsided like a hastily assembled scarecrow, black against the cobalt night sky.

'You slippery, slippery little bitch.' Yet he sounded... pleased? His jaw was rolling, like he was gnawing something. Which was not right, was it?

67

Savage Ballet

BLISS'S SECOND RAID on the Plascarreg Hilton was, of necessity, low-key. He parked in front of the shops, got himself a bag of chips from the chippy. Went on foot through the estate, listening to kids' voices bouncing off the flat-pack walls, the urban birdsong of the night.

First thing he noticed was all the vehicles parked at the far end, on the derelict land separating the Plas from the Barnchurch trading estate. Cars and vans and four-by-fours. Fifteen, twenty of them.

Like there was a party at the Hilton, but there obviously wasn't. Few lights on in there, and only a couple of cars on the forecourt, where a young lad was sitting on the wall smoking. Tossing Bliss a glance.

'What you want, pal?'

'Come to see Goldie. You gorra problem with that?'

'She's not in.'

'You obviously don't know her very well, son.' Bliss offered the kid a chip. 'She's always in.'

'She's resting.'

The kid took a hot chip, bit nervously at the end.

'Goldie rests like an owl rests, till it eyeballs a mouse,' Bliss said. 'I know these things on account of I'm her nephew. From the north. You go and ask her. Tell her it's her nephew Francis.'

The kid slouched away, leaving Bliss counting the cars. Minute or so later he was back, shrugging, and Bliss went in to find

Goldie in the chintzy, brassy lounge watching TV. *EastEnders*, or some similar shite, in fifty-inch plasma. She sat up when Bliss came in but never took her eyes off the screen. The remote was on the chair arm, but she made no move to turn down the sound. She wore a black silk robe and had a steaming mug that smelled of chocolate and alcohol.

'Why you keep pestering me?'

'I'm an auxiliary with Help the Aged.' Bliss crumpled up his chip paper. 'Where do I put this?'

'Stink the bloody place out. En't good for you, all that vinegar.' Goldie pointed at a velvety basket. 'I gived you what you wanted, din' I?'

'Almost, Goldie. Almost.'

On the TV, a squat, bald twat was threatening somebody. Whenever you accidentally switched on *EastEnders* there was always this same squat, bald twat threatening somebody.

'Turn it down, Goldie.'

'Leave it.'

Bliss pulled up a cream leather chair next to Goldie's, sat himself down.

'Victoria Buckland, Goldie. How long you known her?'

Goldie kept on watching TV.

'Since her was smaller than me.'

'That'd be before she started school, then. Now, you've been known to have a… what we might call a *wairking relationship* with Victoria, haven't you, Goldie?'

Goldie mumbled something that Bliss couldn't hear for the noise of the squat, bald twat knocking over furniture.

'Sorry, Goldie?'

'I said I wouldn't go that far.'

'As I understand it, she's occasionally been useful when your guests neglect to pay their bills or complain about the standard of service.'

Goldie sipped from the mug, like a crow at a birdbath.

'See, the situation is,' Bliss said, 'that we now know for sure that Victoria and an associate had gone to administer retribution to the Marinescu sisters. For the personal reasons you'll know about.'

Goldie said nothing. On the box, the squat, bald twat said, *'Cause you've always been a bleedin' slag, is why.'*

'Now, I really don't believe that Victoria intended it to end the way it did, Goldie, if one of the sisters hadn't been discourteous enough to die on them. Leaving poor Victoria with no option – as she saw it – but to ensure the other one was too dead to make a capable witness.'

Goldie spun round at him, chocolate-mouthed.

'And, y'know, Goldie, I can't help remembering what you said the first time we discussed it. You said they were good girls who only went out on the town one night a week. Now, obviously Victoria knew *which night that was.* Who told her that, Goldie? Who told her which particular pubs they went to?'

Nothing.

'I'm willing to accept,' Bliss said, 'that all Victoria said to you was that she wanted to punish the girls. Maybe a broken arm, flattened nose? On previous evidence, Victoria doesn't do knives, so nothing life-threatening... which obviously you wouldn't've gone along with anyway, seeing corpses don't require accommodation and how useful those girls were to you for errands and stuff. And anyway, you could come over all mumsie when they got back... bathing the wounds, applying some of your old herbal remedies – think the world of you after that.'

'You en't getting me on this.'

Goldie was up in a corner of her chair, her eyes blacker than the bald twat's on the box. Bliss smiled.

'When d'you last see her? And don't say you can't remember, Goldie, because selective memory syndrome, we've gorra treatment room for that at Gaol Street. You want to get dressed, apply a smudge of lippie, or go as you are?'

Goldie didn't move.

'Cured already, then,' Bliss said.

'I gived you a name. Thass all I knows.'

'Not interested in what you *know*, I'm open for conjecture, rumour, gossip. That's why I'm on me own. What's the latest word on Victoria, Goldie?'

'New boyfriend.'

'I heard that, too.'

'Big Pole.'

'Yeh, he'd need one. He also got a name?'

'They've gone. Left the country.'

That was a jolt.

'Where've they gone, then?'

'Dunno.' Goldie shrinking back. 'Dear Lord, I don't know. I ever finds out, I'll tell you.'

'Tell me now, Goldie.' Bliss stood up, snatched the remote and snapped off the sound. 'Where you do *think* they might've gone?'

Tossing the remote from his left hand to his right, Goldie leaping up.

'Geddout! Juss geddouter my hotel!' And then – *Mother of God* – she was ripping open her robe. 'You don't get out, look, I'll say you was messing with me!'

'Aw, *Goldie*—'

'Should've brought a woman copper with you, ennit? Wasn't smart enough, was you? Now *get out*!'

Making a lunge for the remote, Bliss holding it over her head. Never seen her like this before. Victoria must really've put the shits up her this time. Bliss jumped back and…

'Hello…'

He stepped behind the sofa, switched the set off completely this time, and the noise didn't stop, a party buzz. Under his feet. Under the white carpet. A party under the carpet.

Bliss smiled.

'And you never invited me, Goldie.'

'All right…' Goldie pulled her robe across her chest. 'They's taken a car across to France.'

'Kind of car?'

'A red one.'

Bliss felt a tingle in both hands.

'Where's the door to the cellar, Goldie?'

'*No!*'

'All right, do it the long way, I'm not fussed. Gwenllian Cecilia Andrews, I'm arresting you on suspicion of—'

Goldie marched across to the TV, switched it on, prodded around till the sound went up, way higher than it was before.

'They just rented it off me, thass all!'

'The cellar?'

'I don't ask no questions. Nobody can afford to ask too many questions these days.'

'Where is it, Goldie? Where's the door?'

'They made me, ennit?' She was up close and her voice had gone small and tight. 'Threatened me, see. Threatened to torch me out if I didn't let 'em 'ave the cellar, again and again, so I just sits tight and turns up the telly till they've—'

'*Where?*'

'In the yard. Steps down, for the coal.'

'Ta.'

'But I'm tellin' you… you go down there on your own, Mr Frannie, you're fuckin' dead, you are.'

'I'm not planning to go down *there*, Goldie. That would alert your little friend outside. I'm assuming there's a more discreet way in, from the house. Maybe more than one – must've been three cellars at one time.'

'Please… go away…'

But were her eyes saying, *don't* go away?

Well, well. Bliss folded his arms.

'Tell you what, let's both go down.'

'Like fuck I will. You should've had her by now. Useless, the cops.'

Bliss followed Goldie into the kitchen, with its big shiny chip fryer and globe lights that made your head ache, then through into a utility room with two washing machines and three steps down to a door at one end.

'That's it?'

Goldie staying well back. Bliss sensed she wasn't unhappy now. If anybody was listening they'd reckon she'd done every-thing she could to get rid of him, all the same knowing – as she would – that the harder she tried to get him out the more he wouldn't want to go.

The noise was like what you could hear coming out of Edgar Street when Hereford United were actually winning. Maybe more like Anfield, really. Anfield underground.

'Put the lights out,' Bliss said.

'You don't wanner do this. Not on your own.'

It made sense. He stood watching his iPhone, waiting for Karen to call him back, or Darth Vaynor. Left messages for both. The bloating noise was making him physically irritated, like a rash, his palms hot but dry as dust, his head fizzing with static. A roar of what sounded like approval made the door shake and Bliss's guts jitter.

Goldie said, 'You go back. Leave me your number. I'll call when they's leaving.'

'Oh, I see.' Bliss smiled. 'Just so nobody gets nicked on your premises.'

'Least you can do.'

'Piss off, Goldie.'

Bliss pocketed his phone, turned the key, eased the door open a crack, then slid out onto the top step where the fetid atmos-phere picked him up like oven gloves.

Five steps down there was a concrete platform, a bloke on it, hunched over a substantial videocam on a tripod, pointed down into the circle of light made by big lamps, like in a dope factory.

Which it wasn't. Nobody wanted to watch grass grow. This would be the kind of video you only found on the Internet, and maybe some gutter cable channel.

Bliss flattened himself against a wet brick wall and saw that it was an actual circle down there, inside a metal barrier, waist-high, like a giant sawn-off-drum. Maybe sixty people around the metal ring. All men, as far as Bliss could see, except he could hear a woman's voice, high and whiny, like a bandsaw when it first touched the wood.

'Finish 'im, boy! Get fuckin' stuck in, you bastard, we en't got all night!'

Now he saw her, taller than many of the men. Saw her black-gloss lips working.

'Go for the eyes, go for the eyes, that's it!'

Was it his birthday?

Bliss started to laugh, and then he was coughing on the smoke and the fumes of booze and sweat and nasty, twisted excitement at what was going on under the hot lights: the flapping and the stabbing, the spinning and circling, the darting head-to-head, peck-and-thrust, like some savage ballet in sandy dust and scattered twigs and roars and little jewels of flying blood. One of the cocks had the other one against the barrier, stabbing with its reddened beak. In his rattling beanbag head, Bliss heard that voice again.

That's a bugger, we're... gonner have to do the other one now.

The cameraman must've heard him coughing and turned, and Bliss raised a hand – 'You're all right, pal' – and the man turned back to his camera, and it was all like slow-mo after that.

Some bloke catching the movement from the floor and looking up and nudging his mate, and he was looking up, too, but that was all right, Bliss didn't think he'd ever nicked either of them. Smiling kindly at them, wondering how he was going to stop this and contain them. Contain *her.* Probably needing to get back-up, get on his phone.

It was only when more eyes were raised that it occurred to Bliss that, not only was he the only feller here in a suit and tie, he'd been doing – in this same suit and tie – a fair bit of telly these past couple of days. His was a face they all realized they knew from somewhere. So when the cameraman turned for a quick second glance, something inside Bliss snapped like old rotted elastic, and he pushed himself back against the wall, brought up his left knee and slammed the sole and heel of his shoe into the cameraman's back.

Watched the guy go skidding down the steps, the camera flying up and then toppling into the ring where he saw both cocks going for it.

Couldn't contain a big caffeine beam as he was pulled to the floor. He rolled away, his back finding the wall.

'Bliss.'

'How's it going, Victoria?'

She came towards him through the crush.

'On your own, is it?'

'Do I *look* thick, Vickie? Wall of coppers halfway to Tesco.'

Victoria sniffed.

'He's on his own.'

She turned away, borrowing someone's cigarette, and then they were on him, half the scum in the cellar, the first boot arriving like a log-splitter in his spine before they started on his face.

Victoria going, 'Don't arse about, boys. You don't wanner get nicked. Just do what you gotter and clean it up.'

68

Punching at Smoke

THE INSIDE OF Annie Howe's Audi was more chaotic than you might have imagined – maps and papers down the side of the passenger seat, a plastic sandwich wrapper on the floor. Merrily watched her driving quite aggressively through the diminishing evening traffic. Perhaps the only detective she'd ever seen in a trench coat, light grey, belted, the collar pulled up against the pale hair.

'How do you know he's going to be there?'

'I had someone ring him, number withheld,' Howe said, 'and ask for Julie or somebody – wrong number. Fate's on my side for once. I thought Mr Bull might have been at Savitch's dinner, where he would have encountered Mr Jones, and I want to get at him first.'

Sollers Bull, brother of Mansel. Both men born to the county in the fullest sense, Merrily was thinking. Names swelling and flexing with the muscle and sinew of the land.

'So he's either on his own or with his girlfriend,' Howe said.

'Girlfriend?'

'The official story is that his wife, Catriona, has picked up the two boys from their boarding school and they've all gone to stay with her parents. To keep the kids out of the glare of publicity. But she's spent an implausible amount of time away lately. It's either a marriage in meltdown or they've come to an understanding.'

Howe's Audi had left the suburbs behind, and the night-time

countryside was gathering them in. The amorphous vastness where the street lights ended. You could go in with a flashlight, but you'd better have a stack of batteries.

'Sollers Bull,' Howe said, 'is not a man who likes to pass up on the fringe benefits of fame.'

'How does he connect with Jones?'

'For a start…' Annie Howe played the washers over the blotched windscreen, applied the wipers. 'I shouldn't be doing this at all. As DCI, I'm an executive, an administrator. But tonight there aren't many detectives unoccupied. Nobody I could trust with this, anyway.'

'This, presumably, is to do with the murder of his brother.'

'Oh, yes. I think we're more or less convinced he *didn't* kill his brother. He has a convincing alibi and there's no DNA match at the crime scene. But… I'll admit I'm punching at smoke, but there are some questions I'd like to ask him, and I'd like you to hear the answers. You did rather well, in the end, with Jones.'

'Not from where I was sitting.'

'You think against the grain,' Howe said. 'My grain, anyway.'

'That sounds like a subtle way of saying I'm a licensed crank.'

Annie Howe didn't deny it.

'It *may* be that Jones has been in touch with Sollers Bull by now, and he knows what we're moving towards. Or it may be that there's no link between them at all. I don't know. We'll see.'

'What does Frannie Bliss think?'

'Why do you ask that?'

'Just that there seems to have been quite a concerted effort to discredit him over this. Sollers Bull and Countryside Defiance? Whoever they are.'

'Most of the time,' Howe said quietly, 'Francis Bliss is his own worst enemy.'

'He's had a bad few months. Domestically.'

'So I understand.'

The Audi was alone now on the Brecon road, where it sliced through invisible Magnis. Night clouds were gliding like flatfish in the aquarium of a big pale sky. The Easter full moon was up there somewhere. Merrily was remembering her first meeting with Annie Howe. The clinical interrogation of Jane in the search for a missing girl. A bad start, getting no better, as she'd conspicuously sided with Bliss through the years of attrition.

Howe took a left towards the Wye. One of those lanes that you never had cause to go down because it didn't lead anywhere apart from farms. Howe slowed, keeping the headlights dipped. Merrily dragged herself out of drowsiness, peering through the windscreen, following the headlights as they opened up the road, bleaching the grass at the verges. Annie Howe was talking again.

'... under no obligation to cover up what Jones and Mostyn have been doing, but I intend to take it slowly. If you see any indication that Sollers knows more than he should about unconventional religious practices, I'd be grateful if you kept it to yourself until we're out of there. And, yes, I *am* aware that you don't work for the police.'

'God tends to take a dim view of murder,' Merrily said.

If only to see Annie Howe wince. The car slowed. A private-looking sign on a right-hand bend said: *Oldcastle*.

'*Was* it a castle at one time?'

'No idea,' Howe said. 'Does it matter?'

'Just wondered how long-established the family was.'

'Long enough. Even for this area.'

Merrily checked her mobile. She'd left messages for Lol and Jane. Lol said he'd be in the Swan. Jane, presumably, was out with Eirion.

Near the top of a wooded rise, the full moon sprang out between the tall chimneys of the lightless farmhouse. It looked like a shell. A dead house. Merrily thought, who *could* live, unconcerned, overlooking the yard where a previous owner had been slashed and hacked to death? How long before the stain faded into a historical talking point, a footnote in a tourist guide?

Annie Howe drove down beyond the house, between well-grown oaks.

'Sollers lives in a converted coach house.'

'But he inherits Oldcastle?'

'Seems likely. Doubt he'll live there, but nobody can see him selling it. More likely turn it into a hotel or some sort of conference centre. Maybe even the official citadel for the increasingly wealthy Countryside Defiance. Their website carries a photograph of him in hunting pink with all the trimmings. And handcuffs.'

'Huh?'

'The countryside in manacles – the foxhunting ban and other issues. Sollers Bull lives to hunt.'

A caged bulkhead light came on over the porch as Annie Howe parked in front of a metal gate next to a small car. By the time they got the gate open and reached the porch door, a woman was coming out, wearing a calf-length sheepskin coat, its collar held together over her chin and mouth. Annie Howe stood in silence and watched her.

'Thank you, Mr Bull,' the woman said, her back to them now, 'and I'm sorry to have bothered you. Goodnight.'

As the woman got into the small car and its engine started up, a man appeared in the doorway.

'Oh,' he said. 'Annie.'

'I tried to call, Mr Bull,' Howe said. 'But you were engaged.'

'Bewildering times, Annie. The phone only ever stops when I unplug it.' His voice was pitched up higher than you expected; you could hear it lofted across the fields, over the mêlée of a hunt. 'You got something to tell me?'

'To ask you. If you can spare the time.'

'Of course. Coffee?'

'No, thank you, Mr Bull. I suspect we've had rather too much of that today.'

The overhead light made a twinkling star in an ear stud as Sollers Bull turned to examine Merrily. She saw a man of a little over medium height. A keenly pointed face, with deep bevelled cheeks. He was wearing tight black jeans and a red T-shirt with a message on it in black: *Not a fox-hugger.* The small car pulled away, headlights on full beam. Maybe the woman was a journalist.

'This is Merrily Watkins,' Annie Howe said.

Didn't explain further. She had her mobile out; it had evidently been on vibrate.

'Excuse me.' She took a step back on to the path, speaking into the phone. 'DCI Howe.' And then, after a silence, her voice low and deliberate, 'When was this, Karen?' before moving further away.

'Erm...' Merrily looked up at Sollers Bull. She was cold. 'Would you mind if *I* had a coffee?'

'I'll put some on.'

She followed him into a very classy designer kitchen.

'This an old house, Mr Bull?'

'Not particularly. Nineteenth-century and fortunately not listed so I've been able to do what I like with it.'

'The farmhouse must be listed, though.'

'Grade Two. Starred.'

'*Was* it a castle?'

'No. Older than that. The site was known as Oldcastle because of what was there before. Don't know what it was, but the stones are probably in the foundations.'

'I see.'

Through a window, Merrily saw Annie Howe, in the light grey trench coat, up against a ranch-style fence, listening to the phone. When she came back, her face was paler than the coat, but no less grey.

'Meant to ask you, how's Charlie these days?' Sollers said.

Sitting with his back to the red Aga, stretched out almost diagonally, feet under the hardwood table, hands behind his head. *Charlie?* This would explain him addressing Howe as Annie. It very much figured that the Oldcastle Bulls would be familiar with her dad.

'I'll come straight to the point, Mr Bull. Colin Jones – how well do you know him?'

Sollers looked blank. Genuinely so, Merrily thought, studying him: younger than he looked in the papers and not so distinguished: too flash for that.

'*Byron* Jones?' Merrily said.

'Oh, well, I know *him*,' Sollers said. 'Though not particularly well.'

'Have you ever done business with him?' Howe asked.

'Kind of business?'

'Cattle, for example. Ever sold any cattle to Mr Jones?'

'I wasn't aware that Mr Jones was even in the livestock business. Or the meat trade, come to that.'

'That's not quite answering the question, is it, sir?'

Annie Howe began unbuckling the belt of her coat, unhurried, like she was prepared to stay until she got what she'd come for. Only Merrily, sitting next to her, opposite Sollers, saw that her fingers were unsteady, fumbling it.

Sollers straightened up in his chair. His sleek, pointy face looked… foxy.

'No, I've never sold any beasts to Mr Jones.'

'Or maybe given him one?'

'Do you know what Hereford cattle are worth?' Sollers glanced from Howe to Merrily and back to Howe. 'What exactly is this about?'

'Just so that we have this clear, Mr Bull,' Howe said, 'you're saying that, as far as you're aware, no animal bred at Oldcastle has ever been sent to Colin Jones's establishment. Sent either to Jones or his business partner, Kenny Mostyn.'

'How would I know?'

'As far as you're *aware*.'

'I think you'd better explain.'

'I don't have to explain anything,' Howe said.

Her skin looked cold as bone.

She hadn't said what the phone call had been about. But then, police business, why would she?

69

Law of the Hunt

'Thank Christ,' Danny said.

Kenny Mostyn, and he was on his own and no longer wearing a dinner jacket.

Dressed for action, in fact: dark jeans, black fleece. Likely his suit was in the overnight bag over one shoulder; Danny had been worried that Mostyn might be staying the night at The Court and they'd still be sitting here when the sun come up, stiff as corpses. But mabbe Mostyn wasn't overnight-guest material.

'Looks like you was right then, Gomer.'

They had the old Jeep parked under a willow tree, edge of the parking area. Only a couple of dozen vehicles left. This was a select dinner party. Gomer had ID'd Councillor Lyndon Pierce, fellers on that level, usual suspects.

'Mostyn just showin' his face,' Gomer said, 'but he got business elsewhere to see to.'

'Don't switch on yet, let him get clear of the gate.'

'En't daft, boy. Keep our distance all the way.'

'Only thing worries me,' Danny said, 'is what if the Scotch bloke's told him about a feller lookin' for him with a cock to put in the ring. Best I could think of at the time, see.'

'Too late to get fussed about that.'

There was a furry growl under Gomer's voice now. Likely due to seeing Mostyn dressed much the same as he had been that night in the snow. Everything coming back, and the worst of it was that – for just a short while, surrounded by these lithe, prowling young guys – he'd felt just a bit scared. And even worse than that…

… mabbe like an old man.

Gomer was gonner hold that against Kenny Mostyn for ever.

It was like Cornel was gobbling up the night, wildly excited as he guided Jane, limping, through the gap in the high wire fence. Holding her hand inside his, which was big and dry. The moon lit an open space, with army-type huts, metal gates leading to fields and woodland.

'What is it?'

'Big boys' playground.'

Jane gave up. The way his mood had altered, she could only think he'd taken something. Maybe when he went off, apparently for a pee in the woods and she hadn't heard anything. Snorting coke from a folded tenner.

'Training centre,' Cornel said. 'Assault course, big pond they cross on ropes, professional shooting range… and all the things they daren't do at The Court because it's too close to the village.'

'And cockfights?'

'Cockfights, yeah, yeah, sure.'

'So this is connected with The Court?'

'Court's just paintballing, clay-shooting, a few pheasant shoots and all that regular shit. And then you're asked discreetly if you'd like to do some *real* shooting. Not for the wimps and the veggies. And that's when you meet Kenny for rough shoots in the woods, back of The Court and then maybe this other guy, ex-SAS, leads a weekend in the Black Mountains or the Beacons, which is a *lot* tougher, and the hunting's on a whole different level – you don't kill, you don't eat. And that's where you start paying for yourself.'

'You did that?'

'Sure, sure, sure, but all the time – this is what pissed me off – you're aware of other guys getting handpicked for *really* heavy shit. I *wanted* that – more than any of them.'

Cornel had his wire-cutters around a strand of barbed wire where a hole had been cut in the fence. Kept leaning on the handles, snipping bits off the wire. 'When I was at the LSE, used to read all these SAS books. I identified with that. Different jungle, that's all. And these other guys are going off at midnight in a Land Rover, and I go to Kenny – *what about me*? And he's going, We don't think you're quite ready, Cornel, and I'm like, What exactly do you want me to prove? *Name it.*'

Jane was trying to ease her hand away, without making it seem like a snub, but Cornel kept squeezing it, words spurting out of him.

''Cause I thought he was like my mate. He'd start taking me on one side, whispering the kind of thing you appreciate knowing when you're on a shooting trip and the others are all upper-class bastards who've been handling shotguns since they could walk. Thought it was him and me. One time I saw what I thought was this fox in the woods, about to pop it when I realized it was a dog. And that night, in the pub, when I was alone with Kenny, he said, why didn't you just shoot it?'

'Shoot a *dog*?'

Jane's fingers stiffened.

'"Lost a few points there, Cornel," he said. And after that I was always aware he was watching me, making these little remarks, asking could I hold my drink, stuff like that. Like testing my resolve, how determined I was to move on. So I'm drinking more and I'm blasting off at anything that moves. Mostly missed, but not always. Getting better. Bought my own shotgun. Getting there. And he kept asking for more money, and I kept giving it to him. It's a rite of passage, he'd say. Cost me over a grand for the cockfight, and that was before the betting started. That was him in the yard at the Swan. That was Kenny. My mate.'

His *mate*? Telling him his balls had fallen off and to go back and cry himself to sleep? *Come and see me again when you're grown up.*

There was something horribly wrong about all this. Cornel's fingers were easing Jane's apart, pushing between them. Didn't like that; made her think of sex. Jane let the hand he was holding go limp, thinking to slide it out of his grip and get the hell out. Her ankle wasn't broken, only twisted. She could do this. Best to run into the conifers. He was fit and had long legs and he could get to her easily if he could see her. The trees were her only chance. Be like midnight in there.

Cornel said, 'You ever meet Kenny?'

'I've never even been in one of his shops. Look, Cornel, I didn't lie. That night at the Swan, I didn't actually *see* anything. It was too dark. I just heard some of it. From the bottom of the yard. And, like, I didn't tell you because I didn't want it to sound like I was trying to humiliate you or anything, OK?'

'Absolutely fine. Fine, fine, fine.'

'It's actually *not* fine, is it?'

'It's answered a few questions.'

'Like I keep telling you, I just want to see Savitch brought down.'

'Sure you do.'

'I *do.*'

Cornel stood in the space where the wire had been cut, looking down into the clearing as if he was trying to think what had happened next. Jane could see his jaw working in the moonlight, hear his teeth grinding.

'So it was Kenny took me to the cockfight. Bunch of us were supposed to be going, but in the end it was just him and me, and a bunch of gyppos and local trash. Some experience, though. Booze and coke everywhere. Crazy. Like something from another century. And you get drawn in – it wakes you up, the excitement. *Incredible* violence. Real energy. Came over with the Romans, cocking, did you know that?'

'They seem to have got off on cruelty,' Jane said. 'The Romans.'

She could feel the sweat forming between their fingers.

'I was drinking pretty heavily,' Cornel said. 'Had a few hundred on this cock and the bastard lost. Felt pretty pissed off, and Kenny says, put it in a sack. Get Barry at the Swan to cook it for

you. Losers get eaten. Law of the hunt. Makes perfect sense.'
Cornel looked around. 'Right. It's clear. Come on.'

Finally letting go of her hand, but before she could move away
and maybe start running, his big hand was around her left buttock,
steering her, his fingers lingering on the wet seat of her jeans.

'Round there. The door's in front of you.'

A big padlock was hanging loose.

'Ha… good. Didn't think they'd have time to fix it.'

Cornel pulled off the lock, tossed it over his shoulder. Jane
looked up. It was just a big shed with a convex roof and heavy
doors set into a wall of concrete blocks.

'Are you sure—?'

'This is it. Go on… *push.*'

He prodded Jane with his torch and she went up against the
doors, which immediately opened a body's width, and she went
stumbling through, down some steps he hadn't warned her
about. Pain jabbed into her ankle. She sank to her knees holding
on to the step above her.

Heard the doors close behind her. Didn't move.

'Go on,' Cornel said. 'Go down.'

'The dead bird in the sack,' Barry said, 'I just thought, get this
bastard out of my bar. I'd had a bellyful of Cornel. Never once
thought of cockfighting. Gomer sure about this?'

'Doesn't usually make mistakes,' Lol said. 'Not where Jane's
involved.'

'Would Savitch do that on his own doorstep? *I'd* like to think
it was him, and, yeah, if Cornel was involved… He's not exactly
compos mentis is he, Cornel? That makes sense – always needs
somebody to blame. Fighting cock lets him down, he wants it
cooked for his dinner. Juvenile. Well, worse than juvenile. I tell
you what happened after that incident with Jane?'

'I don't think so.'

Lol felt the pull of the stitches in his wrist, remembering
Cornel peering into the bar. *Wherever you are, you little bitch, I
just want you to know it doesn't end here.*

'This is while everybody's talking about Mansel Bull,' Barry said. 'Cornel – very drunk, if you recall – goes into the Gents', presumably in search of paper towels. When he only finds a hot-air hand-dryer, he forces the lock on the cleaner's room and then he smashes his way into a couple of cupboards to locate the necessary, which he leaves scattered all over the floor. Then he strips off his wet jeans and his underpants and marches upstairs to his room, naked from the waist down. Not long afterwards, a guest opens the door of her room to see a half-naked man pissing down the stairwell.'

Lol winced.

'What did you do?'

'I know what I *wanted* to bleedin' do, but I'm a genteel hotel manager now. I did a mop-and-bucket job and then I rang the guy at the bank who booked Cornel's room and said perhaps they should think twice about the kind of people they send on these courses. And he puts me on to another guy, and I tell *him* what happened, and he apologizes and says, in this meaningful way, to leave it with him. Obviously, I never heard from him again, and Cornel left the next night. At least I thought he'd left. Until he shows up with the bird in the bag.' Barry finished his beer. 'Odd that Danny hasn't told you what they found at The Court.'

'To be honest, so much has happened since that until you mentioned Danny I'd kind of forgotten about it.'

'If you've got Danny's mobile, give him a call.'

'I'll do it now.'

But when Lol brought out his phone it was playing the riff from 'Sunny Days'.

'Lol? That you, man?'

'Eirion?'

'I've been everywhere,' Eirion said. 'Left messages. She doesn't do this. I mean, you never know which way she's going to jump, but she doesn't stand you up. You know?'

'Jane?'

70

Pot... Kettle... Black

ANNIE HOWE – YOU thought you knew how she was wired, but now it was as if something in the system had gone awry. This normally emotionless woman pinched and twisted by some painful, insistent electricity. She'd had a shock and she was still getting aftershocks. Her questions were fluid and focused but some of them seemed disconnected and illogical, and somehow not...

... not *police* questions.

Merrily drank a second cup of coffee – too much, but she needed to be on top of this.

'I can't quite believe what you're implying,' Sollers Bull said. 'You really think I've been serving up pedigree livestock for some kind of ritual slaughter?'

'Somebody has, Mr Bull.'

'We're not talking about halal?'

'We're *not* talking about halal.'

'Then perhaps you should be looking at rustlers rather than poor bloody farmers. That hidden heap of uninvestigated crimes in the countryside.'

Sollers was on his feet, leaning back against the Aga's chromium bar. Annie Howe sitting next to Merrily at the table, the long coat hanging open.

'Do you know Kenny Mostyn, Mr Bull?'

'I've bought items from his shops.'

'What kind of items?'

'Guns. A shotgun for me, an airgun for my son.'

'How old's your son?'

'Were you thinking you might want to arrest him, Annie?'

Annie. That was it. That *small county* thing again. Howe and Sollers Bull knew each other socially, but how well? Had it ever been more? They were around the same age.

Howe looked down at the table, her white-blonde hair turning rose-gold in the kitchen light. Then she looked up slowly.

'The woman who was leaving as we arrived…'

'A neighbour. Collecting for a local charity.'

'So soon after your brother's murder? *She* must've been keen.' Annie pushing a straying strand of hair behind an ear. 'Mr Jones's peculiar religion… did you know about that, Mr Bull?'

'No.'

'Does it surprise you?'

'Nothing like that surprises me. Country areas are full of eccentrics who think they can get away with whatever they're doing more easily out here.'

'How did you feel when your brother sold the top field to Magnis Berries?'

Sollers blinked, then expelled an impatient breath, shaking his head as if he found the question meaningless. Annie Howe didn't move.

'You don't have to answer *any* of my questions, Mr Bull, but—'

'But it might look suspicious if I don't? For God's sake, Annie, I've cooperated fully from day one. I've given you a DNA swab for elimination purposes, I've explained exactly where I was when my brother was killed and who was with me…' Sollers upturned his head, bit his lip, sniffed, looked back at Howe. 'All right, I don't like selling ground, and I did not understand why my brother had done so.'

'You took it up with him.'

'Of course I did. He was my brother.'

'And?'

'He glossed over it. He'd actually bought that land some twenty years ago from a neighbour, and he said he'd never really felt it was part of the farm, so when he was offered a good price he chose to get rid of it.'

'And that satisfied you?'

'Look, my brother and I were different people. His kind of farming was more of its time… instinctive…'

Merrily said, 'What does that *mean*, Mr Bull?'

'He'd often follow his feelings rather than agricultural economics. Farming was in his blood. He used to laugh at my business degree – in a *good-natured* way, I should add.'

'Was he superstitious?'

'What a ridiculous question.'

Annie Howe said, 'Is it possible that your brother supplied bulls to Mr Jones?'

'As for *that* suggestion—'

'But he did keep Herefords.'

'You know he did. What are you doing, Chief Inspector – trying to prove in front of your subordinate that us being old friends in no way prejudices your inquiries?'

'We were friends of friends,' Annie Howe said. 'That was all.'

Subordinate. Merrily smiled. At least it showed that Sollers had no idea who she was. She turned the smile on him.

'The boss doesn't have anything to prove to me, Mr Bull.'

A faintly amused twitch at the corner of Annie's mouth, but it didn't last.

'You feel happier now about your neighbours, Mr Bull? Magnis Berries?'

'And I *certainly* don't see how *that*—'

'I'm told you've been a regular visitor. In a manner of speaking.'

'I like to keep an open mind about these things,' Sollers said.

'What things?'

'Polytunnels. Much condemned.'

Howe nodded.

'And the migrant workers? You suggested to my colleague, DI Bliss, that migrant workers might be at least partly responsible for the increase in rural crime.'

'I was saying all kind of things that night. I'd just seen my brother's butchered body. And I'm sure your *colleague* exaggerated my comments.'

'We'll come back to that, if you don't mind. How well do you know Ward Savitch?'

'We're acquainted.'

'What do you think of him?'

Another odd question.

'I'm just interested,' Annie Howe said.

'He's just a rich man in search of an identity. Wants to recreate the countryside as somewhere that makes him feel welcome. Lots of them around, in the so-called New Cotswolds, some of them TV celebs, like Smiffy Gill. And now they have an official voice.'

'Countryside Defiance.'

'Ostensibly the voice of the local people. In fact financed and run *by* incomers *for* incomers. I believe it began as a kind of business-class social networking site on the Internet. Then various resources got pooled, and they were away. Good luck to them.'

'But you're their figurehead, and you're not an incomer.'

Sollers bent forward, ear stud winking.

'I'm their much-prized well-known local person, who can get them into both grass-roots farming circles and hunt balls.'

'And what's in it for you?'

'I don't like being treated like a suspect, Annie.'

'This is really not how I talk to a suspect, Mr Bull, but if that's how you want to—'

'Some of us *need* incomers. They buy meat from my farm shop, they eat in my restaurant...'

'And I suppose it means you get to dictate some of Countryside Defiance's policies?'

'Don't like the word *dictate*. They listen to me.'

'Influence, then. The campaign against rural policing, for example?'

'The campaign *for* rural policing.'

'Which particularly targets DI Bliss.'

Sollers snorted.

'Man's a liability, as I'm sure your masters are beginning to realize. A crass little man, who was particularly insensitive on the night my brother died.'

'Why do you think that was?'

'Because he's in the *wrong place*. Because he has no sympathy with country people.'

'Especially,' Annie Howe said, 'when they're shagging his wife.'

Merrily knocked her cup over.

Annie Howe said, 'That *was* Mrs Bliss, wasn't it, on her way out as we arrived? The woman you identified as a neighbour. Not exactly a *close* neighbour. Well, in a manner of—'

'Don't you fucking sneer at me, Annie. Kirsty and I... we've known each other many years, long before her marriage to that...'

'Oik?'

'... which had turned sour long before she and I got together again.'

'And your wife...?'

'My wife knows. We've had separate lives for some time, but we're being responsible about it. We'll stay married until the children leave home.'

Merrily righted her cup, pulled out a tissue to mop up the coffee. Bloody *hell*.

'And Kirsty's family also know,' Sollers said, relaxed again now. 'And approve. Everyone who needs to know knows... except, presumably, for Bliss.'

Annie Howe said nothing, but something in her face quite visibly flinched.

'Too busy hiding his own indiscretions,' Sollers said.

Annie Howe had started to say something. It appeared to catch in her throat. For a moment she looked almost nauseous, and maybe Sollers glimpsed that, too; he slid lithely away from the stove, switched on more lights.

'My information is that a physical relationship between serving police officers in the same division is normally frowned upon to the extent that, should it become known about, one of the officers is immediately put on the transfer list. Who would you rather left Hereford, Annie: Bliss, or—'

'I *think* you should consider...' Annie Howe's voice cold, even for her '... very carefully before you continue.'

The lights were unhealthily bright, halogen hell. Sollers dragged out a chair and sat down directly opposite them.

'Bliss?' he said. 'Or Sergeant Dowell?'

Annie Howe was motionless.

'Pot... kettle... black,' Sollers said.

'You have any proof of this, Mr Bull?'

'Mrs Bliss has been aware of it for quite some time. And she should know, don't you think?'

Annie was silent for a couple of seconds.

'Yes,' she said quite slowly. 'She should know.'

'And all this,' Sollers said, 'relates to the murder of my brother *how*?'

'Did your brother know?'

No hesitation from Annie. In the pink light, Sollers Bull's face froze for just an instant.

'Your brother,' Annie said. 'Did he know about the resumption of your friendship with Mrs Bliss?'

'My brother and I didn't discuss social life. We moved in different circles. And you know what, Annie? I'm not putting up with this any longer. I'm going to ask you to leave.'

'*Did* your brother know?'

'Get out,' Sollers said.

Annie Howe drove the Audi back up the track with the headlights on full beam, took the left at a fork, let the car crawl up to the stone gateposts and a cracked sandstone sign.

OLDCASTLE

The metal gate to the drive was closed, no lights. Rearing beyond it, the house looked to Merrily like a derelict nursing home: three storeys, a flat sheen of moonlight like tin plate on its highest windows.

Annie Howe flashed the Audi's headlights at the gates and waited, lowering her window as a uniformed policeman emerged from a smaller gate to the side of the main entrance.

'Don't bother with the big gates, George, I'll leave the car out here.'

'Ma'am, you do know they're looking for you?'

'I can imagine. I'm not here.'

'Bad night, Ma'am.'

'Yes.'

'I never trust a full moon,' George said.

'Nonsense.' Howe turned to Merrily. 'You spare me another hour?'

'You had a phone call. Before you started talking to Sollers Bull.'

Annie Howe pushed her hair back.

'Yes. I had a phone call.' She parked to the left of the gates, leaving the engine running. 'The woman Bliss was looking for, the prime suspect in the Marinescu case... he found her.'

'Oh.'

'She was attending – if not running – an illegal cockfight in the cellar of a well-known flophouse and brothel on the Plascarreg. The woman is a large, violent sociopath, and the cellar was also full of men who have no reason to love the police. For reasons known only to himself, Bliss went down there. On his own.'

'Oh God...'

'At 19.20, a 999 call was made by the elderly woman who owns the place. Uniform turned out in force, blocked all the entrances to the Plascarreg, caught the suspect trying to smash someone else's car through a security fence. Five other arrests. Males.'

'And...?'

'Bliss was found in the ring. He was taken to Hereford and then transferred to the ICU.' Annie Howe's face was tinted in the bitter-orange haze of the dashboard lights as the engine died. 'They say he's in what, in a few hours, will probably qualify as a coma.'

Shouldering open the car door, ejecting herself into the night.

71

Something Insane

IT WAS COLD now; there might even have been a frost. A stray cloud was draped like a washed-out rag over the bowl of the moon, the only lamp was in the farmyard at Oldcastle.

'You haven't got a coat?' Annie Howe said.

'It was actually quite springlike earlier on. I just jumped in the car.'

'I've got a spare one in the boot, if you…'

'Listen,' Merrily said, 'shouldn't you be back in Hereford?'

'I'm not a doctor.'

Annie Howe walked away into the centre of the yard. She had a flashlight but hadn't switched it on. The mobile incident room was parked at the top of the drive, the bulk of it concealed by an extended barn.

The yard was far too quiet for a farm.

'We had to get the livestock moved,' Annie Howe said, 'so forensic could spend some time in the sheds and barns. Not that they turned up anything useful.'

The flagstones were slick underfoot as if the blood was still here, still wet. Merrily thought about those apocryphal stories where the blood from a murder never dried.

'Are they going to call you, if… if there's any change?'

'Dowell's at the hospital.'

'You do know there's no truth in what he said about Bliss and Karen Dowell?'

Yet was it so unlikely that Frannie Bliss, in the long nights of the coldest winter for many years, would seek refuge with someone who spoke his language? Maybe why he'd been so remote lately?

'Dowell has more sense,' Annie Howe said. 'Either Bull's lying, or Kirsty's got the wrong end of the stick. Not that... there necessarily is a stick.'

The edge had gone from her voice. Drained of attitude, she looked waiflike in the moonlight. The long coat was buttoned around her throat; she sank both hands into its pockets, staring at the ground.

'Jesus Christ, I thought he *knew* Sollers was sleeping with his wife.'

'How could you know and he didn't?'

'It emerged during routine inquiries. Stagg found out. Couldn't wait to tell me. I couldn't imagine how Francis could fail to know about his wife's former relationship, but you forget how secretive rural families can be. I realise now that if he *had* known he would've been very polite and distant with Sollers and unloaded the investigation on someone else long before he was ordered to.'

'To give himself some space to stitch Sollers up from behind?'

'You really do know him, don't you?'

'I'd probably have been more help in there if I'd known what you were looking for,' Merrily said.

'I've never known anyone break down and confess to a serious crime. You know you're actually getting somewhere when they start to say no comment, meaning yes, I did it, now prove it.'

'Did he *say* no comment?'

'He told us to get out. If he was entirely innocent he'd be determined to carry on talking until he'd convinced us of it. "Get out" means "I need time to think."'

Annie Howe gazed at the moon's bevelled reflection in one of Oldcastle's attic windows. Merrily was thinking that if this was anyone else she'd be asking if they could pray together for Frannie. Most of them would humour her.

'Nobody's allowed in to see him,' Annie said. 'When they are, I'll be there.'

'Good.'

Merrily looked up at the cold-haloed moon, recalling the first time she'd met Bliss. The spiritual cleansing of a country church which had been desecrated: a crow's entrails spread over the altar, a stench of urine. Early days for her, then, in deliverance; she'd asked if they could send a cop who might believe that what she was doing wasn't a joke. Bliss had been a detective sergeant then, with a fullish head of ginger hair. *I'm a Catholic. That all right for you?*

Merrily prayed silently, alone, eyes wide open, head still fogged with shock.

Annie Howe said, 'I need to get a feeling for what might have happened on the night Mansel Bull died. I think I actually need to get yours.'

She walked away, across the flags, to a taped-off area halfway between the biggest barn and the house.

'You can waste a lot of time looking for a motive. Forensics have overtaken psychology. You no longer need to show why someone did it, just that they did. Most convicted murderers come out of court in the back of the van and we still don't know why.'

'You still seemed to be presenting Sollers Bull with a selection of motives.'

'Oh yes. *Did* Mansel know about the affair with Bliss's wife, and how did he feel about that? He and Kirsty's father were the biggest farmers in the area – were they friends or was there rivalry? Did Sollers want Mansel out of the way because the growing divergence of their ideas on the future of farming was threatening his plans? Was he afraid that Mansel was going to marry again, maybe this time producing offspring? And then there's the sale of the land to Magnis Berries. Did Mansel really do it without consulting Sollers? Now – why did you ask Sollers if his brother was superstitious?'

'You won't like this.'

'I didn't even like you asking the question.'

'It was when Sollers said Mansel didn't feel it was part of his farm. An old-fashioned farmer. Instinctive. Meaning he followed his feelings. The implication was that he didn't like that ground, even though he'd bought it himself. Was it just not productive... or what?'

Annie Howe said, 'You'll need to explain, as if to an idiot.'

'Everything here is built on or around the Roman town Magnis. There are superstitions connected with parts of the area. It's unlikely that Mansel hadn't heard the stories. A particular field gets a reputation for being unlucky. Crops failing, stock dying, tractor accidents...'

Merrily sensed a dampening of the air between them.

'It's what I do, Annie. The alternative path. You get tired of being defensive in the face of the secular society. Even your copper down there...'

'Didn't trust the full moon.'

'You get the same with paramedics and nurses in A and E. Night of the full moon, increased violence. Surveys prove it. Apparently. So tell me, where does irrational superstition begin? There's an old farmer out at Bishopstone or somewhere who's seen misty figures in the river mist, and some appear real and some don't. He talks of one with a bird's head. Followers of Mithras would wear masks to signify whichever grade they'd attained. One of the grades is the raven.'

Men who had been reappearing.

'So who was the hallucination drenched in blood?' Annie said.

When they reached the barn doors, two spotlights blazed into life high up on the house wall. As though a play was about to begin on the stage of weathered stone flags. Annie Howe fingered the police tape.

'Around six forty-five p.m., on the night of the storm, Mansel Bull sets out for his parish council meeting, then receives a call on his mobile from the council clerk to say it's been called off because of the weather. Mansel turns his Range Rover round and heads home. Who knew he'd be attending a council meeting? The other councillors and the clerk. And his brother, Sollers.'

She moved to the double doors opposite the farmhouse.

'In both these barns there were cattle. Herefords. Including, in a separate stall, one bull.'

'You know that?'

'From Sollers himself who initially was pointing us at rustlers. Now if – for the sake of argument – there *was* a plan to take some of Mansel's cattle, the night of the parish council, which Mansel never missed, might be seen as the most appropriate time.'

'Wouldn't Sollers know if something on that scale was happening? It would take several people.'

'The coach house is lower down the hill, screened by trees and reached by a different turn-off from the main drive. They could easily get up here without being seen. And, on a night like that, without being heard. Perfect conditions, in fact, for crowbarring a barn door.'

'*Was* the barn door forced?'

'No. Perhaps because it didn't get that far. Because Mansel returned in the middle of it.'

'And they killed him?'

'Could easily be that simple. If Jones and his Mithraism are irrelevant. Now give me your take on it.'

'Me?'

'Tell me something insane.'

From the top of the farmyard you could make out, in the moonlight, the silver eel that was the River Wye. Always venerated, sometimes claiming sacrifices. Part of the landscape that the Romans knew.

Oldcastle was part of it, too, a vantage point, perhaps built inside the long-flattened ramparts of a minor Iron Age hill fort. Or a Roman site, with Roman masonry now built into the foundations of this house. Sollers hadn't been specific. Perhaps he didn't know. Perhaps he did.

Back at the edge of the police tape, Merrily bent and lit a cigarette. She was wearing Annie Howe's checked woollen coat. The
sleeves were too long, but it was a cold night.

'In weather like that, most of us prefer to go home and bar the
doors against the wind, but when you're encouraged to go out
and use its energy…'

'Paganism again.'

'Most kinds of paganism work with natural energy. If you're
in what might be considered a haunted landscape, or one that
you believe to be conditioned by over a thousand years of military endeavour… I'm just giving you the received wisdom. Tell
me to stop whenever you like. I was interested in Byron's
description of sacrificial ritual that doesn't end in blood.'

'This is the man who makes his own way here, camps in a
field, goes on a fast… Is it necessary for the sacrifice to be done
in the temple?'

'I don't know. If this was a Roman site, part of the extended
Magnis… then they might find some justification for doing it
right here. Leave quite a mess though, wouldn't it?'

'Rustlers have been known to butcher animals in the fields,'
Annie said. 'That's what it would look like – butchery. For the
meat. All right. So, developing the idea that there was a plan to
take Mansel's bull and have it slaughtered…'

'The candidate arrives at the height of the storm. Maybe
accompanied, maybe not. Part of the challenge? You have to
imagine someone who's been through all the grades – the heat
and the cold and the near-death, whatever – has now reached
the point where he's ready to take on, for a short time, the role
of the god himself. He's on fire.'

'But these are…' Tension creases in Annie Howe's spotlit face
illustrating the hard time she was having with all this. 'These are
educated men?'

'Annie, high-level Freemasons, ritual magicians… they're *all*
educated men. Businessmen, financiers, guys in massively
competitive industries, powered by testosterone, not known for
their sensitivity… And right now they're angry and

disillusioned, reeling under accusations of collapsing the Western economy and walking away with their massive undeserved bonuses.'

'Fallen masters of the universe. OK, I'll buy it for the moment. How might this escalate to the murder of a man? Anybody can be a killer if there's enough anger, greed, ambition, repressed sexuality. How about the candidate?'

'You get drawn into something and if it's changing your life for what seems like the better, you're not going to jump off when it starts to get... extreme. Artificial stimulants might also be involved. The Romans seem to have used something called, I think, haoma.'

Miss White's drug of war. Combined with dogma and ritual and a physical regime built around commitment to a deity, real or symbolic. Could it be recreated? Bull's blood and magic mushrooms.

'Nothing like a brew.' Merrily smiled wearily. 'As they say in the Regiment.'

Chemically-enhanced excitement in the middle of a raging wind where you could hardly hear yourself think.

Annie said, 'Suppose Sollers knew about this. Told them what night his brother's going to be out, what time he leaves, what time he usually comes back from the council. Or was actually there, when his brother was killed? There's time. All we know is that he was at his restaurant at seven-thirty and he wasn't covered with blood. What if Sollers was here to see it? Extreme blood sport.'

Male model in hunting pink, Merrily thought. Ridiculously vain. A figurehead for Countryside Defiance, which he both supported and despised.

'And then Mansel's back unexpectedly,' Annie said, 'and here's his beloved little brother and a man with a large knife.'

Merrily closed her eyes, watched Mansel Bull's headlights blasting between the bars of the gate, Mansel barrelling towards them through the wind-whipped night.

Who's this?

It's Mansel. Mansel Bull.

The Bull. The Bull in his citadel.

The symbolism was both insane and inescapable.

Annie Howe was standing at the high point of the farmyard, looking down between the bare trees at the moonlit Wye. Her face latticed with white light and shifting shadows.

'He has to come through this.' Barely a whisper. 'Bliss.'

'Yes.'

72

Sham

THE SMELL REACHED Jane first. Didn't smell like any church or temple she'd ever been in or imagined. Not herbs, not incense. More like a meat store. The smell of raw meat always made her feel slightly sick now, and she thought about the beautiful dead cockerel with his golden mane.

Cornel shone his torch around for her. It was smaller than it had looked in the picture on his phone. Half the size of a chapel, one of those cold Welsh Nonconformist chapels. Jane could hear echoes of her own hyped-up breathing.

'Go on,' Cornel said. 'Go down.'

'Hold on.'

The torch opened up a panel of light in front of her. She was in the wide trench down the middle.

'This is it?' Carefully, Jane stood up. 'This is where they hold the cockfights?'

It was like a car workshop, with a pit where the car was ramped up. There was a long rectangular gulley down the middle of the floor. On either side of it, rough ledges or benches like seating areas. Much of this below ground level, sunk into the foundations of the hut. So it was a Nissen hut built over a rectangular pit or a trench, as dug by archaeologists.

Cornel was jumping down the steps, pushing past her and strolling along the trench like he owned the place. Pretty clear now that he'd been snorting coke. Talking faster, moving weirdly. Eirion had done coke, just the once – well, as far as

Jane knew. Eirion had said it was like ten minutes of cloud nine and then an hour or so all pumped up before you needed some more.

The knowledge that Cornel was on something… that was actually quite comforting. Like, inasmuch as there was any comfort to be had for a vegetarian woman down here. She called across to him.

'So it's happening later… or it's already happened?'

'What?'

'The cockfighting.'

No doubt about that now. It stank of it. Somewhere down here there would be blood, there would be feathers. Jane pulled out her phone, checked the battery – still functioning but getting low, and the signal was down to one blob, which often meant you could manage to make calls but not receive them.

'What are you doing, Jane?'

'Pictures.'

A stone plinth jutted from the end wall of concrete blocks. Below the plinth, a rudimentary sink, like a font, but with more of a sense of altar about it. Above the plinth, a kind of stone plaque or tablet, quite big, with figures on it in relief.

'Wait,' Cornel said. 'I'll give you some better ones in a minute.'

He unslung his big rucksack, unzipped it, started taking things out. It was really cold in here, half in the earth.

Jane curled her hand around the phone in her jacket pocket and moved along the gulley. It was lined with stone. Some of the marks near her feet did look like patches of dried blood.

'Can you shine the torch down there for a minute?'

Cornel didn't move. In the ambient light, Jane tried to make out the marks on the stone benches.

'They're divided into segments, like individual seats. I suppose the… audience sits up here and, with both ends blocked so the birds can't escape.'

There were chisel marks, carvings in the surface, figures like you saw in pyramids, only more crudely drawn into the concrete. Probably done before it dried, but chipped now. Some were in circles, like astrological symbols. It was actually pretty interesting. Or it would have been if she'd been here with Eirion rather than…

Jane limped up to the sink. A shallow pool in there. Dipped a finger into it, then held it up and sniffed. Looked like water, smelled of nothing much. There was a flake of something like mud on the edge of the sink; when she flicked it off it made brown liquid scribbles in the pool.

'Could this actually have been a Roman cockpit?'

Her knowledge of Roman deities was fairly basic. As an archaeologist, she was a one-trick pony: stone circles, henges, Bronze Age burial mounds.

She brought out her phone again.

'Could you just, like, shine the torch here for just a minute? I want to see if the light's strong enough.'

Cornel made an impatient noise and came over with his torch, directed the beam at the plinth. Jane saw that one corner had been knocked off, and it was all powdery.

'It's concrete! It's not stone at all.' She tried to see his face behind the beam. 'What *is* this place?'

'Been rebuilt.'

'It's a sham!'

'Absolutely.' Cornel bent over her shoulder as she took a shot of the corner with her phone. 'Thank you.'

'What are you—'

He'd just lifted the phone out of her hand.

'I've told you I'll give you some better ones. Stand back, girlie.'

His arm went back, and then there was the sound of something hitting the wall and bouncing off and…

'That wasn't my phone, was it?'

'Probably wouldn't work down here, anyway.'

'*What've you done?*'

The echo came back at the same time as Cornel's arm, and then it got lost in a bang and another bang and a splintering crunch, and then Cornel had hold of Jane's arm and he was dragging her back, and she was shutting both eyes against a rising storm of grit, and the inside of her mouth was like in the yard at the Swan when she'd been choking on the cobweb full of flies.

Cornel pulled her away, screaming, down the aisle, pointing the torch ahead of them into a dust storm.

Jane erupted in coughs, only half aware of the stone tablet with the figures on it beginning to wobble. As she watched, it tilted slowly and began to topple towards them.

'What're you *doing*?'

Cornel was on his feet. He was laughing, the torch in one hand, its beam almost solid with dust, a short-handled lump hammer in the other.

'Haven't even started yet,' he said. 'Girlie.'

Engine noise.

'Where are you?'

Lol shouting, the way you couldn't help doing when the voice at the other end was faint and kept cutting out.

He was on the phone in Barry's office, standing up. He heard Danny telling Gomer to slow down, and then Gomer's voice saying they didn't want to lose the bugger.

'Who?'

'—ostyn. Kenny Mostyn.'

Danny did some explaining. Lol kind of got the gist. He saw Barry in the doorway, standing very still, the way only Barry did.

'Danny,' Lol said, 'listen to me. It's not possible you've got Jane with you?'

No, it wasn't.

Lol could've wept. When he came off the phone, Barry waved him to the swivel chair.

'Slowly,' he said.

'Gomer and Danny,' Lol said, 'are in Gomer's Jeep. They're following Kenny Mostyn because they think he's going to a cockfight.'

'Where?'

'Danny thinks they're probably heading for the Stretton Sugwas route towards Hereford, but obviously he can't be sure. Lots of tracks and old farm buildings.'

'Let me get this right,' Barry said. 'The rock 'n' roll farmer and a man well into his seventies…'

'Why they think there's a cockfight on and this Mostyn's on his way to it, I don't know. I suggested that when he stopped, they should just drive past and then call me back. Don't go up any tracks.'

'Good advice, Laurence.'

'But then, this is Gomer,' Lol said. 'Like there aren't enough problems with Jane missing.'

Cornel had his back to Jane now, fiddling with something. She heard the familiar repeat clicking of a stubborn cigarette lighter.

'He wasn't my mate after all,' Cornel said.

He stepped away from the altar, where two curling flames were sending shadows coiling over the walls and up to the curved ceiling.

Two small bowl-shaped lamps – like twin miniature men's urinals – were sitting on the edge of the altar

Jane backed away. There was still dust in the air,

'Cosy, eh?'

'You took my phone.'

'In this world, girlie, you have to take what you want. Kenny taught me that. Kenny, my *mate*. Take it when you want it, where you want it. That's what Kenny said, *my mate*. Taking pictures of me holding up the dead cock in the ring. My *mate*. Where do you think those pictures ended up?'

'I don't know.'

'You don't know.' Cornel's face was fingered by shadows. 'Well, you know I'm not sure about that. You know what I think? I think I haven't actually got any mates.' He threw something to the concrete. A bundle of something soft. 'Least of all you, girlie. You were never my mate. You're a slippery, duplicitous little slag.'

'Look, I don't know what you're—' Jane steadied her voice. 'I'm not your mate, but I've got nothing… If you just give me the torch and the phone, I can take some pictures, and then, like, if you just give me a day or so to expose the cockfight situ—'

'You *stupidlittlefuckingbitch*!' A bright sprinkle of spit in the thin lamplight as his body arched at her. 'There was never any cockfighting here! Never! You got that?'

73

Raven

He'd done it all. Cut the wire, smashed the CCTV camera. He'd been here before. Well, of course he had.

There was a horrible smell from the lamps. Like rancid, molten butcher's-shop fat. Cornel was leaning against the altar, the lump hammer still in his hand, the rucksack at his feet.

'Thing is, girlie – and I've thought about this a lot – the night you humiliated me in the pub, I do believe that's when it all started going wrong. Me standing there with my trousers soaked, as if I'd pissed myself. And all my *mates* laughing. You started it. You could've walked away anytime, and you didn't. Well in the frame for a shag. Who put you up to it, girlie? Which of *my mates*?'

'Nobody. Swear to God. I was just fishing for information – about what happens at The Court.'

'Bull*shit*. Kids your age, it's just clothes and clubbing and baby booze. And the teen-witch bit in your case, though I'd've thought—'

'I have *never* been a bloody teen—'

'And your boyfriend, the big-time journalist. You think I didn't ask people if you had a boyfriend? Yeah, yeah, she knocks around with some fat Welsh student.'

'He *knows* a lot of journalists, and he's not—'

'Oh, shut up.'

'No, I'm sorry.' Jane moved back into the lamplight. Not having this. 'I'm sorry, but you're wrong. You're—'

'*Shuddup!*'

Jane flinched a little but didn't move.

'If it's not cockfighting,' she said, 'what is it?'

'Took my money, and they hung me out to dry.'

'Who?'

'One of the other guys was washing in the Gents' and he had his sleeves rolled up. I thought it was a tattoo. He'd been *branded*. Branded like a bull, and it was still fresh and livid. The pain of that, and he didn't... he didn't care. Pain works. It's a man thing.'

His teeth were gritted again. Jane recalled how, at the back of the Swan, the man with the ashy voice had told Cornel, *It's about manhood.*

'This is some kind of temple, right?'

'I thought you knew all about it. But you don't know shit, do you?'

'Don't know much about Roman stuff.'

'Holy of holies. Just smashed the holy of holies, and it's not over yet.'

'*Why?*'

'Made it to raven, and then it stopped.'

'Huh?'

'Took me out to the top of a hill. Had to spend the night on the top, naked. All night. Alone, but I knew they were watching, so I couldn't creep off. No food all day. They gave me something to drink so I stopped feeling the cold, and then I'm seeing things, fucking terrifying, but when the sun comes up... God... Next night, we go out lamping hares. It was *spectacular*. I'm wearing like...' Cornel cupped his hands around his face, like a funnel. 'The raven? Then ate raw meat, fresh-killed.'

His body was vibrating again. He was grinding his teeth. Then his jaw fell to his chest.

'And that was it. Covered truck still comes maybe twice a week, close to midnight. There might be fifteen guys on the course, but only two or three will go. And I'm, like, when's it my turn? Why not me? Was that *it*? There's higher degrees, another six. But it stops. It fucking *stops*.'

Oh God, it was about frustration.

It all came out. They wouldn't let him move up to the next grade. They took his money, but they wouldn't let him move on. He'd kept on at Kenny Mostyn who he'd thought was his mate – what did he have to do, what did they want? He'd gone around the countryside, demonstrating how hard he was, shooting at people's pets, following Kenny one night, to a cockfight. Thinking back, Kenny must've been really pissed off when he turned up, but he congratulated him on his initiative, bought him drinks, helped him place his bets. Of course he lost, making a fool of himself, got into the car legless but made it back, trying to persuade Barry to cook the poor bird. He'd become half-mad with frustration, he really didn't understand and, oh for God's sake, Jane didn't either.

'Twenty-six.' Cornel's big jaw thrusting out, his face all sheeny. 'Twenty fucking six, with a mortgage half the size of the national debt, a car that cost fifty K, not half paid for. I'm *fucked*!'

He laid the hammer on the altar. Bent down to the rucksack and pulled something out. Like a folded jacket or something, Jane couldn't see.

'Got the push, girlie, did I tell you? *Necessary rationalization.* Had a message to ring my boss. He wasn't even apologetic. *Difficult times, old boy, difficult times.* Then off to his villa in Tuscany, the bloated fucking toad.'

Jane watched a fist rebunching out of the same hand that had held hers, knuckles shining with grease.

'They shafted me. Mostyn. And Savitch and all the public-school cunts who were egging me on to give you one.' Cornel reached down and tugged on something. 'I followed the truck. Hired the van, so nobody would know it was me. Easy to follow people on these roads. And then I came back. Hey, but you know what was weird? Got in last night. Being really, really careful. And the police came. The actual police. I'm crouching there behind the altar, they flash their torches around very quickly and then bugger off. I creep up to the door, and they've nicked some other bloke. Couldn't believe it. I felt—' Cornel punched his left palm with his right fist. 'Magic!'

When he started to laugh, it was like a yelping. He snapped on the torch and shone the beam at the ground, where he'd thrown down the bundle.

'Strikes me you're the first woman ever to come in here.' His livery lips wet. 'Or you will be.'

Kicking the bundle on the ground, and Jane watched the sleeping bag slowly unroll.

'Sacrilege.' Cornel's shadow was a momentary black bloom on the curved roof. 'Think of it like that. We're gonna have ourselves some sacrilege, girlie.'

Jane's recoil knocked one of the lamps off the altar, hot fat splashing up as it went out, and she bit her top lip so hard she felt the blood come.

Cornel's face, in the mean light, was creamy with sweat. Cornel was a mess, Cornel was a tosser. Keep telling yourself that. Jesus, tell *him*.

'Cornel,' Jane said – even though she knew it was the wrong, *wrong* thing to say, she said it. 'You're an educated guy. You ever think this could be making you just a little bit insane?'

Don't waste time looking for his reaction, look for a way out of here: those stepped concrete blocks, the seating, the back row seemed to be some distance from the wall. Would have to be, because this was a Nissen hut and more than half the wall was curved, part of the roof, so there had to be a space.

'You'll get another job.' Stepping back, her raised voice gathering echoes. 'Look at the totally bent, disgraced politicians who keep bouncing back. And they're, like, *old*?'

So there was likely to be a concealed channel – walkway, crawlway – around the perimeter. Follow that and you'd get back to the doors.

Cornel said, 'Don't try to engage me in conversation, Jane – we're way past that.'

A two-one from the LSE: he wasn't a complete idiot, was he?

Jane saw him place something on the end of the concrete bench and pick up the hammer. Each time he smashed it down, with a dull, metallic splintering, she winced and jerked and backed a bit further away. It had to be her mobile.

'Please, Cornel…' Suddenly near to tears, and they were seeping into her voice. 'You can't rape me.'

The word was out, pathetically, but carrying a long echo.

…*ape me.*

Jane zipped her jacket all the way up as his voice came back at her, petulant, along with a spurt of torchbeam.

'Doesn't have to be *that*.'

'Just because you feel sorry for somebody,' Jane said steadily, 'doesn't mean you… doesn't mean you can fancy them.'

Well, she didn't feel sorry for Cornel at all. He was a victim of his own greed, his own obsession. She hated him. She sank slowly down and fitted both hands under one of the shards of concrete which had flown off under the lump hammer. It was too heavy to throw at him, but she had nothing else; she held it against her stomach, letting her body take some of the weight as she backed away from the lamp.

'And this place is horrible. It stinks and it's not even a proper ancient site. It's just cobbled together out of old… building supplies, and you know what? I… I think you've got this all wrong, Cornel. I think you've been conned. This is just a scam to make money out of guys like you.'

Jane flattened herself against the rough bottom wall and began to drag herself along it, thinking maybe Cornel wanted this place to bring out a side of him he still wasn't sure was there. As if just *being* here, doing violent *man* things…

'It's just a scam, Cornel, to make money out of rich, gullible—'

'Do you see what's in my hand, girlie?'

Jane screamed.

'I'm not looking!' Aware that he was pointing the torch at himself – *oh please* – down there. 'You come near me, Cornel, I swear I'll have your eyes out.'

74

Sleeper

As THEY DROVE up towards the Brecon road, the clouds had fled. The still-wintry moonlight was spread like sour cream on the fields where the man who slaughtered the Bull might have gone running, his head floating inside the feral fury of his haoma high.

Try explaining that to the Crown Prosecution Service, Annie Howe had said.

'Even if Sollers had no hand in the killing, if he was there he did nothing to stop it. Then into his car and off to his restaurant to fix himself an alibi.'

'What was he like when he arrived at the restaurant?'

'Stagg talked to the staff. They were agreed that Sollers was in one of his reorganizing moods. Calling the team together – we should do this, we need to do that. Busy, busy.'

'Hyper. That figures.'

'Then, after a suitable period of time, he comes back and, according to his statement, hears the cattle making a noise in the sheds, walks up with his shotgun and discovers the carnage.'

'Shotgun?'

'Common enough reaction for a farmer at night. Especially in an area portrayed by Countryside Defiance as the badlands. Expect the worst. Be ready. Don't expect any help from the police.'

'How did it all go sour?'

Merrily sank back against the headrest, thinking of Arthur Baxter and his smallholding. *The good life, eh? Where did all that go?* The Baxes, in their shapeless home-made sweaters replaced by the Mostyns in killer camouflage.

'And where's Mansel's murderer now?'

'Conceivably in some London nightclub or the theatre,' Annie said. 'We'd need a list of Jones's clients, present and past. It'll take work, liaison with the Met, manpower, overtime… money. Even before we try to penetrate the well-protected, lawyer-lined heart of the City.'

'Will that be so much harder than penetrating the old farming families of Herefordshire?'

The car climbed the last hill to the Brecon road.

'You know why he explained in detail – Jones – how the candidate came alone and slept in a tent and fasted for a day? You know why he told us all that, instead of delivering his *need to know* line? That's just in case this guy really did do it. Killed Mansel.'

'So Jones could say he was on his own? Nothing to do with me, guv.'

'You could be in the wrong job.'

'I thought the entire clergy was in the wrong job as far as you were concerned.'

Annie Howe laughed and drove out onto the Hereford road, put her foot down. Before leaving Oldcastle, she'd rung the hospital. Frannie Bliss had come round for about five seconds.

It was enough.

Annie Howe had smoked one of Merrily's cigarettes.

The lump of ridged concrete was too heavy, and it was hard for Jane to think how she could smash it down on Cornel if he came for her. But he hadn't, he'd gone quiet and she'd lugged the slab with her into the gap behind the seating blocks, sinking down there, feeling like a rabbit hiding from a rabid fox.

The space was narrower than she'd expected; maybe Cornel wouldn't fit in here. She packed herself into it and waited in silence, hearing him moving around and then a double grunt as if he was heaving himself up on something.

She heard a muted *thuck, thuck.*

Oh Christ, he was barring the doors.

Jane let the slab slide down between her feet, shut her eyes and prayed for help, but when Cornel spoke again his voice was quieter.

'Wherever you are, girlie… don't move. If you don't want to get hurt.'

But there was a kind of anticipation, his voice like the whisper before a performance. Jane said nothing in case he was still just trying to find out where she was. She hunched herself up, back against the curving metal, arms around her knees, the chunk of concrete between her feet. Could see the top of the long concrete bench above her, black against a grey haze. If she stood up, she'd be able to see over it. But if she stood up, Cornel could reach her, get his arms around her.

She shrank into herself, and there was more silence. She could hear him breathing, one long gritty… snort.

Oh God, more coke. Jane grabbed the opportunity to squirm a little further down. Heard Cornel moving around on the concrete bench, breath coming in little spurts now. All pumped up, Superman. *Oh please, please, please, please…*

A creak from the top end of the building, where the doors were, and Cornel went quiet. Nothing for a while, and then, unmistakably, soft footfalls on the steps.

What?

Jane saw the torchbeam bouncing erratically across the metal roof, and she didn't think it was Cornel's.

The torchbeam steadied.

'Evening, Kenny,' Cornel said.

Merrily unlocked her car in Gaol Street and sat behind the wheel, discovering that she was no longer tired. Perhaps the relief: Bliss, nothing life-threatening. She called Lol and then Jane. No answer from either. She left messages.

She had a cigarette half out of the packet and then pushed it back, in no mood to relax. She called Huw Owen. It took nearly half an hour to update him.

'I think we can work this out,' she said. 'We have enough to work it out.'

'Lass, go home, it's dark, it's cold…'

'And it's Good Friday tomorrow, and I'll be locked into a meditation cycle. You don't have to do anything. I just need you to listen. Could be selling myself a scenario. I'm just sitting here, no Bible, no Bergen, no cross. Just old jeans and trainers and a coat borrowed from an atheist.'

'Hardly the time for a crisis of faith, lass.'

'When would be a good time?' Merrily coughed. 'Sorry.'

'Who's the adversary?'

'Does there have to be one?'

'Did wi' Spicer.'

Merrily looked around the empty car park as if there might be a shadow with horns and claws prowling the edge of her vision. Knowing that horns and claws wouldn't scare her half as much as what she'd once seen in the eyes of an old, dying man on a hospital ward.

'Start with elimination,' Huw said. 'Is it Mithras?'

'A sun god consigned to a cellar by the Romans? I'm not sure he's not one of the injured parties.'

'What if she's right, the Witch of Hardwicke, and the Roman Mithras *is* an insidious form of Antichrist? The mole. The sleeper inside the Church. What if the sleeper's been awakened? Going after Spicer in the night? What does he see?'

Merrily stared into the moon.

'He sees three men standing round his bed. One with blood where his teeth should be, one with shards of glass in his face. One with a rope around his neck and his tongue hanging out.'

Greg and Jocko and Nasal. It had to be.

'He told you he was oppressed by the presence of someone who was known to him, a flawed person. He was just being careful. I'm guessing he meant three people. His gang. An SAS operational team are very close. Sharing their individual skills. A unit, a single entity. Now, add to that the chemistry of Mithras. According to Byron, it was Syd who got into it first, and Syd was the only survivor – because he went away and threw himself in the opposite direction.'

'There's another survivor, Merrily.'

'Byron? Was he as close as the others? Was Byron ever on a mission with Syd? It's a four-man team, usually. I think the other guys were – in Mithraic terminology – Syd's brothers. Now all dead in bad ways, and Syd feels responsible.'

'Unquietly dead? That's what you're saying?'

'They are when he comes back to the Regiment. Sleeping in his army house under Credenhill. And then… the *technicality*. Which has to be Mithraism. He tells you about what he calls a strong, negative energy behind the apparitions, manifestations, whatever. These guys were his mates, his brothers, his gang. But one of them killed his own wife, and Syd doesn't know, since Mithras, if Jocko, Greg and Nasal are at all benign any more.'

'And the negative energy? The fuel?'

'All around? Athena White called it a landscape quietly dedicated to war, but it's also, at various points in its history, been dedicated to the Roman Mithras. I mean… more realistically, I think Syd discovered what Byron was doing. *Selling* Mithras? What could come of that but serious evil?'

Merrily gave in and lit a cigarette.

'I think if Mithraism had still been spreading inside the SAS, he would've known about it. He'd have been watching and he had contacts – probably with the last chaplain. Whether he knew what Byron's doing now, before he took the chaplain's job, I don't know. But when he was at Credenhill he must've had a powerful sense of something, horribly familiar. Amplified.'

'And senses the old team back together. But not in a good way, eh?'

'Bad nights, Huw. Racked with guilt, frightened for the future, and he doesn't know how to deal with it. He *thought* he did. In the end, he turns, in desperation, to the chapel.'

'Happen finding it easier because the chapel's in the Beacons, the old SAS training ground.'

'And even while he's there, trying to arm himself, what happens? Back home, that same stormy night, a man gets murdered, in the true Mithraic manner. What kind of night's sleep would *you* get after learning about that?'

There was a long, flat, mobile-phone silence.

'He rings *you*,' Merrily said. 'Yielding a bit more information. If he can only get Nasal and co. out of his dreams – let's call them dreams – he might feel sane enough to...'

The advice Huw had given him – how sane was that? Denzil Joy had been straightforward compared with this situation.

'To do what?' Huw said.

'Take on Byron Jones, I suppose. Sooner or later he knows he has to take on Byron.'

75

Plug

JANE TASTED COBWEB and dead flies.

Came with the voice. The soft, ashy voice from the yard at the Swan. The mottled accent of a man from the Birmingham area who'd been living round Hereford for a long time.

'I'm cool,' Cornel said.

'And this is all your work, is it? I'm impressed, mate.'

Kenny Mostyn. The famous Kenny Mostyn, of Hardkit. Had he followed them? Jane didn't see how he could have, which meant he'd probably been nearby all along, and Cornel couldn't have known that or he wouldn't have laid down his sleeping bag.

And yet Cornel didn't sound in any way dismayed. He sounded, if anything, pleased. Up for it. Cocaine. Good old Charlie.

Cornel said, 'Seen what's left of your idol, Kenny?'

Kenny sniggered. He'd switched off his flashlight, put it down somewhere. It was only the lamp now on the half-smashed altar.

'Dust,' Cornel said. 'He's dust.'

'And that makes me feel gutted, does it?'

Cornel didn't reply. No indication of either of them moving. Then there was another scornful noise in Kenny's throat.

'Know what, Cornel? Yow… are a wanker.'

'And you are gonna…' in the pause, you could hear Cornel's rapid breath, could imagine his long body quivering '… gonna regret that, Kenny. Gonna regret a lot of things before too long.'

'Found the petrol, Cornel.'

Huh?

'Torch the place, was that it? On your way out?'

'Fire's good,' Cornel said. 'Fire destroys DNA.'

Another pause, then Kenny's voice had changed its tone, somehow.

'What's that in your hand, mate?'

'This?' Cornel's gleeful indrawn breath was overlaid by a crisp ratcheting sound. 'What it is, to be exact, Kenny, is a Glock Gen4 Safe Action. *Safe... Action.* I like that, don't you? *Safe.*'

Cornel's voice all gleaming with excitement, like a kid with a new Xbox, but Jane knew what a Glock was. One of those brand names you didn't forget. *Oh, for God's sake...* She was frozen with the reality of it. This was what he'd had in his hand? What he'd had in his rucksack with the wire-cutters and the lump hammer?

Kenny wasn't fazed.

'Where'd that come from, Cornel?'

'Got it in London weeks ago. Two and a half, cash, with four clips.'

'Yow was robbed. Had a go on it yet?'

'Saving it,' Cornel said. 'For somebody who told me to come back when my balls had dropped.'

Kenny laughed. It didn't sound faked. Cornel didn't join in.

'You just laugh while you can, Kenny, 'cause your brains are going on the ceiling. How's that sound? *Mate.*'

'Childish.'

'On your knees, I think.'

Jane stiffened. Kenny's voice came back merely quizzical.

'On me knees, to *yow*?'

'See, if this was a shotgun, I could blow your head clean off at this range, but a head shot with a handgun's riskier, so if you stay on your feet I'll have to go for the body and that could take a bit longer, and a lot of pain. Make sense?'

Oh God. Jane was hugging herself tightly. He was kidding, right?

'Best for you if you kneel down and close your eyes. Eh? Mate?'

What did you do? What could you do when he was, quite plainly, preparing to go through with it? What did you *do*? Which of these was the least-bad guy? Which of them wouldn't rape you? What was the *right* thing to do?

Very quietly, Jane stood up, her hair brushing the curved metal where wall became roof. The air was fogged, the light meagre from the single smelly lamp on the altar and the torch between Cornel's feet directing a beam too narrow to reach her.

Kenny Mostyn stood in the gulley, his back to her. A shortish, dapper-looking guy. He wore a leather jacket and a watch cap, and his jeans were tucked into leather boots.

While Cornel... Standing on the concrete bench with his legs apart and both hands swaddling the grey pistol, Cornel just looked demonic in a ravaged kind of way, with his sagging, fleshy mouth, his hair spiked with sweat. Like a big puppet, some mindless voodoo doll being worked by someone else.

It seemed entirely likely that he'd forgotten Jane was here. She slid down, lifted up the lump of concrete, fingertips finding two smooth depressions, and stood up again as Kenny spoke.

'Yow been snorting again, Cornel?'

'Doesn't exactly slow me up.'

'Just don't do anything rash, eh?'

'Hey, you're really *scared*!' Little whoop from Cornel. 'You're scared shitless, aren't you, Mr Mostyn? Now tell me you don't deserve it – taking my money, never serving up the goods, just leading me on, sending pictures to my boss, feeding all kinds of poison up the line to London? How many other guys you do that to?'

'Never done that to nobody, Cornel.'

'You're a liar!'

'I ripped you, off, yeah, 'cause I was owed that money. Fair's fair. And no way was you going further than raven. Not after I found out where you were from.'

'Don't get you, Kenny.' Cornel was bobbing, the pistol shaking. 'Make it quick.'

'Sod's Law. Just one of them things, look, just another casualty of the recession. I was likely just one of a hundred small businessmen they pulled the plug on that week.'

'Who? What are you saying?'

'Nothing Landesman's don't know about lies and false promises. *Yeah, we'll help you, you stick with us, Mr Mostyn, we'll see you right.* Until the help's needed, then yow don't see the knife go in, just feel it come out, and there's your friendly financial adviser wiping the blade on his pinstripes and asking if you've thought about bankruptcy. So don't yow... go talking to *me* about getting led on with false flamin' promises.'

Pulled the plug. Jane remembered the phrase from the article on Savitch in *Borderlife.* How the bank was close to *pulling the plug* when Savitch stepped in to save Hardkit. So all this was...

... just a kind of scapegoat situation? Cornel paying for what some loans manager had done to Kenny Mostyn? Just a male-pride thing, a petty vengeance trip turned toxic?

The stinking air was suddenly thick with a sour alien insanity. Jane brought the lump of concrete up to her chest. It was round and smooth on one side, but heavy like a cannonball, and her arms were aching already.

'You piece of *shit*! They're never gonna get me for this. Likes of you, low-life scum made good, it could be anybody. Spoiled for choice, Mostyn.'

Cornel's hands throbbing around the gun. Kenny shrugged.

'I'm only human, Cornel. En't the holy man here, just the help. You can go back to London, tell them what I did, why I did it, and no harm done, just a few red faces, and they might even remember my name this time.'

'I've lost my fucking *job*. I've lost everything. You think I'm going to start again, go in as some little high-street fucking bank clerk? That what you think? On your knees, you little piece of shit. Now! *On your fucking knees!*'

The whole place suddenly seemed brighter, as if Cornel was generating his own electricity, shining, his slack lips parted to reveal those gritted teeth, all his resentment and bitterness pouring down those rigid, outstretched arms, and the stink from the lamp was putrid as Kenny Mostyn, almost in slow motion, went down on one knee on the stained floor of the gulley.

No choice now. Panting so hard that she was afraid they could hear her, Jane sucked in her stomach and lifted the ball of concrete, hands underneath, thrust it up over her head, watching Cornel bringing up the gun, his long bony hands together, as if in prayer, around it. As if – for just a moment – as if he was relenting, and Jane held back, swaying under the weight of the concrete.

Then realized that, although she was deep in shadow, the concrete between her hands was gleaming palely in the lamp-light, and Cornel looked up and saw it, looking for a moment puzzled, confused.

As Kenny Mostyn's knee lifted from the floor and Kenny's arms shot out, fingers clawing the air as if to throw himself forward. Like he was finding himself again, Cornel backed up and brought the barrel of the gun down in direct line with Kenny's half-bowed head.

Jane pushed herself forward, and her pathetic little arms gave way and she had to let go of the concrete.

76

Night of the Last Supper

THE CLOUDS HAD cleared and the moon lay cold as rock salt over an alley of conifers. Barry stood inside the wire, looking at the three of them, shaking his head.

'How your life turns on its head. Not much more than a kid, and you're out in the field with a handful of crack professionals, all with special skills – linguistics, engineering, advanced first-aid, bomb disposal. *None* of them much more than kids. Or that's how it looks to me now, at the age of fifty-eight.'

'Fifty-eight, eh?' Gomer said. 'So what point you tryin' to make yere, boy?'

'Forget it,' Barry said.

Doing his recce, Lol thought. Standing among close-packed conifers on the edge of the compound, with its buildings and footpaths, taking his time. Lol was very agitated now, but Barry wouldn't be hurried.

'Four big sheds, one concrete, no windows, so I'd guess equipment in there. Three caravans, say two for staff accommodation, and the other one looks like a canteen. Two tents in that sloping field up towards the woods – might be people in there, can't rule it out. Small toilet block.'

They'd started talking in whispers now, Lol noticed. The air among the conifers was sharp and damp and acrid. The surface of a big pond, off-centre, was shining dully like tinplate under the non-committal moon.

'No cockfight here,' Barry said. 'That's for sure.'

By the time the call had come through from Danny, Barry was changed into his running kit, had his old Freelander waiting outside the Swan, leaving Marion in charge.

'Tell me again,' he said to Danny.

'We come out onto the Credenhill road, and we done mabbe two hundred yards and Mostyn suddenly stops, and we gotter pass him, see? So we turns round and creeps back on sidelights, and he's found this ole van in the bushes side of the road. And then he gets back in and he's off along the lane like a bullet then, up this track.'

No compromises on this track. It was steep and unmade. Without a four-by-four you'd be in trouble. Halfway up, that sign, black on white.

THE COMPOUND TRAINING CENTRE

TRESPASSERS UNWELCOME

The moonlight was so bright on it this time that Lol made out a small amendment, half scrubbed-out. It actually said:

TRESPASSERS ~~UNWEL~~COME.'

'Trespassers here seem to have had their uses,' Lol said.

He'd also told Barry on the way here about the smashed CCTV camera and the cut wire. How the police had thought it was him. Barry had said he was a stupid bleeder for even getting out of his truck.

'*Gomer*,' he hissed now. 'Stay in the trees.'

'Looks like an ole JCB down there, boy, back o' the big shed.'

'Yeah, well, leave it alone for now. In the absence of poultry, the best thing is probably to get the hell out.'

'He's got a bloody cockfight *somewhere*,' Gomer said. 'Sure to. We was told.'

'We'd hear something, would we not? And frankly I can't see Byron permitting it. He don't do entertainment, on any level.'

'Might not start till later, boy. This en't bingo. And he's *in* yere. *Mostyn.*'

'He *works* here. Bleedin' hell, you never give up, do you, Gomer?'

But it was clear they were going in.

Lol wondered if it would feel any different entering the compound by what passed for an actual entrance. Going in mob-handed, unblooded. He checked his mobile to see if there was anything from Jane and found a short text from Merrily.

This is getting weird.
please don't go
anywhere

***

It was on the way home, anyway.

Almost.

Still wearing the atheist's coat, Merrily stood close to the grave of Jane Winder, whose potted history was spotlit by the moon.

AND DIED AT *BRINSOP COURT,*
IN THIS PARISH, OCTOBER 16, 1843.
IN THE 43 YEAR OF HER AGE.

Poor Jane. A stranger. From Off. No age at all. By night, the stone was a monolith in front of the trees on the dark pond – which was labelled *moat* on the map – and all the mysterious humps in the moon-scratched fields below Credenhill. And you held on to it to steady yourself against what seemed like an irreversible madness.

Brinsop Church was locked for the night, of course. Merrily had thought about calling the local team minister, Dick Willis, but she wouldn't have got away this time without an explanation.

She stood there, an arm around Jane Winder's cold shoulder,

and took in the long view to the right, where it was as though the whole wide area overshadowed by Credenhill had been stripped back by the full moon. Nothing but a skim of soil and rock and clay over what remained of the Romans. *The men that have been reappear.* A poet's imaginative exercise, probably nothing more than that. Nothing about a brutalized religion reinvoked from the soil. But the poem had been there, in the book left out by Syd.

A rabbit hopped across the graveyard and sat by the church porch, sniffing the night.

No Bible, no Bergen, no cross, Merrily slipped away out of the churchyard and over the stile to the field where the Dragon's Well lay in sodden grass, its round stone like a small cider wheel. A modern metal drain cover was embedded in the stone.

Ewes and big lambs were watching her from the hedge. Round eyes like lamps. Could be innocence, could be cynicism. If you were looking for an adversary, it could be the dragon but was more likely, in this place, to be George.

Merrily lit a cigarette.

'Advice, Syd?'

In her darkest moments she thought that, if exorcism hadn't found her, she might not have stuck this job. How feeble was that, if the only way you could convince yourself that you were more than just another badly paid professional carer was by re-enacting medieval rituals and seeing what happened? The psychic *son et lumière* and the bangs and whistles that real mystics discounted as foreplay.

'But that wasn't you, Syd. You didn't want any of it. Came out of the army, looked back in horror.'

Leaps I can't make, he'd said to her, smoking in his church. *Aspects I can't face.*

'Any more,' Merrily said. '"Can't face any more" – that was what you meant.' She sat down on the wellhead, watched the smoke rising from her fingers towards the moon.

'The Bible in the Bergen, Syd. This is what I think. A reminder of which side you were on now. Well, sure. But going up Credenhill with that on your back, it's like Christ carrying his cross. A *constant* reminder, every step you take – the tug of the pack, the weight of the book, brass-bound, bulky, uncomfortable. Every step you take up that hill, you feel it. Who you are, what you're about. The weight of responsibility.'

She felt Syd moving up Credenhill, like Thomas Traherne in the blazing stained glass. Bump, bump of the Bible on the spine. Total consciousness.

Why, if he wanted to confront the shadow of Mithras, had he gone up Credenhill rather than come here? Perhaps he didn't know. Hadn't worked it out.

Whatever, something had found him. Death had found him. *Idiopathic Hypertrophic Cardiomyopathy.*

Merrily stood up, folded her arms, looked down at them, swaying a little, then looking up at the moon in its halo of pagan complacency. She felt profoundly empty inside, like a sucked-out seashell. The night before Good Friday, the night of the Last Supper. Always tainted with the sour odour of failure and betrayal.

Bending to pick up her bag from the well-cover, she thought for a moment that it wasn't there, that the well water was exposed and the full moon, a perfect pale disc, was reflected in it.

Merrily straightened up, gazed down for some time and then nodded, remembering. She slipped a hand down one of the back pockets of her jeans and found splinters. Crumbs of faith.

Always a rational explanation.

Slowly, she bent and retrieved the moon.

77

Migraine Lights

THE PIECE OF concrete fell short. Inevitably. Even desperation hadn't produced the necessary strength.

Jane watched it landing on the edge of the bench, rolling into the gulley at the same time as the torch rolled off and died, and the only light was from the Roman lamp on the altar, the air thick and fetid with hot animal fat. One small lamp had done that.

But Jane was bone-achingly cold, looking down at Cornel lying in the gulley with his knees drawn up, foetal.

Kenny Mostyn was standing slightly away from Cornel, quite calm with his arms by his side. But loosened up, springy, watching as Cornel began to roll away, and his hand came out and even Jane could tell what he was trying to reach and knew he wouldn't make it.

Kenny's knee rose up and his foot cracked down on the clawed hand, and Cornel screamed hideously, rolling helplessly onto his back as Kenny kicked something away.

'We don't need this, do we, mate? We're men.'

'I was just—'

'What?' Squatting down. 'Tell your Uncle Kenny.'

'Just trying to scare you, that's all. That's all it was.'

'Course it was,' Kenny said softly.

Cornel was sobbing. Jane hated anybody sobbing. A sob was not something you could fake, and she could feel his fear.

'Kenny, listen, it really was just a joke. Like one of your tests, one of your exercises, where you're thinking you're gonna die, and at the last second…?'

'Sure.' Kenny crouched down next to Cornel. 'You're all right, mate. I understand.'

Jane saw Kenny's face for the first time – actually, *not* for the first time; she realized she'd seen him several times in Hereford, maybe among the Saturday scrum in High Town or sitting outside one of the pubs where they had tables. Short, round-faced guy with a moustache and the hint of a beard which made a dark circle around his mouth.

He was looking up towards the gloss-painted metal ceiling but saying nothing, no expression on the face, and his eyes were white, like a blind man's eyes. He seemed to be stroking Cornel's hair, calming him down, then abruptly he turned his head away, looking up. Not at her, perhaps at the smears of movement which she could see as though through old, speckled glass.

Jane shook her head and the glass brightened and then fragmented and then coalesced and broke apart and coalesced again, like migraine lights, and there were human forms, wet naked men, glowing greasily like in some rugby team's communal bath, a fatty stew of nudging, squirming, white-eyed men around her, touching her skin, and she like shrank into herself in disgust, all her senses full of the steam and the stink of sweat and the disconnected cries from a long way down in her mind, and then one man stepped out of it and became Kenny Mostyn.

He was holding up a short blade which he briefly inspected before nonchalantly folding it and putting it away in an almost military fashion, not once looking down.

But Jane did.

She saw Cornel move. Cornel was lying bent like a burst pipe, and it was as if he was laughing. Shaking with laughter. Just another scary exercise, a test for a hard man. *What happens is anything you want.*

His body jerked once, in spasm, that big chin jutting out like a shelf of rock over a waterfall. Jane felt the pressure of a scream in her throat, but no sound came out. She just stood there, watching from the gallery, watching all the blood belching out of the hole in Cornel's long neck, filling up the gulley.

Kenny Mostyn was sitting down now, on the concrete bench opposite, wiping his forehead with the back of a hand. Blank-faced as the blood ran past his boots, spreading almost the width of the gulley but never quite reaching the other face on which Cornel's glassy eyes were focused.

A face without a head or a body. A straight nose, a petulant twist to the mouth and a hat like a caterpillar.

The face sculpted into the shard of concrete that Jane had grabbed from the rubble after Cornel had attacked the altarpiece with his lump hammer. She thought a smile formed for a moment on the face in the concrete, as her scream passed into echo and all she could hear was the thin, wet sound of Cornel dying.

78

The Wafer and the Moon

THE SCREAM HAD been muffled, choked off, but it was still reaching for Lol like an imploring hand and, for just a moment, he'd thought it was Jane.

It sent him to the Nissen hut. The padlock had been broken, but the big doors were firm. A wall of wood, new oak that would break your shoulder. He turned in desperation to Danny who was alongside him, hands exploring the panels.

'Bolted, it is, from inside.'

'What do we do?'

'All right,' Barry whispered. 'Options. We could bang on the door, shout "police, open up now".'

'But that'd warn 'em,' Danny Thomas said. 'We wanner do that?'

'It would, yeah.'

'And when they seen us… if there's a whole bunch of 'em in there…'

'True.' Barry turned to Gomer, pointed across the compound to the biggest shed. 'That old JCB… you reckon…?'

'Oh aye.' Twin moons floating in Gomer's bottle glasses. 'Sure to. Less he's broke.'

'You can hot-wire it?'

'Don't need no hot-wire.' Gomer had dragged out a jangle of keys on a ring. 'Digger that age, one size fits all.'

'Try it. Go with him Danny, eh? If it don't look promising, get out before you make too much noise and we'll try something else.'

Barry moved away from the doors and Lol followed him to the original hole in the barbed wire, its ends springing free like brambles. Barry ran an uncertain hand across his jaw.

'Bit too much like the old days, Laurence. But this is not the old days, it's not warfare, it's not terrorism… and I'm not your gaffer. Bearing in mind there could be very serious repercussions, you don't have to do what I say, none of you.'

Lol threw up his hands. 'You want *me* to make decisions? The songwriter? Barry, I don't give a *shit* about repercussions. There's something here makes my blood go cold.'

'All right. Let's quickly go over the situation one last time. What's the worst we *know* happens that might be happening in there?'

'They kill a bull.'

'With?'

'A knife. In theory.'

'How many people involved in that?'

'No idea.'

He looked back at the Nissen hut. *Underground*, Athena had said, *to simulate a cave. Certainly no windows.* It was a possibility.

'If this was Regiment business,' Barry said, 'we'd have smoke bombs, masks and automatic bleedin' hardware from Heckler and Koch.'

'And one of us might even know what to do with it.'

There was a metallic clang from the JCB, then silence. Barry gazed across the compound, light as a dull day down there.

'Jeez,' he said. 'Look at us, Laurence. Even you'd be too old to qualify for selection.'

From behind the big shed, they heard the slow clatter of an old, cold engine being coaxed back into active service.

'And as for *him*…'

The moon lay in the palm of Merrily's hand, its symbolism fully apparent.

The night before Good Friday was the night of the Last Supper.

This is my body.

Merrily looked down at the tiny full moon. Two of them, in fact, both consecrated. Must've fallen off the communion plate last Sunday morning and she'd found them when she'd come in at night for the meditation, slipped them into her back pocket and forgotten about them. One – still intact, she guessed because it had lodged near a seam – must have fallen out of her pocket when she'd sat down on the stone over the well. The other was already in pieces.

She looked towards the church porch, directly across from the well, and recalled the sorrowful shadow over the door on the inside, the weary, defeated Jesus, drained and desiccated, *in the act of dying.* Fading into the wall and into history. And soon, the way things were going, out of history and into myth and legend sooner than anyone would have imagined, least of all Mother Julian, who in some way had experienced the reality. An anchoress, a solitary, not part of a religious community. They spent their lives in prayer and contemplation, in a particular place which was felt to be blessed by their presence there, the way the atmosphere of an area could be darkened by the shadows of violence.

Merrily held up the intact communion wafer until it covered the moon, so that it looked like the fan of white-gold rays were spraying from the wafer.

Like, when a place gets into disaster mode, expecting the worst all the time, the worst just seems to go on happening. Unless you step in with an act of sacrifice.

Jane. Who'd been known to venerate the moon as Mother Goddess – how seriously Merrily was still unsure, but it was a very different concept from Julian's Mother God. Who, in an odd way, was more like Syd Spicer's God, the SAS commander in the field, on first-name terms with his team. Your best mate, none of that *sir* crap, no salutes. In the same way, back in the days when God was seen as a touchy tyrant with a pile of plagues and thunderbolts at his elbow, Julian had sensed only a source of infinite kindness and patience and politeness, without which, she'd insisted, it would be impossible for this flawed world to exist.

Merrily closed her fingers on the wafer. It felt warm. She had the surreal thought that here, in a place whose sanctity pre-dated both Christianity and Mithraism, there could be some act of fusion between the wafer and the moon.

It was cold now, her trainers crunching on frost as she went back over the stile and across the field to the car, where she took off Annie's coat and laid it on the back seat. She stashed Syd's books, Lol's map and the compass from the glove com-partment in her bag, checked her manicure case for nail scis-sors and went back to the churchyard, and now it was *very* cold.

In the swivelling seat of the old JCB, Gomer lit up a ciggy and then was still, looking across at Barry like an old toy dog with glass eyes.

Barry took a breath, held it for several seconds. They listened. There was no sound from inside the hut.

'Remember the steps,' Lol said.

'And afterwards, Gomer, leave your lights on full-beam, *but don't get out*. Danny, see he don't get out.' Barry moved back. 'OK, off you go.'

Lol clocked Danny's worried eyes over the beard, gave him a tight nod and slammed the cab door as the big shovel wobbled, the cig came spinning out of the window, the engine noise changed into a minor-key growl.

'Back off till it's done,' Barry told him. 'There'll be flying splinters.'

But the hinges were weaker than the doors. The shovel, nearly as wide as the doors, just punched them off the side walls, and they collapsed into the void.

Job done.

Lol crouching, an arm thrown across his face, turned for guidance to Barry, but Barry had already gone. Lol saw him flattened against the wall at the entrance to the Nissen hut as the

JCB roared and trembled massively in the entrance, like some wounded charging animal.

Barry made a backwards turning motion with his fingers, and Gomer switched off the engine but left the lights on. Danny had his window down, leaning out, yelling,

'*Body...*'

Barry said, 'Dead or alive?'

'Dunno, blood everywhere.'

Barry shouted into the hut.

'Out now, please. Everybody. Slowly.'

A patch of silence and then one small voice.

'Gomer?'

Jesus. Lol's feet threw him forward, stumbling for the doorway, whispering, *Jesus, Jesus, Jesus.* Barry grabbed his shoulder, spun him round and away.

'It's Jane—' Lol stumbled round the digger's caterpillar tracks to Danny's door, under the open window. 'Danny, it—'

'Best for Jane, boy, if we don't get killed.'

'If this thing goes down them steps,' Gomer was saying, 'and there's anybody in the way...'

Lol saw Barry emerge on the other side of the digger, staying out of the lights, his back to the inside wall of the hut. A single sharp crack and its rapid echo and the headlight on Gomer's side had gone out and Barry's urgent hiss came out of darkness.

'Geddown! Everybody! *Down!*'

Lol slid onto hands and knees between the digger and the remains of one of the doors. Couldn't just do nothing. He began creeping slowly forward. Ahead of him, a meagre ochre glow like a nursery night light wrapped in dusty muslin. A moment of waxy silence and then a long, torn cry, and that *had* to be Jane, and Lol was back on his feet, squeezing past the JCB, clambering up the broken wooden door.

Then he stopped. A man about his own height was facing him, knees slightly bent, arms extended like short girders in front of his face.

A spatter of impressions coming at Lol, questions answered

almost as soon as they were formed, like, *What's that between his hands? Why are the hands wearing red gloves?*

He was halfway along the big wooden door now, and the door was hanging half over the steps, seesawing. Legs apart, battling for balance, he was going up and down, and the man's extended arms were tracking his movements, and the man's blank eyes, inside a red mask, found his for an instant, and Barry was screaming at him.

'Down. Lie the fuck *down!*'

And then something hit Lol and he did go down and, while he was falling, the arms of the man, his face glistening scarlet, swung round, away from him, and Lol registered Barry's silhouette in rapid motion and a twitch from the man's hands, then a small, gas-jet flash and the sound of a single massive handclap.

The shot's echo died.

Lol turned sideways, his cheek against the wood. He saw Barry's face twisting back.

Barry sinking to his knees, a red halo misting around his head.

'Oh… oh for God's sake…'

This was Danny Thomas's voice from inside the JCB, all fractured, as Barry's heavy body toppled back across the shovel's blade.

Part Seven

GOOD FRIDAY

They did not lose themselves, as did the other sects, in contemplative mysticism; for them the good dwelt in action.

Franz Cumont
The Mysteries of Mithra

…the perfect soldier of Mithras, non-attached, passionless, disciplined, inured to hardship, sleeping for whole months on the frozen snow and hard earth; ambitious, cruel and ruthless, but possessed of immense personal courage…

Esme Wynne Tyson
Mithras, the Fellow in the Cap

Nothing can be what it was
But through the drifting mist of loss
You hope to find a home.

Lol Robinson
'Tanworth-in-Arden'

79

No Fuss

UNCLE TED WOULD say call it off, but then Uncle Ted had been against it from the start, the whole idea of dumping Evensong and replacing it with this swami stuff. Uncle Ted was probably also suspicious of Mother Julian, a woman with a man's name and torrid crucifixion fantasies, but he'd said nothing about that.

Anyway… it was going on. Although a stand-in had been arranged for today's early services, Merrily, striving for normality, was up while the early sun was still struggling in twisted ropes of cloud and the village was as silent as an empty film set.

Standing in her dressing gown at the scullery window with *Revelations of Divine Love* open on the desk and Ethel curled between her feet. Watching a fox slide off home, the way Lol had half an hour ago, while it was still dark, another neurotic damsel-fly episode.

Don't have long to decide before something makes the decision for you. And that may not be the one you hope for.

Not now, Athena.

The Julian meditation would begin at two, and Jane would be there and Lol, where Merrily could see them. And she would do her best. Better than she had last night in the moonwashed churchyard at Brinsop while, less than a mile away, Jane… her daughter… eighteen… was watching men being killed.

She gripped the window sill until her fingers hurt.

Jane had gone, finally, to her attic about four hours ago, and if Eirion was up there too, instead of in the guest room, that would be no bad thing. When they had finally got home, they'd found him asleep in his car on the square and, for the first time, Jane had wept. *Catharsis?* Well, it was a start. Even as a child, Jane had never been a weeper.

Merrily watched the fox, a familiar visitor, creeping away between the church wall and the shed.

And no, she wasn't naive. She wasn't expecting a warm radiance rising in the nave as they all welcomed Easter after tomorrow night's vigil – beatific smiles, villagers embracing one another. That was *Lark Rise to Candleford*. This was Ledwardine, on the border.

Jane had already been offered professional counselling, and Merrily had said, *It wouldn't be a sign of weakness, flower, these people—* And Jane, stone-faced, had cut her off. *You* are *kidding, right?*

The new jacket Jane had worn for the first time on her day out with Charles Cornel had been put out for the wash and was destined for the Oxfam shop. This was all going to take time, lots of it, but compared with any one of several things that might have happened last night to close your whole life down, time – weeks, months, years – didn't matter at all.

Mid-morning, Annie Howe came to the vicarage door, alone, her grey trench coat streaked with red mud and wrinkled as if she'd slept in it, although her eyes didn't look as if she'd slept at all.

'Some things I need to go over again,' Annie said. 'With Jane. I'm sorry about this.'

'She doesn't make things up,' Merrily said irrationally. 'She just sometimes sees them from... a different place.'

'I won't keep her long. This is not official.'

So much that Annie Howe had done and said since yesterday evening that was not official – blindingly, uncharacteristically not official. One day there might be an explanation unconnected with the full moon.

'Is Frannie Bliss…?'

Merrily waited, kettle in hand. A sunbeam from the highest window was pale and coffin-shaped.

'The Chief Constable's on his way over. Have his picture taken going into the hospital, hold a press conference. Two results in one night. Well worth interrupting his holiday weekend for.'

'So Frannie…?'

'His voice is very slurred. He's lost two teeth, his nose is broken and they think there may be brain-stem damage.'

'Oh God. What's that mean?'

'Doesn't mean he'll be a cabbage, but functions like balance could be impaired. Speech, eyesight, coordination. It will all improve with time, they say, but Bliss isn't noted for his patience. He—' Annie Howe's smile was swift and crooked. 'He says that if the Chief shows up at his bedside he'll strangle the, ah, twat, with the nearest drip tube. Or I may have mis— Oh.' Annie glanced at the door. Jane had come in.

Hair unbrushed, tied back. She had a deep scratch all down one cheek. At the refectory table, her sugary tea going cold, she described again what had happened when the managing director of Hardkit had cut a young man's throat.

'All my fault.'

Jane said that twice.

Gently – for her – Annie Howe said, 'All you did was throw something which distracted Cornel before he could…'

'He might not have. Might not have shot Mostyn. I think he just wanted to see him crawl.'

'Jane, nobody carries a loaded firearm—'

'You weren't there,' Jane said.

Merrily flinched. Because Jane *had* been there. And Lol had been there, and so had Gomer Parry, wielding a digger like heavy artillery at the age of… whatever age Gomer was.

While *she* had been faffing about in a churchyard, cutting up a communion wafer with nail scissors, trying to alter the *spiritual balance*. Just one slippage of a gear, one shift in the pattern of events, one stalling of momentum in that hellhole last night, and she could be burying Jane, raking out the last cold ash in Lol's wood stove. She was worthless, a sham. Failing to see what she should have seen. Being someone who people *didn't want to worry* because she was too busy unscrambling the thought processes of a man who was dead and hadn't wanted her to know about it anyway. She wanted a cigarette.

'He kept asking me to come out,' Jane said.

'Mostyn?'

'He said it was OK, Cornel had just tripped and fallen and hurt his head and they needed to call an ambulance.'

'And what did you say?' Annie asked.

'I didn't say anything. I knew he was just trying to find out where I was. I went down on hands and knees again. I thought, even if he finds out where I am he can't come in after me, it's too narrow, but he can... he can climb up and look down on me and just... shoot me. I was just lying on the floor and covering my head with my hands. For all the use that would've been.'

'What happened next?'

'There was this... you know, the noise of a big engine outside the doors? Like a JCB?'

'That was what you actually thought?'

'I know what a JCB sounds like. And then both doors just came in with this massive crash and that's when I stood up, and I saw Gomer straight away. And Lol and...' Jane smiled feebly. 'It was like the best moment of my entire life. For about two seconds.' The smile turning wintry. 'Before it was the worst.'

'When did you first see Mr Bloom?'

'Barry – I heard him first. He was calling to everybody, telling them to keep down. And then I saw Lol. I was, like... going insane because Kenny Mostyn... I saw him standing up with the gun levelled and I could see he was pointing the gun at Lol, and I just... lost it. I started climbing over the top of the concrete bench, and the next thing I saw was Barry, just falling back, and half his face was...'

'All right. In your first statement, you said you saw another man where Lol Robinson had been standing. Had *he* been there all the time?'

'I don't know. Lol was, like, standing on one of the doors that Gomer had smashed in, and this guy just… he just came out of nowhere and rammed Lol out of the way. All in dark clothes and this balaclava with just a slit for the eyes?'

'What did Mostyn do?'

'I've told you all this once…'

'Tell me again.'

'Nothing. He did nothing. He had the gun by his side. Just standing with his legs apart, kind of… relaxed. And the gun by his side.'

'As if he knew the man? Saw him as an ally rather than an adversary?'

'Yeah.'

Merrily could see it all in her head. The balaclava to hide the giveaway white hair and the cold intent in his blue eyes.

How sure *were* they that this was Byron Jones?

Annie sipped her tea, casual, unofficial.

'What happened next?'

'I didn't see exactly… I was looking for Lol. The next thing I saw, Kenny didn't have the gun any more, the other guy did. I'd been looking straight into the JCB lights, so when I turned round I couldn't see properly.'

No one else had seen it, Merrily knew that. Not Lol, nor Gomer, nor Danny. Barry had told them all to get down, before…

Annie said, 'You're sure there wasn't more than one gun?'

'Pretty sure.'

'What happened next, Jane… is something we need to be absolutely sure about because only you—'

'Every time I close my eyes I'm *still* seeing it. He was standing behind Kenny, then it was like pieces of Kenny's head came flying out. And his knees were, like, buckled and he just… you know like they say someone was dead before he hit the ground. That's how it was.'

'How many shots?'

'Two. And then this other guy slipped the gun in his jacket pocket and walked out. He stopped for a moment and bent over Barry, and then he turned away and he was… gone. He was just, like… no fuss, you know? He just did what he did and walked out. Like, the way I'm telling it, it must sound like it took ages, but it was just… barely seconds. He was so sure of what he was doing. Like he didn't have to think?'

'No struggle for the gun or anything like that? I'm sorry to keep going over these points, but it's impor—'

'I keep telling you,' Jane said, eyes wide. 'Kenny Mostyn wasn't expecting it. There was no struggle. It was like an execution?'

They left Jane in the kitchen. Annie Howe stood at the door in the hall, next to Holman Hunt's *Light of the World*.

'They, ah… they're still trying to save Barry Bloom's right eye. They're not hopeful. Made a mess of one side of his face but the bullet didn't enter his brain. At that range he was, I suppose, very lucky.'

'Lucky,' Merrily said dully.

The worst could have happened, and it hadn't. Not quite.

'I…' Annie took her hand off the doorknob. 'I'm not sure why Jane feels in some way responsible. I don't know her particularly well, but it seems… slightly odd. We can still arrange some professional counselling. Sometimes it helps to unload it all on a stranger.'

'I'll ask her again, but I'm not optimistic.'

'But then again,' Annie said, 'I suspect *you* might have an idea why she blames herself. Is there something I should know?'

'If I tell you, you'll wish I hadn't.'

'I'll chance it.'

'She seems to feel she was the instrument which brought all this together. If she hadn't become obsessed with tying Savitch into cockfighting. Which led—'

'Ah, yes…' Annie Howe raised a hand. 'Just so you know. In a storeroom behind one of Mostyn's shops we found a consignment of what you might call cockfight gift-sets – leather cases containing a selection of polished spurs. Brand new. Originally prized, apparently, by cockers in the travelling community. Now finding a new market, it seems.'

'So that links Mostyn to it.'

'There's also the established fact that Victoria Buckland, the woman charged in connection with the Marinescu murders, used to work for Mostyn when he was running canoeing and mountaineering courses for young people. Buckland's believed to have been organizing periodic cockfights at the Plascarreg Hilton for a couple of years. It'll all come out at some stage.'

'And Savitch?'

'Savitch is now attached like a Siamese twin to his London solicitor. He denies all knowledge of Mithraism, cockfighting, badger-baiting or any other illegal country pursuits. Appalled to discover the truth about Mostyn, who was contracted purely as an instructor and a supplier of equipment. Horrified that some of his own clients were into these foul practices.'

'Hanging it on the dead.'

'Don't they always. So Jane…?'

'Jane thinks that if she hadn't pursued Cornel with a view to nailing Savitch they would never have wound up in the mithraeum.'

'And yet Cornel went tooled up. He'd lost his job, he'd been humiliated, he was at the end of his rope. He went prepared to kill somebody, and Mostyn's the most likely candidate. From Jane's version of what was said, it seems likely that Cornel was *hoping* Mostyn would appear. He certainly seems to have believed he'd get away with it.'

'Yes, but what about Jane? Jane would've seen everything.'

'You might want to think, in retrospect,' Annie said, 'that the heavy object Jane threw down might, in the end, have saved her life. Now, what were you going to tell me?'

Jane had said that instinctively she hadn't liked the face. She hadn't even known then whose face it was supposed to represent. She'd said that raising up the rounded shard of concrete, she must have had her fingers in its supercilious eyes, below the remains of its cap. Jane had picked up an image of Mithras and taken him with her, away from Cornel. The kind of stupid detail that lodged in your mind and inflated itself into a crazy significance.

'Annie, maybe you could tell me something first. Why were you asking Jane if there was a struggle for the gun between Mostyn and the man you think was Byron? Why didn't you want it to be... an execution?'

'It's not that simple.' Annie thought for a few moments. 'All right. But not here.'

80

Slasher

SHE CLIMBED INTO Annie's Audi on the edge of the square. The shops had opened into gold bars of welcome sunlight and – even more welcome – Easter tourists.

Lol was walking up Church Street from the river, with Jane and Eirion, Merrily felt momentarily disconnected, as if this might be a mercy-dream softening the truth: dead Lol lying across from dead Barry on a mortuary trolley. Jane awakening, stiff and raw, to the memory of a night in the rape suite. Athena White was right. *It must not go on much longer, do you hear me?*

Annie parked the Audi at the bottom of Old Barn Lane, half on the grass verge. Her mood was hard to read.

'So you're saying Savitch is in the clear?' Merrily said.

'You studied law. Tell me what he's done wrong.'

'What about Sollers Bull?'

Annie Howe stared uninterested at conical Cole Hill, straight ahead and looking almost volcanic, wreathed in smoke-ring clouds.

'The last thing certain prominent people want is for Sollers to go down. I'd have to number my father amongst them.'

'What's it got to do with Charlie?'

'Rang this morning, confiding that Lord Walford, that respected ex-chairman of the Police Authority, was concerned about my "astonishing behaviour" towards his son-in-law. Never mind that Sollers is notoriously unfaithful to Walford's daughter, he's *one of us*. "I really can't see what your problem is,

Anne," my father says. "It's open and shut." With the emphasis on shut.'

'Shut as in—' Merrily twisted in her seat. 'Annie, this is the murder of Mansel Bull. Who also, surely, was very much "one of us". It's *shut*? As in case closed?'

'As good as. Remember hanging it on the dead? Two knife killings – two *slasher* killings within a few rural miles – how could there *not* be a connection? Mostyn's an SAS-fantasist who runs hardcore adventure courses for men who want more risk in their lives, has obscure religious beliefs and likes to hang out with he-man celebs like Smiffy Gill. His love of violence is implicit. Walking time-bomb.'

Annie Howe glared angrily at the dash.

'What if he has an alibi?' Merrily said. 'What if there's someone who knows he couldn't have been at Oldcastle at the time?'

'He was with Jones. Who told us that? Jones did. Jones who shot Mostyn dead and is still out there – somewhere. We even have a possible motive. Seems Mansel Bull persistently refused to allow Mostyn and his clients to use his land for rough shooting, prompting a number of angry exchanges. Mostyn seemed very frustrated about that.'

'Where did that one come from?'

'Sollers Bull.'

'You're not serious?'

'Who phoned someone… over my head… to remind them. Why didn't he mention it to Bliss? Well, *of course* he mentioned it – doesn't Bliss remember? You see? Are we looking for anyone else? Why would we?'

'What about the London clients?'

'I told you how long it would take to track them down. How costly. And why would we need to? London bankers and financiers worshipping some ancient Roman god of war? Oh *please*.'

'This is—'

'I know what it is. I'm sorry – I really am no fun, am I? Famous for it. Severe, po-faced, strait-laced, entirely without imagination and destined to walk on eggshells for the rest of my indifferent career because… because of my father.'

Merrily couldn't summon any kind of smile.

'So Mostyn killed Mansel Bull?'

'Mostyn killed everybody except himself. Mostyn is Derek Bird and Raoul Moat and the Hungerford man and the Dunblane man… and just as dead as all of them.'

'But Byron knows the truth. Wherever he is.'

'His bungalow's empty. He hasn't been officially seen since he walked out of Gaol Street. We're searching.'

'What are your feelings… about this whole mess?'

'What would you imagine?' Annie Howe said. 'Sick to my stomach and determined to preserve my increasingly contemptible career for as long as it takes to nail Sollers Bull. And I was never here, and we never had this conversation.'

Christ always died on the cross at three p.m., British Summer Time. Just over an hour to set things up for the Julian meditation.

The Rev. Martin Longbeach, who'd been hauled in to take over the routine services, had left around noon, refusing lunch at the vicarage. Not the time, he'd said, patting Merrily on the arm. Then they closed the gift shop in the vestry and pulled the moveable pews into a circle below the rood screen for however many other parishioners had decided to tough it out with Mother Julian.

The beeswax candle on the altar flared under the Zippo, and Merrily felt its heat and that gentle sense of handmaiden.

She knelt for a moment. Last night she'd felt, on two occasions, that another woman was with her in Brinsop churchyard, stepping lightly between the gravestones. But for the horror of what had followed, those memories of Brinsop might have retained a slightly baffling glow.

And a smudge of guilt.

It had seemed a bit silly at first, using Lol's map – which he'd left in the car – and the compass to determine the rough positions of the four most convincing leys passing through the church, but once you identified them you could almost see them unravelling across the moon-creamed fields.

Channels for prayer.

Pagan prayer, doubtless, when – *if* – the leys had been created, back in the Bronze Age or earlier. And yet Merrily had felt that Mother Julian would have approved. Things were different in the Middle Ages; the Christian Church had no problems with magic.

She'd heard Jane's voice. *You're playing with the Big Forces here.*

Quartering the communion wafer with her nail scissors, she'd placed a segment on what she'd perceived as each of the leys, around the edge of the churchyard.

The prayers had been for... serenity, Merrily supposed, restoration of balance, and the God had been Julian's God, without whose warmth and gentility the human race would never have survived. *Mother God.*

And the energy had come, unequivocally, from the full moon. *Mother Goddess.*

A female thing.

Up yours, Mithras.

She'd walked away feeling the terrifying rightness of it, thinking that when things were calmer she'd have to tell Jane what she'd done.

Felt obliged.

And there was something else for Jane. When she'd rung Neil Cooper, as promised, to tell him about the possibility of Mithraic remains at Brinsop, he already knew. The police had asked for someone to come along when they excavated the temple and surrounds to see what was there.

Merrily had also told Neil about Jane and university. Why Jane was reluctant to go and thereby miss the excavation of Coleman's Meadow. Neil said he'd talk to the guys hired for the dig to see if they could use somebody to make the tea and stuff. Probably not a gap year but maybe a gap six months, on peanuts pay.

Earlier today, Jane had been palely determined: *I will go to university. I'll work like hell, get the grades and go as far away from here as I can. I'm no good for this place, I'm a bloody liability.*

Like that. She'd come round.

Resurrection of Christ. Resurrection of Ledwardine. Resurrection of Jane.

At key moments in the Julian meditation, Merrily would hold in her head an image of the crucifixion stain on the wall of Brinsop Church.

If it all fell flat – and she'd know – then last night had been the first signs of a dangerous eccentricity, and it might be time to think about getting out of the job.

The vestry door was ajar, the way it was never left any more. The smell of mud and sweat came to her. Merrily froze. The voice at her shoulder was not a voice you wanted to hear, alone, in the dimness.

'A few minutes of your time, please, Mrs Watson.'

81

The Toxic Dilemma

THE ENERGY-SAVING BULBS in the vestry sputtered in nervous dawn-like tints as he shut the door.

'Lock it,' he said.

He wore a black woollen hat, hiking gear, a pack too light-weight to be a Bergen. Just another long-distance walker, although the sweat suggested he'd been running and the mud spatters suggested it hadn't been along established footpaths.

Across the room, from which there was no easy escape, Merrily didn't move. On one side of her a table with prayer books, on the other a carousel of 'Beautiful Ledwardine' post-cards. Above her, a window that didn't open.

He said, 'Just do it, please.'

'Byron...' Keeping her eyes on him, her voice low. 'Don't take this the wrong way, but I'd really rather not be in a locked room with you.'

He smiled, revealing all the black lines in his teeth.

'Want your help, that's all.'

'I really don't think so.'

Perhaps she should have been afraid, but she was just annoyed. About everything. He didn't seem to notice.

'Do you know what Power of Attorney means?'

'I do, actually. Studied law for a year, before... life took over.'

He reached into an inside pocket, lifting out a long buff envelope.

'I want to give you Power of Attorney.'

'Over what?'

'Disposal of my property. Which is not inconsiderable these days. All the land, all the buildings, the bungalow, all paid for. Also a small apartment in Hereford. Surprising how much money you can make in a short time, isn't it?'

'I wouldn't know, I'm a vicar.'

He didn't smile.

'If I appeared irritated with you, back at the cop shop, it was only because I could see you catching on. Picking up on too many things, joining too many ends. But then, your religion and mine do have a lot in common.'

'Not really, Byron. Ritual murder might be a point of contention.'

He didn't seem to hear.

'Of course, you're also part of the problem. Women priests and guys like that nancy who was filling in for you today. But I did come away admiring you, the way you put your finger on the worm in the apple. Now…' He extracted the contents of the envelope. 'I had this done some while back. I've always been tidy that way. Had a bloke in mind to expedite things, but we fell out. Go on… read it.'

Merrily moved to pick up the paper, never taking her gaze off him, and backed off with it.

THIS GENERAL POWER OF ATTORNEY *is made this*
day of **by COLIN JONES** *of The Compound, Brinsop,*
Herefordshire.
I APPOINT MERRILY WATKINS *of The Vicarage, Ledwardine,*
Herefordshire, to be my Attorney in accordance with Section 10 of the
Powers of Attorney Act 1971
IN WITNESS *whereof I have hereunto set my hand the day and year first*
before written
SIGNED *as a Deed and delivered*
by the said **COLIN JONES** *in the presence of:-*

'This authorizes you to act in my name. Sell all the property and see that the proceeds are distributed, fifty-fifty, to the people I shall name to you.'

She said, ludicrously, 'You got my name right.'

'I always knew your name. Legal stuff, you don't make mistakes. I'm going away, Mrs W, and wish to dispose of my property meaningfully. I shot a man. As you know.'

'Yes.'

'Be pictures of The Compound in all the rags. TV, the Net. Truth is, it was as good as over when they killed Farmer Bull. Bloody Kenny. What a mistake he was.'

'Because he wasn't a soldier. Because he had no discipline.'

'Kenny was the worm in the apple. Hanging out with that clown from *The Octane Show*, appearing on promotional videos. Fame and fortune. That was never what this was about.'

'But Kenny didn't kill Farmer Bull. Or—'

'He let it *happen*. He was doing stuff on his own, taking men through the degrees. Stuff I didn't know about. At first, when you take a civilian through the degrees, you think it'll change them. Nah. Not in the right way.'

'It changed you.'

She was thinking, *Some men win at snooker and some at poker, too...*

He sat on the edge of the table.

'I was responsible. You accept that, then you take action. Mithras doesn't forgive. Couldn't exactly fire Mostyn when he owned half the company. Better there was an accident. Not here. Somewhere remote. Beacons, maybe. Just biding my time. Another mistake. Unless you take immediate action...'

He pushed the form towards her. His fingers touched hers, briefly; she looked up into his lined face. Part of him was watching her, impassive, beyond stimulation. She felt that another part of him was already going away, something receding.

'I still don't understand why me.'

'Don't have many choices. I believe you won't double-deal. And you know the people concerned.'

'It needs another signature. A witness.'

'Someone here you can trust? Preferably not your boyfriend.'

Whose life he might have saved. He just might.

'Byron, there are several people I can trust. None of whom I'm prepared to expose to a man who I have every reason to think may have a gun with him.'

He grinned, turned his back on her. When he turned around again, it lay across the palm of his big, leathery hand.

'The Glock.' He placed it carefully on the table, pushed it towards Merrily. 'I may ask for it back before I leave.'

She didn't touch it. They both knew she could pick it up, point it at him and call the police. Always assuming it was loaded, and somehow, she thought, it would be.

Byron placed the pistol in the centre of the table, took a stack of prayer books from the pile and arranged them around the Glock on four sides, finally placing one on top.

'You got a phone on you?'

'Yes.'

'Phone for a witness.'

Merrily pulled her mobile from her jeans then put it down on the table.

'Can I ask you a question?'

'Long as you're not playing for time so your congregation turns up.'

'I wouldn't expose a congregation to this. We have about forty minutes.'

'Go on.'

'When you tried to pass your religion off as just a series of exercises, a discipline – was that just for Lockley and Howe, or do you believe that?'

'You've just reminded me why I found you so annoying.' He stood up. 'It's a secular age. It doesn't matter what you believe, it's how you sell it. You have to use acceptable terminology. Nobody likes a crank, certainly not the men I deal with.'

'I don't think you're that cynical.'

'Who's your proposed witness?'

'Gomer Parry.'

'Sensible choice. Could've wrecked my digger last night, but he didn't.'

'He would never wreck a digger. You know him?'

'*Of* him. Make your call. Keep it casual, and he comes alone. If an armed response unit arrives, I'll just bite the barrel. You don't want that in here.'

God.

'And there'll be no money for Fiona.'

She stared at him.

'Fiona Spicer?'

'Make your call. And I'll be listening for nuances.'

Merrily put in the number and waited. It was surreal. Be easier if she could feel an accessible evil: the night stench in the tower room, the squirming male miasma assailing Jane in the mithraeum, which Jane had talked about only once when they were alone, staring blankly into the fireplace, disconnected, as if she was repeating someone else's story. Jane, whose knowledge of Mithraism had been virtually non-existent then.

'*Gomer Parry Plant Hire.*'

'Oh. Sorry. Gomer, it's me. You… got a few minutes to spare? Over at the church.'

'Sure to, vicar.'

'Thank you. I'll be in the vestry.'

Simple as that. When the line cleared, Byron was nodding. Merrily put the phone on the table next to the stack of prayer books.

'You really think Fiona's going to accept anything from you?'

He blinked just once.

'She can give it to her daughter, or a charity of her choosing. I liked Syd. You could only quarrel – on that level of intensity – with someone who was a brother.'

'And Fiona? What was your quarrel with her?'

He looked at Merrily for a long time, his face blank. Then he transferred his gaze to the wall behind her. She tensed in horror. *Mithras always looks away.*

But then he turned back to her, his blue eyes steady.

'I take full responsibility for everything I've done. No papering over cracks. No sentiment here. No apology. I don't do that.'

'Was that why you left Liz? Because you realized the elements you were dealing with…'

'… were unsuited to a domestic situation. I'll confirm that much. I had respect for my wife.'

That's why you were so very publicly screwing your way around Hereford?

'And when Mostyn killed the banker, Cornel, did he do that on his own? You know what I'm asking, don't you? I understand he turned his head away when he did it. Do you think he was entirely responsible then for his own—?'

'You're back to the same question.'

'I'm not a cop. These things matter to me.'

Confronting the impossibility of her own job. The toxic dilemma she'd tried to evoke for the students in the chapel. *To what extent you want to demonize this is up to you.*

Byron shook his head.

'Nah.'

'No, he wasn't entirely responsible? No, he'd surrendered his—?'

'How's Barry?'

'He'll lose an eye. They think.'

'But he'll live. That's what it said on the radio.'

'So I believe.'

'That was regrettable.' Byron looked mildly affected. 'He was a good soldier. Shot, unarmed, by a man who wasn't fit to clean his boots. I'm taking responsibility. He'll be the second beneficiary. Fiona, Barry. See to that, would you? Might be enough for a down payment on a big old pub. If there happened to be one on the market.'

'You've thought it all out, haven't you?'

'No sentiment, no apology. We take action, then we walk away.'

'How will you live?'

'That's my business.'

'All right.' Merrily shook herself. 'Tell me one more thing. When Syd died on Credenhill... you were there, weren't you?'

He thought for just a moment.

'Yes.'

'What was that about?'

'No comment.'

'You must've been worried when you heard he was coming back, as chaplain.'

'I never worry.'

She heard the squeak of the church doors. There was no time. There *had* to be time.

'As far as I could see, Byron, there were two ways of looking at this – at Syd coming back – and one would be an opportunity. The chaplain's the only direct feed into the spiritual life of the Regiment. If there was *anything* left of Mithras in Syd... if he was, to any extent, in denial... you might still see an old ambition realized. That John the Baptist side of you.'

He shrugged.

'Did you ask to meet him on Credenhill? Just two recreational runners, paths crossing. Or did he ask you?'

'Does it matter?'

'Not really. All I'm feeling, very strongly, is that if you wanted to know where his innermost allegiances lay, there was only one thing you could say to him. Only one thing you could tell him, as a test. You'd tell him...' she put both hands on the table, leaned forward, smelling the sweat and the mud and nothing else '... when and where and... and how... you'd had sex with his wife... right?'

His eyes closed briefly in his weathered sandstone face, and she half expected him to smash the pile of prayer books to the ground.

A tapping on the door.

'*Vicar?*'

'One minute, Gomer...' She looked into Byron's eyes, hissed, 'You knew exactly what kind of interior eruption that would cause. This savage inner conflict between the soldier who wanted to beat you to a pulp and throw you down the fucking steps and the Christian who—'

'And now we'll never know.'

'I think we do.'

'Let Mr Parry in,' Byron said.

Merrily turned away from him, nodded.

Now she could smell it.

82

Revelations

WHEN SHE GOT back to the vicarage, nobody was home but Ethel.

The phone was ringing.

She'd have to be back in church in less than half an hour. She'd agreed to give Byron Jones ten minutes to walk away – like just another Easter hiker – before she called the police.

She picked up the phone. It was Dick Willis, minister in charge of the Credenhill cluster.

'I do rather wish you'd given me a hint of this, Merrily.' There was no anger in his voice. 'Might even've been able to help you.'

'Dick, it all moved too...'

And was still moving. Gomer had known as soon as he saw the name on the document. She'd told him it was all right. Byron had stood in the farthest corner of the room looking as unthreatening as a man like Byron could ever look. No fear in Gomer, only concern.

She'd firmly squeezed his hand and said it was OK. *OK*.

'Don't suppose they've got him yet,' Dick Willis said.

'Not as far as I know.'

'Frightening,' Dick said. 'Merrily, look, I'm sitting here on a chancel pew, waiting to take a service and I... I think I'd rather go into it with a clean conscience. Especially on Good Friday. When I told you that Colin Jones hadn't been in Brinsop Church during a service, that was a blatant and unforgivable lie. He came once. Memorably. Though I wasn't there.'

'When was this?'

The ten minutes were up. She should be ringing Annie Howe. And if she was late for the service, Gomer Parry, who'd signed on the dotted line and then walked out with her and a murderer and rapist, would start raising hell.

'About a year ago,' Dick Willis said. 'I was approached by Colin Jones and asked if he and some other "army colleagues" might borrow St George's for an evening service. He offered what I can only describe as a remarkably generous donation towards the maintenance of the church. *Remarkably* generous.'

'What kind of service?'

'He didn't explain in detail. He just called it a service of thanksgiving, which could mean anything, as you know. I presumed some of the chaps had come through a fairly dicey situation abroad and it was something they couldn't talk about. I put it to the churchwarden and also ran it past the Bishop's office. No objections – SAS, you know?'

'Mmm.'

'They also said they'd be bringing their own minister. A chap called, if I remember correctly, Adrian Barclay turned up. I'd never seen him before. Said he was from London. And then it was made clear that I was not required in any capacity. Then the congregation arrived in their cars. All men. About twenty of them.'

'How long were they in there?'

'Couple of hours. When the churchwarden thought he'd better check that everything was all right, he found the door locked from the inside. We never found out what that service was about. And, you know, some of the chaps in that congregation… most of them didn't look like SAS men at all. You can tell a Regiment man, somehow – seldom huge muscular chaps, but there's a *look*… somehow.'

'But you kept quiet for the, erm…'

'For the money, Merrily. You know how things are. What I did do afterwards was to check on the Reverend Barclay. Rang the church he said he was from.'

'Which church was it?'

'St Stephen, Walbrook, in London. The minister there said they'd never had an Adrian Barclay there, but when I described him – tall, shaven-headed chap in his early forties – he fitted the description of a curate who'd lasted six months before he was asked to leave. Wouldn't explain why. Curious, wouldn't you say?'

'But you didn't ask any questions… locally.'

'It didn't seem appropriate,' Dick Willis said. 'Locally.'

Merrily phoned Gaol Street, asked for Annie Howe.

Not available. She spoke to DC Vaynor and explained briefly. She said she'd last seen Colin Jones walking from the square into the alley which led to a stile which led to a footpath into the remains of the old Powell orchard.

What happened now would be an exercise for Byron. A discipline.

DC Vaynor told her not, on any account, to go anywhere, but she told him she had to be in church in twenty-five minutes and could not be disturbed. Not for anything.

She changed quickly into a black skirt, black cashmere jumper, pectoral cross, then sat down and Googled St Stephen Walbrook.

Never been, but she'd heard of it.

There was a colour photo of an angular City church with a campanile. Built by Sir Christopher Wren, it said, to replace one destroyed in the Great Fire of London. The first recorded church on the site near the River Walbrook, now underground, had dated back to the seventh century.

According to Wikipedia, the banks of the River Walbrook had yielded spectacular Roman remains, the best known of which was an impressively well-preserved monument now moved to Temple Court from its original site and open for public viewing. The London Mithraeum.

Its original site, apparently, had been close to the foundations of the Bank of England.

Merrily switched off the computer as if it was about to explode.

She couldn't think about any of this until after the meditation.

Or Easter.

The vestry was locked now, but she didn't know whether the pistol remained at the centre of the pile of prayer books.

She looked up at a movement in the window, saw Lol coming past towards the back door, in an actual jacket.

Flitting in and out of one another's energy fields.

She felt warmth, relief, guilt, a touch of shame… folding the Power of Attorney document and sliding it inside her copy of *Revelations of Divine Love.*

Credits

THE WALES/HEREFORDSHIRE BORDER is not exactly rich in Roman ruins, but Magnis did exist. In 2010, excavations in connection with a Herefordshire Council flood-alleviation system turned up some remarkable relics, including the remains of a very large woman, identified in parts of the media as a female gladiator – possibly a remote ancestor of Victoria Buckland. Thanks for additional information to the archaeologists George Children, Jodie Lewis and Francis Pryor.

Particular thanks to Tracy Thursfield, who directed me to the wonderful Brinsop Church, made some *very* significant connections there and uncovered illuminating aspects of Mithraism

And to Mairead Reidy who provided some crucial, half-forgotten books on the Romans and Mithraism (including the fascinating *Mithras, The Fellow in the Cap* by Esme Wynne-Tyson) as well as endless Internet data, while spreading the word, along with Anne Holt, via the Merrily Watkins Internet discussion forum on Yahoo… as does Caitlin Sagan on the Facebook PR appreciation society. Many thanks to them, and all in Greater Ledwardine.

Thanks also to: John Moss, of The British Society of Dowsers, Mark Townsend, author of *The Path of the Blue Raven,* the great forensic pathologist and crime-writer Professor Bernard Knight, Duncan Baldwin (Byron Jones's legal adviser) Neville Meredith from Herefordshire Council and Polly (tunnels) Rubery on migrant workers and fruit farms. Arno Gundisch, native of

Transylvania, for Marinescu-linked background. Peter Brooks for *the wafer* and other crucial spiritual devices, which Merrily and I may have misused. And John Whitbourn for reminding me what I was supposed to be doing.

On the subject of cockfighting, which has not exactly died out in some areas, my thanks to someone who, for obvious reasons, would rather not be named. And any SAS-linked sources, where not obvious, must remain in the shadows. I've heard many stories over the years, most of them unverifiable. The ex-Regiment men I've encountered at various times have been great blokes, full of ideas and dark humour, but I made a point of *not* attempting to run the central idea in this novel past anybody in, previously in or currently connected with the SAS. If anybody needs to be disposed of, it'll have to be me.

Re Julian of Norwich, the quotes under the headings to parts two, three, four and six, are taken from the Penguin Classics edition of *Revelations of Divine Love*, translated by Clifton Wolters.

The Lol Robinson songs mentioned here can all be found on the full-length CD *A Message from the Morning*, for which many, many thanks to Lol's talented producer, arranger, bandmate and co-writer Allan Watson, to the ingenious Bev Craven who designed the package and to tireless Terry Smith who markets it via the website, www.philrickman.co.uk.

Finally, thanks to Nic Cheetham, who relaunched the Merrily series with flair and commitment, to Mathilda Imlah at Corvus, to my agents Andrew Hewson and Ed Wilson and, of course, my wife and editor Carol who burned endless candles at both ends and in the middle getting this one right.

Incidentally, in the week during which *The Secrets of Pain* was finished, West Mercia Police in Hereford launched Operation Ignite to combat rural crime close to the Welsh border.

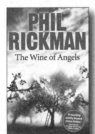

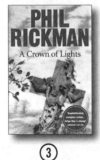
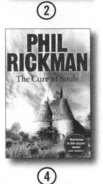
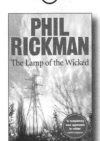
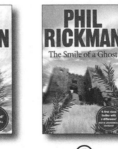